Myster

The Vanishing Skinny-Dippers

MYSTERY OF

THE VANISHING SKINNY-DIPPERS

G. James Quandt

Publishers Note

This is a work of fiction. All characters, locations, and events are portrayed in this book as fictional, and any resemblance to real people, places, or incidents is purely coincidental

ISBN 978-1-7329419-1-5
(Paperback)

First Edition, December 2018

From the author...

The story in this book was conceived and developed in my mind over the last few years, until I started entering the outline of the story into my computer, in my spare time. The outline grew into a rough draft of a story, and I then began expanding it, and smoothing it out several times over.

The final story contained in these pages has been read by me at least a half dozen times, with changes being done each time, in an attempt to make the story flow more smoothly. With each proof reading of the story, I tried to correct any typographical or grammatic errors, so I hope there are few, if any problems, that English language enthusiasts would feel a need to point out.

I offer this fictional story to the public, and hope that a majority of those who read it, will enjoy it as much as I enjoyed creating it. Please feel free to visit my website at: '**https://www.GJamesQuandt.com**'.

Thank you,

G. James Quandt

Contents

PLANNING A TRIP

"Hey, Jeremy, wait up!" Charlie called out as he half walked, half ran down the hallway, waving to his best friend. Jeremy stopped and turned around, smiling and waiting for his best friend to catch up to him. "What's up?" he asked with a grin. Charlie took a deep breath and exhaled before speaking. "You have a free period right now, don't you?" he asked. "Yes, I do. Why do you ask?" Jeremy replied. "I was hoping that we might go to the library and talk over the plans for our camping trip next month" Charlie answered. "Sure, we can do that" Jeremy said, "I have most of my homework done already, and the rest I can work on when I get home. Plus, I wanted to talk to you anyway. I've heard of a new place that I think would be great for our trip, and I wanted to see what you think of it for the trip. It's supposed to have a small lake that will be great for swimming, if we camp there."

The two proceeded to the library on the second floor of the school, and found an empty table in the back where they could sit and discuss their plans, and not be overheard by anyone else. After they were seated in the chairs at the table, Charlie looked across the table at his friend. "Okay, so where is this new place you have in mind for camping at?" he asked. "Well, it's about eight miles west of town" Jeremy answered, "You know those woods just past the bend in Highway 22? The lake is supposed to be in the middle of those woods." Charlie stared back at his friend with a look of shock. "Eight miles!" he exclaimed, "That's kind of far out, don't you think? How far into the woods is the lake?" Jeremy smiled back at his friend. "The lake is in the center of the woods, about a two-mile hike from the highway. We talked about finding a secluded location that would be far away from where anyone else might go, didn't we?" "Yah, but how are we supposed to get all our supplies and camping equipment that far out of town, and then through the woods to the lake?" Charlie responded. Jeremy grinned back at his friend. "I already worked that out" he said, "I asked my mom if she could drive us out to the woods in her pickup, and she said yes. That just leaves us with getting our stuff through the woods. I figure we can carry our personal stuff in backpacks, and I'll have the rest loaded into that cart I used for delivering newspapers a few years ago. We should be able to handle a two-mile hike through the woods that way, after my mom drops us all off."

"That plan sounds like it might work" Charlie responded with a smile, "And, it sounds like you've been thinking this all over and making plans, just like you always do for our camping trips. So, what supplies are we planning on taking with us?" "We'll take extra clothes, a swimsuit, and personal stuff in our backpacks" Jeremy replied, "The tents, sleeping bags, tarps, cookware, cooking grate, rope, food storage bag, food and drinks, tools, radio and batteries, first-aid kit, shovel, and any other necessary things will go in the cart." "Are your sister and her friend still planning on coming along?" Charlie asked with a grin. "Yes, they're both planning on joining us yet, and they'll each have to carry a backpack with their own clothes and stuff" Jeremy replied.

"So, when are we planning on leaving?" Charlie asked. "I think it would be best to leave early in the morning, the Thursday after school lets out for the summer" Jeremy answered, "I have to start working at the grocery store eleven days later, the Monday after we get back." A frown came over Charlie's face. "That won't work for me" Charlie exclaimed, "my cousin Alvin is graduating that Thursday night. My mom says I have to be at the graduation ceremony with her, so I can't leave until the next day, on Friday morning." "Shush, quiet down!" came a disapproving hiss that caused both boys to jump in their chairs. "You two boys are getting a bit too loud, please try to keep your voices down" scolded the librarian. "Sorry Ms. Marsh" Charlie replied with a red face, realizing that he had raised his voice a little too much. "We'll try to be quieter" Jeremy added. They watched Ms. Marsh walk back to the librarian's desk before they returned to their discussion. "We'll have to wait until Friday to leave" Charlie whispered. "Maybe not" Jeremy said with a grin, "The girls and I can still leave on Thursday morning, like I said. We'll take the supply cart and our backpacks, and when we get through the woods, we'll get the camp setup taken care of. When you get there on Friday, hopefully around noon, you can join us at the camp site for lunch."

"Yeah, okay. That sounds like it might work" Charlie replied, "if I can find the spot where you and the girls have set up the camp that is. Remember, I've never been to this place before, and it sounds like you've never been there before, either. You won't be able to draw me a map to where you'll be, so how will I find you?" Jeremy thought for a moment, then started grinning. "Markers, that's how!" Jeremy whispered. "You already know how to get out to the woods by the highway" Jeremy explained, "Once you get there, you just follow the markers that I leave for you." "What kind of markers?" Charlie asked. "I'll tack some yellow ribbons to the trees as the girls and I hike through the woods, then leave stone trail markers for when you come out of the woods" Jeremy explained. Charlie smiled. "That actually sounds like a good idea" Charlie responded, "I think that might work, and I won't have to help set up the camp site that way." "You'll still get plenty of stuff to do, once you get there" Jeremy replied with a grin, "you won't miss out on all the work." Charlie's grin disappeared, "Great, I have to go to my cousins' graduation on Thursday night, get eight miles out to the woods on Friday morning, hike two miles through some woods by myself, and then work when I get to the camp site." "The camp site will already be set up" Jeremy growled, "All you'll have to do when you get to the camp, is your fair share of the daily chores that need to be done, including breaking down the camp when it's time to come home."

Charlie was grinning, "I was just playing around with you, buddy, you know that don't you" he chuckled, "It sounds like a great plan." Jeremy smiled back, "Yeah, I figured you were just being a drama queen again" he said, "Oh! When you come through the woods, be sure to move the ribbons around to the opposite side of the trees as you pass them. That way they'll be facing away from the road, and we can follow them back out to the highway again when we leave." Charlie grinned at his friend, "Right, and that way no one else will see them and be able to follow us to our secluded camp site. We'll probably have the whole place to ourselves, right?" "Right" Jeremy agreed. The boys got up from the table and walked out of the library, since it was time to head to their next class. "See you later" they said to each other as they separated out in the hall.

PACKING FOR THE TRIP

Jeremy finished putting everything he thought he would need, into his backpack. He stood up straight and stretched his arms up over his head. "I hope I packed everything" he thought to himself, "I wonder how the girls are doing." They were all packing their own personal stuff for the camping trip, into their own personal backpacks. They would be leaving the next morning, and he decided to go and check on his sister and her best friend. Walking down the hallway, he came to his sister's bedroom door and knocked on it. "Who is it?" came his sister's voice from inside. "It's me, Jeremy" he answered, "can I come in?" "Wait a minute" his sister yelled back to him. He could hear movement and some whispering inside of the room, as he stood outside the door and waited. "Okay, you can come in now" his sister finally called out to him.

He slowly opened the door and peeked around the edge. He saw his sister sitting on the bed as he stepped inside. "What do you need?" his sister asked. "I just came to check on how you and Jenny were doing with your packing" he answered, "Where is she by the way?" "She's in the closet, changing back into her clothes" Amanda replied. "Changing into her clothes. What were you two doing before I knocked?" "Jenny was trying on one of my swimsuits" his sister answered, "I thought it best for her to change back into her clothes in the closet, before letting you come in." "Oh, right" Jeremy said, "Well, I just wanted to check on what all you two were putting in your backpacks." "Why?" his sister asked with a frown. He grinned back at her. "Well, since we'll be hiking two miles through some woods tomorrow with backpacks strapped on, we don't want to carry any more weight than we need to" he replied. "So, what do you suggest we pack?" Jenny asked as she came out of the closet with a big smile. Jeremy smiled back at her. "Some extra clothes, a swimsuit, and whatever personal stuff you really need to have along" he answered.

Jenny smiled at him. "I put six pairs of clean clothes and a swimsuit in my backpack" she said, "plus a hair brush, soap, deodorant, sun screen, a pair of flip flops, a radio, and a few books. Does that sound okay to you?" "I think you could make it a little lighter if you leave most of the books out, along with the radio" suggested Jeremy, "The sun screen is something I need to add to my own backpack yet. Unless you plan to do a lot of reading, you don't want all the extra weight of the books and radio on your back. I'm packing a radio in the supply cart anyway, along with spare batteries, so you shouldn't need a radio. You could probably do with fewer clothes, too." "You can't expect us to wear the same clothes for over a week?" his sister suddenly exclaimed, “We’ll end up stinking if we wear the same things for the entire camping trip.” Jeremy smiled at his sister. “Besides what you wear on the way there, you can actually get by with two or three extra sets of clothes. We can take dirty clothes down to the lake and rinse them out in the water each day, then hang them up on a rope to dry. That way we don’t need to take a lot of clothes along, and our backpacks will weigh a little less.” “That actually makes sense” Jenny said, “We’ll be like pioneers who only had a couple sets of clothes, and did laundry every day.”

Jeremy grinned. “I’m just making suggestions though” he said, “You can pack as much as you want, but each of us has to carry whatever weight we put in our backpacks.” “So, you’re just trying to make it easier on us” Amanda stated. “Yes” he replied, “The fewer clothes and unnecessary items, the better, weight wise. Besides, if it’s nice weather all week long, we’ll probably be spending most of our time in swimsuits.” “Well, in that case, we should probably pack more than one swimsuit” Amanda said to Jenny with a grin, “I’ll take along my black bikini, besides the one piece I already packed. You can take along the orange bikini that you just tried on, I think you looked pretty good in that one.” “Are you and Charlie taking along more than one swimsuit?” inquired Jenny. “He only has one pair of swim trunks” Amanda said. “I have my regular swim trunks, plus my swim team suit" Jeremy said, correcting his sister, "I think you made a great point about taking an extra swimsuit, so I'm going to add my swim team suit, and I'll call Charlie to suggest it to him."

"So, what all are you packing in the cart?" Amanda asked, "Just so we don't duplicate anything else, and end up carrying extra weight in our backpacks." "I'm packing all the food, drinks, and ice in two coolers, more food in paper bags, two tents, four sleeping bags, the radio, a couple of battery powered lanterns, flashlights, spare batteries, rope, tarps, a shovel, and a CB radio" Jeremy recited, "I'll also bring matches and paper for starting the camp fires, plus a first aid kit in my backpack." "Why the CB radio" Amanda asked with a chuckle, "You need to keep in touch with your friends back in town?" "No, it's for emergency use only" Jeremy replied, "In case something bad happens, and we need to call out for help." "Oh" Amanda mumbled, "I guess that sounds like a pretty good idea after all." "You really thought this all out, didn't you" Jenny commented, "You're making sure we'll be safe, and not over-worked." "I just want all of us to have a good time" Jeremy replied with a smile, "And being safe is a really important part of having fun."

After his talk with the girls about packing sensibly, Jeremy left the room with the girls chatting enthusiastically about how anxious they were to get going the next day. “Jeremy seems pretty good at planning trips like this” Jenny commented. “Yeah, my big brother is a Boy Scout” Amanda responded, “he reached the rank of Eagle Scout last summer, just after turning sixteen. He enjoys going on camping trips, and always watches out for the younger scouts in his troop. You know what, though, I think he really hopes that you have a good time on this trip.” “Why do you say that?” Jenny asked. “Well, it’s just that I’m pretty sure he likes you a lot, and not just as my friend. I think he wants you to have fun on this trip, so maybe you’ll want to go on more trips with him” Amanda explained, “I think he’s been sweet on you for a long time.” “Really?” grinned Jenny. “Yes, really” Amanda answered, “And I think you’re sweet on him too.” “Is it that obvious” Jenny said with a grin, and the two of them started giggling.

Jenny was staying overnight and sleeping in Amanda’s room, so that they would all be ready to go early in the morning. The girls got ready for bed as soon as they had their backpacks ready, then went downstairs to watch some television. At nine o’clock, they decided to go back up to the bedroom, where they laid out their clothes for the next morning, then climbed into bed to get some sleep. After Jeremy got back to his own bedroom, he added a few bottles of sunscreen and the second swimsuit to his backpack, then called Charlie to suggest he be sure and pack the same. He then went down to the garage, where he had placed the cart, and began loading as much stuff as he could into it, for the night. The coolers were packed empty at the back of the cart, and he would put the food and ice into them in the morning. He got to bed around ten o'clock and finally drifted off to sleep soon after. He was positive that he had planned for everything that four people would need on an eleven-day camping trip, and he slept soundly through the night.

STARTING ON THE TRIP

Jeremy was up extra early the next morning, around five-thirty, so he could finish packing supplies in the cart. He placed the food that was in a refrigerator, along with some ice, into the coolers. The non-refrigerated food stuff was in paper sacks, and he packed those into the cart also. When he finally had everything packed into the cart, he spread a tarp over the top of the cart, and secured it in place with a rope. He then got out the ramp they always used for loading the lawn tractor into the back of the pickup, secured it to the tailgate, and proceeded to pull the cart up the ramp and into the bed of the pickup. After the cart was loaded, he detached the ramp again and slid it into the back of the pickup with the cart, so they would be able to unload the cart when they got out to the woods. He made sure that everything was secure in the back of the pickup, and then went inside of the house to join the others for a nice hot breakfast, which his mother was preparing for the girls and himself.

When he walked into the kitchen, the girls were already sitting at the table eating breakfast, so he sat down and began helping himself to some of the hot food that his mother had ready on the table. "I think I have everything loaded in the pickup" he announced, "we just need to grab our backpacks, and we'll be ready to leave." "Good, I'm ready to go myself" Mrs. Andersen stated, "so, as soon as you're finished eating, you can go get your backpacks, and we'll start out for the woods. You girls can sit in the front of the pickup with me. Jeremy can climb into the back with the cart, so when we pick Charlie up, he can simply jump into the back along with Jeremy." "But Charlie isn't coming with us" Amanda exclaimed, "He's going to his cousin's graduation tonight with his mother." "Oh, that's right, mom, I forgot to tell you about that" Jeremy added "he'll be joining us tomorrow instead."

Mrs. Andersen looked directly at her son with a look of surprise on her face. "Really, Jeremy? You forgot to tell me?" she said with a grin, "Gee son, you seem to be getting pretty forgetful in your old age." "I'm really sorry mom" he apologized, "I just got so busy planning what supplies and food we needed on this camping trip, that it completely slipped my mind to tell you about Charlie. I probably should have told you last month, when Charlie first told me. We decided that he would come a day later, and the three of us would setup the camp site without him." "So, how is Charlie planning to get all the way out to the woods?" his mother inquired, "And how is he going to find the rest of you in the woods?" "I'm not sure how he's getting out to the woods, but I'll be leaving him trail markers to find his way to the camp site" Jeremy answered, "I didn't think to ask him how he was getting out to the woods." "Well, if he needs a ride tomorrow, I can pick him up, and drive him out to the same spot I drop you off at today" she offered. "You can? That would be great, mom! I'm sure he'll really appreciate that!" Jeremy exclaimed with a smile. "Well, write down his phone number for me, and I'll call him when I get back from driving the three of you out to the woods" Mrs. Andersen said, "I don't want to call him this early in the morning."

The three teenagers finished eating and headed upstairs to get their backpacks, while Mrs. Andersen headed out to start the engine of the pickup. The kids came out the back door a few minutes later and started towards the pickup. "Jeremy" his mother called to him from the truck, "please be sure the back door is closed and locked." "Okay mom!" he called back to her with a grin. He ran back to the house and checked the door, which was properly closed and locked, while the girls climbed into the cab of the pickup. Jeremy ran up to the back of the pickup truck and jumped into cargo bed along-side of the cart, then knocked on the roof of the cab to let his mother know he was ready. "You girls all set?" Mrs. Andersen asked. "All set!" the girls chorused together.

The trip out to the woods took about thirty minutes, since they were starting out on the east side of town and had to go through downtown to get to the highway heading out to the woods. The woods came into view as they came around a bend in the road, and when they were all the way around and along-side of the wooded area, Mrs. Andersen pulled the truck off on the side of the road. When they came to a complete stop, Jeremy climbed out of the back of the pickup and began pulling the ramp out as well. His mother and the girls got out of the cab and came around back to see what they could do to help unload the supply cart. "Once I have the ramp secured to the tailgate, I'll climb in, grab the pull handle, and start pushing the cart back to the ramp" Jeremy said, "When it starts down the ramp, just make sure it stays on and doesn't come down too fast. They got the cart out of the back of the pickup and down the ramp without much difficulty and were then ready to start the two-mile hike through the woods. Amanda and Jeremy kissed and hugged their mother goodbye, receiving the usual instructions from her to stay safe, and be good. They all watched Mrs. Andersen climb back into the pickup and start the engine again. She U-turned the pickup around and yelled "goodbye" again to the kids as she started back towards town.

The three teens watched the pickup go around the bend in the road and disappear behind some trees. Jeremy slipped his backpack on and grabbed the handle of the supply cart. He smiled at the two girls who were slipping on their own backpacks, "You guys ready for a long hike through the woods?" he asked. "Yes!" they both answered together, then giggled at having answered in a chorus together. "Okay, this way then" he declared as he began pulling the cart towards the woods. The girls followed along, close behind him, while trying to shift their backpacks into more comfortable positions as they walked. Jeremy stopped when he reached the first tree at the edge of the woods. The girls watched, as he took a yellow ribbon out of his pocket, and then used a large red tack to pin it to the front of the tree, before walking on into the woods.

"What's the ribbon for?" called out Jenny from behind the cart. Jeremy turned around for a moment and smiled at her, "That's a marker for Charlie" he answered, "so he can find his way through the woods and to the camp site tomorrow." "That's a good idea" Amanda exclaimed, "he shouldn't have too much trouble following a trail of bright yellow ribbons, right?" "Right" Jeremy replied. About forty feet further into the woods, Jeremy tacked another yellow ribbon to another tree, he wanted to place the ribbons so Charlie would be able to spot each one up ahead from each previous tree that had a ribbon attached to it. He continued walking along, selecting a path that was wide enough to allow for the passage of the cart, and using a compass to guide them in the right direction through the woods.

He was humming a tune to himself as he tacked the ribbons to the trees. Amanda and her friend Jenny continued to follow along behind the cart, chatting to each other, but keeping an eye on Jeremy, so as not to lose track of him. They did not want to get left behind and lost in the woods.

The trees started getting denser, and it was getting darker as they walked deeper and deeper into the woods. The sun was hidden from view above the canopy of branches and leaves that hung thickly over their heads. It wasn't dark like at night, there was still enough light filtering through to allow the group of teenagers to find their way along the path. "Guess we don't need much sunscreen while we're walking through the woods" Amanda commented to Jenny with a smile. "Nope, we shouldn't need any until we get to the lake" her friend replied. The girls were following closely behind the cart, not paying much attention to where they were, they fully trusted their guide to not get them lost, since he was an Eagle Scout, and had been hiking and camping quite a bit over the last six years. They could also see that he was using a compass to find the way, and not get lost. As they made their way through the woods, the girls kept chatting about different things, like boys, clothes, school classes and activities, and all the other summer vacation plans they had planned.

When the three teens had left the house earlier, around six-thirty, the temperature had been somewhere around the mid-seventies. Now it was almost eight o'clock, and they had been hiking through the woods for close to an hour. Even in the shade of the trees, Jeremy estimated that the temperature was somewhere in the mid-eighties already, maybe even nearing ninety. The humidity felt high, and he was working up a good sweat. Pulling the supply cart along through the woods, loaded with the groceries and other camping supplies was hard work. The cart seemed to be getting heavier and heavier, and Jeremy finally decided that it was time for them to rest for a little bit and have a drink of cool water. When he stopped at the next tree, he attached a ribbon like he had the earlier ones, then sat down under the tree, resting in its shade. "Time for a break" he said to the girls. The girls came around the cart and sat down against the tree next to him. They had also been feeling hot and tired, and had been hoping that they could stop for a rest soon. They all took out water bottles from their backpacks and sipped some of the cool liquid from inside of them.

Jeremy wiped the sweat from his face with a handkerchief and leaned back against the tree trunk with his eyes closed. "We've been hiking for about an hour now" he announced, "I figure it will take no more than two hours to get completely through the woods, so we should be at least half way through by now." "Are you okay?" Jenny asked with concern in her voice, "You've been pulling that cart for an hour now, and you look awfully hot." "I'll be okay after a little rest in the shade here" he responded with his eyes closed, "I think we're all getting tired. The humidity here in the woods is a lot higher than outside of them, that's what's tiring us all out so fast. We may have to take another break before we reach the end of the woods, but I think we'll be at the lake soon after that. We'll rest here for ten minutes, then continue on." "When we get to the lake, do we have to set up the camp site right away?" Amanda asked Jeremy. "No, we'll rest again, and then we'll search for a good place to set up the camp" he answered. "Can we go for a quick swim in the lake after finding a camp site, and before getting the camp set up?" Amanda asked.

Jeremy opened his eyes and looked at his sister. "Maybe we can go for a quick dip in the water, to cool off" Jeremy replied, "it will depend on what time it is. It's just going to be the three of us setting everything up, and we'll need to get the tents put up, and prepare a fire pit, with rocks around it. We'll also need enough firewood to cook supper tonight and provide some heat for overnight. We don't want to be trying to do any of that when it starts to get dark out." "But it doesn't start to get dark until after seven o'clock" Amanda said, "If we get to the lake by noon, we should have plenty of time to get everything done." "It'll probably start to get dark sooner at this place" Jeremy responded, "The mountains on the west side of the lake, and the woods surrounding us on the east side will block out the sun earlier. We should plan on it getting dark as much as an hour earlier, when the sun starts going down behind the mountains. We want to cook supper before it gets dark."

"What time is Charlie supposed to get to the camp tomorrow?" Jenny inquired. "If he leaves early enough, he should get here sometime before lunch tomorrow" Jeremy answered, "And if my mom drives him out, she'll want to leave early enough so she can get to work on time. Why? Are you anxious for him to get here? You aren't kind of sweet on Charlie, are you?" Jenny looked at Jeremy for a moment before answering. "He's a real nice guy, Jeremy, and I know he's your best friend, but I'm not interested in him as more than just a friend" she replied. "That's right big brother" Amanda laughed, "I happen to know that she's kind of sweet on someone else. I'm the one that's sweet on your best friend, and I think he already knows it, but is too shy to ask me out."

"Well, I think we've rested enough" Jeremy announced, as he got up on his feet, "We should get moving again." He slipped on his backpack as the girls got up also, moaning after having sat on the ground for several minutes. They put their own packs back on as Jeremy grabbed the pull bar of the cart again and started pulling it through the woods again. “So, how did Jeremy find out about this place with the lake in the middle of these woods?” Jenny inquired of Amanda. “Oh, we both heard about it from our two twin cousins” responded Amanda, “They were visiting with our aunt and uncle over spring break, and they kind of casually mentioned that there was a great place for swimming down in this valley. They said it was hidden in these woods. Jeremy thought it sounded like the perfect location for a camping trip, and I thought it sounded pretty good too, so I kind of invited you and me along.”

“I’m really looking forward to the next eleven days” Jenny giggled, “Imagine, actually camping out by a lake in the middle of the woods, with no one else around except my best friend, and two cute boys.” “Me too, except for the work of setting up the camp site, and then taking it back down when we leave” Amanda said with a grin, “But, we’ll be able to swim as much as we want and relax when we want, without our parents around, giving us chores to do.” “That’s right” Jeremy called back from up in front of them, “Once we have the campsite setup, with plenty of firewood gathered, all we will have to worry about is cooking meals, cleaning up after meals, and keeping the camp site picked up. Plus, gathering more firewood when we start to run low, washing our clothes, and having as much fun as we can handle, and relaxing when we get too tired to have fun."

Half an hour later, Jeremy called for another rest break and sat down under the tree he had just marked with a yellow ribbon. The girls sat down and leaned back against the same tree that Jeremy had chosen. "Oh! I don't know if I can go much further" Amanda exclaimed, "I'm so tired that I'm practically dragging my feet." "Me too" Jenny said. "Let's take about a twenty-minute break this time" Jeremy suggested as he poured a little bit of his water on his head. "Sounds good to me" his sister responded. "And if you want to take even longer, I'm okay with that" Jenny added. Twenty minutes later, Jeremy was thinking that an additional ten minutes would be better, but as he sat there relaxing, he suddenly realized that the air did not seem to be as humid as before, and he felt a slight breeze coming through the trees, from ahead. He suddenly felt a lot more energetic and stood up. "Is it time to go already?" moaned Amanda. "Yes, but I think we're pretty close to the end of the woods now" Jeremy exclaimed. "What makes you think that?" Jenny asked, as she got up on her feet. "I can feel a little breeze coming through the trees" Jeremy explained, "That means we have to be getting close to the edge of the woods. Amanda suddenly looked up at her brother,

"You mean we're really almost there?" she asked. "Yes" Jeremy answered, "Come on, get up. I want to get going again."

Amanda got up on her feet, "Okay, I'm ready" she said. They started out through the trees again with a renewed determination. Jeremy chuckled as they proceeded along. "What's so funny" his sister inquired. "I was just thinking" he answered, "We were so tired a little bit ago, now we're moving along pretty good again because we're near the end of our hike through the woods. "So" Amanda said. "So, I was thinking how much we are like a group of people in a movie I saw on television. They were crawling along through the dessert, then they reached the top of a sand dune and saw a dessert oasis on the other side, just down the hill." "I saw that movie too" declared Jenny with a chuckle, "They were all suddenly up on their feet and running down the sand dune to the spring in the oasis. You're right, we are kind of like that."

About ten minutes later, Jeremy saw some light flashing through the trees up ahead. He kept watch on the bright, flickering light, and soon let out a grateful sigh of relief, when he realized that it was the sun reflecting off of some water up ahead. "We're here!" he exclaimed, as they approached the edge of the woods, where they could all see the lake ahead, through the trees. It was around nine o'clock when they walked out of the woods. The temperature was definitely in the nineties, but there was a nice cooling breeze coming off of the lake. Jeremy was hot and tired again, and as they came out of the woods, he stopped at the edge of the clearing, and stood in the shade of the trees behind him, enjoying the cool breeze. They were all hot, tired, and sweaty from the long hike through the woods, but Jeremy was the most exhausted, from having pulled the supply cart all the way. He just stood in the shade of the trees. The trees had blocked the wind when they were in the woods, but now that they were out in the open again, they could enjoy the wonderfully refreshing breeze that was gently blowing against their sweaty faces. They all slipped off their backpacks, set them down next to the cart, then located a large grassy spot that was shaded by trees, and sat down for a good rest.

FINDING A CAMP SITE

The girls watched Jeremy as he sat on a grassy spot under the tree. He was leaning back against it with his eyes closed, breathing in deeply through his nose, then slowly exhaling through his mouth. "Do you need some water?" he heard someone ask of him. Opening his eyes, he saw Jenny smiling over at him and holding out a bottle of water. She was very attractive, not just pretty, and had a great personality. He had known her for a long time now, ever since his sister became best friends with her, and he'd come to enjoy her company quite a bit. "No thank you" he responded with a smile and holding up the water bottle he already had, "I already had some water when we first arrived. Thanks for asking though, but for now, I just need to rest and cool down for a little while." He closed his eyes again and started breathing in and out the same way as before.

Jenny turned and started talking to Amanda again after he closed his eyes and started his breathing in and out. Jeremy smiled to himself as he listened to the two girls chatting away and giggling. "Is he okay? Why is he breathing like that?" he heard Jenny whisper to his sister. "He's fine, he's just doing some breathing exercises that he learned in karate, to help him relax" Amanda answered her, "he uses that breathing method a lot for sports, too." "Does it really work?" Jenny asked. Jeremy opened his eyes, and looked over at the girls, "Yes" he said with a smile, "breathing in deeply through my nose and exhaling slowly through my mouth really helps me to relax and feel more rested." The three relaxed in the shade of the trees for nearly half of an hour, resting and cooling off from the long hike through the woods. The cool breeze that was coming off of the lake felt so good, and it was making Jeremy feel sleepy. He awoke a short time later, opening his eyes wide when he realized that he had fallen asleep. His sister and her best friend were watching him, and he smiled back at them. "Have a nice nap" Amanda asked with a grin. "How long was I asleep" he inquired. "Only about ten minutes" Jenny replied with a smile. "Oh, that's okay, I guess" he said. "You probably needed a little nap" Jenny said, "You were up later than us last night, got up before us this morning, and pulled that cart all the way through the woods by yourself." "You're right" he replied, "And I do feel a little better now."

"So, do you have any other plans for this summer" Jenny asked him, "besides this camping trip I mean?" "Not really" Jeremy answered, "I'll be working at the grocery store almost every day after we get back home. I work Monday thru Friday, and every other Saturday, bagging and carrying the groceries out to customers' cars, plus stocking the shelves. Other than that, I plan to just take it easy, and hang out with my friends." Jenny smiled, "My family usually goes on a vacation trip for a couple weeks every summer" she said, "My dad tries to plan a two week vacation at some fun place, where there are neat things for us to do." "That sounds pretty cool" Jeremy responded, "we go and visit our grandparents sometimes, and our aunt, uncle, and cousins always come to visit us during Easter, Thanksgiving, and Christmas, but mom likes us to help out with the family business, so we don't get away very often." "That's true, but we also get paid for working in the store." Amanda added, "So, we earn some money to spend on things that we want."

Jeremy glanced at his watch, "Well, I think It's time for us to get going, again" he announced, "We need to find a good spot for our camp site." "Do we have to?" grumbled Amanda. "Yes, can't we rest for just a little bit longer?" Jenny asked, "You still look awfully tired." Jeremy smiled back at the two girls, "It's around nine-thirty right now", he said, "if we can find a good spot and set up most of the camp site before noon, we should be able to take a few hours off this afternoon to go swimming in the lake, and then relax on the shore until supper time." "Oh! I like the sounds of that" squealed Amanda, "let's get going then!" Jeremy pointed to the cart, "We'll leave the cart and our backpacks here in the shade until we can find a good camp site" he explained, "then we'll come back to get everything. That way we won't be dragging all of our stuff around with us while we search for the best camp site."

They set off towards the lake shore, then headed south, looking up towards the area between the lake and the woods to see if they could find a good place to set up their camp for the next ten days. After about ten minutes, they had checked out two locations which did not meet with Jeremy's approval. One was too small of an area, he said, and the other was too rocky, which would make for a pretty uncomfortable area to sleep on. Reversing direction, they walked back along the shoreline the way they had come, until they could see the supply cart up near the tree line. Continuing north, they soon heard a distant roaring sound up ahead of them. "What's that sound?" Jenny voiced aloud. "It sounds like it might be rushing water" Jeremy responded. "It's the waterfall!" squealed Amanda, "Remember Jeremy? James and John mentioned that there was a waterfall at the lake." "Oh, yeah" he replied, "wouldn't it be neat to have our camp site near the waterfalls?" "Not too close though" Amanda said, "I wouldn't want the sound to be so loud that it keeps me awake all night."

Another five-minute walk along the shore, and they

spotted a location that looked like a good possibility for them. “This spot looks good enough to me” Amanda declared, obviously getting tired of looking. “It’ll work if we don’t find a better location” Jeremy replied. “Well, why don’t we just use this one then” his sister asked. “Because it lacks one thing that I think we need, so I think we should check further on” he answered her, “the next one might be better than this one, otherwise we’ll come back to this one, alright?” “Alright” Amanda grumbled, “but I don’t see anything wrong with this one.” “Nothing’s wrong with it, except that I’d like a place that has a tall tree in or near it” he explained, “We need to hang a bag with our food supplies in it, from a high tree branch, to keep the food away from any animals that might come into the camp when we’re away.” “Oh” Amanda replied, “okay then. But just a little further, right?” “Yes, just a little further” he agreed, “Besides, we don’t want to get too much closer to the waterfall.”

They located another possible spot, after following a path from the shore, through an opening in the bushes running along the shoreline. The path went up a way, then curved around and into a clear area. Jeremy looked the area over with a grin, noting that it was large enough for their use, the ground was clear of anything that would make sleeping on it too uncomfortable, and it had a couple of trees just inside of the cleared area.

"This is a perfect location for our use" he announced. The girls were over-joyed, as he proceeded back down the path to the shoreline, to mark the path up to the camp site with an arrow shaped trail marker made of stones.

They continued walking south along the shore, back towards where they had exited the woods originally. They walked up towards the woods again and retrieved their backpacks and the cart with the supplies. When they got back to the edge of the woods, Jeremy marked the tree he had rested under earlier, with another yellow ribbon. When they all had their backpacks on, Jeremy grabbed the pull bar of the cart and they all headed back to their chosen camp site, with him tying yellow ribbons in the bushes, down to the shoreline. At the beach, he created another arrow marker that pointed north towards the camp site. When they reached the path that led up to the camp site, the girls ran on ahead, while Jeremy pulled the cart up the path after the girls. It had only taken them about an hour to find a suitable camp site location, and then get all of their supplies back to that location. It was now about ten-thirty, and they would probably need a couple of hours yet, to get the site all set up before lunch time.

SETTING UP CAMP

Jeremy pulled the supply cart into the center of the camp site clearing. "Okay" he called out, "first thing we need to do is put on some sunscreen. We are going to be working out in the sun most of the time now." They all got out their sunscreen and applied it on their arms, legs, and faces. "The next thing is to decide where to put everything. The fire pit will be located in the center of the camp, away from anything that might melt or catch fire" he explained. "I think we should put the tents on the south side of the camp" Amanda said, "over there by those bushes, so the sun will be to the back of the tents most of the time." Jeremy looked at his sister with disbelief, "That's a good idea" he said, "what made you think of that?" "I've been looking up information on camping" his sister replied with a grin, "My information also says that the 'latrine area' should be on the opposite side of the camp, away from the tents, and behind some bushes or trees for privacy." "That makes really good sense to me" Jenny put in with a grin, "and maybe a separate place for the boys, and one for us, so we don't worry about the wrong person walking in on our personal business."

Jeremy untied and removed the tarp from the cart, and placed it on the ground, in one of the chosen tent locations. He got one of the tents out of the cart, and the three of them started getting all the parts out of the bag. Under Jeremy's instructions, they soon had the first of the two tents assembled on top of the tarp, and it had only taken them twenty-five minutes to complete. He got another tarp and the second tent out, and they began setting up the second tent, taking only twenty minutes to finish this time. "Good job" Jeremy said to the girls, "now, get your sleeping bags out of the cart, and put them in the tent that you two want to share, along with your backpacks. I am going to start staking and tying down the tents, so they can't fly away if it gets windy."

The girls gathered up their stuff and began putting it into one of the tents. When they were finished, they checked on Jeremy, who had the first tent already secured with stakes. "Can we help you with the second tent?" Jenny asked, "I'd like to know how to do the staking down part, too." "Sure, just take two stakes and one tie-down cord" he said, pointing to the items as he named them, "then just watch me, and do like I do." They grabbed the items and watched as he proceeded to stake down one of the four tent pole corners to the ground. They followed his example and staked two of the other tent corners down in the same way, while he secured his tie-down cord to the tent, then staked it to the ground a couple feet away from the tent. "I didn't see how you did that cord" Amanda complained.

"That's okay" Jeremy said with a smile, "watch me as I do the last corner of the tent." He staked the last tent pole down, then slowly proceeded to secure the tie-down cord to the last side of the tent. The girls watched, then followed his example to finish their corners of the tent also.

"Good work" Jeremy complimented them. "Now, can you grab the last two sleeping bags, and put them in this second tent?" he asked, as he grabbed his backpack and put it inside of the same tent. While the girls put the sleeping bags inside of the tent, Jeremy got one of the coolers out of the cart and put in the tent also. The girls helped him unload the rest of the supplies, storing everything except the paper grocery bags in between the two tents. "I'm going to store the dry groceries in a canvas bag and hang it from that tree over there" he said, pointing to one of the trees at the edge of the camp site, "That should be high enough to keep animals from getting into our groceries." "What should we do?" asked Jenny. "You two can relax for a little bit if you want to" Jeremy said, "when I'm done with the groceries, we still have more setup work to do." "Okay with me" Amanda said with a smile, "just call us when you're ready. We'll be down by the lake looking around a little bit." Jeremy smiled back at the two girls, "Okay, it'll take me about fifteen minutes to finish this" he said. "We'll be back in about fifteen minutes then" Jenny replied, as the two girls headed down the path to the lake.

Jeremy pulled the cart over by the trees on the east side of the camp site and took a rope from the cart. He carefully tossed the rope up over a limb of the tree so it was hanging down on both sides of a good-sized branch. Taking a canvas bag from the cart, he reached inside of it and pulled out four cords that he attached to the four eyelets on the corners of the canvas bag, using carabiners at the end of each cord. Next, he took a piece of wood from the cart, and placed it in the bottom of the bag to stretch the bottom open. Slipping one end of the rope that was hanging from the tree branch, through the metal loops on the other end of each cord, he securely tied a knot to hold them all together. "Okay" he muttered to himself, "now, let's get the groceries inside of this bag and pull it up into the air to get this chore done." With all the groceries inside of the bag, he pulled out the attached canvas flap from inside the bag and draped it over the groceries inside. He pulled the draw cord tight at the top of the bag, closing up the opening, and secured it with the sliding lock. Finally, he pulled down on the loose end of the rope that was over the branch and raised the food bag up off the ground. When the bag was hanging about twelve feet above the ground, he wrapped the rope around the tree trunk, and secured it with a knot. The groceries were now hung up out of reach of animals.

While Jeremy was securing the groceries up in the air, the girls had gone down to the lake shore to wade around in the cool water. “Let’s go up around that bend up there” Amanda suggested, “I’m sure the waterfall is in that direction.” “Okay, but we can’t go any further than the bend” Jenny told her friend, “we have to get back to camp in less than fifteen minutes, remember?” The two ran up along the shore together. As they got near to the bend, Jenny stopped, “What’s that other sound, besides the rushing water?” she asked. Amanda stopped along-side of her, and listened, “It sounds like voices” she replied, “kids’ voices?” They walked up behind some bushes at the bend and looked around them to see the waterfall up ahead. Then they spotted two figures out in the water, young kids splashing each other and playing around. One of the kids was white and the other appeared to be dark skinned. “They must be here with some adults somewhere” Amanda whispered, “but I don’t see anyone except those two kids.” “There have to be some adults around here somewhere” Jenny whispered back, “who would let their kids swim in the lake by themselves?”

The girls watched the kids for several minutes, as they played out in the lake, but failed to see any adults in the immediate area. Suddenly, Amanda gasped and placed her hand up to cover her mouth. “What’s the matter?” Jenny inquired. Amanda looked at her friend and started giggling, “Didn’t you see the kids when they jumped high up, out of the water?” “See what?” Jenny said, “I was looking over towards the shore for adults that might be around.” Amanda pointed out at the two kids and grinned, “They’re naked” she whispered, “I saw their bare bottoms when they jumped up out of the water.” “Really?” gasped Jenny, “They were actually naked?” “Yes” her friend replied, “just keep watching them. When they jump up high enough again, you’ll see for yourself.” They watched the kids for several minutes before they began jumping up and down in the water again, splashing each other. “Oh!” Jenny exclaimed, “You’re right, they are naked, and at least one of them is a boy.” “They’re both boys” Amanda said, “I saw them both from the front this time, and they’re definitely not girls.” The girls watched several more minutes, as the two boys bounced around out in the lake, then Jenny tapped Amanda on the shoulder, “We need to get back” she whispered, “Jeremy will be waiting for us.” “Okay” Amanda giggled, “wait until he hears what we found.”

“We only have about thirty minutes until it’s noon” Jeremy announced when he saw the girls coming up the path, “We need to get started gathering rocks for the fire pit”. He grabbed the pull bar on the cart, which was empty now, and walked towards the two girls. “Wait a minute” Amanda exclaimed, “we want to tell you what we saw in the lake.” She and Jenny started giggling together. “What did you see that could be so funny?” Jeremy asked. Amanda grinned at her brother, “We saw two kids swimming out in the lake by the waterfall, and they were naked” she exclaimed. “Really?” Jeremy said with doubt in his voice, “You expect me to believe that there are naked people out in the lake.” “Yes” Amanda said, “come with us and we’ll show you.”

The girls quietly led him out to the bushes at the bend and told him to look around the side and out towards the waterfall. He kneeled down and peeked around the bushes for several seconds, then moved more around the bushes and looked around for about another minute. “There’s no one out there” he declared, “I don’t see anyone.” “Oh, no! They’re gone” exclaimed the girls in unison, after looking for themselves again. “Nice try” Jeremy said, “But we don’t have time for jokes right now, so can we get back to work again?” “But they were there.” Amanda insisted, “We saw them, and they were bare butt naked.” “Sure” her brother replied, “well, maybe they’ll be back for another show later. Come on, we have to build the fire pit yet, and when it’s done, we’ll be finished with setting up the camp site, and we can go for a swim. We’ll gather the wood later.”

The girls were disappointed about Jeremy not believing them about the two boys they had seen, and they were a little depressed, but the idea of finishing the camp setup had lifted their spirits. “All right!” they yelled together, “Let’s get this done, you just have to show us what to do.” The three teens went back to camp and retrieved the cart, then started out south along the shore to gather rocks for the fire pit. Jeremy picked up a rock from the ground and showed it to the girls, “This is about the size of rock that we need, or slightly larger” he said. They located a few more rocks from the immediate area and put them into the cart, then started out along the shore again. Jeremy pulled the cart along, while the girls found rocks of the size he had indicated, placing them into the cart. “Aren’t you going to help pick up rocks, too?” his sister asked. “I would” he replied, “but then one of you would have to pull the cart.”

Amanda smiled, as she took the cart handle from her brother, and started pulling it along. Jeremy smiled knowingly, as he joined Jenny in selecting more rocks to put into the cart. After about ten minutes, Amanda stopped, wiped the sweat from her face, and looked at her brother. “Okay, you can take the cart again” she told him, “It’s getting too heavy for me to pull, now.” Jeremy grinned at his sister and laughed, “I was wondering how much longer you would want to pull the cart” he said, “It must be getting pretty heavy by now.” “Yes, it is” Amanda replied. “Maybe I should pull it for a while”

Jenny offered. "No, I think I should pull it" Jeremy answered her. "Yeah, Jenny, let him pull it" her friend agreed, "it really is too heavy for us right now, with all those rocks in it. I was going to give it back to him earlier, but I knew he would tease me about it." "Amanda's right, Jenny" said Jeremy, "You can tell it's getting heavy by how deep the wheel tracks are in the sand. I'll pull it back to camp, we'll get these rocks unloaded, then we can come out again to look for more rocks. You can pull the cart then, okay?" "Okay, it's a deal" smiled Jenny.

They picked up a few more rocks on the way back to camp and unloaded all of them near the location for the fire pit. Jenny grabbed the cart handle when it was empty and headed down the path to the beach. "We'll go north towards the waterfall this time" Jeremy suggested, "we don't want to go over the same area to the south again." "There should be plenty of rocks by the waterfall" Jenny suggested. "Yes, probably, and maybe the naked kids will be back" chuckled Jeremy. "Oh, shut up!" exclaimed his sister. They found more rocks as they continued north, but after about ten minutes, Jenny stopped. "You're getting tired of pulling the cart, aren't you?" Jeremy said. "Yes" she answered, "I think you should take over again." He smiled at her as he took over pulling the cart. About five minutes later, as they rounded the bend, he stopped. "What's the matter, tired already?" his sister teased. "No, I'm not tired" he answered, "I'm just admiring the waterfall."

"It's beautiful, isn't it" Jenny commented. "Yes, it is" he replied, "and I can see plenty of rocks around the hillside, too. We should take this load of rocks back to camp, then return here for one more load of rocks. That should be about all that we'll need to collect for the fire pit." "Why don't Jenny and I wait for you over by the waterfall, while you take the rocks back to camp" Amanda suggested. "Oh, now that wouldn't be fair to Jeremy" Jenny said, "He shouldn't have to do all the work of getting the cart back to camp and unload the rocks, while you and I sit around relaxing." "You're right" Amanda groaned, "that wouldn't be fair." "That's okay" Jeremy said with a big smile, "you two have been working pretty hard, and it's already past twelve-thirty. We've been collecting rocks for nearly an hour, so I'll take this load back to camp while you two go over by the waterfall and relax. Just look around for rocks we can use while I'm gone. When I come back, I'll bring some lunch with me. We'll fill the cart again after we eat, take it back to camp, and then go for a swim to cool off." "Oh, you're wonderful. Thank you!" the girls exclaimed as they headed off towards the waterfall.

Jeremy reached the camp site about fifteen minutes after leaving the girls back at the waterfall. He didn't have to pick up any rocks along the way, and when he got to the camp site, he unloaded the cart, placing the rocks with the previous load they had gathered. Then he went over to the tree they had the food stores hanging from and lowered the bag down to the ground. He opened the bag to retrieved some bread, a jar of peanut butter, a paper bag, and a knife. He put the food and knife into the paper bag, placed the bag in the cart, and pulled the cart over to the tents. He went inside his tent, and got three water bottles from the cooler, and put them in the cart also. With the food and drinks in the cart, he started back down the path to the beach, and towards the waterfall where the girls would be waiting for him.

TIME FOR RELAXING

"Here he comes" Jenny shouted, "I can see him coming around the bend now." Amanda looked up and saw her brother approaching, then picked up the rock she had found, and walked towards Jenny. The two girls had started gathering up rocks about ten minutes after Jeremy left to head back to camp with the last load of rocks. He'd been gone about half an hour and was finally returning with the empty cart and their lunch. She and Jenny had been piling up rocks in one spot, to hopefully fill the cart for the last time. They would eat the lunch Jeremy was bringing back, then load all the rocks into the cart and take them back to the camp site. Once back at camp, they were hopefully going to get in a little swimming time in the lake, before beginning the work of creating a fire pit with the rocks they had gathered.

"Welcome back" the girls chimed, as Jeremy reached them, "We found a lot of good rocks over by the waterfall and carried them back here to this pile." "That's great," Jeremy responded, "it looks like more than enough to be able to finish the fire pit. We can load them into the cart after we eat and take them back to camp." He reached inside of the paper bag that was in the cart and took out the bread, peanut butter, and knife. He opened the jar of peanut butter and started making sandwiches, handing one each to the girls as he made them. They all sat down on the sandy shore and ate their sandwiches, washing them down with the water Jeremy had also brought along. After they finished eating, they put the remaining groceries back in the bag, and started loading all the rocks into the cart. When the cart was full enough, Jenny picked up the grocery bag to carry it and Jeremy picked up the pull bar of the cart so they could start back to camp. The girls were following along behind the cart, giggling and chatting about how anxious they were to go swimming in the lake, and how great it would be to finally cool off properly.

When they arrived back at their camp site about fifteen minutes later, Jeremy pulled the cart over by the pile of rocks that they had already collected and dropped the handle on the ground. "Okay, you two go ahead and get ready to go swimming, I'm just going to put the groceries back up in the food storage bag" Jeremy said. Jenny handed the bag of groceries to him and the girls dashed over to their tent to change into swimsuits, and apply more sunscreen. When they stepped out of the tent again, ten minutes later, Jeremy had just finishing tying the rope to the tree trunk again, to hold the storage bag in place. "We're ready" the girls squealed excitedly. "You two look absolutely gorgeous" he told them, "Go on ahead to the lake, "I'll be there in a few minutes, after I get changed into my swim trunks." The girls ran down the path with their towels flapping behind them, heading for the lake, while Jeremy slipped into his tent to change into swim trunks. Ten minutes later, all three teenagers were in the lake, jumping around and splashing each other, yelling and screaming, as they played in the cool water.

After twenty minutes of playing wildly in the lake, the three friends were starting to get tired, so they sat down in the water at the edge of the lake and just relaxed in the gently lapping water. "This is great" Amanda said with a grin, "this feels really nice after all the work we've done, setting up the camp." "It's a great place" Jenny said, "It's so peaceful here, with just the birds singing, the rippling sound of the lake water, and the rushing sound of the waterfall in the distance." "Yeah, and the water is so clear" Amanda added, "I just love how crystal clear it is." "Clear, cool, and refreshing" Jeremy declared, "But don't forget, we still have to construct a fire pit." "You're a party pooper" his sister growled with a smile, "did you really have to remind us of the work we still have to do?" "Well, I just want all of us to remember that we'll need that fire pit if we want to be able to cook our supper later" he replied. "I don't know about you two" Jenny exclaimed, "But I'm going to enjoy the lake for as long as I can before doing more work." "Me too" Jeremy said as he splashed some water at his sister. Amanda returned the favor and splashed water back at him, and there was soon a water war going on between the two siblings.

Jenny stood up in the water and started walking out into the lake. "I think I'll go for a swim further out in the lake, to get away from this feud between you Andersen's" Jenny said with a chuckle, "when the war is over, and peace is again present in this wonderful land, maybe you two will come out and join me." "I'm finished already" Jeremy quickly responded while standing up, "I surrender to my lovely sister. May I come with you now, beautiful princess of peace." "Are you coming too?" Jenny asked Amanda?" "No, not right now" Amanda replied with a sly grin, "I think I'll stay here, and relax some more. You two go ahead. Have a nice swim, together." Jenny glanced back at her best friend as she and Jeremy wadded out into deeper water, "I saw that sly grin of hers. What's she up to now" Jenny thought to herself. Amanda grinned as she watched her best friend and brother walk out into deeper water together. "Those two need some time together, alone" she thought to herself, "and when Charlie gets here tomorrow, I going to make sure that he and I get some alone time together, too."

Jeremy grinned as he looked at the slender, blond haired, blue eyed girl who was walking in the water beside him. They continued walking until the water was waist deep, then dove in and began swimming out towards the center of the lake. He was glad that his sister had stayed behind, allowing him to swim alone with Jenny. Maybe he would work up the courage to ask her out, yet. He had always liked his sister's best friend, but over the last year, he had grown a lot fonder of her, and wondered if she could possibly like him enough to say 'yes' if he were to ask her out on a date. Jenny noticed the smile on Jeremy's handsome face and was overjoyed that he had come along on a swim with her. She hoped that the muscular, brown haired boy with green eyes, liked her as much as she like him, and that he would ask her out on a date someday, soon.

The two had been swimming steadily for ten minutes already. Jeremy felt like he could swim forever with this beautiful girl beside him, but he noticed the signs that indicated she was starting to get tired. He'd been on the school swim team for the last three years and was considered one of the team's best swimmers. He was the team captain now, and he could easily swim further, and still make it back to the shore, but he worried that Jenny might not be able to make it back to shore if they went on much further. He stopped swimming, and treaded water, "Jenny" he called over to her, "I think we've gone out far enough, we should head back to shore." Jenny stopped swimming, and looked over at him, “You getting tired?” she asked him with a grin. “Yes” he answered, “Let’s head back to shore.” “You’re not being honest with me” she said, “you’re not that tired at all, yet. But you can see that I’m starting to get tired, and you’re worried that I might not be able to make it back to shore.” “Well, yes” he replied with a guilty look on his face, “So, are you ready to head back in?”

“Yes, I am tired. And I’m ready to go back” she answered him, “but I think you are so sweet to be worried about me.” “Well, I think a lot of you” he said to her, “you’re my sister’s best friend after all.” “Oh? Is that all” Jenny asked him, “I’m just your sister’s best friend?” Jeremy started blushing, “Well, no, you’re a lot more than that to me. You’re my friend too” he replied, “and I like you a lot.” “I like you too” she responded, “A lot. I think you’re a great guy.” He grinned at her comment about liking him a lot. “So, do you like me enough to go out with me?” he inquired. “Are you asking me if I would go out on a date with you?” she said with a grin. “Well, yes. Yes, I am” he answered, “When we get back from this camping trip, I would like to take you out to a café, and then maybe a movie.” “I’d really like that” she replied with a big smile, “I’ve been waiting a long time for you to ask me out.” “Really?” he gasped, “Because I’ve wanted to ask you out for a while now, but I’ve been too afraid that you might say no.” She swam over to him, and put her arms around his neck, "I think you are the most wonderful, sweetest guy that I know, and I would definitely love to go on a date with you." Jeremy was grinning from ear to ear. "Thank you. That's great, really great" he exclaimed, "I can't wait! But now we really should head back to shore, Amanda is going to be wondering what happened to us." "Oh, I don't think she will be too worried" Jenny replied, "She might be wondering if her plan worked though." "Plan? What plan?" Jeremy asked.

When the two teens were close enough to shore, they stopped swimming and stood up, then began walking towards the beach where Amanda was still relaxing on the sand. Amanda saw them approaching and stood up. She watched her brother and her best friend coming towards her, holding each other's hand. "How was the swim?" she asked with a big smile. "Very nice" replied Jenny with a straight face, "The water was great and we had a nice swim and chat. After all the work we've been doing today, it was very enjoyable." "A nice swim?" Amanda exclaimed, "Is that all?" "We just went for a swim out and back, what else were you expecting, sis" asked Jeremy. "Well, I thought, I mean, oh just forget it" Amanda exclaimed. "No!" exclaimed Jenny. "What?" gasped Amanda. "I don't want to just forget it" Jenny responded with a grin, "I don't just want to forget that your brother asked me to go on a date with him, after we get back from this camping trip." "What? Really?" squealed Amanda with a big grin, "Did he really asked you out?" "Yes, he did" answered Jenny, "Wasn't that what you were planning to happen, you little schemer." "What? Who, me?" Amanda chuckled, reaching out to embrace her best friend. Both girls giggled happily, as Jeremy just stood by with a huge grin on his own face.

Finally, the girls separated, and Amanda turned to her brother with a stern look on her face, "It's about time you got around to asking her out" she growled. "What do you mean?" Jeremy asked. "I've known for a long time, that you really liked Jenny." "Yah, and how would you know that?' he inquired. "Really, brother dear. I could tell by the way you act when you're around her, of course" his sister replied with a grin, "It's been pretty obvious to me, for a long time. And you better treat her good, she's my best friend you know." "I know that" Jeremy said, "and I wouldn't do anything to make her unhappy, I happen to like Jenny too much to hurt her, and not just because she's your best friend."

"Hey, let's sit down on the beach, and relax for a little while, I'm tired after that swim with your brother" Jenny declared. They all walked back up on the sandy shore and sat down on the sand. Jeremy sat close to Jenny and put his arm around her. "This is really great" he exclaimed, “the best trip I’ve ever been on. We found a great place for our camping trip, and I have my girlfriend and my favorite sister with me.” “I’m your only sister” Amanda said with a laugh, “And, Jenny had better be your ‘ONLY’ girlfriend.” “She is” he replied, looking admiringly into Jenny’s eyes. They all laid back on the beach, and let the sun wash over them, warming and drying them at the same time. After about thirty minutes, Jeremy sat up and looked at the two girls relaxing beside him, “I think I’ll head back to camp” he announced, “I’ve relaxed enough, and I want to get started on the fire pit.” “Do you want us to come along?” Jenny asked with a smile. “Not yet” he answered her, “You two can head back in about fifteen minutes, that should give me time to dig a hole for the fire pit.” “Okay with me” piped in Amanda with a grin. Jeremy stood up and began walking back towards the camp with a new spring in his step.

BUILDING A FIRE PIT

Jeremy slipped into his tent when he got back to camp and changed out of his wet swim trunks, and into a dry pair of shorts. He grabbed the shovel that he had brought along and went over to where he wanted the fire pit to be. He began shoveling away the sand in about a four-foot radius, tossing the sand out about three feet away from the edge of the hole he was creating, so it would not slide back into the hole again. About eight inches down, the sand changed to black dirt, and he started placing that over the outside six inches of the hole he was digging. The remaining three-foot wide hole he dug down at an angle towards the center until he had dug down about another four inches deeper. The fire pit would end up being about six to ten inches deep when it was completed and lined with the rocks they had collected from around the lake. The six-inch ring of dirt would allow him to set the rocks in place for the sides, starting at the bottom of the hole and going up the edges of the pit. A ring of rocks on the surface, going around the fire pit would help to keep sand from sifting back in.

The girls showed up while he was still finishing the last four inches down in the pit. They went into their tent to change out of their wet swimsuits, while he continued digging. When they came back out of the tent, they came over to the edge of the hole he was still digging. “What do you want us to do?” Amanda asked her brother. Jeremy looked at the girls and smiled. “I’m not quite done digging yet” he answered her, “why don’t you guys go and look for some dry fire wood around the area for about five minutes. When the hole is finished, we can cover the bottom with rocks, and then build up the sides of it with more rocks from what we’ve collected.” “What do you mean by, ‘you guys’” Jenny asked with a smile, “do we actually look like ‘guys’ to you?” “Oh, no. N-no w-way” Jeremy answered with a stutter in his voice, “you definitely do not resemble ‘guys’. I should have said, you two gorgeous gals.” “Nice save” Amanda chuckled, “Come on gorgeous friend of mine, let’s find some fire wood.” Jeremy went back to digging, as the girls headed off to look for fire wood in the brush around the camp site. He estimated that he was about a foot deep so far and needed to dig down another two inches yet before they started putting the rocks in place.

The girls returned about five minutes later with an armful of wood each. Jeremy had just finishing digging the hole and was ready to start putting in the rocks. “Hey, handsome, where do you want this wood?” Jenny inquired with a smile. “Pile it up over there by the edge of the camp, gorgeous” Jeremy replied with a grin, “the hole is finished, so we can start lining it with rocks now.”

Jeremy tossed a thin layer of sand back into the hole to cover the bottom of the pit, then had the girls start bringing him rocks. "The flattest rocks first" he instructed, "then I'll need larger rocks for the bottom of the sides, and then the smaller ones to finish up the sides to the top." He placed the flat rocks they brought him down in the bottom, on top of the sand, then started building up the sides of the hole with the larger rocks. Soon, they had the hole lined with the rocks and he threw some more sand over the rocks in the bottom to fill in any holes or gaps. The last of the rocks were arranged around the top of the fire pit, forming a ring all the way around the edge of it. He pushed more sand up against the outside of the top ring of rocks, so it tapered off to the ground all around. He placed a couple large rocks in the bottom of the pit, so the wood they put inside would be raised up a little and allow air to get under the fire and help it burn better.

"Are we done, now?" asked his sister. "Not quite, we still need more wood" he replied, "We need enough wood to cook supper tonight, breakfast tomorrow, and maybe to keep a fire going if we want to sit around a campfire tonight. When we have enough wood for all of that, we should be good. We can gather more wood tomorrow morning after breakfast again." "So, how much wood do you think we'll need?" Jenny asked him. "Well, if we take the cart along and fill it up good"

Jeremy said, "that should be enough for tonight." They headed off down the path with Amanda pulling the cart, and Jenny and Jeremy picking up dry wood as they went along, piling it all into the cart. When the cart started getting too heavy for his sister, Jeremy took over, while the girls continued gathering more wood. They went south along the lake shore, going up paths where they had searched for camp sites earlier. Finally, the cart was filled with enough wood, and they headed back toward the camp site again.

They arrived back at camp with the cart full of fire wood and left it by the small pile of wood the girls had collected earlier. Jeremy took some of the wood over to the fire pit and laid it down at the side. He placed some smaller pieces in the bottom of the pit, with a couple larger pieces on top, then went and got some newspaper and matches out of his tent. He tucked the paper under the larger wood pieces and around the smaller stick type of wood, then used a match to ignite the paper. After the fire was burning good, he put a couple more larger pieces of wood on the fire and set a collapsible fire grate over the fire so they were now ready to start cooking. It was almost five o'clock, and everyone was hungry from an afternoon of swimming and working. "What are we having for supper?" Amanda asked. "I think something simple, like hot dogs on bread, with some chips" Jeremy suggested. "That sounds pretty good to me" she replied back. "You can get the hot dogs from the cooler in my tent," he directed her, "Jenny and I will go over to the grocery store hanging up in the tree and get the plates, bread, chips, and condiments. "The grocery store" Jenny repeated with a chuckle, "do we have enough cash to pay for everything?" "Oh, no. I forgot to bring some money with me" Jeremy said with a grin, "We'll just have put it all on credit." Jenny giggled as she followed him over to the tree, while Amanda went to the tent to get the meat from one of the coolers.

The fire was burning pretty good by now, and Jeremy adjusted the grate over the fire so the meat could be cooked on it without it burning. "I'll get the hot dogs started" Amanda offered, "you two put the plates, buns, and other stuff on a blanket. "Sorry, no buns" Jenny replied with a smile, "the grocery store didn't have any buns, so we've got to use slices of bread instead." When Amanda had the hot dogs completely cooked, she placed them on a forth plate, and brought them over to the blanket. Each person prepared their own hot dog the way they wanted, using packets of ketchup and mustard, and some shredded cheese. They had cheese puffs to go along with the hot dogs, and of course water to drink. When they finished eating, they tossed the paper plates into the fire to dispose of them. The remaining food stuffs were taken back to the grocery store, which was then pulled up in the air again. With their first day coming to an end, the three teens sat down on the blanket again to relaxed around the crackling fire for a while.

After half an hour of relaxing by the fire, Jeremy stood up and looked down at the girls. "I think I'll head down to the lake again" he announced, "I feel like going for a swim before it gets too late. Anyone else want to go with, before it starts to get dark?" The girls immediately jumped up and ran into their tent to change back into their swim suits again, while Jeremy slipped into his own tent to change also. They all had a little trouble slipping into their still wet swim wear, but soon emerged from the tents and raced down the path towards the cool lake water, splashing through the water until they were able to dive in. The air was still hot, so the water felt great. Amanda began splashing Jenny and her brother, and soon they were all three splashing each other, and screaming in fun. They spent nearly an hour and a half in the lake, swimming around, playing tag, and splashing each other. When the sun started going down behind the mountains at around six-thirty, and it was beginning to darken, the air started cooling down also. They decided it was time to go back to camp, change into dry clothes, and sit around the warm fire again before bedtime. The girls dried off a little more after getting back, then slipped into their tent to change out of their wet suits. Jeremy did likewise, and after they were all back out, they hung their suits and towels over some bushes. Jeremy put more wood on the fire, then joined the girls on the blanket at the edge of the fire pit.

They sat around the fire and talked, as the darkness of night slowly engulfed them. "So, what are you two going to do on your first date?" Amanda asked. "We don't know for sure, yet" Jenny answered, "Jeremy was talking about dinner at a café, and then maybe a movie." "Hey, maybe I can find someone to go along as my date, and we can have a double date" suggested Amanda. Jeremy starred at his sister for a moment, shaking his head. "Sorry, sis. When Jenny and I go on our date, we're going alone. I'll behave, I promise. You don't have to come along and chaperone us" he said with a grin. "Are you sure?" Amanda asked with a chuckle. "Yes, he's sure" Jenny replied to her friend, "And so am I. We'll be fine with just the two of us. Maybe next time we can double date with you, okay?" "Okay" Amanda said with a grin, "And maybe I'll actually be able to find someone by then." "Not to worry there," Jeremy said, "A guy would have to be crazy to not want to go out with my gorgeous sister." "Well, I think she might have a specific someone in mind" Jenny giggled, "and that guy seems to be a lot like you Jeremy, afraid to ask her." "So, maybe we'll have to help him past his shyness, like Amanda did for me" Jeremy said, smiling at Jenny,

"Some of us guys just need a little push." "More like a little shove" Amanda said with a chuckle.

After a couple hours of relaxing around the camp fire, the girls were starting to feel sleepy. "I think I'll go to bed" Amanda announced with a big yawn, "It's been a long day, and I'm already starting to fall asleep right here. I need my beauty rest." "Me too" Jenny said, "I need my beauty sleep, too." "I think you're both beautiful enough" Jeremy said, "but you're right, we need to get some sleep. Five o'clock comes pretty soon after all." "FIVE O'CLOCK?" shrieked both girls together, "We have to get up at five o'clock?" Jeremy looked at the two girls with a straight face for a few seconds, then began laughing. "Gotcha!" he said. "That was mean, Jeremy" Amanda scolded him, "We got up early this morning to come here, and we've been working hard all day. You think that was funny? I might just get up at five o'clock, just to throw some cold water on you." "You wouldn't?" Jeremy said with concern in his voice, "I was just joking around, you know that, don't you?" "Don't worry, Jeremy" Jenny laughed, "have you ever known your sister to get up that early in the morning?" "No" he answered, "But I can imagine her doing just that to get even with someone."

SKINNY-DIPPERS AGAIN

The sun rose over the trees around six o'clock, the next morning, with the birds chirping and singing in the nearby woods. Jeremy finally crawled out of his comfortable sleeping bag about an hour later and slipped quietly out of the tent. He headed over to the far side of the camp and walked about ten feet into the bushes, to the spot they had designated as the boy's latrine. After finishing his business there, he headed back to his tent, and crawled back into his sleeping bag again. He awoke about two hours later to the sounds of voices. Deciding that it was time to get up and get the fire going again for breakfast, he rolled out of the sleeping bag. After rolling up the sleeping bag and putting it back into the cover bag, he exited the tent and spotted Jenny coming up the path from the lake. She saw him also and held up a finger to her lips to signal him to remain quiet. Next, she motioned for him to follow her back down the path towards the lake.

"Good morning. What's up?" he whispered to her, as then silently walked north towards the waterfall. She smiled at him, "Amanda and I woke up a little while ago and heard voices coming from down at the lake" she replied, "We got up and followed the voices this way towards the waterfall. Remember us telling you yesterday about the naked boys we saw swimming by the waterfall, well, they're back." Jeremy stopped in his tracks, "Are you two trying to get back at me for last night, when I kind of made you think we had to get up at five this morning?" he asked. "What?" she whispered, "No. No, I'm serious Jeremy, those kids are back out there near the waterfall again. Amanda and I think they're the same ones as yesterday, only there are three of them today." "So, where's Amanda?" Jeremy whispered back. "She's up ahead, behind the bushes, keeping an eye on them" Jenny answered, "Come on, hurry before they disappear again." Two minutes later, he spotted his sister crouching behind the bushes at the bend. She was occasionally glancing around the edge of the bushes at something, and the kid voices he could hear were coming from beyond those bushes.

Jenny quietly came up behind her friend and placed her hand on Amanda's shoulder, then bent over close to Amanda's ear. "I'm back with Jeremy" she whispered softly. Amanda looked back over her shoulder and stared straight at her brother, with a smirk on her face. "Okay big brother, now you'll see for yourself that we weren't trying to pull a joke on you yesterday. Just look around the edge of these bushes." "But, be careful so they don't see you" Jenny instructed him. Jeremy moved around his sister as she moved to the right side of the bushes and sat down on the sand. He glanced around the edge of the bushes but didn't see anything except the waterfall a little further up the shoreline. He started turning back to the girls with a grin on his face, when two heads bobbed up out of the water, followed by a third head a couple seconds later. His grin vanished, as he watched the three kids splash around out in the water. “Okay, I see three kids swimming out in the lake” he whispered to the girls, “but what makes you so sure that they are naked out there?” “Just keep watching them” Amanda instructed him, when they start jumping up in the water, and get high enough, you’ll see for yourself.”

He continued to watch the three kids swim and play around in the water, and after several minutes saw two of them jump up out of the water enough so they could dive back in and swim away from the third child. The third one followed suit and swam after the first two. “You’re right, they are naked!” Jeremy gasped, “I saw their bare butts.” “See” Amanda whispered to him, “we weren’t lying to you yesterday, we did see naked kids swimming out there, except yesterday there were only two boys, and now there are three of them.” “No, there’s still only two boys” Jeremy said with a grin, “Look, they’re all running out of the water now, and I’m sure one of them is a girl.” Jenny and Amanda crowded around him to look down the shoreline at the three kids that were coming out of the water and up onto the beach. “Oh my” gasped Amanda, “that one is a girl.

Why is a naked girl swimming with naked boys? Why are they all naked?" "Maybe they're all nudists" Jenny suggested, "a nudist goes naked all the time, boys and girls together." The three teens continued to watch as the kids ran around on the beach, playing tag. Suddenly, the girl stopped and called out to the two boys, signaling for them to come over to her. When the boys reached her, she pointed in the direction of the bushes that the spying teenagers were behind. "Oh no, I think they spotted us" exclaimed Amanda. They watched as all three kids ran back into the water and began swimming towards the other side of the lake.

"What do we do now?" asked Amanda. "We go back to camp and have breakfast" Jeremy casually replied. "But, what about those kids?" Amanda asked. "Well, they're out in the water now, and we can't chase after them in the water" Jeremy replied, "none of us is wearing a swimsuit." "So, we just go back to camp?" Amanda grumbled. "Well, we can keep our eyes open for the kids from now on" Jeremy suggested, "They must be camping with some adults somewhere around here. When Charlie gets here, we'll go looking around the lake for their camp site." They all stood up, looked at the kids that were retreating across the lake, and began walking back to their own camp site. Jenny glanced back as the waterfall was slipping out of site, and stopped. "Hey, they're gone already! I don't see them anywhere" she exclaimed. They all looked back and scanned the lake surface in search of the kids. “Where’d they go?” Jeremy asked, “There’s no way they could swim all the way across the lake already.” “Not unless they’re faster swimmers than you, brother dear” Amanda said with a snicker.

CHARLIE ARRIVES

When the three teenagers arrived back at camp, the girls went into their tent to get dressed for the day, while Jeremy went to get some food from the grocery storage bag up in the tree. When he got back, the girls had come out of their tent in clean clothes and were ready for something to eat. "What do you have there for breakfast?" Amanda asked. "Just some dry cereal for today" Jeremy replied, "you can choose from sugar glazed corn flakes, puffed chocolate balls, or crunchy sugar squares." "Cereal!" exclaimed Amanda, "I was kind of hoping for something more like sausage, eggs, and toast." "Not this morning, sis, we're not at home with a full refrigerator available. We had to pack lite for this camping trip, especially since we plan to spend eleven days here" Jeremy replied, "Do you realize the extra weight we'd have had to haul out here if we wanted to eat the way we do when we're back at home?" Amanda looked at her brother and saw that he was a little upset by her reaction. "I'm sorry" she apologized, "I've never really gone camping like this before, I guess I didn't consider that." Jeremy looked at his sister and shook his head a little. "I'm sorry, too" he said to her, "I forgot that you've never been camping for more than a weekend before. I didn't think to explain to you before we started out on this trip, what you'd be giving up to come along." "I still don't regret coming along" Amanda replied, "I knew I'd be sacrificing things on this trip, and I still would have come along even if you'd told me about everything. I wanted to spend some time with you, because in another year you'll be going off to college, and I'm going to miss having you around all the time."

"So, I suppose this means no cheeseburgers and French-fries, with chocolate malts for lunch?" Jenny said with a chuckle, to relieve the tension. Jeremy and Amanda looked at Jenny and started laughing, "We might have cheeseburgers and chips, with water" Jeremy said, "but no French fries, and double chocolate shakes are definitely not going to happen out here." "Oh! No double chocolate shakes?" the two girls cried out dramatically while grabbing each other and pretending to sob. Jeremy grinned at their little play-acting episode, and they all sat down together on the ground to eat their breakfast of dry cereal and water. It didn't take them long to finish, and the empty cereal boxes were tossed into the fire pit. The girls whispered back and forth between themselves for a few seconds, then looked at Jeremy. "Thank you for the wonderful, gourmet breakfast" they giggled together. He smiled back at them and bowed, "You are most welcome, mademoiselles" he replied with a grin, "you are most welcome 'ere at 'Chai Jer-O-Mee' any time, where our goal ez to pleaz all of our cus-tow-mairs, all of zee time."

The girls started laughing at his attempt to imitate a French waiters' accent.

Suddenly, a worried look came over Jeremy's face. Jenny looked at Amanda, then back at Jeremy. "Jeremy, what's the matter?" she asked. "Well, don't get too upset with me" he replied while staring at the ground, "but I have some disturbing news for you girls. We need to gather up some more fire wood again." The girls started giggling. "Is that all?" Amanda said. "Yeah, Jeremy, is that all?" Jenny repeated after her friend, "We already knew that we needed more fire wood. So, let's get started finding some, and get it over with for today, okay?" He looked up at both girls, and they were smiling at him. He smiled back at them, "Okay" he said, "I'll get the cart." The three headed out with the empty cart and went south to look for fire wood. They were gone for about an hour and returned with the cart filled almost to overflowing. Jeremy had actually stuck branches upward along the inner sides of the cart, so that they could get more wood stacked up inside of it. They were walking slowly along the shore on their way back to camp, but when they reached the entrance path, they heard music coming from the camp site up ahead. "I think someone is up in our camp site" Jenny whispered to the others.

Creeping slowly around the last bend in the path to

the camp site, the three teens began looking around for where the music was coming from. The girls suddenly stood up straight and ran into the camp. Jeremy followed them, still pulling the cart of fire wood behind him. "Charlie!" the girls both exclaimed together. Charlie was sitting on the ground next to the boys' tent, leaning back against a boulder and listening to music on the radio. He jumped up at the sound of his name being yelled by the girls and stood up to face them as they ran over to him. "You're here earlier than I was expecting" Jeremy called over to him, as he pulled the cart of fire wood over to the pile of wood that was still left from the previous day. "Well, your mom called me yesterday morning and offered to drive me to the edge of the woods where she left you yesterday" he replied, "She told me I had to be ready to go by six-thirty this morning though, so she could get to work on time after dropping me off." "Oh yeah, it's only Friday" Jeremy snickered, "she had to go to work today." "Unlike some people" giggled Amanda. "Huh? What do you mean?" asked Jeremy. "Well, mom had to go to work, and we have all been out gathering fire wood this morning" she replied, "I don't know about Charlie there, what work has he done today?" "Hey!" exclaimed Charlie with a smile, "I had to get up at six o'clock this morning, shower and get dressed, and eat breakfast. All after having to stay up late to celebrate my cousin Alvin's graduation. It wasn't so easy getting up that early. And then I had to hike two miles through the woods to get here. I've been sitting here worrying about where my friends were for almost forty-five minutes, because when I arrived the camp site was deserted."

"Oh, you sweet thing, were you really worried about us?" Amanda asked with a smile. She walked up to him, gave him a hug, and a kiss on the cheek. "Do you feel better, now that we're all back?" she asked him. He looked at her with a grin, "I feel a little better" he replied, "but another hug like that would make me feel even better." "OH! Of course." Jeremy exclaimed, as he walked towards his best friend with his arms out stretched, "Let me help you feel better." "No! No! Not from you" Charlie exclaimed, backing away from him, "Your sister is right here, and another hug from her will do just fine." Jeremy stopped and grinned at his friend as his sister moved back over in his place. "Oh, of course, Charlie, I'd be more than happy to give you another hug" she said as she embraced him in an even longer hug, plus another kiss on his cheek.

Jeremy and Jenny smiled at each other as Amanda finished hugging Charlie. "How's that? Feeling better, now?" Amanda asked the blushing boy. "Um, yeah. For now," Charlie said with a big grin, "I might need some more of that later though." Everyone started laughing. Jeremy went back over to the cart and started unloading the fire wood from the cart, onto the wood pile. "Do we have anything more for chores" Amanda asked Jeremy. "No, no more chores that I can think of for the two of you" Jeremy answered her, "We'll probably just head down to the lake after this wood is stacked." The girls proceeded into their tent while the boys took care of the fire wood, and soon stepped back out wearing bikini swim suits. They applied some sunscreen, and then were ready to go, so they started heading off, down the path. "We'll be down at the lake, boys" they exclaimed with giggles, "join us when you're done with that. "Wait!" Jeremy called out to them, "We should take our dirty clothes from yesterday, and rinse them out in the lake water. Charlie and I will put up a rope clothes line, to hang them on when we get back to camp." "We'll wash out our clothes when we get back from checking out the waterfall again" Jenny called back. "Waterfall?" Charlie said, looking at Jeremy, "Why are they in a hurry to check out the waterfall, without us along?"

Jeremy smiled at his best friend, "There's a waterfall to the north of the camp site, you can hear it, right?" "Yes, I hear it" Charlie replied. "Well, I don't think it's really the waterfall the girls are going to check on. I would guess that they actually want to see if the naked kids are back again" Jeremy said. "Naked kids!" exclaimed Charlie, "What naked kids?" Jeremy grinned at his friend, "Oh, just a couple of naked boys they spotted out in the lake yesterday, by the waterfall. We saw them out there again this morning, and they had a naked girl with them." "Naked boys, and a naked girl?" Charlie exclaimed, "So, what are we doing here, let's get down to the lake." "Hold your horses" Jeremy chuckled, "We have to put up the rope clothes line first, remember. Besides, the naked boys and girl are just kids. Little kids about ten to twelve years old." "Little kids" Charlie said with disappointment, "I guess that means there is someone else here at our secret camping spot, and they let their little kids swim bare bottomed." "We haven't seen any adults yet" Jeremy responded, "just the kids so far." "So, why are the girls so interested in a few skinny-dipping kids?" Charlie asked. "Well, these kids keep disappearing whenever they see us" Jeremy answered, "and we haven't figured out where they are disappearing to." "Well, it sounds like we are going to have an interesting week" Charlie said, "Camping out with the girls, and a mystery for us to solve." "That's right" Jeremy responded, "We have the mystery of the disappearing skinny-dippers to solve."

When the fire wood was all stacked up in the wood pile, the boys took a rope from their supplies, and tied it up between two trees to act as a clothes line for hanging wet clothes from. They slipped into their tent and put on their swim trunks, then applied sunscreen and exited back out of the tent. They ran down the path towards the lake shore, Jeremy turned right at the end of the path, followed by Charlie, and headed north to where the girls would probably be waiting for them. As they neared the bend in the shoreline, Jeremy slow down. The bushes he and the girls had hidden behind that morning were just ahead, but the girls were nowhere in sight as they crept towards the bushes. "Where are the girls?" Charlie asked. "I'm not sure" Jeremy replied, "I figured they would be here behind the bushes, if the skinny-dipping kids were back again. If the kids aren't back, then the girls probably went on ahead to the waterfall. We'll just look around the bushes first, before we go on." He peered around the edge of the bushes, with Charlie right behind him, and they spotted the girls out in the lake.

"There they are, out in the water" Jeremy said, "No kids though, just the girls. Let's go and join them." The boys ran around the bushes and headed towards the girls. The girls spotted them and began swimming towards the beach. When the four were together on the beach, Amanda hugged Charlie again, and Jenny gave Jeremy a hug also. "So, no kids around this time?" Jeremy inquired. The girls glanced over at Charlie. "Does Charlie know about the kids already?" asked Amanda. "Yes, I told him back in camp, while we finished our work" Jeremy answered. "Yeah, sounds like a cool mystery to solve" Charlie said, "we can call it,

Mystery of The Vanishing Skinny-Dippers." "Well, we'll have to wait until they come back before we can start solving the mystery" Amanda declared, "Right now, I just want to swim and have fun for the rest of the day."

A LOOK AT THE FALLS

"I've done enough work today" Amanda declared as she turned and ran into the water. She was about twenty paces out before the others reacted and ran after her, all of them screaming for her to wait for them. They swam far enough out into the lake so that they had to tread water to keep their heads above the surface. The girls joined forces and started a water war by splashing the boys and laughing. The boys joined together and began splashing back at the girls in return. Several minutes passed as the water war went on, then Jeremy looked over at his friend and suddenly yelled "Dive! Dive!" and then disappeared underwater. Charlie disappeared below the water also, and the girls were suddenly left alone, treading water and looking around for where the boys might resurface. "Where'd they go?" Amanda questioned. "I don't know" Jenny replied, "They just... Oh!" Jeremy suddenly came up right behind her and embraced her in a hug as Amanda shrieked in surprise as well. Charlie surfaced behind Amanda and grabbed her in a hug as well. Jenny spun around in her captor's arms and looked at his smiling face. "Do you surrender?" he asked her with a grin.

"Yes, we give up" Jenny responded with a smile of her own, "You win, we surrender." "We were getting tired of the war anyway" Amanda added. "Why don't we go back to shore and rest for a while then" Charlie suggested. The others all agreed that a short rest on shore would be a good idea, and they began swimming back to the beach. Once back on the beach, they all sat down on the sand to rest for a while. After about ten minutes, Charlie decided to start inquiring a little more about the skinny-dippers that his friends had apparently seen that morning and the day before. "So, tell me all about the skinny-dippers you think you saw" he said with a chuckle, "Where do you think you saw them?" "We saw them right out there in the lake, near the waterfall!" Amanda declared, pointing to where they had all just been swimming a few minutes earlier. "And we don't 'THINK' we saw them! We 'DID' see them!" she added, as she gently punched him in the arm. "Yes, we 'DID' see them" Jenny stated firmly, "And, Jeremy saw them with us this morning, right Jeremy." "Yes, I really did Charlie" he declared, "They're telling the truth. I thought they were trying to pull one over on me yesterday, but I did see them for myself this morning." "But you didn't see them until this morning?" Charlie asked his friend, "Just the girls saw them yesterday?" "That's right" Amanda said, "except that Jenny and I only saw two boys yesterday, we all saw two boys and one girl this morning." "And, how do you know they were swimming 'naked'?" Charlie asked. "Because, when they jumped up to dive under the water, we could see their bare-naked butts" Jenny answered. "So, you're all absolutely sure they were swimming naked" Charlie chuckled. "Yes, we are" Amanda said with a scowl, "they jumped up out of the water far enough yesterday for us to see that they had boy parts." "And this morning when I saw them, they actually came up on the beach to play tag for a little bit" Jeremy added, "I saw two young boys and one young girl, and they were all completely naked."

Charlie looked at his three friends, studying them for any sign of a smile, which would give away that they were pulling a joke on him. "Okay, so you all saw some naked kids swimming out there" he finally conceded, "But you have to admit, it's kind of hard to believe." "Well, when they show up again, maybe you'll get a chance to see them for yourself. Then you'll really have to believe us, Mr. Doubting Thomas" Amanda growled. "Yeah, Mr. Doubting 'Charlie'' Jenny said. Charlie knew better than to irritate the girls any further, so he decided to drop the subject for the time being. Jeremy, however, wasn't ready to drop it just yet. "When they spotted us watching them this morning, they ran back into the lake" he explained, "None of us had a swimsuit on, so we couldn't follow them out in the water, and we headed back to camp. Before we got very far, Jenny looked back for them, and they had disappeared again, from out in the middle of the lake." "You didn't see where they went to?" Charlie asked. "No, we didn't"

Jeremy replied. "One of us should probably have stayed back to see where they were going, but we didn't think of it at the time" Amanda answered.

"I've rested enough, let's go swimming again" Jenny suggested, in order to change the subject. They all got up and headed back into the water. "I wonder" Charlie suddenly muttered. "What?" Jeremy asked. "I was just wondering if there might be a place to hide, behind the waterfall" Charlie responded, "If there is, those kids could have swum back to it, under water, and you guys wouldn't have seen them doing it." "You're right, that might be possible" Jeremy declared, "why don't we all swim over and have a look?" "Yeah, let's do it" the girls chimed in excitedly. The four teens started swimming towards the falling water, Jeremy and Jenny swam to the east side of the waterfall, while Charlie and Amanda swam over to the west side. Jenny and Jeremy got over by the falls and saw that the water flowed into the lake from about eighteen feet up, out of the rocky surface of the hill behind it. They swam back to a couple feet from the rock wall, and looked under the waterfall to the other side, waiting for their friends to appear. "There they are, I see them on the other side now" Jenny exclaimed, pointing towards their friends. "I see them, too" replied Jeremy, and he waved over to them. As their friends finished swimming closer to the hill side behind the waterfall, Jeremy and Jenny began to swim towards them, under the falling water. Jeremy stopped swimming suddenly, after glancing at the rock wall just above them, "Look" he shouted to Jenny, "there's a ledge in the side of the hill." He swam closer to the rocky surface and reached up towards the ledge. "It's just out of my reach" he said to Jenny. "Try jumping up to reach it" she suggested.

Charlie was watching his friend on the other side of the waterfalls when Jeremy suddenly dropped down below the surface of the water. "What's he up to?" he mumbled softly, "Has he found something?" Suddenly, Jeremy came shooting up out of the water again. Charlie watched him grabbing at the hillside, and then he was hanging from the side of the hill, partially out of the water. "There's a ledge in the hillside!" exclaimed Amanda. "Yes" responded Charlie, "and it comes all the way down to this side of the waterfall. But look what's on this end of the ledge? Come on, let's go." He and Amanda started swimming towards the hillside under their end of the waterfall. Jeremy had been able to grab hold of the ledge with both hands and was now hanging down from it. He was still in the water from the bottom of his rib cage down. "Can you pull yourself up?" Jenny asked from below him. "I think so" he panted, "I just need to catch my breath first." After a few seconds, he pulled with his arms, and slowly lifted himself up until he was able to pull himself completely up on the ledge.

He sat down on a ledge that was cut into the hillside three feet deep and looked down at Jenny, "Need a hand up?" he asked her. "Yes, please" she replied, raising her arms up towards him. He grabbed hold of her wrists, and slowly pulled her up, until she was able to grab onto the ledge, then he stood up, reached back down to grab her wrists again, and pulled her up until she was able to sit down on the ledge. He sat down on the ledge beside her to rest for a bit, then looked back towards where they had last seen their friends in the water.

"Where did Amanda and Charlie go!" Jeremy exclaimed, when he failed to see his sister and best friend out in the water. "We're right behind you" came Charlie's voice from his left side. Jenny and Jeremy looked back along the ledge they were sitting on, and saw their friends walking towards them. "How did you two get up on this ledge so fast?" Jeremy asked, "You were still further out from the hillside when I started climbing up here. "We found a better way to get up here" his sister answered with a grin. "A better way up?" Jeremy inquired. Charlie smiled at him, "We found a kind of stairway, down on our side of the waterfall" he said, "looks like it was chiseled out of the rock. We just climbed up the steps to the ledge." Jeremy starred at them in disbelief, then started laughing, "Sure, of course, it makes perfect sense that you would find an easy way, doesn't it?"

"So, do you think the kids climbed up to this ledge, and went into a cave?" Jenny asked. "There's no cave in the hillside though" Amanda said, "we didn't see any as we walked down here on the ledge." "So, your kids didn't disappear back here" Charlie added. Amanda punched him in the arm for the second time that day, "They aren't 'OUR' kids, you lunkhead" she growled at him. "Alright, alright" he exclaimed, rubbing his arm, "I was just referring to the kids that you saw, but that I haven't seen yet. Now, will you please stop hitting my arm like that, you're going to cripple me." "Well, we weren't joking with you about seeing them" Jenny replied. "Hey, they still could have disappeared back here" Jeremy exclaimed. "What?" his friends chorused together. "They may have disappeared by hiding back here on the ledge" he said with a smile, "Think about it. They swim back here underwater, like Charlie suggested, then climb up those stairs to this ledge, and sit here out of sight until we are gone." "They were swimming towards the side of the falls with the steps" Jenny added. "So, after we were gone, they could jump back in the water and swim away in any direction, back to where they came from, and we wouldn't know where they went" Jeremy finished. "Of course, that makes sense" Charlie chuckled, "Okay, the case of the disappearing skinny-dippers is now solved, right?" "Not quite" Amanda corrected him, "we still need to find out where they are actually coming from and going to."

"Yeah, but not today" Jenny said, "I'm tired of mystery solving for now, I'm going to get in some more swimming, and then work on my sun tan." "Good idea" Jeremy said, "Let's just enjoy the lake for the rest of the day, we can continue with the mystery solving tomorrow."

AN EXHAUSTING AFTERNOON

Everyone agreed that the mystery solving would wait until the next day, so they could enjoy themselves for the rest of the current day. "Hey Charlie, wouldn't this ledge be a great place to dive from" Jeremy said, "after we dive off the ledge, we can use the steps you found at that end to climb back up again." "You're right" Charlie exclaimed, "It sounds like it would be fun too, let's give it a try-out." "Sounds good to us too" Jenny and Amanda added together. Jeremy was the first to give it a try, diving into the water, with a loud "Whoopee!" After surfacing about five feet out from the rock wall, he began swimming back down towards the ladder that his sister and friend had located. Charlie followed him into the water in a near perfect dive, then followed after his friend. The girls simply jumped into the water feet first, screaming gleefully and swimming after the boys. Jeremy climbed up the steps, and began walking back along the ledge to the other end, so he could dive in again. He stopped half way along the ledge and turned around to face his friend who stopped a couple feet behind him. Charlie looked at his friend, "What's the matter?" he asked. "I was just wondering what the water depth is all along the ledge" Jeremy replied, "It looked to be about twelve feet deep where I climbed up onto the ledge the first time, that's where we just dove in from, but we can't be diving in like that anywhere else until we've checked the depth all along the ledge first." "You're right" Charlie replied, "why don't we check it now, before doing any more diving."

The girls came up behind the boys at that moment, "What's up?" Amanda inquired. The boys looked at the girls. "We just realized that we need to check the water depth all along the ledge, before we can do any head first diving anywhere other than where we just dove in at" Charlie answered. "Just to be sure it's safe all along the ledge" Jeremy added, "You two can jump in feet first if you want to though." "You're saying that you boys shouldn't have dived in head first before checking the water depth, right?" Amanda said. "Jeremy already checked the depth where he climbed up on the ledge the first time" Charlie said, "that's where we just dove in. We're going to check the depth all along the rest of the ledge, to make sure it's all safe for diving." "After we've verified that it's all deep enough, we'll be able to dive in head first, anywhere that it's deep enough" Jeremy explained. "Oh, okay" the girls said together, and they all headed down to the far end away from the ladder, except Charlie, who went back to the ladder end. The girls reached the far end with Jeremy, where he had already verified the depth, and after jumping in again, the girls proceeded to swim towards the ladder, while

Jeremy swam down under the water, and began checking the bottom depth from his side towards the ladder. Charlie was already in the water and checking the depth from the ladder end towards Jeremy. They agreed to check the area from the rock face and out to about three feet short of the crashing water of the waterfall. When they finished checking the entire area, they decided that it was safe to dive anywhere along the ledge. The waterfall had worn the lake bottom down to a good diving depth for them.

The four teens spent about another hour, jumping and diving off of the ledge, and swimming around behind the waterfall. They were tiring, and finally decided it was time to head back to shore, for a rest out in the warm sunshine. They swam out from behind the waterfall and headed towards the beach. As they all walked out of the water and up onto the sandy beach, Amanda realized that she was hungry. “Is anyone else getting hungry?” she asked. “Yeah, I am” Jenny replied. The boys admitted that they could go for some lunch, also. “It’s almost one o’clock, and we’ve all been going since early this morning, on just dry cereal” Jeremy stated, “Let’s go back to camp, and get something to eat. After lunch, we can return to the lake, and rest for a while in the warm sun.” “Actually, I had bacon, eggs, pancakes, and orange juice for breakfast” Charlie declared with a grin, “but, I’m hungry too, so that sounds like an excellent plan to me. Let's go and eat." They all proceeded along the beach, walking back towards their camp site for some lunch.

When they arrived back at camp, they all enjoyed sandwiches, chips, and water for lunch, while sitting around in front of the tents and chatting. "Anything else happen around here before I arrived?" Charlie inquired cautiously, as they talked, "Besides the skinny-dipping kids that is." Jenny and Amanda glanced over at Jeremy with big grins on their faces. Charlie noticed the looks and the grins, turned towards Jeremy, and stared his best friend in the eyes. "Okay buddy, what else unusual happened" he demanded, "I can tell that there's something else." "Well, I don't know if I'd call it unusual" Jeremy replied with a grin. "It was unusual for you" Amanda exclaimed, "And, something you should have done sooner, but you were just too shy." "What is it? What happened?" Charlie pressed his friends. "Well" Jenny answered with a big smile, "It's just that Jeremy asked me to go out on a date with him when we get back to town. That's all." "Really? You did?" Charlie asked, staring at his best friend with a grin, "You finally got up the nerve to ask her out? It's about time." Jeremy just looked over at Jenny with a big grin. "I know" he said, "I guess I'm just the shy, quiet type. But once we finally had some time alone together, without friends hanging around and listening, we got to talking, and discovered that we both liked each other a lot. So, I kind of asked her out, and she said yes." He looked at Jenny, grinning, "And, I'm really happy you said yes."

After a little more conversation, Amanda started standing up, pulling Jenny up with her. "We need more sunscreen if we're going to head down to the beach again" she announced. "Yeah, we better grease up some more, too" Charlie said to his friend, as he got up. A short time later, four greased up teenagers were on their way down the path to the lake, with towels in hand. They reached the shore of the lake and spread their towels out on the sand, then laid down on the towels to let the warm sunshine wash over them. "Oh, this feels so good" Amanda mumbled, as she laid back on her towel, "I should have a pretty good tan by the time we get home from this trip." "It does feel good to relax, and not worry about homework" Charlie added from her right side. After they had been laying there on the beach for about half an hour, Jenny sat up and looked down to her left. "Hey Jeremy, I'm going to go for a little walk along the shore" she said, "Would you like to come with me?" "Oh, that sounds good, I'll come too" Charlie replied, as he opened his eyes and looked over towards her. "No, you won't" Amanda exclaimed, glaring at Charlie, "Jenny was asking her boyfriend, not you. You can stay right here and be my bodyguard." "Your bodyguard?" Charlie exclaimed, "Since when do you need a bodyguard?" "Since Jenny obviously wants to be alone with my brother" Amanda growled. "Oh, right" Charlie mumbled, blushing.

Jeremy and Jenny started walking south along the shoreline together, holding hands. When they were far enough away from their friends so that they couldn't be overheard, Jenny looked at Jeremy. "You know, I think Charlie is the one who might need a bodyguard" she chuckled. Jeremy burst out laughing at her comment. "Yeah, from my sister" he replied, "I think you're absolutely right about that. But, then again, I don't think he'll mind being my sister's bodyguard. And, I think you're trying to give them some time alone together, aren't you?" Jenny just smiled back at him without answering his question. "How about we swim for a little bit" she suggested, as she pulled him into the water, "I like swimming, especially when you're swimming along beside me." "That's strange" he responded with a smile, "I like swimming with you along too." They both wadded out into the water together, still holding hands, "Then again, Jenny, I believe I would enjoy doing almost anything with you along" Jeremy added.

Amanda waited several minutes, until she was sure her brother and Jenny had walked far enough away, then she sat up and looked at the handsome boy lying beside her. “I’m sure glad Jeremy and Jenny finally got together” she stated, “He’s liked her a lot for a long time now. He just needed an opportunity to be alone with her, to finally talk to her and let her know how he felt about her.” “And that chance just happened to come yesterday” Charlie asked, with a grin. “Well, it didn’t just happen” she said, “I kind of arranged for it to happen, a little.” “And, just how did you manage that?” Charlie asked, sitting up beside her. “Jenny said she wanted to go for a swim, and Jeremy was going along with her” replied Amanda, “When he asked me if I was going with them, I simply said I wanted to stay on the shore to relax some more. That allowed them to be alone together, so they could talk without anyone else around, listening to them. And it worked. When they got back from their swim together, they were holding hands and smiling, and had decided to go on a date together.”

“You’re a regular match maker” Charlie chuckled. “Not really” she replied, “The match was already made. It was so obvious that they liked each other, I just gave them an opportunity to be alone together, so they could both get past their own nervousness.” “Well, you did a great job” Charlie said to praise her. “Oh, sure” she said with a sigh, “Just wish I could get a boy to ask me out on a date.” Charlie looked at the beautiful, brown haired, green eyed girl sitting beside him, and suddenly realized something. “I think I’ve been pretty stupid” he mumbled. Amanda looked at him, "Why, what did you do" she asked with a smile. "It's not what I've done" he replied, "It's what I haven't done. Something I should have done a long time ago, just like your brother." "What's that" she asked with concern in her voice. "I've been like your brother" he answered, "I've liked a certain girl for a long time, but have been too afraid to ask her to go out with me." "Oh, do I know the girl" she asked. "You should know her, since she's you" he answered, "I should have told you a long time ago how much I like you, but I've been afraid that you wouldn't feel the same towards me." "And I've just been waiting for you to ask me out" she said with tears in her eyes, "I was starting to think you might not like me as much as I liked you."

"Well" Charlie said with a smile, "if we both like each other so much, maybe we should go out on a date, too." "I'd like that a lot" Amanda replied. "Hey, maybe we could double date with Jeremy and Jenny" he said. Amanda looked at him and started laughing. "What's so funny" he asked. "Just what you said" she answered, "I already suggested to Jeremy and Jenny yesterday, that I should find a boyfriend, so we could double date with them." "So?" he said. "So, they both said 'no', and explained to me that they didn't need a chaperone along on their first date" she replied with a giggle, "For some strange reason, they want to be alone on their first date, so they can get to know each other even better." Charlie smiled, "I guess that makes sense" he said, "matter of fact, it sounds like a good idea for our first date too."

Jeremy spotted his sister and best friend sitting up and talking, back on the beach. "Hey, look at Amanda and Charlie on the beach" he pointed out to Jenny. "Looks like they're having a good talk" Jenny said with a grin, "Maybe they're getting to know each other, like we did yesterday." "I hope so" Jeremy replied, "I know Charlie likes my sister a lot, but he's as shy about telling her, as I was in telling you." "She's laughing about something" Jenny noted, "do you suppose that's a good sign." "I hope so" Jeremy replied, "Hey, I think Charlie's pointing back this way." He casually waved back to his friend on shore. "They're both waving at us now" Jenny said, "maybe they're ready to join us for a swim." She motioned for the two on shore to join them, then watched as the two got up and ran into the water in their direction. "Let's swim in a little way and meet them" Jenny suggested. The four teens came together out in the lake, where Amanda informed her friend and brother that she and Charlie had been talking and had discovered that they mutually liked each other a lot. "Charlie asked me out on a date" she exclaimed. "It's about time" Jeremy said with a grin. They all had a really good laugh, then decided to swim to the north end of the lake where the waterfall was. When they got there, they swam around behind to the ledge, climbed up the stone steps, and sat down to rest for a while. The girls were tired from the long swim, and they just wanted to sit on the ledge for a while, before doing anything else.

The boys only rested for about five minutes, then decided to start diving off of the ledge. Charlie stood up and launched himself off of the ledge first, forming an arch in the air and entering the water in perfect form. Jeremy followed his friend into the water as soon as he saw Charlie surface and start swimming back over to the steps again. Amanda leaned in close to her friend, "I think they're showing off just for us" she whispered to Jenny. "I think you're right" giggled Jenny, "but I enjoy watching your brother when he dives into the water, he looks good in a swimsuit." "Charlie does too" Amanda said, "but I think he looks even better in his swim team suit." "Oh" Jenny giggled, "Jeremy looks better in one of those too, especially since it shows his cute butt so well." Both girls broke out in a giggling fit. The boys saw the girls talking and giggling and wondered what was so amusing. After about fifteen minutes of diving, the boys finally started to get tired again, and decided to sit on the ledge with the girls for a while. The girls however, were rested up enough by then, and decided to swim back to shore.

The two girls wanted to lay out in the sunshine some more to improve their tans. “So, those kids you saw this morning, do you think they might come back again” Charlie asked, after the girls had left. “Well, the girls saw them for the first time yesterday, we all saw them again this morning, with a girl along” Jeremy responded, “If they’re camping out somewhere around the lake, they might be back again today, but if they’re coming here only once a day, from somewhere else, then they probably won’t be back again until at least tomorrow.” “Maybe we can come out to the lake tonight, after it gets dark, and see if there are any lights or sounds from anywhere around the lake” Charlie suggested. “We can do that if we’re not too tired” Jeremy said, “But even then, only for a little while. I want to spend some time around the camp fire with the girls.” “You mean with Jenny” Charlie said with a grin, “And speaking of the girls, let’s go and join them on the beach”.

The boys stood up and dove into the water once more, then started swimming out from behind the waterfall and towards the shore. “Hey, where did they go, I don’t see them anywhere” Charlie exclaimed. “Don’t worry” Jeremy replied, “They said they were going to lay out on the beach, remember. Our towels are back by the path to camp.” “Oh, yeah” Charlie replied with a laugh, “I guess they would have headed back there then.” “Let’s stay in the water, and swim over to join them" Jeremy suggested. They swam around the bend, then headed south, towards the girls that they could now see a little way down the shoreline. They were tired again after the long swim, so by the time they walked out of the water and over to the girls, they just wanted to drop down onto their towels. The girls opened their eyes and smiled up at the boys, as they came walking up, dripping wet. "Hey" Jeremy said, "would you two lovely girls mind if two handsome guys were to join you here on the beach?" "What handsome guys" Amanda teased. "Amanda!" gasped Jenny, "do you want them to go somewhere else instead?" "Oh, no" Amanda replied, "I don't want that. I was just teasing. I'm sorry boys." Jenny smiled up at Jeremy, "We wouldn't mind if you joined us, not at all" she said with a smile, "Pull up a towel handsome, you can relax right here, next to me. You can even use my boyfriend's towel."

After an hour of laying in the sun on the beach, they all decided that it was time to head back up to the campsite again, to get started on making supper. They gathered up their towels and headed up the path to the camp. Jeremy and Charlie got some wood from the wood pile and placed it near the edge of the fire pit. The fire from the previous night was completely cold now, so Jeremy got newspaper and matches from his backpack, while Charlie arranged some small pieces of wood in the bottom of the pit for kindling. Jeremy tucked the newspaper around in the kindling and lit the paper. As the paper burned, it ignited the small pieces of wood, until there was a small fire burning. Carefully, the boys placed some of the larger pieces of wood over the small fire and allowed them to catch fire also. When the fire was burning good, they placed the cooking grate back in position, which the girls had finished cleaning. The girls went and got a pound of hamburger out of a cooler, formed the meat into four patties, then placed the patties onto the grate to cook. Meanwhile, the boys went over to the hanging grocery bag, and got out a can of beans, bread, chips, condiment packets, and some paper plates and utensils to eat with. While the girls were taking care of cooking the burgers, Jeremy opened the can of beans and placed it on the edge of the cooking grate so the beans would heat up for the meal as well. The smell of the burgers cooking smelled great, and they were all getting hungry and anxious for supper. As soon as the burgers and beans were ready, they all grabbed a plate and put some food on it. They were all seated between the tents and the campfire, with their plates balanced in their laps. They began devouring the food. The burgers, beans, and chips, with water to drink, tasted fantastic to the four hungry teenagers.

After finishing their meal, they tossed the paper plates and plastic utensils into the fire to dispose of them, so the only other thing left was the empty bean can, which Jeremy placed inside of a garbage bag that was staked down between the tents. They would haul that bag back out of the area with them when they left in nine days. They relaxed around the fire for about half an hour, no longer feeling hungry, just tired and wanting to do nothing. "How about going back down to the lake" Charlie suggested. "Not me" Amanda responded. "Me either" Jenny said, "I'm too tired to go swimming right now." "Would you girls feel more like going to the lake, if we had some air mattresses to float around on" Jeremy asked. "Air mattresses!" exclaimed the girls, "Did you really bring an air mattress along?" "Of course, I did" Jeremy chuckled, "You each slept on one under your sleeping bag last night. It's one luxury that I figured we would all enjoy. And, we have four mattresses, one for each of us."

A RELAXING EVENING

Each of the teens grabbed the air mattresses from their tents and headed down to the lake again. They wadded out into the water a short way, placed the air mattresses on the surface of the water, and laid down on them. As they laid there on the mattresses, floating around on the rippling water, they chatted about school finally being out, and the plans they all had for the summer. The sun felt nice, and floating around on the lake water, which was gently rocking them, was extremely relaxing. Since they were all pretty tired from the activities of a long day, they all started dozing off on the air mattresses until everyone was asleep. Jeremy awoke rather suddenly when he rolled over and slipped into the cool lake water. The splash, followed by his sputtering and gasping as he jumped up in the water, woke the rest of the teens. "What happened" Jeremy's sister asked in a concerned voice. "I must have fallen asleep" he answered, "I rolled over on the air mattress and ended up in the water." Everyone except Jeremy burst out laughing over the mishap, and his face turned a couple shades of red as he climbed back up on his air mattress again. "Now, don't fall off again big brother" Amanda said to him, "We wouldn't want you to drown." "Ha, ha. You don't have to worry about that, I'm wide awake now" he responded, "but you better watch out, it might be you that takes the plunge next time."

Jeremy laid back on the mattress again, and began floating around with the others, but decided to start a up conversation with the others, so he wouldn't fall asleep again. "Hey Charlie, what time do you want to head out tomorrow morning, to search around the lake for signs of the camp site of those nudist families." "Families?" Amanda said, "What makes you think there's more than one family?" "Well, two of the kids looked like they were African-American, and the other one was white" he answered her." "Well, yeah" she replied, "but they could still all be from one family if some were adopted." "That's true" Charlie said, "but chances are, they'll be from more than one family." "So, what time do you want to get going tomorrow?" Jenny asked. "Not until after breakfast" Charlie answered, "And I'm planning to sleep until at least eight o'clock." "That sounds good to me" Jeremy said, "We'll head south around the lake, and check for signs of fresh camp sites as we go." "Why are you going south?" Amanda inquired. "Because north is back towards the waterfall" Charlie answered, "and we've looked over that area enough today, and seen nothing. South hasn't been explored yet, it's the unknown territory."

"What time do you think is it now?" Jenny asked of no one in particular, "I'm getting sleepy." "Well, we don't want you following in my brothers' foot-steps, and have you doze off and start sleep swimming" chuckled

Amanda, “So maybe we should head back to camp now and turn in for the night.” “That’s a good idea, except I’d like to sit around the camp fire for a while” Jeremy added, “The sun won’t be going down behind the mountains for a little while yet. When it starts to get dark, we can crawl into our tents for some sleep.” They all agreed to that and started paddling back towards shore on the mattresses. When they reached the shore, they picked up their air mattresses and headed up the path leading to the camp site. Jeremy and Charlie used their towels to dry off their air mattresses, and put them into their tent. The girls followed the boy’s example, towel drying their air mattresses and putting them into their tent as well. The girls remained in the tent long enough to slip into some dry clothes, while the boys put more wood on the dying fire. When the girls came back out, the fire was going good again, and felt good in the cooler evening air. “Oh” Jeremy suddenly exclaimed, “With Charlie arriving this morning, we never got around to rinsing out our dirty clothes from yesterday, and now we have today’s clothes too.” “Oh, that’s right” Jenny confirmed, “do you think we have time to do it before it gets too dark, or should we wait until tomorrow morning?” “I think we have time to do it tonight yet” replied Jeremy, “you girls go ahead to the lake with your clothes, and get started, while Charlie and I get changed. We’ll be down in just a little bit.”

The girls grabbed the plastic bag they had been putting their dirty clothes into and headed back down to the lake again. The boys slipped into their tent to change, putting their clothes into another plastic bag, and then headed down to join the girls. The girls were out in about a foot and a half deep water, and Jenny was dunking pieces of clothing into the water over and over. When she finished with one piece, she would hand it to Amanda, who would give her another piece of clothing to wash. Amanda would then go up on shore again, wring out the cleaned piece of clothing and place it back into the plastic bag. Another soiled piece of clothing was picked up off of the beach, and she headed back out to Jenny again. They used this method until all their clothes had been rinsed and wrung out, finishing up two sets of clothes for each of them, plus two towels. "That looks like a pretty efficient way to do clothes" Charlie commented. "Yeah, let's do ours that way too" Jeremy said, "I'll stay in the water like Jenny, and you can do like my sister was doing." The boys copied the girls' routine, rinsing out a total of three sets of clothes, two sets for Jeremy, and one for Charlie, plus their towels. All four of them then headed back up to the camp site.

When they arrived back at camp with the clean clothes, Jeremy showed the girls a small bag of clothes pins, and they all began hanging the clean clothes up on the rope that the boys had put up earlier that day. With all the clothes hanging up to dry, they went over to the fire pit again, and Charlie and Amanda sat down together, while Jeremy put a couple more pieces of wood on the fire, and then sat down next to Jenny. The temperature was starting to drop now, so the warm fire felt good to them. "What time do you think it is?" asked Jenny. "Between six and seven" Charlie responded. "It's six- thirty-two by my watch" Jeremy said. "How about some music" Amanda inquired, "Can we turn on the radio for a while?" "Sure thing" Charlie said with a smile. He got up to get the radio from the tent, turning it on as he walked back, and turning the selection knob in search of some good music.

Jenny leaned against Jeremy and laid her head on his shoulder as he draped his arm around her shoulders. He held her close, enjoying her closeness to himself. Amanda and Charlie sat a short distance away, and pretty much duplicated their friend's actions. The two teen couples sat in the glow of the fire as darkness descended to engulfed the camp site. They sat in the glow of the fire for a little over an hour, listening to music on the radio, and just chatting occasionally. Soon, they were all having a little trouble keeping their eyes open. "I think we should all go to bed" Jenny suggested with a big smile, "Five o'clock in the morning comes pretty early." "FIVE O'CLOCK! I'm not getting up at five o'clock" exclaimed Charlie. The other three teens all started laughing, and rolled onto their backs, tears filling their eyes. “What’s so funny?” Charlie inquired with a frown, “five o’clock is way too early to be getting up.” “It was a joke, silly” Amanda chuckled, as she sat up and hugged the muscular, black haired, brown eyed boy, “Jeremy pulled that same joke on Jenny and me last night.” “Very funny, buddy” Charlie told his friend with a straight face, “Very funny.”

The girls headed off to bed, stopping at the entrance to their tent. “So, we’ll plan on breakfast at around eight-thirty tomorrow morning” Jenny announced, “What should we prepare?” Charlie looked over at his friend, “What do you think?” he asked, “You know what all you packed.” “I think a hot breakfast would be a nice change” Jeremy responded, “How about scrambled eggs and sausage, with toast, I’ll get up at eight to help you two with everything.” “That would be nice” Jenny replied with a smile, “We’ll see you in the morning then. Good-night.” “Good-night Jenny, good-night sis” Jeremy said. “Good-night big brother, and good-night to you too Charlie” Amanda returned. “Oh, yeah. Good-night Charlie” Jenny said. “What are we doing here, a scene from the Walton’s?” Charlie chuckled, “Well, good-night Amanda, good-night Jenny, and good-night to you too, Jeremy-boy.” They all laughed and slipped into their own respective tents, zipping the doors closed, and crawling into their sleeping bags.

Charlie awoke just after midnight, needing to go out to answer a call of nature, but he realized that he didn't know where the designated latrine was. "Hey, Jeremy" he whispered, as he shook the shoulder of his sleeping friend. Wh...what?" Jeremy asked, as he opened his eyes, "Charlie? What's the matter? It's not morning already, is it?" "No" his friend replied, "I just need to go to the bathroom." "So, go" Jeremy groaned, "You don't have to get permission from me." "But I don't know where you and the girls designated the bathroom to be" Charlie squeaked back. "Oh, right" Jeremy moaned, "Okay, I'll show you where the latrine is then, grab the lantern." Jeremy escorted his friend across the camp site to the designated boys' latrine, "Do you need me to hold your hand?" he chuckled, now that he was almost fully awake. "No daddy, I big boy now, I do it without you" Charlie whispered back with a laugh. Jeremy left his friend to his business behind the bushes and went over to add some more wood to the fire. "Good idea" Charlie whispered, as he came over by the fire, "Now we can go back to bed." "You go ahead, but give me the lantern" Jeremy said, "I think I'm getting a nature call myself." "Do you want me to come along and hold your hand?" Charlie chuckled.

BREAKFAST ALL TOGETHER

Jenny woke up early and quietly left the tent, then walked across the camp to the bathroom area. After finishing up behind the bushes, she headed back to her tent. As she was circling around the fire pit, she noticed that the fire from the previous evening, was down to only some glowing embers now. "I should put some more wood in there, so it doesn't go completely out" she whispered to herself. Going over to the wood pile, she took a few medium sized pieces of wood, and carried them over to the fire pit. "There" she whispered, as she placed the wood on top of the glowing embers, "that will keep it going, if they start burning." She watched for a few minutes to be sure that the dry wood had started to burn, then she went back to her tent.

She quietly stepped back inside of the tent, but as she was zipping the door closed again, a voice came from behind her. "You're up early" Amanda whispered. Jenny spun around towards the voice in the dark, "You're awake?" she said. "Either that, or I'm talking in my sleep" came a reply, "Where did you go?" Jenny smiled at the question, "Behind some bushes on the other side of the camp" she giggled. "Huh?" her friend mumbled, "Oh, I get it. Very funny." "Well, you did ask me 'where' I went" Jenny giggled, "I just went where we are supposed to go, when we have to go?" "Yeah, good one Jenny, I woke up when you left the tent. I was starting to worry, since you were taking so long." "Well, I stopped on my way back, to put some more wood on the fire" Jenny replied. "Oh, well, I'm sorry I startled you when you came back in the tent" Amanda said, as she got up from her sleeping bag. "You don't have to get up yet" Jenny said, "you can sleep for about another hour I think." "No, I can't" Amanda replied, "I need to get up and go somewhere." "Where are you going?" Jenny asked. Amanda giggled, "The same place you just came from." "Oh" Jenny chuckled, "I guess if you have to go, then that's the place to go." Amanda left and returned a short time later to crawl back into her sleeping bag. "Welcome back" Jenny whispered, "Good-night." Good-night" Amanda said, "fire is going good now. Should be okay until we get up to make breakfast."

Jeremy was up around eight o'clock. He slipped out of the tent to check on the fire, and found it still burning. "Can't believe it's still going" he whispered to himself. "That's probably because I put some more wood on it about an hour ago" came a voice from behind. "Huh? What?" he said, as he turned around to find Jenny stepping out of the girls' tent. "I said, I put more wood on the fire, about an hour ago" she replied with a smile.

"You got up to put wood on the fire?" he asked. "No, I got up for something else" she replied with a grin, "The fire was just some glowing embers at the time, so I put a couple pieces of wood on it to keep it going till we got up to fix breakfast." "Oh," he said, blushing, "speaking of which, I'll be back in a moment." Jenny smiled, as she watched him cross the camp site, and slip behind the bushes.

Jeremy returned a short time later, and put some more wood on the fire, then used a branch to lift the cooking grate back over the fire pit. Amanda was just coming out of the tent, as he was getting the grate leveled over the fire. "Morning" she said to Jenny and her brother, "Is Charlie up yet?" "Not yet" replied her brother, "We can wake him up when breakfast is almost ready, if need be." "If need be?" his sister said. "Yeah" Jeremy said with a knowing smile, "In all the time I've been camping with Charlie in scouts, he has never missed breakfast. As soon as the smell of the cooking food gets to him, his stomach wakes him up." "Oh. Well, let's get working on his alarm clock then" Amanda giggled.

Jeremy got a couple of skillets out and placed them on the cooking grate, while the girls went to the cooler to get the eggs and sausage. The girls began cooking the sausage and eggs while Jeremy went to the canvas bag hanging in the tree, to retrieve some bread, plates, and utensils. "Bread?" Jenny asked him, when he came back over with everything. "It's bread now" he said with a smile, "It'll be toast when I'm finish with it." How do you turn it into toast?" his sister asked. "With these" he replied, as he held up a couple of long handled, metal, two-pronged forks. The girls watched him, as he slipped a piece of bread onto one of the forks, then used it to hold the bread over the fire pit. A few minutes later, he turned the fork over, revealing that the underside of the bread had become toasted. "We do each side for one or two minutes each" he explained, "and voila, we have toast. Jenny came over next to him and grabbed the other fork, slipped a slice of bread onto it, and held the bread over the fire in the same manner, "I'll help with the toast" she offered, "It only takes one person to watch the meat and eggs." "Okay" Jeremy said with a smile, "just not too close to the fire, or we'll end up with charcoal toast."

Fifteen minutes after starting to cook the eggs and sausage, they heard some noise coming from the boys' tent. "I think the alarm clock went off" Jeremy chuckled, "the smell of food must be getting to him." Almost immediately, the zipper of the tent door started unzipping, and a head popped out of the opening. "Something smells good out here" Charlie said as he yawned. His friends started laughing. "What's so funny?" he asked. "Nothing Charlie, nothing at all" Jeremy replied. "You're up just in time, as usual, breakfast is almost ready." Charlie sat down on the sand a short distance from the fire, stretching and yawning some more. Amanda came over to him, and handed him a plate, "Here you go, handsome" she said with a big smile, "scrambled eggs, sausage, and toast. Sorry, no coffee or juice, just water." The other three grabbed plates, and helped themselves to breakfast as well, sitting down and joining their still sleepy friend.

"Ah, that was a terrific breakfast" Charlie announced, "My compliments to the chef." "Yes, this is a most delightful restaurant" Jeremy added, "and well worth visiting again. And, the most delightful dining companions I've ever been privileged to have." "I am a wonderful cook, don't you think" Amanda said, looking specifically at Charlie. "Oh, yeah" he replied. "Hey, I helped" Jenny exclaimed, "I helped make the toast." "Yes, you did" Jeremy declared, "And, it was some of the best camp toast I've ever had." She smiled at him, "Thank you" she said, and kissed him on the cheek. "Well, I think I should do the dishes" declared Charlie with a smile, as he tossed his paper plate and utensils into the fire. "That's very nice of you" Jeremy chuckled, "but don't forget the skillets and toasting forks. They won't be so easily cleaned." "Oh, yeah" Charlie mumbled, as he saw all of the grinning faces looking at him, "Right, I kind of forgot about those."

Jeremy grabbed the skillet that had been used for the eggs and started down the path to the lake. "Don't worry Charlie, I'll help you with the dishes" he said, "You grab the other pan, and the toasting forks." Charlie grabbed the other items and followed Jeremy down to the lake, with the girls tagging along. The girls looked confused, as the boys used the pans to scoop up some sand, and then started scrubbing the inside of the pans with it. After they finished rinsing the pans in the lake a few minutes later, they showed the cleaned pans to the girls, which were clear of any food remnants. Then, returning to the camp site, Jeremy got some paper towels to dry the pans with. Then some oil was put on a paper towel and rubbed around the inside of each pan. "That's how we wash them when camping out" Jeremy explained with a smile, "and the oil is to keep the pans from rusting between campouts." The forks were wiped off with the same paper towels, and then the paper towels were disposed of in the camp fire. "Dishes are all done" Charlie proclaimed with a grin.

"Now, are we allowed to relax, and work on our tans?" asked Amanda. "If you want to" Jeremy said, "Charlie and I are going to hike around the lake and look for signs of anyone else that may be, or may have been camping around the lake over the last couple of days."

"Oh! I want to go with the boys" Jenny exclaimed, "they're going to be working on the mystery." "Oh, I'm going too" Amanda said, "I always did like trying to solve a good mystery." "Well, wear your swimsuits and shirts" Charlie said, "in case we get hot and decide to take a dip in the lake along the way." The girls excitedly agreed and slipped into their tent. The boys went into their tent to change also, and were waiting by the fire pit when the girls came out, wearing knee length shorts and t-shirts. "Those aren't your swimsuits" Charlie declared. "No, we thought we would wear something a little more than our bikinis" Jenny explained, "We put our swimsuits on underneath of all this."

MYSTERY INVESTIGATION

"Well, let's get going" Jeremy said, "I've got my sunscreen, a towel, and water and snacks for everyone in my backpack to bring along." "You girls can put your towels and sunscreen in my backpack" Charlie offered, "I'll carry them for you." With everything loaded into the two backpacks, the four teens started off down the path to the lake. They headed south when they reached the shoreline and walked along for several minutes before Jeremy stopped. "Okay, here's where we need to start looking around for signs of another camp site" he said, "We've been over the area pretty good up to here already, looking for fire wood. Beyond this point is where we haven't been yet." "What do you mean?" Amanda asked. "He means, we've been over all of the area from the camp to here already" Charlie answered her. "Right" Jeremy added, "We were all over the area up to here, when we came down from the woods on the day we arrived here, and when we've been searching for fire wood." "Oh, that's right" Amanda agreed, "So, we only have to look around for someone else's camp site from this point on, right?" "That's right" Charlie answered with a smile, "But we need to look for more dry wood that we can use for our camp fire, also." "Any firewood we find between the beach and the woods, we'll take down to the beach, so when we need wood for the camp fire, it'll already be sitting in piles on the beach" Jeremy explained. "Oh, that sounds like a good idea" Jenny exclaimed, "That should make the job of gathering fire wood later, a lot easier."

They walked in the shade of the trees, near the edge of the woods, as they started off around the rest of the lake. They checked the area from the woods down to the beach, and the boys kept checking a little way into the woods also, about ten feet, but they found nothing to indicate that other people might have been camping at the lake also. They did find a few spots that looked as if they would make good camp sites, but none of them seemed to be as good as the one they were currently staying at. They also collected lots of dry wood and piled it up at the edge of the beach next to the bushes. They were a little over three-quarters of the way around the lake, when Amanda and Jenny began to fall behind. "I'm getting tired, can we take a break" Amanda exclaimed. "Yeah, it's getting hot out, I need a rest too" Jenny declared. "We've been going for almost an hour now, but let's go just a little bit further" Charlie replied to them, "I think I can see a clearing up ahead with some trees for shade." The girls followed Charlie and Jeremy along a path through some brush, and ended up in a large shady clearing. They immediately noticed that this clearing was opened up on the lake side, with a large, beautiful, sandy beach area.

“Oh, Wow!” exclaimed Jenny, “This looks like it would be a great place for camping.” “I think it has already been used for a camping spot” Jeremy said, “Look over there by those boulders.” He was pointing over at a ring of large rocks next to three huge rocks, “That looks like a fire pit that someone made by those large boulders” he added. They all walked over to where the three large, four-foot-high boulders sat at the north edge of the clearing. A hole had been dug out in the sand, about four feet in diameter, and was lined with good sized rocks to keep the sand out, and a fire in. “Doesn’t look like it’s been used recently though” Charlie said, “but from the amount of ash in the pit, it’s probably been used a lot by someone.” “This would be a great spot for us to use as our camp site” Jeremy said with a grin, “It’s a lot bigger than where we have our camp right now, it has more shade, and the large beach area is really convenient.” “Yeah, maybe we should use this area the next time we come camping here” Charlie said. “I don’t know” said Amanda, “I kind of like camping over by the waterfall, where it’s peaceful and relaxing, with the sound of the water falling into the lake. Plus, this spot would take a lot longer to get to.” “I can still hear the waterfall from here” Jenny said, “But I agree with you about the extra distance in getting here, it took us about forty-five minutes to get here from across the lake”

Jenny said. "But it wouldn't take that long if we came straight here, instead of searching the entire area between the woods and the beach" Charlie commented. "Let's sit down and relax" Jeremy suggested, "we can talk about all this later, I'm hot and tired right now, and I feel like cooling off with a swim in the lake."

Jenny set down the water bottle she was holding in her hand, took off her shoes, and then slipped off the shorts and t-shirt that she was wearing. She ran screaming into the cool, inviting water of the lake, in the bikini swimsuit she had been wearing under her other clothes. Amanda followed her example, stripping down to her bikini as well, and followed her friend into the lake water. Jeremy and Charlie set their own water bottles down, peeled off their t-shirts and shoes, and joined the girls in the refreshing lake water. They spent about twenty minutes out in the cool water, splashing and playing around, before heading back up to the shady clearing again. They went over to the fire pit and sat down around it to relax and discuss this new camp site, comparing it to their current one. They all finally agreed, that for future camp outs at this lake, they would camp here only if they had more friends along with them. This larger site would be great for larger groups, but otherwise their current camp site was a more convenient location, since it wouldn't be as much of a hike to get to it from the highway.

They enjoyed a short rest, during which time their wet swimsuits managed to dry out, then they got up and brushed the sand off of themselves. They slipped on their shirts, shorts, and shoes, and began hiking north around the lake again. Fifteen minutes later, they found themselves approaching the waterfall from the west side of the lake. “Well, this is as far as we can go” Charlie declared, “and it doesn’t look like anyone else has been camping anywhere around this lake lately, except us.” “So, we still haven’t solved the mystery of where those kids came from or are disappearing to” Jeremy said. “Guess we may as well head back around the lake” Charlie suggested, “Back to our own camp site.” They started the long walk back along the shoreline again, in the opposite direction, and towards their existing camp site. It only took them about twenty minutes to reach the path that led up to their camp, since they had walked straight back along the shoreline, not having to search the area up to the woods this time.

As they were walking up the path, Jeremy looked down and spotted something interesting. He stopped and knelt down to look more closely at some impressions in the dirt. “What you looking at?” Charlie asked from behind him. “Foot prints in the sand” Jeremy replied, “small foot prints that didn’t come from any of us. They seem to go up toward our camp site, and then back down the path again." Charlie knelt down beside his friend, "They look like they were made by little kid's feet" he said. "What's up?" Amanda asked, as she and Jenny came up behind the boys. "We're looking at some small foot prints" Jeremy responded, "we may have had some visitors while we were gone." "Visitors?" Jenny whispered. "Yeah" Charlie answered, "these are foot prints that go up to our camp and then come back down again." "So, someone was up at our camp site?' Amanda asked. "It looks that way" Jeremy replied, "but I don't think they're still there, since the prints come back down the path also." "We better get to the camp and check everything out" Charlie suggested.

Continuing on, they rounded the bend in the path that led into the camp site, and immediately looked around to see if there were any visitors still there. There was no one there, except the four of them. They looked around in the tents, in the coolers, and under the tarp covering their miscellaneous supplies, but they found nothing out of place or missing. Jeremy and Charlie checked out where all the foot prints of their visitors were, and it looked as if their visitors came into the camp only a short way, and then turned around and left again. "They probably found the camp site, called out to see if anyone was here, and then left after no one answered" Jeremy theorized to the others as they all sat down around the fire pit. Since they were all feeling tired, and it was almost lunch time, they decided to have something to eat, and then rest for a little while.

After eating a quick lunch of sandwiches, chips, and water, they sat and rested around the dying embers of the fire pit. About thirty minutes later, they all felt rested and well fed, so decided to head off to the lake with the air mattresses again, and just float around on the lake for a while. They all slipped out of their extra clothes so they had on only their swimsuits. Jeremy placed a couple pieces of wood in the fire pit before following his friends down to the beach. When they all reached the lake shore, they wadded out into the water and got onto their air mattresses. "Hey, let's paddle over to the waterfall on the mattresses" Jenny suggested to the others, "if we go slow and easy, we should still be rested up enough to do some swimming and diving off of the ledge behind the falls." "That sounds like a good idea to me" Amanda agreed, "Let's go." Both girls laid face down on their mattresses and started paddling in the direction of the waterfall, around the bend ahead. Charlie smiled over at his friend, "Are you coming?" he asked, as he started out behind the two girls. "Right behind you" Jeremy replied, as he began paddling.

As the girls neared the bend that would take them around to the waterfall, they stopped paddling. "Did you hear that?" Jenny whispered to Amanda. "Yes" her friend whispered back, "It's kids' voices coming from up ahead, the kids must be back." "You two decide not to go to the waterfall?" Charlie asked as he came up alongside of Amanda's air mattress. "Shush!" Amanda whispered back to him, "Listen, we hear voices from ahead." Jenny signaled to Jeremy, to be quiet, as he pulled up beside her with a big grin. "Listen" she whispered to him. They all laid silently on their mattresses, listening, as the voices of kids playing came to them across the water. "They must be back" Jeremy whispered to his friend. "What? The naked kids?" Charlie asked. "Yes" the other three all whispered back to him. "Head for the shore" suggested Jeremy, "we can check from behind the bushes to be sure it's them. I think you are about to see for yourself, Mr. Doubting Charlie."

Reaching the shore, they quietly crept up as far as they could to the bushes running along the shoreline, then proceeded down to the bushes at the bend. They all sat down behind the bushes. "You go ahead and look first" Amanda whispered to Charlie, "but don't let them see you." Charlie smiled and moved down to the end of the bushes, and carefully looked around the edge. "I see two young kids swimming and playing, out in the water" he whispered back to the others. "Can you see if they're naked?" Jeremy inquired softly. "I don't know" Charlie answered, "they're in the water, so I can't tell." "Keep watching them" Amanda whispered, "if they jump up in the water far enough, you'll be able to tell." He looked around the edge of the bushes again, watching the kids. Five minutes passed, and he was starting to get tired of stretching his neck to look around the bushes at the two kids. Just as he was about to give up, the kids started splashing each other, bobbing up and down in the water, going under water, and then coming up out of the water further. Charlie suddenly tumbled back into his friends. "What's wrong, Charlie" Amanda whispered. "Th-they're naked" he whispered back, "Both boys. One black and one white."

THE RACE

"So, what are we going to do now" Amanda whispered to the others as they all sat hidden behind the bushes. "If they see us again, they'll probably leave again" said Jenny. "Maybe" Jeremy replied, "But every time we've seen them before, we've had to go back to camp, because we couldn't follow them. This time we are all wearing swimsuits, so we could swim after them if we wanted to." "So, what are you suggesting?" Amanda asked. "That we go swimming out in the lake on our air mattresses" Jeremy explained, "We'll walk around the bend like we were planning, and go swimming. If they spot us, we just wave at them and continue on into the water." "But what if they start swimming away again?" Jenny asked. "I'm hoping that they won't" Jeremy replied, "every time before, they disappeared as we were leaving the area. This time we're just arriving, and if they leave while we're here, we'll be able to see where they go, and I don't think they want us to know how they keep disappearing." "I think he's right" Charlie agreed, "They probably won't leave as long as we are here. They might try to stay away from us, but they probably won't leave unless we make them feel threatened."

"So, do we swim out on the air mattresses?" Amanda asked. "Yes" Jeremy answered, "Charlie and I will head out first, you two wait and follow us about five minutes later." "Why don't we all go out together" Amanda inquired. "They might panic if we all go out at once, and since they're boys, and Jeremy and I are boys, they might feel less threatened" Charlie offered, "so they might be less likely to swim away with boys coming towards them, right Jeremy." "Well, that too" Jeremy answered, "Plus, if they do start to swim across the lake again, we can swim after them without the air mattresses. The girls can grab our mattresses, since they will be coming along behind us." "Oh, right" Jenny said, "you two can probably catch them, since you're both on the school swim team." "Right" Jeremy replied, "If we have to, we can swim after them to see where they keep disappearing to."

The four teens gathered up their air mattresses, back tracked a short way, and then proceeded along the shore and around the bend, walking as if they were just heading out for a swim. They rounded the bend and continued on for a short way along the beach before one of the boys pointed towards them. Jeremy casually waved out to the two boys and continued walking along. The boys looked at each other, talked back and forth to each other for a few moments, then they both waved back at the teenagers on shore. "They're not swimming away yet" Amanda whispered, "how much further do we go, before getting into the water?" "We don't want to scare them away" Jeremy replied, "so we'll go about ten or twenty feet more, then Charlie and I will start into the water." A few minutes later, the boys finally turned and walked into the cool lake water. The girls simply sat down on the beach, to wait five minutes. Wadding out until the water was up to their hips, the boys climbed up onto the air mattresses and began paddling towards the two young boys that were treading water out in the lake.

The young boys watched the teenagers coming towards them for a few moments, and then started looking around the lake, like they were seeking a way to escape. The girls were in the water also now, swimming after the boys. The young kids kept talking back and forth and appeared to be getting more nervous about the approaching group of teens. Suddenly, they turned in the water, and began swimming away, heading towards the opposite side of the lake, like the day before. "They're heading for the shore on the other side" Charlie pointed out. "Yeah" Jeremy agreed, "Hey wait" he called out to the fleeing boys, "We won't hurt you, we just want to talk with you." The two boys looked back for a moment, then continued swimming away at an even faster pace. "We better let the air mattresses go, and swim after them" Jeremy said. The two teens slid off of their mattresses and started swimming after the naked boys. "We're gaining on them" Charlie said as he swam. "Yeah" Jeremy replied, "but they're swimming faster than I thought they would be able to. They're going to reach the shore before we catch up to them."

Still about twenty feet ahead of the teen boys, the two young boys reached a point where they could stand up in the water. Their bare bottoms were exposed as they ran through the shallow water to the beach. When they were almost out of the water, they glanced back at the lake once more, then started off at a run towards the brush. By the time the two teen boys reached the beach, the naked boys were completely out of site. "They're gone, we lost them" Charlie said. "We can follow their foot prints" suggested Jeremy, "They went this way, towards the path we were exploring earlier, I think." They followed the trail of foot prints going in the direction of the large camp site they'd discovered earlier. Half way there, the tracks went into the brush again. The two teens followed the prints into the brush but soon lost the trail. "Where'd their foot prints go" Charlie mumbled. "I think they must have covered them up" Jeremy replied, "Probably rubbed them out." "They're good, aren't they" Charlie said with a grin. "Yeah, maybe they're in Boy Scouts, too" Jeremy said, "Let's look around a little bit more in this area. If we don't find any more tracks, we'll head back to the girls."

"Here they come" Jenny exclaimed. "Yeah, but it

doesn't look like they caught up with the kids" Amanda commented. Having returned back to the lake, the boys were now swimming back towards the waiting girls. When they reached the air mattresses, they grabbed hold of one each, and treaded water, panting from their long swim. "You didn't catch them, did you" Amanda said. "No, they got away" Charlie answered between gasps for air. "They had too much of a head start on us, and they were pretty good swimmers" Jeremy added, "they got to the opposite shore too far ahead of us and ran off into the brush." "We tried following their foot prints for a while" Charlie said, "but then their tracks vanished." "Vanished?" Amanda repeated. "Yeah" Charlie said, "we think they used something to rub them out, to hide their trail so we couldn't follow them." "We're kind of tired from chasing after them" Jeremy panted, "How about we just float around out here for a little while, till Charlie and I are rested up."

The boys climbed back onto their own air mattress, and they all relaxed as they drifted around out in the middle of the lake. "So, Charlie, do you believe that we really saw naked kids swimming out here yesterday, and the day before?" asked Amanda. "Yes, I believe you saw them" he replied, "How can I not believe you, now that I've seen them for myself." "Seeing is believing, right?" Jeremy stated with a chuckle, "I doubted the girls too, until I saw the kids myself, yesterday." "Do you think we'll find out where they are disappearing to" Jenny asked. "I don't know" Jeremy replied, "they seem to know this area around here pretty good. It's almost like they live around here." The four laid on their air mattresses, and just floated around on the lake. After about an hour, the boys felt rested up, and decided that they were going to do some more diving behind the waterfall. The girls wanted to lay out in the sun for a while longer, so the boys started paddling towards the beach to leave their air mattresses on shore. With the air mattresses laid out on the sandy beach, the boys started swimming out to the ledge, while the girls continued floating around out on the water.

When the boys got behind the waterfall, they swam over to the steps and climbed up onto the ledge. Charlie looked at his friend, "You ready to start diving?" he asked. "Sure am" Jeremy answered, and both boys got up, side by side, and dove into the water at the same time. Charlie surfaced right away, and started for the steps again, to go back up onto the ledge again. Jeremy stayed underwater and swam just past the ladder before he surfaced. When they were both back up on the ledge, they dove in again. Charlie swam back to the steps and climbed up to the ledge again, but as Jeremy was going up the steps behind him, he slipped on one of the steps, and fell backward into the water again. The sun was coming out from behind some clouds just at that moment, and it shone through the clear water, illuminating the bottom of the lake and the rocky surface of the hillside below water. Jeremy was sinking down in the water after slipping off of the steps, and as he righted himself under water, he glanced down to where the sun was lighting the bottom of the lake and the rocky hillside. He immediately pulled himself upward through the water, to the surface. As he took in a couple of lungs full of air, he heard his best friend laughing from up on the ledge. "Interesting dive, buddy" Charlie chuckled, "was it one you came up with by yourself?" "No, it's one you taught me" Jeremy called back, "Remember our first swim meet last year, you showed me that particular dive right after your first swim event, when you were climbing out of the pool."

After climbing up onto the ledge again, Jeremy sat down for a moment to rest, while Charlie dove into the water again. Charlie climbed back up on the ledge again, and sat down next to Jeremy, "Sorry about laughing at you" he said with a smile, "It was kind of funny though, how you fell backward into the water when climbing the steps." "I slipped on one of the smooth steps" Jeremy explained, "we better be careful when we're climbing up them, since the steps are stone, and wet." "Yeah, you're right" Charlie said, "so, you ready to dive in some more?" "You know what" Jeremy said, "When I was under water, I thought I saw something. The sun came out from behind the clouds and shone down through the water on the hillside. I'm not sure, but I think I may have seen a small opening near the bottom of the hillside." "An opening? You mean, like a cave or something?" Charlie inquired. "Yeah, but it wasn't big enough to be a cave, it was more like the opening to a tunnel" Jeremy replied, "I'm wondering if there might be a tunnel going down to a cave in the hillside. If there is a cave, those kids may be hiding from us in there." "Except today they swam to the other side of the lake, where we lost them" Charlie reminded him. "Yeah, today they did that" Jeremy replied, "but for the last two days, they disappeared out here by the waterfall." Jeremy stood up and prepared to dive into the water again, "I think I'll dive down and have a closer look at where I saw the opening" he said to his friend. "I'll dive down with you" Charlie offered, "safety in numbers you know."

Both boys dove into the water, and swam down the twelve feet to the bottom, and looked at the hillside. They couldn't see very well this deep down, so they swam back up to the surface after a couple of minutes. "It's too dark down there" Charlie said, "how could you have seen anything like an opening in the hillside before?" "The sun came out from behind the clouds when I was down there before" Jeremy replied, "it was easier to see then." "So, let's wait until the sun comes out again" suggested Charlie. "Okay" Jeremy said. They climbed up onto the ledge, and kept a watch on the sky, waiting for the sun to start coming out from behind the clouds again. When the sun was near an opening in the clouds, they stood up and prepared to dive. As the sun started to appear, they both dove in, and went down deep in the water again. This time, it became a lot brighter underwater when the sun came out, and as they looked around at the hillside, Jeremy spotted what he was looking for. He tapped his friend on the arm and pointed to the opening in the rocky hillside.

The boys surfaced again and climbed up on the ledge, "I think you're right" Charlie said, "that looked like an opening to me, too." "But you can't see how deep it goes" Jeremy replied, "We need to get the waterproof flashlights, and check it out better." "I think it will have to wait until tomorrow" Charlie said, "I'm still kind of tired, and by the time we get back to camp, get the flashlights, and come back here again, we'll be too tired to go under and check it out again." "Yes, and it's getting close to supper time" Jeremy agreed with a smile, "All the hiking, swimming, chasing after naked kids, and now diving, has made me hungry. I'm sure you're getting hungry too." "Let's go get the girls, and head back to camp" Charlie said, "We'll have a good meal, and relax for the rest of the night. We can let the girls know what we found, and what our plans are for tomorrow."

END OF A LONG DAY

The boys swam out from behind the waterfall and found the girls floating out on the lake on their air mattresses. "Hey" Charlie called out, as they swam up to the two girls. "Hey" Amanda answered back, "You guys finished with diving already?" "Yeah" Charlie replied, "we decided to head back to camp and get the fire going for supper, you girls want to join us in about half an hour?" "Sounds okay to me" Amanda answered. "Me too" Jenny said, "We'll head back to camp in about thirty minutes." "Okay" the boys said, as they started swimming towards the shore. When they got up on the shore, they went over and gathered up their air mattresses, and carried them back with them to the camp site.

When the girls came walking up the path into the camp site, the boys had a good fire going, and the cooking grate was already in place. They were laying on their mattresses, relaxing next to the fire, and almost asleep. "Hey, guys, we're here" Jenny announced, "What's for supper?" Jeremy sat up and smiled at her, "Grilled chicken breasts, green beans, bread, and soda pop. And, some pineapple for dessert" he announced. "Really" exclaimed Amanda, "Are you serious, because that sounds pretty good, and if you're joking around with us two hungry gals we might just have to get even."

"We just thought you might enjoy something besides burgers, hot dogs, or sandwiches" Charlie said with a smile. "And, chicken doesn't keep as long in the coolers" Jeremy added with a smile, "By the end of the trip, we'll be having sandwiches a lot." "So, we better enjoy the hot meals while they last, right?" Jenny said with a chuckle. "That's right" Jeremy responded. "How long until it's ready" Amanda inquired. "Once it goes on the grate, about twenty minutes" Jeremy replied, "Charlie and I already have the chicken and vegetables seasoned and wrapped in foil, waiting to be put on the cooking grate." "We were just waiting for you two to arrive, so we could talk about our plans for tomorrow, while the food is cooking" Charlie added.

"You can come over and sit down with us by the fire" Charlie said, as Jeremy placed four foil packages on the cooking grate. The two girls put their air mattresses down next to the boys' mattresses and sat down on them like the boys were doing. "Okay, so what's up?" Amanda asked, "You two seem to be too serious, so there must be something important you want to talk about." Jeremy smiled at his sister, and then at Jenny, "We think we found something important behind the waterfall this afternoon, which might help us solve the mystery of the vanishing skinny-dippers." he said. "What did you find?' Jenny inquired. "Well, Jeremy slipped off the stone steps and fell back into the water, over on the left side of the steps, when we were back there diving. He ended up down near the bottom of the lake, and he spotted an opening in the hillside" Charlie began. "We think it might be the entrance to a cave inside of the hillside" Jeremy explained, "It could be where those kids keep disappearing to." "But, if there's a cave down there, how could they stay in it without air?" Amanda asked. "The cave could be higher up, inside of the hill, above the water level where there would be air" Jeremy explained. "So, you're thinking about checking it out tomorrow, aren't you" Jenny said. "Yes, we're going to take a couple of waterproof lights with us behind the waterfall tomorrow" Jeremy answered, "We'll be able to see inside the opening better with the light shining in there, and then determine if it's a tunnel or not." "And, if it's a tunnel, Jeremy will swim into it to see if it goes to a cave" Charlie blurted out.

Both of the girls suddenly frowned, and appeared visibly worried. "Nice going, Charlie" Jeremy scolded, "Real tactful of you to just blurt it out like that." "What? All I did was tell them our plans" Charlie responded, "What's wrong with that?" "You could have let them think about what we found for a little bit first" Jeremy told him, "By blurting out the plans like that, they're probably visualizing me swimming into a dark tunnel with some monster waiting for me." "You can't be serious about this" Amanda exclaimed, "you want to swim into an underwater tunnel? You don't know what might be in that tunnel." "He'll have a light with him" Charlie offered, "so, it won't really be dark inside the tunnel." "He could still get stuck in there, or go too far in and not have enough air to make it back out" Amanda reasoned for them. Jeremy smiled at his sister, "I'll also have a rope tied around my waist" he began, "Charlie will have the other end of the rope and will pull me back out after two minutes." "Jeremy can hold his breath under water for three minutes easy" Charlie added, "so it should be plenty safe." "Two minutes going into the tunnel, and only a minute of air left to get back out" Jenny declared, "I don't think that sounds very safe." "I'll be pulling him back out, which will be faster than when he swims in" Charlie explained, "and if the tunnel looks too deep, he'll start back before the two minutes are up." "It still sounds too dangerous" Amanda declared, "I don't think it's a good idea. You can't do it." "Well, the first thing I will do, is go down and shine a light into the opening" Jeremy said, "Then, decide if I need to go into it if it is a tunnel."

"You'll decide!" Jenny exclaimed, "You don't think that the rest of us should have a say in what you're going to do?" "I didn't say that" Jeremy replied. "You basically did" Amanda exclaimed, angrily, "You said that 'YOU'LL' look in the tunnel with a light, and then decide if 'YOU' are going to swim into it. You didn't say anything about discussing it first." "Well, you girls are obviously against the plan, and it sounds like you're ordering us to forget all about it" Jeremy angrily replied, "Charlie and I had decided to tell you what we found, and then discuss what we thought we should do. You seem to think you can just 'Veto' our plans." Amanda glared at her brother, "Well, we are against it" she growled, "right Jenny." "Well, I'm not sure" Jenny answered. "What! You aren't sure?" her friend gasped, "Do you think they should do something as dangerous as what they're planning?" "No" Jenny replied, "but Jeremy is right, we just told them we didn't like their plan, and that they couldn't do it. We didn't give them a chance to explain everything, and then discuss it. I think we should calmly discuss it with them some more." Amanda opened her mouth as if to reply, but closed her mouth without saying a thing. She looked at her brother, and then at Charlie, then back at her best friend. Jenny smiled back at her friend, "Don't you think they deserve a chance to explain everything, before we try to calmly talk them out of it?" Amanda looked around at her friends and brother, thinking. "Okay, I guess we can discuss it" she replied. "Discuss it calmly?" Jeremy asked, with a smile. "Yeah, sure" Amanda said, "why not?"

"How about we eat supper first" Charlie suggested, "I'm sure we're all hungry, and we'll all be in a better mood after getting some food in our stomachs." The girls sat down by their tent to talk, while the boys finished getting supper ready. The food had been on the cooking grate for ten minutes already and would be ready in another twenty minutes. The smell of the cooking food was already starting to fill the air, and everyone's mouths were watering. "I hope you're making enough" Amanda exclaimed, "I'm real hungry now, and if I don't get enough to eat, don't expect me to discuss your plans in a pleasant mood." The boys went and got some plates, and everything else they needed for supper, from the grocery bag in the tree. "I think we'll have plenty for all of us" Jeremy said, "and we'll all feel better after we've eaten." "Yeah, we did a lot today" Charlie agreed, "and, we still have more to do after supper." "You mean discussing your plans for the tunnel?" Amanda asked with a sneer. "No, I mean some chores that we still have to do tonight" Charlie replied. "He's talking about gathering more fire wood" Jenny said, pointing to the wood pile, "It looks like there's only a couple of pieces left." Amanda glanced over at the depleted fire wood supply, "Oh" Amanda muttered. "Don't worry, it won't take too long to restock the wood pile" Jeremy said, "remember, we left piles of wood all along the beach today. We'll just take the cart, fill it with wood, and bring it back to camp."

Ten minutes later, Charlie announced that the food

was ready. Everyone received two chicken breasts, some green beans, a slice of bread, and a pineapple fruit cup, along with a glass of soda pop to drink. Digging into the chicken after extracting it from the foil, both of the girls carefully tasted the meat. "Oh" both girls moaned. "This chicken is delicious" Jenny declared. "Yeah, it's actually pretty good" Amanda agreed, "how did you boys learn to cook like this." "Boy Scouts" mumbled Charlie, with his mouth full of chicken. Jeremy looked at his friend and laughed, "Yeah" he said, "we learn lots of useful stuff in the Boy Scouts, including how to cook some pretty tasty food." "Well, this chicken tastes really good" Jenny replied. "It's kind of my mom's recipe" he explained, "modified a little for cooking over a camp fire, but marinating it came from her recipe." "Wait till I tell mom she has competition for world's greatest cook" Amanda said with a chuckle.

When they were finished eating, plates and utensils were cleaned by the usual procedure used each time before, which was by fire. The last of the soda pop was used up by refilling their cups, and the plastic bottle was kept for recycling when they got back home. They relaxed while finishing their drinks, then tossed the cups in the fire. Charlie stood up and went over to the cart. "Everyone ready to go and get the fire wood" he asked, as he grabbed the handle and started pulling it towards the path. The others slowly got up and walked after him. Jeremy had been right, gathering the fire wood was an easy task, as they simply picked up the wood from a couple of piles they came to, and piled it into the cart. With the cart full, they headed back to the camp site for the night. When they were finally ready, the girls sat down by the fire pit together, facing the boys who stood a little way away from them. "So, I guess we can discuss your plan for swimming into that tunnel tomorrow" Amanda said. "If you're willing to listen to the entire plan" Jeremy replied, "then we'll explain what we have in mind." "Go ahead" his sister said, "I'm listening." "I'm ready to listen too" Jenny added. "Okay, but let us finish up before you say anything" Charlie insisted, "You start, Jeremy."

"Well, first of all, we're not even sure that there is a tunnel" Jeremy started, "we saw an opening, but we can't tell how deep it goes. We need to take flashlights down there and shine them into the opening first." "And if it isn't a tunnel, then that's it, no need to check it out any further" Charlie added. "Right" Jeremy said, "but if it does appear to be a tunnel, then we want to check it out closer, by going just inside the opening with the flashlights." "The opening looked about four feet wide" Charlie said, "If it's a tunnel, then it should be that wide all the way through it, and if it gets narrower further in, then we can forget about trying to swim inside of it." "If it looks safe, then Jeremy will go inside to check it out some more, since he's the best swimmer" Charlie explained further, "and he'll have a rope tied around his waist, so I can pull him back out if I need to." "Okay" Jeremy continued, "So, since I can hold my breath for about three minutes under water, I'll swim inside of the tunnel for only two minutes, to give me time to get back out. I'll be using a flashlight to see as far ahead as I can, to see if the tunnel ends soon enough to try swimming all the way through." "He'll come back out after two minutes, no matter what" Charlie added, "We can discuss it further after that, when we're all sitting up on the ledge."

"Any questions" Jeremy asked. "Yes" Amanda replied, "You said you can hold your breath for three minutes, right?" "That's right" Jeremy answered. "Okay, but you plan to swim into the tunnel for two minutes, wouldn't it be safer if you swim in for only one and a half minutes instead. That's half of the three minutes each way." "Well, yes" he said, "we can change it to one and a half minutes in to be safe." "You know Jeremy, it would be even safer if you went in for only one minute at first" Jenny chimed in, "and then come out. Then, if it looks okay at that point, you could go back in a second time, for a half minute longer." "You know what buddy" Charlie said, "that makes good sense. We should go slow, for safety sake. You can keep going back in further each time, and you'll have looked ahead with the flashlight each previous time, so you'll know what to expect each time back." "Okay, that sounds reasonable, I'll go in there only four times that way, because I'm not going in more than two minutes max, unless I actually find a cave in there somewhere."

"Any more comments or questions" Charlie asked the girls. "I have a question" Jenny replied, "You said that you would pull Jeremy out after two minutes, right?" "Yes" Charlie answered. "Can you hold your breath for three minutes too" she asked, "because wouldn't you have to stay under water that long also, in order to pull Jeremy out?" "No" Jeremy responded, "he'll be above water for one minute, then dive down to check on me." "But what if you get in trouble" Amanda inquired, "how will he know?" Jeremy looked at his friend, "They're right" he said. "Yeah" Charlie agreed, "so what do we do then?" "If we are all working on this together, there would be four of us out there" Jenny said, "Amanda and I can hold our breath for at least a minute, so if we all take turns underwater, we should have someone down there all the time." "Yeah, in half minute turns, so if something happens, the one under water can signal the ones above water for help" Charlie agreed. "That sounds good" Jeremy exclaimed. "Anything else we need to discuss about the plan" Charlie asked. No one else was saying anything, so Jeremy figured they were done discussing the plan.

"So, everyone's okay with the plan for tomorrow?" Jeremy questioned. "Not really" his sister responded, "I'd still be happier if you didn't go swimming into a dark, unknown, underwater tunnel, if that's what you find down there." "But you just helped us plan it" Charlie exclaimed, "We thought you agreed with checking it out now." The two girls looked at each other and grinned. "We still don't like the idea of either one of you swimming into underwater tunnels" Jenny said, "But, we talked it over before supper, and agreed that you two were going to go ahead with your plan anyway, whether we wanted you to or not." "So, we decided that the best thing to do, was to help you make the plan as safe as possible" Amanda added, "And to be out there with you, to help keep you safe." "You and Jenny are wonderful, Amanda" Jeremy declared. "Of course, we are" she responded with a laugh, "I need to make sure you come back home alive after all. You're the only brother I've got, and I don't want to lose you, and then have to explain to mom how I let you do this."

With the plan set for the next morning, the four friends decided to get ready for bed. They all went over to the clothes-line and removed the clothes that had been rinsed out the day before. The girls went into their tent and the boys into theirs. When they were all back out, in dry clothes again, they took their swim suits and clothes from that day down to the lake and began rinsing them out the same way they had done the previous day. They returned to camp again and hung up the freshly cleaned clothes to dry, then sat down around the camp fire again. Charlie got the radio out and tuned it to a news broadcast for a while, and then found some music for them to listen to. They stayed up for a couple of hours, listening to the radio and talking, until everyone was yawning. "I think it's my bedtime" Jenny announced to the others. "Mine too" Amanda said, "I can barely keep my eyes open." "We should probably all get some sleep" Jeremy declared, "It's getting dark anyway." "What're we going to have for breakfast tomorrow" asked Charlie. "Dry cereal" Amanda replied, "You guys need to eat light, so you're not stuffed with a lot of food when you go exploring that tunnel under the water." "Right" Jeremy said, "we'll see you girls in the morning then. Good night."

Jeremy went over to the wood pile and selected several large pieces, then placed them in the fire pit. "That should be enough to keep the fire going for several hours" he explained, "I'll put some more wood on again later. "They all slipped into their tents and crawled into their sleeping bags for some much-needed sleep. Charlie was the one who got up during the night and put more wood on the fire, after attending to a call of nature around midnight. When Jeremy got up about an hour after his friend, also to answer natures call, he noted that someone had already put additional wood on the fire, so he didn't feel it needed any more, and went back to his waiting sleeping bag.

THE TUNNEL

The girls were up early the next morning, around seven, and proceeded to have some dry cereal for breakfast. They chatted together for about an hour after they finished eating, and before Jeremy came out of his tent. "You gals already have breakfast" he asked as he stepped out of his tent. "Yes, we got some cereal down from the grocery store already. We got some for you and Charlie here too" Amanda answered, "Is Charlie up yet?" Jeremy smiled at his sister, "Are you kidding" he asked, "This early in the morning, when there's no hot food cooking?" "Oh yeah" she giggled, "what was I thinking. So, how do we wake him up than?" "That's easy" Jeremy said as he went back to the boy's tent, stuck his head inside and yelled "Last call for breakfast!" Immediately, the girls heard Charlie moving around in the tent. "I'm coming" they heard him yelling, "I'm coming. Save some food for me." When he finally came out of the tent, everyone was looking at him and grinning. "Dig in" Jeremy chuckled, as he tossed a box of cereal to his friend.

"Cereal?" Charlie exclaimed, "You guys were actually serious when you said we were having dry cereal for breakfast." "We can't have a hot breakfast every morning" Amanda chuckled, "do you know how much food we would have to haul in here to have hot meals all the time?" "He knows" said Jeremy, "his stomach was just hoping for a bit more than cereal." Charlie opened the box and started eating the contents, as Jeremy placed two flashlights and some rope in front of the tent. "Do we need to gather more wood for the fire" Jenny inquired. "Yes, we do" Jeremy responded, "we can gather wood as soon as Charlie is finished with breakfast. We need to wait a while after eating, before we go swimming over to the waterfall." "I'm already done with my breakfast" Charlie said, as he tossed the empty box into the fire pit, "Let's go get some wood."

They went out with Charlie pulling the cart after him and returned about twenty minutes later with the cart full of fire wood. The stack of fire wood was actually growing now, since they weren't using up all that they brought in each time. The girls went into their tent to change into swimsuits, while the boys unloaded the contents of the cart. When all the wood was stacked up in the wood pile, the boys slipped into their tent to change into their swim trunks as well. While the boys were changing, the girls started walking down toward the lake shore to wait for the boys there. The boys arrived at the lake where the girls were waiting for them, carrying the flashlights and rope. "So, how are we going to tie the rope to you when we get out there?" Amanda asked, as they walked along the shore in the direction of the waterfall. "He's got two pieces of rope"

Charlie replied, "the shorter one will go around his waist, and loop down between his legs like a safety harness. The longer one we attach to the loop between his legs, so we can easily pull him out if we need to. Obviously, if we tie it to his feet, he won't be able to swim very well." "Yes, but the rope can't be tied too tight" Jeremy added, "I need to be able to breath, you know." "Wrong" Jenny put in, "It won't affect your breathing that much if it's around your waist, since your chest will not be tied. So, it needs to be tight enough so it won't slip off if we have to pull you back out of the tunnel." Jeremy looked at Jenny, and realized by the serious look on her face, that she was concerned for his safety. "Okay, you're right again" he said to her with a grin.

They walked around the bend in the shore, and saw the waterfall, up ahead. When they were close to the waterfall, but still on the beach, they all began wadding into the lake water until it came up to their hips, then they all started swimming in the direction of the pounding waterfall. They reached the area in back of the waterfall and everyone climbed up onto the ledge. They sat down and rested from the swim out, to be sure Jeremy was not tired when he started out on the task he had come out to do. As soon as Jeremy said he was ready, he and Charlie got the short rope tied and wrapped around him, with the part around his waist nice and snug, then the four teens jumped into the water. Before diving into the water to begin investigating, Jeremy looked at Jenny and smiled, "How about a kiss for good luck?" he said. Jenny blushed at his request, then smiled and gave him a little kiss on the cheek. "You want a good luck kiss from me too, big brother?" Amanda asked with a grin. "Thanks, Amanda, but I'm good for now" he replied."

Jeremy slipped on his swim goggles and stood at the edge of the ledge. Everyone watched him as he took several deep breaths, then, holding the last one, he dove into the water with Charlie right behind him. The girls watched down in the water, and soon saw a light moving around under water. The light moved towards the rock face, moving back and forth in search of the opening the boys wanted to check out. After several seconds, the light remained steady, moving closer to the rocky hillside, until it seemed to move right into the side of the hill as it disappeared. "I guess they found the opening" Amanda commented. A moment later the light from the flashlight reappeared and stayed in place, while another light appeared and began rising up towards the surface of the water. The girls could see Jeremy and Charlie coming upwards toward them, and they soon popped up in the water next to the steps.

The boys climbed up onto the ledge again, and sat

down to rest. Jeremy began describing what they had found so far. “It’s an opening for sure” he said, “I put my arm inside of it up to my shoulder and moved the flashlight around the inside. It’s about four feet wide as far as I could see, but I couldn’t see how deep it actually goes, with my small flashlight.” “Where is your flashlight?” Amanda inquired. “I left it down at the tunnel entrance, still on” he answered her, “So we can go directly down to the tunnel again.” “So, what’s next?” asked Jenny. “I think we need to take the next step in the plan” Charlie suggested, “The plan we all agreed on.” “I’ll swim into the tunnel for about thirty seconds, looking around further in, then come right back out again.” “Okay, as long as you come right back after the thirty seconds are up” Amanda agreed. “I need to rest for a little bit longer first” Jeremy stated, then someone can go down with me, and I’ll head directly into the tunnel.”

When Jeremy was ready, he and Charlie slipped on their swim goggles, then dove into the water and straight down to the tunnel entrance, where the flashlight was still shining. Amanda was going to dive down thirty seconds later, and Jenny thirty seconds after her, if needed. Jeremy quickly grabbed the flashlight that was shining outward from the tunnel entrance and turned it so it was shining back inside of the tunnel. He went right into the tunnel with the light shining ahead of him. In his mind, he was counting the seconds since he went under water. He still hadn't seen any end to the tunnel as he neared the end of his thirty seconds, but as he was about to turn back, he saw a rock wall about six feet straight ahead of him. His thirty seconds were up, and he had to swim back out, but as he was turning around, he noticed something interesting on his right side.

Charlie started pulling on the rope when the thirty seconds ended, to remind and assist his friend in returning back out of the tunnel. The rope seemed like it was too slack though, so he began pulling on it more quickly. Just when Amanda appeared at his side, the rope suddenly became taut and Jeremy appeared, swimming out the end of the tunnel. The three immediately started swimming up towards the surface, then swam over to the ledge and went up the steps. Jeremy was taking deep breaths as he sat on the ledge resting. "So, did you find anything" Jenny asked, "you seem kind of excited." "I think I saw the end of the tunnel" Jeremy answered in between breaths, "It looks like it might actually be only a thirty second swim through the tunnel." Amanda looked at him, "So, does it come to a dead end, or to a cave" she asked. "I'm not sure yet" her brother replied, "the thirty seconds were up, and I had to start back out before Charlie started pulling me out. But as I was turning to come back out, I noticed that the tunnel wall on my right side was missing." "What do you mean, it was missing" Charlie asked. "Well, from where I was, to the wall at the tunnel end, I couldn't see any more wall on my right side" Jeremy explained, "I didn't have time for a closer look though, because I had to start back out of the tunnel, but I think that the tunnel might continue on to the right. I'll have to check it out some more on my next trip in."

The boys were excited about what they had found so far, and the girls actually seemed more interested in what was ahead. Everyone sat on the ledge relaxing for about fifteen minutes, with Jeremy taking in deep breaths to prepare for another dive down to the tunnel. He would be allowed one minute in the tunnel this time, then he would have to swim out once again. When he was ready to go again, he put his goggles on, and he and Amanda went into the water and down to the bottom. Amanda watched her big brother as he went straight into the tunnel, out of sight except for the glow of his flashlight, which seemed to get dimmer as it progressed deeper into the dark recesses of the tunnel. Charlie was counting the seconds since Jeremy's light had entered the tunnel, prepared to dive in and go down to replace Amanda on their end of the rope. He would be ready to get his friend out when he was down there and the count reached sixty seconds.

Jeremy swam as quickly as he could through the tunnel this time. He was able to swim faster than the previous time, since he already knew what to expect up ahead, to the point where he had turned back the last time. He reached the last stopping point and directed his flashlight off to the right, at the missing tunnel wall. His eyes opened wide when he saw that the tunnel did not actually turn to the right, but that there seemed to be an underwater chamber present instead. He began shining the light all around the area, looking for any openings that might be present, but there were none visible for him to see. He only had about another ten seconds before he needed to head back out again, so he quickly shone the flashlight upward along the rock wall just before he started turning around to go back. He stopped moving and was starring upward for several seconds when he felt a tug on the rope around his waist. It was time to head back out to his friends again, but he would be coming back there again, soon.

Jenny had joined Charlie on the lake bottom about the time he started pulling on the rope, just as the sixty-second time limit was up. The two pulled on the rope together until Amanda appeared at his side and took the rope from him. She pointed upward, indicating that he should go up to the surface for air. Amanda and Jenny continued pulling on the rope until it suddenly started to slackened, and then started to come out more easily as they pulled on it. They continued to pull on the rope until Jeremy appeared at the entrance to the tunnel. He smiled at the girls and pointed upward towards the surface of the water. The girls swam up to the surface with him where they saw that Charlie was preparing to dive back down again. A smile appeared on Charlie's face when he saw Jeremy with the girls, and they all swam over to the steps and climbed up to the ledge for another rest.

After about five minutes, Jeremy grinned at his three friends. "It doesn't turn" he said, out of breath. "What doesn't turn" asked his sister. "The tunnel" he replied, "it doesn't just end. The reason for the wall on the right disappearing, is that the tunnel turns into an underwater chamber on the right." The others starred at him for a moment, to let the information sink in. "How big of a chamber does it seem to be" Charlie inquired, "Is it just a flooded cave maybe?" "From where the tunnel enters the chamber, to the rock wall straight ahead, it is about six feet" Jeremy answered, "The length to the right looked about eight to ten feet, I didn't have time to get a closer look." The others continued to look at him, waiting for him to provide them with more information about what he had found.

"What else" Charlie asked impatiently, "does the

chamber have a ceiling to it?" Jeremy grinned, "The chamber bottom is about a foot lower than the bottom of the tunnel. I shone my light all around, but the only opening in the walls, was the one I came in through. When I pointed my light upward, there was no visible sign of a ceiling, and the water appeared to be rippling in the light, like the water surface would do if air was above it. I'm guessing that the chamber is actually a pool of water that is about twelve feet deep, like the water out here next to the ledge is. "So where exactly is this pool" Charlie asked. "Don't know yet" Jeremy responded with a grin, "I'll have to check that out on my next trip in. I'm going to try swimming straight through to the pool, and then up to the surface to look around for a few seconds." Jenny grabbed hold of his arm and looked him in the face. "One more time" she declared to him, "Just one more time this morning. Then you need to rest up back at camp or on the beach. We can come back out here again this afternoon maybe, okay?" Jeremy stared deeply into her blue eyes and just smiled. "Does that sound okay with you?" Jenny asked again. "Huh? Wh-what?" Jeremy stuttered, "Oh, yeah. That sounds fine to me" he replied. "Is something wrong with you?" she asked him, "you seem kind of lost right now." "Yeah. Oh, yeah, I'm okay" Jeremy answered, suddenly blushing, "I guess I got a little lost in those beautiful blue eyes or yours though."

Jenny was blushing now too, but was also smiling. Amanda and Charlie looked at each other and started chuckling. Amanda tapped her friend on the shoulder. "Jenny, I think my brother would do just about anything you wanted him to do, right now" she said. Jenny grinned at Jeremy and gave him a tender kiss right on the lips. "You are so sweet" she told him. Jeremy smiled, then shook his head. "Oh. Oh, right. One more dive this morning" he said to everyone, "I just need a few more minutes of rest before diving down again." "You better sit down to rest, buddy" Charlie suggested, "Get your head clear before you go down again." The four sat on the ledge for about ten minutes before Jeremy decided he was ready for another trip down to the tunnel, and the pool that he had found. "I get a minute and a half this time, right" Jeremy inquired. "Yes" Charlie answered, "and I'll go down with you for the first thirty seconds. "I'm ready" Jeremy said as he stood up and approached the edge of the ledge. "Do you need a kiss for good luck" Jenny asked with a smile. "No!" Amanda suddenly declared as her brother started turning towards Jenny, "Close your eyes if you want the kiss, but do not look into her eyes again. We don't want you getting lost again, before you head down to that dark chamber."

Jeremy stared at his sister in disbelief, as everyone else began to laugh, "Very funny, sis. Very funny." Jenny gave him a kiss on the cheek, and he prepared to dive into the water with Charlie again. The girls watched the boys dive under the water and watched as the light from Jeremys flashlight disappeared into the tunnel again. Jeremy swan straight through the tunnel to the end, then turned and swam upward. A few seconds later he popped out on the surface, and took a few deep breaths as he shone his flashlight all around the small pool that he was in. He appeared to be in a cave, but it was far too big for his flashlight to illuminate much of it. He couldn't see any of the walls, except the one behind him, which was the inside of the hillside behind the waterfall. "Cool" he said to himself, "wait until I tell the others about this." He had used up only about thirty seconds of his time now, but decided to head straight back out to the others. He dove down into the pool and swam to the bottom, then located the tunnel entrance on the pool side and started back down it to the lake side. Charlie had just joined Jenny on the bottom of the lake when Jeremy came swimming out of the tunnel, gave them a thumbs-up, and started swimming for the surface.

Jeremy surfaced behind the waterfall and started swimming directly for the steps to the ledge. Charlie and Jenny surfaced a couple of seconds later, saw Jeremy already heading for the ledge, and followed after him. "You must have been really out of breath" Charlie said to his friend when they were all up on the ledge again, “The way you came out of that tunnel and headed straight up to the surface.” “No, I wasn’t out of breath at all” Jeremy replied excitedly, with a big grin, “I took several breaths of air before I dove down and headed back out here to the lake.” “Oh?” Charlie said, confused. Suddenly Charlie caught on and looked directly at his friend’s smiling face. “Where exactly were you able to take a few breaths, before heading back out to the lake” he asked. “In the cave above the pool, at the end of the tunnel” Jeremy answered him with a laugh. “There’s really a cave?” the girls happily shrieked together. “Yes, there’s a cave” Jeremy replied, “I swam upward as soon as I got through the tunnel and into the pool. I came to the surface of the pool, and into a huge cave.” “What was in the cave?” Charlie asked. “I don’t know” Jeremy answered, “It was too large for my flashlight to show much at all. There was a floor obviously, and a wall between the cave and outside, here. You can’t see anything more with just a small flashlight. We all need to get in there with our lanterns and explore the cave together.” “Well, let’s go back to camp and grab the lanterns then” Charlie exclaimed, “we can be back here in half an hour.”

“Hold it” Amanda exclaimed, “we’re going back to camp, but there are not going to be any more trips into that tunnel until we have all rested up back at camp.”

"Yeah!" Jenny said, "We all agreed to only one more dive this morning, then rest up good before maybe coming back here after lunch." "But, we're not hungry yet" the boys declared together. "Maybe not" Amanda said, "but Jeremy has been into that tunnel three times already, and he; no, all of us need to rest up." Charlie put his hand on Jeremy's shoulder, "Looks like we'll have to wait until later" he said with a chuckle, "unless we want to argue with the girls, which will probably take until after lunch anyway." Jeremy looked at the two girls and grinned. "Okay" he conceded, "We'll wait until after we've had lunch, before coming back out here to dive down and explore the tunnel, pool, and cave area. Does that make you girls happy?" "Yes" both girls chorused together.

Moments later, all four teenagers jumped into the water, and began swimming out from behind the waterfall, towards shore. They exited the lake and walked along the shoreline around the bend. When they reached the path leading up to camp, Jeremy stopped, "Since it's only about ten-thirty, and none of us is actually hungry yet, why don't we get our towels and just relax on the beach for a while" he suggested. "Who's not hungry?" Charlie asked, "all I had for breakfast was some cereal". The other three teens all started laughing. "You're always hungry, Charlie" Jeremy replied, "If it was up to you, there would be a hamburger joint out here on the beach." "Ooh, that would be great" Charlie replied, sending the others into laughing fits again. "Too bad, Charlie, lunch isn't going to happen for at least another hour" Amanda told him. "Let's get our towels and come back down here to the beach" Jenny said. "That sounds good to me" Amanda agreed. "Sounds good to me, too" Jeremy added. "Oh, okay" Charlie grumbled.

The four all returned to the beach a short time later, carrying towels. They spread their towels out on the sand and laid down on them to relax in the warm sunshine. Several minutes later, Charlie turned to his friend, "Hey, Jeremy, I got a question about that pool you found." Jeremy looked back at him. "What do you want to know Charlie, I haven't had much chance of checking it out yet though" he replied. "I know, but could you tell if the pool was natural, or did it look like it was man-made" Charlie asked. "I'm not sure. I didn't look at the sides of it close up, but if it's like the tunnel, I'd say that it is probably man-made" Jeremy answered. "What makes you think the tunnel is man-made" Jenny inquired. "The sides of the tunnel are rough, not smooth" Jeremy said, "If the tunnel was natural, the sides would be smooth from the flowing water that would have worn through the rock and left it that way. Rough would indicate that someone actually chiseled through the rock of the hillside." Charlie was nodding in agreement, “That’s right, if water wears the rock down, it does it gradually over years, and leaves the surface pretty much smooth” he said. “So, since the tunnel walls are rough, it was probably chiseled out by humans?” Amanda asked. “Right” both boys answered together. “Because beavers don’t usually chew through rock” Jenny added with a giggle.

Just before twelve noon, Charlie sat up and glanced around at the others. “Is anyone else getting hungry yet” he asked. Jeremy chuckled and sat up also, “Sure” he replied, “I could go for something to eat, let’s go on up to camp and have some cold-cut sandwiches, and chips.” They grabbed their towels and proceeded to walk up to the camp site for lunch. The girls retrieved some bottles of water and sandwich meat from the cooler, while the boys got the rest of the stuff from the hanging grocery supplies. They ate their lunch slowly while listening to some music on the radio. Charlie and Jeremy both had one and a half sandwiches each, but the girls were fine with just one sandwich each. When they were finished eating, Jeremy put his arms out and stretched. “You ready to head back to the tunnel” Charlie questioned. “No, not yet” Jeremy replied, “I’m actually kind of tired after that meal. I think I’ll lay down in the tent for a while and take a nap.” “What? Are you serious?” Charlie exclaimed, “You were the one that was so anxious to explore the cave again.” Jeremy smiled and yawned at his friend. “I know I was” he said, “But I’m feeling tired right now, and the girls are right, we need to be rested up before going through the tunnel and up to the cave.”

His sister and two friends watched, as Jeremy slipped into his tent. “He must have been more tired than he originally thought he was” Jenny whispered. “Well, I’m going down to the lake for a walk” Amanda declared, “anyone want to come with me.” “I’ll join you” Jenny offered. “You coming too, Charlie” Amanda asked with a smile. “No, I think I’ll take a little nap too” he replied, “I’m suddenly feeling a little tired too.” “Okay, we’ll see you later then” Amanda said to him. “We’ll be back in about an hour, make sure you and Jeremy stay here until we get back, okay” Jenny said. “Okay” Charlie answered her.

The girls decided to take the cart with them on their walk and fill it with fire wood to bring back to camp. They headed south when they reached the beach and headed in the direction of where the group had left the piles of dry wood the previous day. When they returned from their walk and wood gathering a little less than an hour later and unloaded the wood from the cart onto the wood pile, the boys were nowhere in sight. “Do you think the boys are still napping” Jenny asked Amanda. “Yes, since they aren’t waiting outside their tent for us”

Amanda replied, “but I’ll check for sure.” She went over to the boy’s tent, looked in through the mesh door, and could see both of the boys laying on their sleeping bags. She returned to Jenny and confirmed that the two boys were indeed still in the tent. “What do we do till they wake up” Jenny inquired. “We could listen to some music on the radio” Amanda suggested. “Or, we could take the radio down to the lake, and play some music while we relax out on our air mattresses” Jenny said. “That sounds even better” Amanda replied, “with the radio along for some music, when the boys wake up, they’ll hear it and come down to the lake.” “Good plan” her friend said, “let’s go.”

Charlie was the first one to wake up from his nap, and he checked the time on his watch. “Hey, Jeremy! Wake up” he said as he shook his friend’s shoulder, “we’ve been sleeping for an hour and a half.” Jeremy’s eyes flew open and he sat up. “An hour and a half” he mumbled, “Man, I must have been really wiped out. Where are the girls?” “I don’t know” Charlie responded, “maybe they’re in their tent waiting for us to wake up.” The boys climbed out of their tent and went to check the girl’s tent. Finding no one in the other tent, they stood between the two tents, thinking. “Wait, I hear music, and it’s coming from down at the lake” Charlie exclaimed. “It must be the girls down at the lake with the radio” Jeremy said. The two friends went down the path to the lake and found the radio sitting on the sandy beach. "There they are, way out on the lake" Jeremy said, pointing out to the two girls floating on their air mattresses. "Hey Amanda, Jenny" Charlie called out to the girls. The boys waited, but neither girl moved or responded to Charlie's call. "They fell asleep out there" Jeremy chuckled. "Yeah, we better swim out there and make sure they don't roll over and drown" Charlie snickered.

The boys quietly wadded out into the water and then swam in the direction of the girls, who actually had fallen asleep on the air mattresses. Jeremy swam to Jenny while Charlie swam to Amanda, and they each started tickling the girls' ears. When the girls reached up to brush their ears, the boys whispered to them that it was time to wake up. Jenny opened her eyes and looked over at Jeremy beside her mattress. "What time is it" she asked him. "It's about a quarter after two" Jeremy answered. "A quarter after two" exclaimed Amanda from the other air mattress, "We've been floating out here on the water for almost forty-five minutes?" "Jeremy and I just woke up a little bit ago" Charlie told her. "Yeah, we all must have been a lot more tired than we thought we were" Jeremy said. "Do you still plan on going down to the tunnel again?" Jenny asked. "Yes, I do" Jeremy replied, "Charlie and I are going back to camp for the rope, flashlights, and lanterns right now, are you girls coming out to the ledge to help again?" "Yes" Amanda exclaimed, "of course we are." "We'll come back to camp with you" Jenny said, and the four began swimming back towards shore together.

THE NATURISTS

After returning to the camp site, they grabbed the sack with the flashlights, lanterns, and rope inside, and started back out to the lake again. Each of the girls was taking along an air mattress also, so they could put the lights and rope on them to float everything out behind the waterfall. "Wait a minute" Jeremy exclaimed as he ran back toward the tents. He went into the pile of supplies for a moment and returned with another rope. Charlie looked at him, mystified, "We already have the rope here" he exclaimed. "Yeah, I know" Jeremy replied, "but I have an idea that requires a third rope." "What idea" Amanda nervously asked. "To put a guide rope through the tunnel, and up to the cave" he responded, "We'll attach the end of the rope to something outside the tunnel, then I'll pull the other end along when I swim in to the cave again. I'll find somewhere in the cave to tie it to, and we'll have a rope to follow when we swim through the tunnel and up to the cave." "That's a good idea" Charlie said with a smile, "but you could just use the rope that will be tied to you, instead." "Oh, yeah" Jeremy moaned. "But the third rope might still be a good idea" Jenny offered, "He can leave it in the cave, so we have one there in case we should need one inside the cave later." "Yeah. Isn't the Boy Scout moto, 'Be Prepared'" asked Amanda. "Yes, it is" replied Charlie with a smile, "Okay, let's go 'prepared' then."

As they neared the bend in the shoreline, the four teens started hearing voices ahead. The girls looked over at the boys, smiling. "They're back" Amanda whispered. "No need to whisper" Jeremy replied, "If they are back, it doesn't matter anymore. When they see us, they'll either stay, or swim away again. We aren't going to chase after them this time, we're just going to go swimming for a little while instead, okay." "I don't understand" Charlie said, "Why don't we want to catch them?" "Because we're only scaring them" Jenny said, "and that's not what we want. We want them to feel safe around us, so maybe they'll talk to us, right Jeremy?" "Right" Jeremy replied, "We'll just stay to ourselves, swimming. When they feel safe with us around, and they get curious enough about us, maybe they will come closer and talk to us." "And then, maybe we can get to be friends with them." Jenny added. "Okay, so are we going to the tunnel, and the cave right now?" Charlie asked. "No" Jeremy responded, "we'll leave the ropes and flashlights here behind the bushes, then go around the bend and start swimming back behind the waterfall. We can jump and dive off the ledge instead, and hopefully the kids will come and see what we're doing. If they do come back, and they talk to us, make sure none of us says anything about the tunnel or cave, unless they tell us about it first, okay?" "Okay" everyone responded, and the girls laid the mattresses down on top of each other by the bushes, and then the boys laid the rest of the stuff down on top of them.

The four teens walked around the bend and continued down the beach for about twenty feet more, then started walking into the water together. The young boys, the same two from the previous day, watched the group of teens very closely from out in the lake. The four teens simply waved to the kids, but made no attempt to go out to them. When the teens got into deep enough water, they began swimming in the direction of the waterfall. They were watched very carefully by the young boys as they made their way to the waterfall and behind it. Jeremy swam towards the steps on the opposite end of the ledge, with the others right behind him. When they reached the steps, they all climbed up onto the ledge and started diving or jumping back into the water, then climbing back up to the ledge again. They had been behind the waterfalls for about ten minutes, when Charlie noticed the two young boys come into sight further out on the stone steps side of the falls. "They're watching us" he whispered to the others. The two boys remained about fifty feet away, treading water out in the lake, watching the teenagers behind the waterfall as they enjoyed going off of the ledge.

Jeremy and the girls glanced over at the young boys

out in the lake and waved at them, then went back to enjoying themselves as they jumped or dove off the ledge into the water. "I'm getting tired" Amanda said to Jenny, "I need to take a rest break." "Me too" Jenny responded, "Let's sit down on the ledge and relax for a little bit." The girls sat down on the ledge with their legs dangling over the edge and leaned back on their arms. The boys continued to dive off the ledge and into the water, yelling and laughing as they did so. A few minutes later, after glancing back out at the young boys, Jenny turned to her friend. "They're getting closer" she whispered. Amanda looked over at the two boys and saw that they were indeed slowly coming closer to the west end of the ledge. "Hey, Jeremy" she called to her brother when he came close enough to her on the ledge, "looks like company's coming." Jeremy looked over at the boys who were now only about ten feet from the steps, and smiled, "Hey" he called out to them, "Nice day for a swim, isn't it?" The two stared back at him for a little bit, then the black-haired boy spoke back, "Yeah, the lake is always a great place on hot days."

"You boys must be getting tired out there" Jeremy said, "you've been out in the water swimming, since before we got here." "We are a little tired" the red-haired boy replied. "Well, if you'd like to rest for a little bit up here on the ledge, we wouldn't mind" Jeremy offered. The two boys remained out in the water, whispering to each other. “We better stay out here” the black-haired boy finally said. “But, if you’re tired, you should really take a break from swimming” Jenny said, “You don’t have to be afraid of us.” “We know that we scared you yesterday, when we tried to get close enough to talk to you, but we weren’t trying to” Jeremy stated. “And we’re sorry if we did scare you” Amanda added. “That’s not it” the red-headed boy replied with a smile. “Is it because you’re naked?” Jenny asked. Both of the young boys looked at each other. “We’ve seen you swimming out in the lake several times” Jenny explained, “We couldn’t help but notice that you were skinny-dipping, and we figured you were probably nudists.” The boys looked at each other again, then back at the four teenagers. “Naturists” the black-haired boy stated. “What?” Charlie asked. “We’re ‘naturists’, not ‘nudists’ the boy answered. “What’s a naturist?” Charlie asked. “A naturist is like a nudist, just a little different” responded Jenny. “Okay” Charlie said, “So, are they coming up here or not?”

“You guys really don’t mind us joining you up there, when we’re nude?” the red-haired boy asked. “I don’t mind” Jenny answered. “I don’t think any of us would mind if you wanted to take a break up here” Jeremy said, “even if you are naked. Or nude.” The younger boys looked at each other again and whispered back and forth. “Okay, we’ll come up there” the black-haired boy said, "since we're getting awfully tired and need to rest, so as long as you guys are okay with seeing us nude." The young boys swam the remaining ten feet over to the steps and slowly started climbing up out of the water to the ledge, carefully watching all the teenagers. Amanda stared as the two young boys came up the steps and stood on the ledge with water dripping off of their naked young bodies. "You okay" Jenny whispered to her friend. "Yeah, sure" Amanda whispered back, "Why?" "Because you're staring at them with a big grin on your face" Jenny whispered, "you're going to make them feel uncomfortable if you're not careful." "Well it's just kind of strange to have two naked boys standing around" Amanda whispered back. "You've seen naked boys before, haven't you?" Jenny asked. "Sure, when I've been babysitting, but they were just babies and toddlers. Not boys this old" replied Amanda.

The two young boys sat down on the ledge, unashamed of their nudity, in the presence of the four teenagers. "This is my friend, Charlie" Jeremy said, indicating the person he meant, "that brown haired girl there is my sister Amanda, and the blond girl is my girlfriend, Jenny. My name is Jeremy." "We're camping over on the east side of the lake" Charlie added. "My name is Greg" the black-haired boy said. "And my name is Tomas (*Tow-mas*)" the red-haired boy added. "We know where your camp site is, we saw it yesterday" Greg said, “We saw a stone marker pointing up a path and followed the path up to your camp. We called out to see if anyone was in the camp, but no one answered, so we left.” “That was you then” Jenny said, “We saw your foot-prints on the path and wondered if you or someone else had been there.” “We didn’t take anything” Tomas quickly explained, “We didn’t really even go in very far.” “We know” Charlie replied, “Your foot-prints only went a few feet in off the path.” “So, do you guys have a camp site around here too? Are your parents here with you?” Jeremy asked. “We aren’t camping anywhere here” Greg stated, “we came here alone.” “We come here almost every day during the summer” the red-haired boy added. “You’re here all alone” Amanda exclaimed, “How old are you?”

The boys looked at each other, then whispered back and forth for a moment. “We’re both twelve” Greg said, “And our parents know that we come here to swim. They don’t worry about it, as long as we swim with one or more friends along.” “We’re both really good swimmers, so it’s okay with them.” Tomas added. “Well, with the four of us here, you have four more friends with you” Charlie chuckled, “that makes it even safer than with just the two of you, right?” “Well, maybe” Greg answered, “except that we don’t really know all of you yet.” “Yeah” Tomas agreed. “Well, we can fix that” Charlie declared, “Jeremy and I are going to be seniors in school this fall, and we're both on the school swim team, so we can swim really good, too." "And, we already know that you two are really good swimmers" Jeremy added, "Charlie and I couldn't catch up to you guys yesterday to talk with you, remember?" The two younger boys grinned at Jeremy's praise of them. "You probably would have caught us if we weren't so far ahead of you to start with" Greg admitted. "Yeah" Tomas added with a grin, "Greg said you were really fast swimmers, and that you almost caught us." "Well, we are trained to swim fast, to win races" Charlie said, "but you two could be on a swim team too, when you get into high school." Jenny noticed that the boys seemed more at ease now, but were still obviously nervous. "I hope you don't think we would hurt either of you, because we wouldn't" Jenny said, "If you're uncomfortable with us here, we can swim back around the bend in the lake and do our swimming there until you leave."

Greg and Tomas looked at each other and smiled. After a few moments of whispering to each other, they seemed to agree on something. "Okay" Tomas replied, "We think you're okay, and that you don't want to hurt us." "So, you can swim with us, as long as it doesn't bother you that we aren't wearing anything" Greg added, "because, we're not going to put on any uncomfortable, stupid swimsuits." "We think it's dumb to wear anything when swimming" Tomas said, "clothes just feel uncomfortable and weird to us." "Great!" Jeremy exclaimed, "And, I hope we can all become good friends, too." "Okay" Charlie exclaimed, "Now that all that is decided, can someone explain to me what the difference is between a 'nudist' and a 'naturist." Greg looked at Charlie and grinned. "I can" he said, "A nudist goes nude whenever he can, but naturists prefer to live nude all the time, except when they feel like they have to wear uncomfortable clothes. Tomas and I are naturists, because we live au naturel all the time." "Yeah! Vivre au naturel!" Tomas exclaimed with a grin, "Live natural." "Some people say nudist and naturist are the same thing" Greg continued, "but 'naturists' are people who live naturally, without clothes, all the time, not just some of the time." "Okay, I think I might be getting it now" Charlie said, "But I'll have to think about it some more, to be sure." "Do you mind if I ask you a question" Amanda inquired, "Who was the girl that was with you yesterday?" "That was just my sister Karen, she's thirteen" Greg answered.

"I have a question too" Jenny stated, "Are we going to talk all day, or are we going to do some swimming." "Swimming" Jeremy declared, as he stood up and began preparing to dive into the water. "Wait for me" Jenny exclaimed, as she also stood up. They all stood up and jumped, or dove off of the ledge at the same time, creating a cascade of splashes all along the ledge. The six youth all surfaced, laughing, and a water war erupted when Charlie started splashing the two girls, followed by Jeremy. The girls began splashing the two boys back, and the two younger boys joined in on the girl's side. The splashing continued until Jeremy and Charlie suddenly turned, swam for the steps, and went up to the ledge. When the other side realized that they were not being splashed back, they stopped and saw the two teen boys already going up the steps to the ledge. Charlie turned to face the four in the water and smiled out at them. "You guys want to keep splashing the air out there or join us up here?" he asked with a laugh. The girls and young boys began immediately making their way over to the steps, and as they climbed up to the ledge, the two older boys walked down to midway on the ledge and dove into the water.

The six of them spent the next hour behind the waterfall, swimming and diving off the ledge, resting about every fifteen minutes as they tired. Jeremy and Charlie also worked with Greg and Tomas, giving them some pointers on diving properly, so they wouldn't land in the water on their stomachs. The girls finally decided that they needed to go and get their air mattresses and rest out on the lake by just drifting around on them. They left the four boys behind and swam for the beach, but the boys decided to stay in back of the waterfall and keep diving. After about the sixth dive for them all, after the girls had left, they were sitting down on the ledge to rest again when Charlie decided to ask the young boys another question. “Greg, Tomas” he started, “Have you guys ever tried swimming with swimsuits on? I was just wondering, because you said that swimsuits and clothes were ‘uncomfortable’.” The two young boys looked at Charlie and smiled. “Yes, we’ve had to wear swimsuits before, and even clothes” Greg answered. “We wear swimsuits when we go swimming where nude isn’t allowed” Tomas added. “And we wear clothes when we’re in town, so we know what it’s like to wear clothes” Greg concluded. “Have you guys ever been swimming without your swimsuits on?” Tomas inquired, “Do you know what it feels like to swim nude?”

Charlie looked at the young boy that had asked the question. “You mean, s-swim n-naked. No, I don’t think I could ever do anything like that” Charlie replied, “How about you, Jeremy? Have you ever swum naked?” Jeremy stared at the naked twelve-year old boys. “No, I’ve never done anything like that” Jeremy answered, I don’t think I could do it either.” “Why not?” Greg inquired, “Are you ashamed of your body?” “No” Jeremy replied, “I just don’t think I’d be comfortable with going naked.” “Why?” asked Greg. “Because someone might see me” Jeremy answered. “You mean like your friend Charlie?” Greg inquired. “No, he’s seen me naked in the shower, after swim practice, and I’ve seen him taking a shower" Jeremy answered. "So, if you've both seen each other nude before, why don't you try swimming nude here, right now?" Tomas inquired. "I don't think it's a good idea" Jeremy said, "The girls might come back here and see us naked?" "But they just left so they could relax out on the lake on air mattresses, they won't be coming back here again for a while" Charlie teased Jeremy with a grin on his face. Jeremy stared at his friend. "You do know that they're talking about both of us going nude?" Jeremy declared, "not just me." Charlie's smile vanished, and he looked over at the two young boys. The boys looked back at him, nodding their heads to confirm that they were suggesting both teen boys try skinny-dipping. "No. No way. I can't do it" Charlie said. "Why not?" Jeremy said with a scowl on his face, "You said that the girls won't be coming back." "Are you saying that you'll do it?" Charlie asked his friend with a sneer. Jeremy looked at the young boys who were grinning, then back at his friend. "Sure, why not. I'll try it, if you will" he challenged Charlie.

The two teen boys stared at each other for about twenty seconds. "You first" Charlie said. "No, we do it together, at the same time" Jeremy declared, "After all, you're the one who started all this with your question." "Okay, okay" Charlie replied, "We'll jump in the water, take off our swim trunks, and try swimming naked for a minute." "Would that be good enough to say we tried it?" Jeremy asked the two naked young boys. Greg smiled back at them, "It would be better if you got naked up here first, then jumped into the water and left your swimsuits here on the ledge" he replied. Jeremy looked at Charlie, "Well?" he inquired, "you want to give it a try?" "Okay, but we should check on where the girls are first" replied Charlie. The two teen boys walked down to the east end of the ledge, jumped into the water, and swam out from behind the waterfall until they could see down the beach. The girls had retrieved the air mattresses from behind the bushes at the bend and were just climbing onto them out in shallow water. The boys watched them for a couple minutes as they paddled further out into the lake and then laid back on the mattresses. They then began to swim back behind the waterfall, along the ledge.

Jeremy climbed up the steps to the ledge with Charlie just behind him. They both walked a few feet onto the ledge, then looked at the two naked boys that were waiting for them on the ledge. Jeremy looked at his friend, "You ready?" he asked. "If you are" Charlie replied, "We can leave our trunks right here and jump in." "Okay, let's do it" Jeremy said, and he untied the cord to his trunks. Charlie followed suit and untied his as well, then the two of them pulled down their swim trunks, stepped out of them, and stood there completely naked, looking over at the two younger boys. The young boys nodded at them, and then jumped off the ledge and into the water. Jeremy walked over to the edge of the ledge, looked towards both ends of the waterfall to be sure no one was there, and finally jumped into the water, with his friend right behind him. When their heads popped back above the surface, they looked at each other and laughed, then they looked for the other two boys. “We’re over here” Greg called out as he and Tomas started up the steps to the ledge, “Come on, lets dive in this time.”

Charlie began swimming over to the steps, with Jeremy right behind, and the two went up the steps to the ledge. Greg and Tomas were already at the edge of the ledge, motioning for the two teens to come over and join them. Charlie started reaching down for his swim suit on the ledge, but Jeremy stopped him. “Let’s wait and try diving in like this a couple times” Jeremy suggested. “You want to stay naked?” Charlie muttered. “Yes” Jeremy replied, “When we jumped in a moment ago, I noticed how different it felt to not have swim trunks riding up on my legs. I want to try diving in naked, and see how that feels.” “You’re kidding, right” Charlie inquired. “No, I’m not” Jeremy said, “I’m going to dive in without my trunks on. If you don’t want to, then go ahead and put yours on.” Jeremy proceeded over to the ledge in the nude and stood along-side the two young naturists that were waiting. Jeremy looked back at his friend to see if he was going to join them. Charlie was just standing there, staring back at him, then he suddenly looked down to both ends of the water fall and put his swim trunks back down on the ledge. With a little huff, Charlie started towards the other three boys, still completely naked.

"Okay, I'm ready" Charlie said, "Let's do this, again." Jeremy grinned at his friend, "Okay, on three we all dive in" he stated, "One. Two. Three." All four naked boys jumped up from the ledge and out to the water, arching mid-air, and then going down with arms ahead of themselves. The four swam back over to the steps again and proceeded up to the ledge. Up on the ledge again, Jeremy looked at his friend, "How did it feel" he asked. "What do you mean?' Charlie replied. "It felt different to me" Jeremy explained, "When I slipped into the water, I felt less drag, without a swimsuit on. I slid into the water without feeling my swimsuit trying to come off." "I didn't notice anything" Charlie responded. "You probably weren't really paying attention" Jeremy said, "you were only thinking about how naked you were. I'm going to dive in again and see how it feels, why don't you try it again, and try to concentrate on how it feels this time." "Alright, one more time" Charlie replied, "then, I'm putting my suit back on." "Fine" Jeremy said, "but pay attention to how it feels this time." The four boys dove in again, surfaced, and swam back to the steps and climbed up onto the ledge. Charlie immediately started putting his swim trunks back on. Jeremy slipped his trunks on also, and then went to the edge of the ledge, ready to dive in again. "Come on Charlie, let's dive in again, but pay attention to how it feels with your trunks on this time" Jeremy urged his friend.

The boys did another dive into the water. When they came above water again, Jeremy looked over at Charlie. "Well, does it feel any different to you now" he asked. "Yes, you're right" Charlie answered, "There's more resistance from a swimsuit when diving, than there is when diving in naked." They got up on the ledge again, and this time Jeremy just stood for a little bit. "You okay?" Charlie inquired. "Yeah, sure" Jeremy answered, "I was just noticing something else. "What's that" his friend asked. "Well, we went into the water three times with nothing on and came back up here to the ledge for another dive" Jeremy stated, "This time, when we get up here on the ledge, I can feel my wet swim trunks kind of hanging on me. It felt nicer when I didn't have the suit on." The two younger boys were standing nearby, grinning at Jeremy's observations. Jeremy looked over at the two naturist boys, "You're right, swimming with nothing on does feel better" he admitted, "but I don't think I'll get much chance to try it much more, with my sister and girlfriend around."

"Let's rest for a little bit" Jeremy suggested, "Then we can do some more diving. We'll have to quit and go get the girls in a little while, so we can get back to camp and fix supper." "Hey, Jeremy, do we have enough food so Greg and Tomas can come and have supper with us." "Sure" Jeremy responded. "Tomas and I have to go home for supper" Greg declared, "Our parents will wonder where we are if we don't." "Okay" Jeremy said, "Maybe some other time then. We'll be here for about another week." "How about for lunch tomorrow?" Charlie suggested. "Okay, we'll ask our parents about it when we get home" Greg replied. "So, where is home" Charlie asked, "how do you get there from here?" The two young boys looked at Charlie. "Sorry, we can't tell you that" Greg replied. "We're not supposed to tell anyone where we live" Tomas added, "It's a secret." "That's okay" Jeremy inserted into the conversation, "But, we can still be friends, right?" "Sure" both boys replied enthusiastically. "So, we'll plan on you for lunch then. If you can't join us then, just let us know somehow, and we'll just not fix any extra hotdogs." "Hotdogs!" exclaimed Tomas, "Oh, I hope we can have lunch with you guys, I love hotdogs."

After resting for another ten minutes, the boys began diving off of the ledge some more, then decided to swim out and check on the two girls. They swam around the waterfall and spotted the girls floating around on the air mattresses, out on the lake. They began swimming in the girl's direction, and as they approached them, the girls turned over on their stomachs to see who was coming. "Hey guys" they shouted out as the four boys swam towards them. "Hi" Jeremy exclaimed as they swam up to the two air mattresses, "Want to come to shore with us for a little bit?" "Sure" the girls said, and they all headed in towards the beach. When they reached the shoreline, they all walked up onto the sandy beach and sat down. "So, did you boys have a good time in back of the waterfall" Amanda asked. "What? What do you mean?" Charlie replied. "I mean, did you all have a good time diving, without us there" Amanda replied. "Oh, yeah. We had a great time" Charlie said, "we had to rest up a couple times in between sets of diving, but we had a good time." "These two young guys are really getting good at diving" Jeremy added, "They might do good on a swimming team someday." "Great" Jenny said, "And by the way. Amanda and I were talking and thought maybe Tomas and Greg might want to eat supper with us."

Greg and Tomas started laughing together. "What's so funny" Jenny asked, looking first at the two young boys and then at Jeremy and Charlie. "They're going to check with their parents about having lunch with us tomorrow" Charlie replied with a grin. "We already invited them" Jeremy added, "So, I guess you two don't have any objections about guests coming for lunch." "Thank you all for asking us" Greg said, "We'll check with our parents about tomorrow." "That's great" Amanda said, "I sure hope you can, and maybe we can spend the day together." "Well, I think Greg and Tomas probably need to start back home" Jeremy said, "And we need to get back to camp and start getting our supper ready. We'll head back to camp so our new friends can head out, without any of us spying on them." "What" Amanda exclaimed, "Spy on them." "I think they know we're curious about where they go when they leave here" Jeremy stated, "But they're not supposed to show or tell where they go." "Right" Tomas said, "It's a secret." "Just so you know though, we won't spy on you anymore, but we'll still keep looking around to try and figure out where you go, okay" Jeremy said. "Okay" Greg replied, "but I don't think you'll be able to find our secret place." "Okay, we'll hope to see you tomorrow" Charlie said, as the four teenagers got up and headed back to their camp site. "Bye" the girls called back to the young boys. "Bye" the young boys called back to them as they got up and walked the other way. "They both have such cute butts" Amanda whispered to Jenny. "Amanda!" Jenny replied with a giggle.

JENNY'S SECRET

Jeremy, Charlie, Amanda, and Jenny all headed back to camp, stopping behind the bushes at the bend to gather up the sack with the ropes and lights, which they had stashed there earlier, when they spotted Greg and Tomas swimming out in the lake. They got back to camp and put the stuff back in the storage area under the tarp between the tents. Jeremy proceeded over to the grocery supplies in the tree, the girls got some ground beef for hamburgers from the cooler, and Charlie started building up the camp fire again. Once they had supper ready, they ate and started discussing the events of the day. Jeremy was disappointed that they had not been able to get back to the tunnel, so he could get to the cave to explore some more, but everyone seemed to be elated that they were actually able to talk with and befriend two of the naturist kids that they had spotted in the lake over the last four days.

Everyone seemed to agree that Greg and Tomas were great kids. They all realized also, that they had gotten so used to the boys' being naked, that they had actually forgotten that the young boys were completely bare the whole time. Jeremy and Charlie had decided not to mention anything about their skinny-dipping behind the waterfall earlier, while the girls were out on the lake. "I wonder how people can do that, go naked all the time in front of other people" Amanda said, "especially boys and girls naked together." "Maybe it's just natural for them" Charlie suggested, "They're just used to it because that's how they were raised by their parents." "Yeah" Jeremy agreed, "For someone that's never been nude around other people, it's hard for them to imagine, I guess. Unless they try it for themselves, maybe." "Really, Jeremy?" Amanda gasped, "Have you ever been naked around other people?" "Of course, he has" Charlie exclaimed with a big grin. "What? When?" Amanda demanded. "At school" Charlie chuckled, "After gym class and swim practice, all the guys have to take showers without clothes or swimsuits on. You take showers without clothes too, don't you?" "Well, that's different" Amanda declared, "It's all boys in the shower for you two, and all girls for me and Jenny, right Jenny?" "Yes" Jenny replied quietly, "But we are naked in front of other people, and you wondered how people could do that."

Amanda looked at her friend, then at the boys, and then back at Jenny again. "Okay, so there are times when it's normal to be naked in front of people of the same gender" she said, "but do you all think it's okay for people to go naked all the time? To be a nudist, or naturist as the boys said." "Well, they think it's okay, at least for them" Jenny said. "But would you go naked like that, in front of other people, boys, girls, men, and women?" Amanda demanded to know. Jenny stared at her friend, blushing, then looked over at the boys. "I knew you wouldn't" Amanda declared triumphantly. Jenny looked down at the ground and sighed. "I've already done it once" she said. "Done what?" Amanda inquired. "I've gone nude around other people before" Jenny answered. "What? When?" Amanda gasped. "When I was about twelve" Jenny replied, "I was on vacation with my family, and my dad decided we should all visit a clothing-optional beach in Florida." "So, you actually went naked with other people around?" gasped Amanda. "Yes, my whole family went nude at that beach" Jenny answered, "There were hundreds of people at the beach, almost all of them nude." Amanda stared at her best friend. "How come you never told me about this before" she mumbled.

Jenny felt afraid now, she had just revealed something she thought she never would, and not only to her best friend, but also in front of Jeremy and Charlie. Jeremy reached over and put his arm around her, and pulled her closer to himself. "I can't believe it" Amanda declared, "You've never said anything about this to me before." Jeremy glared at his sister. "Amanda, shut up!" he exclaimed angrily, "You're supposed to be Jenny's best friend, and you talk to her like that? Like she did something wrong?" Amanda looked at Jenny and saw the tears in her friend's eyes.

"Oh, Jenny, I'm sorry. I didn't mean it like that. I didn't mean to hurt you" she apologized, "I was just so surprised. I don't know what I was thinking. My mouth was running, while my brain was frozen in shock."

Jenny started sobbing on Jeremy's shoulder, her body shuddering with each breath. "Now you all think I did something bad" she said. Amanda came over and put her arms around Jenny and her brother, "No Jenny. I'm so sorry I hurt you like this. You didn't do anything wrong, I was just talking stupid." "None of us thinks you did anything bad, Jenny" Jeremy said, "There was nothing wrong with you going nude on a nude beach. Nothing at all." "You're just saying that to make me feel better" Jenny replied, "You'd never go nude around other people like that." Charlie started chuckling, then seemed to choke a little and cough. "What's wrong with him?" Jenny asked, regaining some control over herself. Jeremy looked over at Charlie, then at his sister, and then back at Jenny. "He just thought what you said was kind of funny" Jeremy explained. Jenny looked up at his face, "Why does he think it's funny that I went to a nude beach?" she asked. "That's not what I thought was funny" Charlie started to explain, as he looked at Jeremy and nodded his head. "He thinks it's funny because, well, because he and I were skinny-dipping behind the waterfall with Greg and Tomas this afternoon" Jeremy stated softly, "While you and Amanda were out on air mattresses, floating on the lake, we tried skinny-dipping." Charlie put his head in his hands and started shaking it back and forth. Amanda looked at her brother in shock. Jenny looked up into Jeremy's eyes, and could tell that he was telling the truth.

"You were really swimming nude back there?" Amanda said, "Why?" Jeremy smiled back at his sister. "Charlie was talking to Greg and Tomas, and asked them if they had ever tried wearing swimsuits or clothes. They told him that they had, but that they didn't feel comfortable in them" he told her, "Tomas then asked us if we knew what it felt like to swim nude, and that kind of made us feel like we should try skinny-dipping." "Jeremy thought we should try it" Charlie interjected, "And, since you two were gone, he talked me into trying it with him." "So, you two went skinny dipping back there" exclaimed Amanda. "How did it feel? Did you like it?" Jenny asked. "Well, I don't think Charlie liked it very much, but I thought it felt kind of nice" Jeremy replied, "I liked how it felt, not having a wet swimsuit on every time I came out of the water, and when I dove into the water, I felt less drag without my trunks on." "I remember when I was twelve, at that nude beach" Jenny started, "I felt really nervous at first, but everyone else was naked, so I finally took my suit off after about half an hour. I got to playing with other kids on the beach, and forgot I was completely nude in front of hundreds of people. By the time we had to leave the beach, I didn't feel like putting my clothes back on. And when I did get dressed, it felt so uncomfortable." "Would you ever want to go back to that nude beach" Jeremy asked. "I don't know. It was a long time ago" Jenny answered. "Well, I think I might like to visit a nude beach someday, and try skinny-dipping again, with more people around" Jeremy exclaimed, "It might be fun."

Jenny felt a lot better after hearing about Jeremy and Charlie's brief skinny-dipping experience earlier. Amanda was still in shock, but seemed a lot more understanding towards her friend. She had to agreed that Jenny hadn't done anything wrong four years earlier, when she was at the nude beach with her family. She was also thinking about what her brother had said about how it felt to swim nude, and how Jenny had indicated that it felt good. Amanda was wondering whether she might consider skinny-dipping someday, either alone or maybe with her best friend along.

A little later, after giving Amanda some time to think things over, Charlie came over to where she was sitting and asked if it was okay for him to join her. "Of course, Charlie" she said to him, "why wouldn't it be okay?" "Well, after what you found out about your brother and me skinny-dipping this afternoon, I thought maybe you wouldn't want to be around me anymore." "Oh Charlie, no. I'm okay with what you and my brother did" she responded to him, "But, I guess I can see why you'd be a little worried, the way I acted when Jenny told us her secret. I was stupid." "So, we're still okay?" Charlie asked. "Of course, we are" she answered as she kissed him on the cheek, "You still want to be my boyfriend, don't you?" "Of course, I do" he replied with a grin. "So, Charlie?" she whispered. "Yes?" he whispered back. "Jeremy kind of said that he liked skinny-dipping. How did you really feel about it?" she asked. "Oh" Charlie responded while blushing, "I guess it wasn't too bad. Jeremy was right about it feeling better without wet swim trunks on, and also about there being less resistance when diving in the water. I just don't know if it's something I want to do again." "Well, I was just wondering, because I might want to try it myself" Amanda giggled, "since I'm the only one of us four that has never tried it yet." "Really?" Charlie said, "Would you want someone along with you, when you try it?" "Yes" she replied, "I might ask Jenny to join me when I try it." She laughed when Charlie looked disappointed. "Hey, what's so funny over there?" inquired Jeremy.

"Nothing much" Amanda replied, "I was just telling Charlie that I might try skinny-dipping myself, but with Jenny along, instead of him. You should have seen the look of disappointment on his face." Jeremy glared at his best friend, who was now blushing a deep red.

"Amanda" Jenny called to her friend, "Would you like to go swimming for a while now, before it gets dark out?" Amanda looked nervously at her friend, "Well, sure. Why not" she replied, "But, just the two of us" she added, looking back and forth between her brother and Charlie. "Don't worry" Jeremy pipped up, "I'll make sure Charlie stays right here in camp, along with me." "Okay then, let's go" Jenny said to Amanda. The two girls got up and started down the path to the lake, while the boys put more wood on the fire, and turned the radio on. The girls reached the beach and looked all around, up and down the shoreline. "Are you ready?" Jenny asked. "I don't know, I'm having second thoughts already" Amanda muttered. "Let's walk further up the beach" Jenny suggested, "Maybe if you're not so close to camp, you'll feel better about getting naked and skinny-dipping." They walked along for about five minutes before Jenny stopped again. "How about now" Jenny asked. "I don't know" Amanda replied, "I'm still having second thoughts about this." "Okay, you think about it, and do whatever you think best" Jenny finally declared, "I'll just be out in the lake, waiting for you." Amanda watched, as her friend started slipping out of her swimsuit. Jenny dropped her suit onto the sandy beach and stood there in just her birthday suit for a few seconds before starting into the water. When she was knee deep in the water, she turned around, "The water's great, are you coming in for a swim?" she asked.

Amanda looked out at her nude friend in the lake, and finally decided. She started removing her own swimsuit, dropping it onto the beach beside Jenny's, and ran out into the water towards her best friend. They wadded out in the water until they were waist deep, and then dropped down in the water to their chins and started swimming further out in the lake.

The two girls swam around in the water together, occasionally splashing each other, and talking. After about an hour and a half, the sky started to darken, "I think we should head back to camp" Jenny suggested. "So soon?" Amanda responded, "Let's swim for just a little longer, the water feels so refreshing." "Okay" Jenny replied with a grin, "But we have to get back to shore before it gets too dark. We need to find our swimsuits and put them back on before we go back to camp again." Amanda gasped, "Oh, I forgot" she exclaimed, "We're naked, with nothing on out here." "You forgot that we were skinny-dipping?" Jenny chuckled. "Yes" Amanda answered with a grin, "It feels so much better without a swimsuit on. So, so..." "So natural" Jenny finished for her friend. "Yes, that's it" Amanda replied, "So natural. And so free." The two swam for another ten minutes, Amanda savoring the free feeling of swimming without a swimsuit. Jenny led them back towards shore to locate their towels and swimwear on the beach. "Our swimsuits are all full of sand" Amanda stated as she picked her suit up. "Let's rinse them out in the water then" Jenny suggested, "We'll carry them until we get close to the camp site, and then put them on." "You mean walk naked out here on the beach?" Amanda asked. "Sure" Jenny replied, "After rinsing the sand out of our swimsuits, they'll be wet and difficult to put on. If we wring them out good and carry them back with us, they'll be drier, and a little easier to put on." "Well, okay" Amanda agreed, "but the boys had better still be in camp and not out looking for us."

When the girls came strolling back into camp, they were talking and giggling. The boys got up, smiling, and welcomed them back. "How was your swim" Jeremy asked. "Wonderful" the girls responded together. "We had a great time" Amanda said with a grin. "And? Did you try it?" Charlie asked. "Try what" Amanda said with a straight face. "Skinny-dipping" whispered Charlie, "Did you actually try swimming with nothing on?" "Maybe" Amanda replied with a grin. "Oh, come on" Jeremy said, "You know you tried it, so just admit it. You tried swimming nude and you enjoyed it, didn't you?" "How do you know I did?" Amanda exclaimed, "Were you spying on us?" "No" Jeremy answered with a smile, "Charlie and I were here the whole time that you two were gone. We probably would have enjoyed a nice swim ourselves, but we agreed to stay in camp to let you two go alone." "Then how do you know I was actually swimming nude?" Amanda demanded. "Because I know you, sis" he responded with a grin, "I know that if you had gone by yourself, you probably wouldn't have done it. But with your best friend along, you would be braver. And even if you were scared to try it, Jenny would probably go ahead without you, and then you'd have to prove that you were just as brave as her." "Well! Mister Know-it-all" Amanda said with a smile, "You're right, I did try it. We both went skinny-dipping. Now, are you happy?" "That's not the question" Jeremy stated, "The real question is, are you happy? Did you enjoy skinny-dipping?" "Well, it was different" Amanda responded. "Yes, she liked it" Jenny declared, "She even forgot that we were swimming nude, when I mentioned it was time to head back to camp."

The girls got changed into some regular clothes, hung their swimsuits up on the clothes line, and then sat down around the fire pit with the boys. They all began to discuss their plans for the following day and decided to check out the tunnel and cave early in the morning, after having breakfast. After another hour and a half, the girls decided that they were tired, and headed off to their tent to get some 'beauty sleep'. Jeremy and Charlie put some more wood on the fire and stayed up for about another half hour, listening to music on the radio, before deciding to head off to bed as well. They slipped behind the bushes to the boys' latrine to take care of business, then headed back to their tent, slipped inside, and crawled into their comfy sleeping bags. "I can't wait to see what's in that cave" Jeremy whispered to his friend. "Well, you better forget about it for tonight" Charlie responded, "or you won't sleep well, and then you'll be too tired in the morning." Both boys got comfortable in their sleeping bags, closed their eyes, and slowly drifted off to sleep.

THE CAVE

Charlie and Jeremy woke up early the next morning, around six-thirty, put on their swimsuits, and slipped out of the tent. They visited the restroom area, and then began gathering up everything that they would need for their cave exploration after breakfast. As they finished placing everything near the path to the beach, the girls exited their tent, stretching and yawning. They looked at the fire pit, with just some glowing embers, then at the boys. “A light breakfast, this morning?” Amanda inquired. “Yes” Jeremy answered, “cereal again. We don’t want to be too full when we go through the tunnel, right?” “Right” Jenny answered, “Maybe we can have a better lunch?” “We’re having hot dogs for lunch” Charlie declared, “At least that’s what we told Greg and Tomas we were having, when we invited them to join us.” “Oh, that’s right” Amanda exclaimed, “We invited them for lunch, didn’t we? Do you think they will join us?” “We’ll have to wait and see” Jeremy answered, “But, we better have breakfast and get going, so we’ll be back here in case they do come.”

After everyone had finished up their cereal, the boys gathered up their exploring supplies, and the four teens headed down to the lake. They turned north towards their destination when they reached the beach, then walked for about ten minutes until they reached the waterfall. The boys piled the supplies onto the one air mattress that Amanda had carried along, and they all started out into the lake towards the area behind the falling water. When they reached the ledge behind the waterfall, they carried the supplies up with them and sat down to rest. "How do we keep the air mattress back here when we all go into the cave?" Jenny inquired as they rested. "The mattress has a loop on each end of it" Charlie answered, "We'll tie the rope to the air mattress before going down to tie the rope to a large rock on the west side of the tunnel. That will keep it from floating away." "I'll take the other end of the rope through the tunnel and up to the surface of the pool in the cave" Jeremy continued, "I'll find something near the pool to tie that end of the rope to, and then I'll swim back out to the rest of you."

Charlie started tying the rope to the air mattress as they sat resting up on the ledge, then pushed the mattress off the ledge and into the water. "You ready?" he asked Jeremy. "Ready" Jeremy responded as he grabbed the free end of the rope and stood up. "Okay" Charlie said, "I'll be in the water holding onto the mattress, you take the rope down and fasten it to the rock down there. If the end to the surface needs some slack, I'll tug on it and you let some rope out for more slack before tying it to the rock anchor." "Okay then, let's go" replied Jeremy. Charlie slipped into the water next to the air mattress, and Jeremy dove off the ledge with a lantern and the free end of the rope, to head down to the tunnel. Jeremy swam down to the bottom and quickly located the tunnel entrance with the help of the waterproof lantern. He pulled down more of the rope from above until he felt a tug on the rope from Charlie up at the surface, then let out a little slack before proceeding to wrap the rope around the rock they had designated as the anchor for this end of the tunnel. He tied the rope off to keep it in place, then tossed the rest of the rope into the tunnel before starting up for the surface.

The girls had been carefully watching everything the boys were doing, although they couldn't really see much of Jeremy when he was down at the bottom of the lake. When Jeremy surfaced, he and Charlie swam over to the steps and climbed up onto the ledge again. They sat down next to the girls on the ledge, and the four of them stared at the mattress floating in the water. "So far, so good" Jeremy declared, "Next step is taking the rope through the tunnel and up to the cave. "Is there enough rope to go all the way in?" Jenny asked. "Yes" Jeremy answered her, "It's a fifty-foot rope, and I figure we need about thirty to fifty feet, depending on how close to the pool I can fasten it." "Yeah, plus we tied a loop on the end of it, so we can attach another rope to it with a carabiner, if needed" Charlie added. He showed them the carabiner that was already attached to the second rope they had brought along.

Jeremy grabbed a flashlight and stood up on the ledge again. "Okay, I'm ready to go" he announced. Charlie grabbed another flashlight and stood up beside his friend. "I'm ready too" he said, "I'll wait thirty seconds, and be right behind you." "You girls okay?" Jeremy asked. "Yes" they answered him nervously, "Be careful though." "We will" Charlie said with a smile, "We'll be back in about ten minutes or so, try not to worry." Jeremy jumped off the ledge and into the water. The others watched him in the light of the lantern that was still on the bottom. He descended down to the tunnel opening and turned on his flashlight, then headed towards the rock wall below them. His light paused near the tunnel entrance, as he grabbed the end of the rope, and then proceeded into the tunnel and out of sight. Charlie waited patiently for thirty seconds, then jumped into the water after his friend. The girls watched him descend also, turn on his flashlight, and then go into the tunnel as Jeremy had done. "I hope everything goes alright" Amanda mumbled softly, as she looked over at the worried looking face of her best friend.

Jeremy had slipped the loop on the end of the rope over his hand and up his arm so that he could hold the flashlight and have at least one arm free to help him swim through the tunnel. He swam quickly through the tunnel with the flashlight illuminating the way ahead, and when he reached the pool at the end of the tunnel, he looked back into the tunnel and saw a light just entering the opening out at the lakeside. Charlie was on his way through the tunnel just behind him. He looked up, pointing his flashlight up also, and pushed off the bottom of the pool to head for the surface. When he reached the surface, he looked back down into the pool, waiting for Charlie's light to appear at the end of the tunnel. When he saw that Charlie was near the end of the tunnel, he moved his light around the edge of the pool, to see if there was anything that they would be able to attach the guide rope to. He spotted a rock at the edge of the pool, above the corner of the pool where the tunnel exited below. The floor of the cave seemed to slant downward from the back, outward side of the cave, and towards the rest of the cave, so that the edge of the pool was closer to the surface of the water away from the wall of the cave. He swam over to that edge of the pool and waited for Charlie to surface.

Charlie surfaced in the pool about the same place that Jeremy had, and took several deep breaths as he shined his own flashlight around, looking for his friend. "Over here" Jeremy called out, as he pointed his flashlight in Charlie's direction. Charlie spotted him and began swimming over to Jeremy. When he reached Jeremy, he directed his flashlight all around the cave to see what it looked like. “Can’t see much in here” he said. “Yeah, too dark.” Jeremy responded, “There’s a rock over there that we can attach the rope to though” he said as he pointed his flashlight across the pool. “We should be able to get out of the water here and go around to tie the rope to the rock” Jeremy instructed. “Okay” Charlie responded, “We better get moving then, the girls are going to start worrying about us if we don’t get back out to them.” The boys climbed out of the water and stood up at the edge of the pool. “Better be careful” Charlie suggested, looking at the rock floor of the cave, “This rock floor will probably be slippery with our feet being wet.”

Both boys carefully maneuvered across the floor and over to the rock that Jeremy had identified as the best possible place to attach this end of the rope to, here inside of the cave. The rock was shaped like a small Christmas tree, and had a blunt point at the top. It also had a groove or notch running around it about a third of the way down, which would be a perfect location to attach their rope to. They had plenty of rope at this end, so they formed a lasso type end to the rope, slipped it over the rock to the notch, and tightened it up. “Perfect” Jeremy announced, “We couldn’t have found a better anchor on this end for the rope. “It should work great" Charlie responded, "We better get back to the girls now though." "Okay" Jeremy said, and he dove into the water with his flashlight aimed ahead of him. Charlie followed Jeremy into the pool, and the two swam down to the bottom together. When they reached the tunnel down at the bottom, Jeremy motioned for Charlie to go into the tunnel first. Not wanting to waste any time objecting, Charlie swam into the tunnel and proceeded through it with his flashlight. Jeremy placed his own flashlight down at the opening to the tunnel with the light shining outward, then swam into the tunnel also and followed his friend through, keeping an eye on the light ahead of him.

Charlie exited the tunnel and turned around in the water to make sure Jeremy was behind him. He saw the light of a flashlight way back in the tunnel, and a dark shape coming through the tunnel towards him. Jeremy exited the tunnel, saw his friend waiting, and signaled that they should head up to the surface of the water. They popped up in the water, to the relief of the girls, and swam towards the steps up to the ledge. As they walked along the ledge towards the girls, Jenny and Amanda came over to them. Jenny grabbed Jeremy in a hug, and Amanda grabbed Charlie. The girls held onto the boys for almost a minute before releasing them again. "What's the matter?" Charlie inquired, "You two act like you haven't seen us in a long time." "You two have been gone for over ten minutes" Amanda exclaimed. "We were starting to worry about you" Jenny added. "We couldn't have been gone for much over ten minutes" Jeremy said as he looked at his watch, "Thirteen minutes as of right now, and we've been out of the water for a couple of minutes." "Well, it seemed a lot longer to us" Amanda tried to explain. "It's okay, sis. We understand." Jeremy replied, "But we're back now, and everything is okay. The rope is tied off on both ends, so we can all use it to swim into the cave now."

"We're all going in this time?" Jenny asked. "Yes" Jeremy answered, "You and I will go through first, with Amanda and Charlie coming in five minutes later." "I don't know if I can swim under water long enough" Amanda exclaimed. "You can do it, sis" Jeremy said, "All you have to do is take a deep breath and hold it as you dive into the water, then swim down to the light of the lantern at the tunnel entrance, and into the tunnel towards the light at the other end. Use the rope to pull you through if you have to." "It's not really that far" Charlie added, "I got through it in less than thirty seconds my first time." Amanda looked at her best friend. "What do you think?" she asked. Jenny smiled back. "Well, I think we can do it Amanda. And I'd rather be with the boys, instead of out here worrying about them while they explore the cave in there." "Well, okay. I guess I can stay under long enough to get in there"

Amanda conceded.

They all sat down and rested on the ledge. "What does it look like in there?" Amanda asked. "Not sure yet" Charlie replied, "It's too dark to see much of it, we'll have to have all the lanterns and flashlights with us to see better." "You can grab the lantern at the tunnel entrance, when you start in" Jeremy said to Charlie, "I'll carry this second lantern in with me, to help light the way a little. Jenny, when you get to the end of the tunnel, grab the flashlight I left there, and head up to the surface of the pool, I'll be right behind you." "Okay" Jenny responded. "It will take Jenny and I about thirty seconds to get to the surface of the cave pool, and a few minutes for me to help Jenny out of the pool and waiting at the edge for Amanda. After I make sure Jenny is okay, I'll wait until about five minutes have passed since we jumped into the water out here, then I'll swim back down to the tunnel in the pool with the lantern, to give you and Amanda a light to swim towards" Jeremy said to Charlie, "As long as no one panics, we should have no problems."

Charlie smiled at Amanda. "There won't be any problems" he declared, "I'll be right behind Amanda, helping her through the tunnel." Amanda smiled back at him, "I'll be fine Jeremy" she said, "I've got a big handsome guy along to take care of me." Jeremy looked at his sister and best friend, "Okay, so is everyone ready to go then?" he asked. "I am" replied Jenny. "We are" Amanda and Charlie declared. "Okay then. Jenny, stand alongside me on the edge of the ledge here" Jeremy instructed, "We'll dive in on the count of three, and swim straight down to the tunnel. You head into the tunnel, towards the light, and I'll be right behind you. Don't forget to get the flashlight." Jenny stepped up to the edge, alongside of her boyfriend and smiled at him. "I'm ready, on three" she said.

Jeremy slowly counted to three, and he and Jenny leapt off of the ledge and into the water. The two teenagers swam swiftly down to the tunnel entrance, and Jenny went into it without any hesitation. Jeremy grinned to himself as he followed his beautiful girlfriend into the opening. "Brains, beauty, and brave too" he thought to himself. He followed Jenny through the tunnel to the end and watched her grab the flashlight at the end of the tunnel. She entered the pool at the bottom, turned to look at him, and pushed off from the bottom to swim up to the surface, with Jeremy right behind her. They came to the surface of the pool together, shook the water off of their heads, and took in several deep breaths of air. Jeremy pointed to the opposite end of the pool, "Head over to that side" he instructed, "It will be easier to get out of the water there." Jenny began swimming to where he had indicated, with Jeremy right beside her. When they reached the edge of the pool in the cave, they grabbed hold of the edge for a moment and smiled back at each other. "How did I do?" Jenny asked him. "You did great" Jeremy answered, "Now, let me help you up, out of the water, so you can wait for Amanda, and help her out of the pool too."

Jenny put the flashlight up on the cave floor so it shone on the edge of the pool, then grabbed the edge of the pool with both hands. Jeremy put the lantern up on the edge of the pool also, then put his free arm around her waist and lifted her upward as she pulled herself out of the water. Jenny slid out of the pool and laid on her stomach, on the cave floor for a moment, then slowly turned over and sat up. "Okay, I'm good now" she told him, "How long before you have to go back down to the tunnel?" Jeremy looked at the waterproof watch on his wrist, then looked up at her. "We jumped in about two and a half minutes ago" he announced with a grin, "I have two and a half more minutes before I dive down again." "You better get some deep breathing in then, before you have to go" she told him, "I hope Amanda comes through okay, I know she's nervous." "It only took us about forty-five seconds to surface on this side" Jeremy responded, "She can do it, as long as she just swims through without getting scared."

Jeremy kept breathing in and out for the next couple minutes, keeping an eye on his watch. When the time came to dive down, he smiled up at Jenny, "See you in a minute or so" he said, then took a deep breath and dove under the water of the pool. Jenny watched the light of the lantern, and Jeremy's dark outline behind it, as he descended down into the pool and over to the tunnel opening. She could make out the opening of the tunnel in the light of the lantern and watched as Jeremy waited for his sister to appear out of the tunnel. The end of the tunnel started lightening up, and a few seconds later another form swam out. Jeremy grabbed his sister's arm, pulled her upright, and pointed upward as he gave her a push towards the surface. Amanda swam up to the surface, and as her head came out of the water, Jenny heard her gasp in a deep breath. "Over here" Jenny called out, "swim over here to me and I'll help you out of the water." Amanda shook the water out of her hair and looked in the direction of Jenny's voice.

Amanda spotted her friend across the pool, and as she swam towards her, Jenny got on her knees at the edge of the pool, preparing to help her friend out of the water. Charlie had surfaced alongside of Amanda and was swimming along with her to where Jenny waited. When they got to the edge of the pool, Jenny took Amanda's hands and pulled her upward, while Charlie boosted his girlfriend from below. Jeremy got to the edge of the pool as his sister was turning around to sit on the edge of the pool. Both boys stayed in the water for a little bit, catching their breaths, then they hoisted themselves up onto the cave floor and sat next the girls. “Well, that wasn’t so bad, was it?” Jeremy inquired of his sister. “No, it was actually pretty easy” she replied, “I thought it was going to take longer though, and I would have trouble holding my breath long enough.” “She did great, Jeremy. She swam down to the tunnel and right into it without any hesitation at all” Charlie boasted on Amanda’s behalf. “I knew she could do it” Jeremy replied, “but I could tell that she was a little nervous about going into an underwater tunnel.” “Well, what now?” Jenny asked, “Are we just going to sit here, or are we going to check out the cave?” “I need a little break before we start exploring” Jeremy said, “I need to catch my breath.” After resting for about ten minutes, Jeremy stood up, indicating that he was ready to start exploring. They decided to split into two groups, so Charlie and Amanda headed off to the left side of the cave while Jeremy and Jenny took the right side.

Each pair took a lantern and a flashlight with them, the boys held the lanterns up to illuminate the area they were exploring, and the girls hung the flashlights around their necks, turned off to preserve the batteries. Even with the lantern to light up the immediate area around them, the cave still seemed very dark and ominous to

Amanda, and she kept as close as possible to Charlie as they walked along the left side of the cave, about ten feet away from the smooth rock wall. They were being very careful, watching for any dangers that might show up within the light that the lantern was generating. They could see the light from the lantern that their friends were carrying on the opposite side of the cave, but they could only see the outline of their friends' figures. "How big is this cave anyway?" Amanda whispered. "I don't think it will turn out to be as big as it seems right now, in the dark" Charlie answered her. Amanda smiled, "Do you think we could setup a camp site in here if we wanted to?" she asked. "Probably, but I don't think we would be able to build a campfire" he replied, "I don't know if there's any fresh air getting in, and the smoke from a fire would need to get out, or the cave would fill up with the smoke. Plus, we would probably want a few more lanterns for light, too." "What about if we bring in a gas cook stove" Amanda suggested, "then we'd be able to cook, and have some hot food to eat." "Maybe" Charlie replied, "but we would still need fresh air coming in first, or we would run out of oxygen."

Jeremy and Jenny had gone about seventy-five feet back, along the right side of the cave, when Jenny pointed over to where the light from Charlie and Amanda's lantern was. "I think they've stopped over there" she said to Jeremy. Jeremy looked over to confirm what she had said, and a puzzled look appeared on his face, "They couldn't have reached the back of the cave yet" he said, "unless this side goes back even further than their side." "Should we head over there and find out?" Jenny asked. "No" he replied, "Not unless Charlie signals to us that he wants us to join them." A few minutes later, they spotted the other lantern moving again, towards the back of the cave. "Maybe they just stopped to tie a shoe lace" Jeremy said with a laugh. "But they aren't wearing any shoes" Jenny replied, "we all swam in here barefoot, remember?" "I know" Jeremy said with a chuckle, "I was just trying to be funny. We'll find out why they stopped, when we meet them at the back side of the cave."

When they had gone another sixty feet, Jeremy noticed that the cave wall had started curving to the left. He glanced across the cave towards Charlie's lantern on the other side, and a few minutes of watching confirmed that the two pairs of teenagers were coming towards each other. "We've reached the back of the cave" he said to Jenny, as he pointed, "See, they're coming towards us now." Moments later, the two groups met up around the middle of the caves' back wall. "We didn't find anything on our side of the cave" Jeremy exclaimed to the other two as they met up, "How about you two? We saw your light stop for a little bit back there, did you find something?" A big grin appeared on Charlie's face. He looked as if he had just won the lottery or something, and Amanda was practically dancing in place from excitement. "So, what's up" Jeremy asked, "Did you guys actually find something?" Charlie jabbed his thumb back over his shoulder, towards the left side wall of the cave, "I think we might just have found something at that" he answered, "We found some steps leading up to what looks like another tunnel back there in the wall, and it has been cut out with tools."

Charlie lead the way back along the left wall, over to a section of wall where there were some steps going up to a four-foot wide opening about three five deep. "We were walking by here, and spotted the steps, and thought it looked strange" Charlie explained, "When we got closer with the lantern, we saw the opening back there." Charlie held his lantern up higher, so they could all see the obvious opening, about four feet wide and five feet high. Jeremy stepped closer, holding his own lantern up high, and saw what appeared to be another tunnel passing by the opening in the cave wall. The steps had been carved out of a section of the wall that jutted out from the rest of the rock wall about five feet. Jenny stepped in for a closer look also, "Steps?" she asked. Jeremy looked at his best friend with a smile, "So, where does it go" he asked, "Did you check it out yet?"

"No, not yet" Charlie replied, "Amanda and I decided to finished checking the rest of this side of the cave first, so we could all come back together to check it out." "So, let's find out where it goes" Amanda exclaimed excitedly. Jenny was nodding her approval at the suggestion. "Hold on" Jeremy said while looking at his watch, "We've been gone from camp for about an hour already. It will probably be about another hour to get back." "So?" Amanda asked. "So, it's eight-thirty now, and that means we'll get back to camp at about nine-thirty. And we don't know what time Greg and Tomas will be coming for lunch. If we go exploring that passage back there, we may not be around camp when they show up, and they might not want to wait for us." "Oh" Amanda replied. "We really should be back at camp when they show up" Jenny agreed. "Jeremy's right" Charlie said, "We can come back here later, or tomorrow, and explore the new tunnel." "Well, we can explore it for a little bit right now" Jeremy declared, "We just have to set a time limit. Fifteen minutes in, and fifteen minutes back here. That gives us an hour to get back to camp by ten o'clock." The four teenagers agreed on the fifteen-minute time limit and started up the steps to the new tunnel.

The new tunnel turned out to be about a twelve-foot wide passage, and they decided to take the passage to the right first. Charlie led the way with Amanda beside him, and Jenny and Jeremy followed behind them. Charlie lead the way through the passage, holding his lantern up ahead of them, to provide light. They followed the passage as it went deeper into the hill at a slight incline. They walked for about three hundred feet before it came to an end, with an opening into another cave. Charlie stopped at the entrance to the second cave, and when everyone else was caught up behind him, he slowly poked his head around the corner and looked around for any possible dangers. "I think it's another cave" he whispered back to the others. Amanda poked her head inside, "But this one must be up higher than that first one with the pool in it." she said. "How much higher up do you think we are" Jenny inquired of no one in particular. "We've probably walked about three-hundred feet at an upward angle" Jeremy answered, "I would guess that we are about twelve to fifteen feet higher up than the first cave." Jenny smiled at him, "You always were good at numbers." His face turned a little red at her compliment, "Thanks" he said. "Should we look around?" Amanda asked. "We can't" Jeremy said from behind the others, "Our fifteen minutes are almost up, we should head back now." The other three looked disappointed, but knew he was right, and they had all agreed to turn back after fifteen minutes.

Jeremy led the way back down the passage to the

lower cave, and they all headed back to where the entrance pool would be. When they reached the pool of water, Jeremy went over and untied the guide rope from the rock where he and Charlie had attached it. "Why are you untying the rope" Jenny asked, "Won't we need it when we come back?" "No, I don't think we will need it next time" he answered, "Nobody really needed it the first time. We all swam through the underwater tunnel without actually using it, so I think we should take it back to camp, so Greg and Tomas won't see it when they use the tunnel." "Will we need to bring it back next time?" Charlie asked. "Yes" Jeremy replied, "We'll bring it, in case we need a rope for anything else, while we are exploring tomorrow, or whenever we get back here."

Charlie jumped into the pool first, along with Amanda, and the two swam down to the tunnel with one flashlight and one lantern. Jeremy and Jenny watched the lights disappear into the tunnel, and then they jumped in and followed their friends through the tunnel with the other lights. When Jeremy and Jenny surfaced out in the lake, they looked around and saw the other two already over by the steps and climbing up to the ledge. When the four teenagers were all up on the ledge, they sat down to rest and talk, while Jeremy coiled up the rope he had brought back with him. "When do you think we can go back in and explore some more" Amanda inquired. Jeremy and Charlie looked at her and chuckled. "Gee, sis. You sure are anxious to swim through that underwater tunnel now, aren't you?" Jeremy said. "Yes" she answered him with a stern look on her face, "I was nervous the first time, but I know I can get through there without a problem now. You were a little nervous your first time, weren't you?" "Me?" Jeremy asked with a puzzled look, "Did you see me look nervous when we all went in a while ago?" "No" Amanda answered him with a grin, "But that wasn't your first time in, either." "She's right" Jenny added, "Your first time was yesterday, when you didn't know where that tunnel down there went to, remember?" "Oh, yeah" Jeremy groaned, "I guess I was nervous my first time going into the tunnel." "I don't think any of us were 'nervous', I would say that we were all just 'cautious' about our first time going into an unknown place" Charlie offered. "Yeah, we were all just feeling cautious" Jenny said with a chuckle.

Jeremy looked at his watch, then looked around at the others. "It's just after ten o'clock now" he said, "Let's head back to the camp site and put all this stuff away. We can do some swimming in the lake by the path up to camp until lunch time." The others agreed, and they loaded the ropes and lights onto the air mattress and headed back out from behind the waterfall and towards camp. Arriving back at camp, the girls put the supplies in the storage area while the boys gathered some wood by the fire pit and got a fire going. They wanted a fire already going when their guests showed up for lunch.

GUESTS FOR LUNCH

Charlie and Jeremy had the fire going and the girls had the supplies put away under the tarp between the tents. The four teens decided to head back down to the lake with the air mattresses and just relax while floating around out on the water. As they were relaxing on the air mattresses, Amanda suddenly splashed her brother, who was floating next to her. “So, Jeremy, when do you think we’ll be going back into the cave to explore some more” Amanda asked. Jeremy looked over at his sister. “Depends on how things go with Greg and Tomas” he replied, “If they stay around after lunch and spend time here with us, talking and swimming, then we probably won’t be able to get back to our exploration until at least tomorrow. Otherwise, we might be able to go back again this afternoon.” “I think we should just wait until tomorrow” Charlie interjected, “If we head out again tomorrow morning, we’ll have most of the day to explore. If we go this afternoon, we’ll have less time to look around.” “What do you girls think about that plan?” asked Jeremy. “I think Charlie’s right, we should wait until tomorrow morning” Jenny replied. “I’m anxious to get back into the caves” Amanda said, “But Charlie is right, we’ll have more time if we wait until tomorrow.” “Alright then” Jeremy said, “We’ll plan on exploring again tomorrow after breakfast, and take along something for lunch.”

The four teenagers laid back on the mattresses, peacefully floating around out on the lake water and enjoying the warm sunshine. Suddenly, they heard some splashing in the water, coming closer. They all looked up and towards the north and spotted two boys swimming towards them. "It's Greg and Tomas" exclaimed Amanda. The two younger boys swam up to the group of teens and grabbed hold of two air mattresses. "We're here" Tomas exclaimed with a smile, "What time do we eat?" "How about in about fifteen minutes" Charlie declared, "We'll all head back to shore and go up to our camp to start cooking everything." "Great" Greg replied, "Should we come with and help you?" "You can" Jeremy replied, "You don't have to though. The girls will start cooking the hot dogs while Charlie and I get the rest of the stuff out of the tree. You two can just relax and wait for everything to be ready." "What stuff do you have to get out of a tree?" asked Tomas. "Bread, condiments, some beans, plates, and cups" answered Jeremy. "You have your food and other stuff in a tree?" inquired Greg. "Yeah" Charlie said, "We keep our food in a canvas bag, hanging in a tree to keep it away from any animals that might come looking for it." "That's a good idea" Greg said, "Where did you learn to do that?" "Boy Scouts" Charlie answered.

Tomas and Greg decided to return to the camp site

with the four teens and wait for lunch to be served. The teens slid off of their air mattresses and they all proceeded to swim back to shore. When they reached shallow water, they stood up and walked the rest of the way out of the water to the beach. Jeremy and Charlie started up the path to camp with Greg and Tomas right behind them. The girls followed the younger boys, smiling and admiring the cute bare butts of the two young boys walking in front of them. When they reached the camp site, the teens placed the air mattresses around the fire pit, between the fire and the tents, and told the two naturist boys they could sit on one of the mattresses while they got lunch ready. Charlie put some more wood on the fire and the cooking grate over the fire pit, while Jeremy went over to the hanging grocery supplies, and the girls went into a cooler to retrieve some hot dogs. "How many hot dogs does everyone want, one or two?" Amanda called out. Everyone seemed to be hungry, and wanted two a piece, so the girls brought a dozen franks over to the fire. They put six hot dogs in a fry pan, and set the others aside, deciding to cook the second six when the first ones were ready and being eaten. Jeremy and Charlie returned to the fire with the rest of the needed items, and Charlie opened a can of beans to place on the cooking grate to heat.

As the food began heating up, the smell of the hot

dogs and beans filled the air. "We told our parents about meeting you guys" Greg told the teens. The four teenagers looked at the younger boys. "Were they okay with you coming here for lunch with us?" Jenny asked. "They were worried about you finding us swimming" Greg replied, "But we told them you were all real nice, and were okay with us being naturists." "We even told them about you guys showing us how to dive better yesterday" Tomas added, "And how you two boys even tried swimming and diving with, um, um…" Tomas looked at the girls and seemed lost as how to continue. The girls were staring at Tomas with smiles on their faces. "Tomas" Jeremy said, "It's okay. We already told the girls that we were skinny-dipping back behind the waterfall, and naked while diving." Tomas looked at the two grinning girls. "You know about it?" he questioned. "Yes, we know that the boys tried being naked to see how it feels" Jenny answered. "They told us last night, after Jenny told us that she has been to a beach where everyone went naked" Amanda added. "It was four years ago, when I was twelve" Jenny said, "My father took my whole family on vacation, and wanted us to visit a clothing optional beach."

"We were discussing how some people can go naked around other people" Jeremy said, "Jenny thought it was okay, but Amanda wasn't so sure." "Amanda asked Jenny if she would go naked with other people around, and that's when Jenny told her she already had" Charlie continued. "I was pretty shocked by that" Amanda interjected, "I hurt my friends' feelings by the way I reacted. I didn't mean to, and I'm really sorry about it." "But, when my sister and Jenny went swimming alone together last night, Amanda tried skinny-dipping for herself" Jeremy said with a big grin. Greg's eyes popped open real wide. "Really?" he asked. "Yes, really" replied Amanda, "Everyone thought I should try it before condemning it, so I gave it a try last night." "So, you've all tried skinny-dipping now" Greg exclaimed, "Don't you think it feels better when you're swimming without a swimsuit?" "I think it feels great" Jeremy offered, "It's nice to not have wet swim trunks on when I get out of the water. It feels so free." "I liked it that time I went to the beach with my family" Jenny said, "And again last night with Amanda. I remembered again how wonderful it feels. I think Amanda kind of enjoyed the free feeling to." "Well, it was nice" Amanda confirmed, "but I don't think I would want to go naked with boys around." "How about you Charlie?" asked Tomas, "What did you think of skinny-dipping yesterday." "I don't know yet" Charlie answered, "I'll admit that it didn't feel bad, but I'm not sure if I actually enjoyed it, or if I would try it again."

"The food is ready" Jenny announced, as she took the six cooked hot dogs out of the pan and put the second six into it to start cooking. They all grabbed a slice of bread and put a hot dog and whatever condiments they wanted on it, along with some beans. Jeremy passed out cups and filled them with orange soda, so they had a drink to go along with the food. By the time they had finished their beans and first hot dogs, the second six hot dogs were ready. When everyone was finished eating, they all tossed the plates and plastic utensils into the fire, and Jeremy poured more soda into everyone's cups. They all sat around the fire, relaxing on the air mattresses. Greg and Tomas finished off their sodas while whispering back and forth. Finally, Greg stood up. "Well, Tomas and I want to do some swimming yet, before we have to head home again" he said, "do you guys want to go swimming too, or do you have something else to do?" "I could go for some swimming" Charlie announced as he stood up. "Me too" the girls declared together, also getting up. "Count me in" Jeremy said while standing up. Greg looked at the four teens and grinned. "Are any of you going to skinny dip with us?" He asked. The four teens all blushed and looked back at the naked young boys. "I don't think any of us are ready to go swimming co-ed together, without swimsuits on" Jeremy responded. The other three teens all nodded their heads in agreement. "Maybe someday we'll give it a try" Jenny added.

"Okay, just thought I'd ask" Greg said with a chuckle.

"So, let's head for the water" Jeremy said as he picked up one of the air mattresses and started for the path to the lake. Greg and Tomas ran ahead of the teens and were already out in the water a little way, waiting for the teens. The four teens entered the water with the air mattresses, and all six of them swam out further, and then headed north for the waterfall, with Greg and Tomas sharing Jeremy and Charlie's mattresses. As they rounded the bend, the waterfall came into sight, as well as another swimmer out in the water. "Hey, it's my sister, Karen" Greg exclaimed, "She said she might come to the lake after she had lunch." Karen must have seen them coming, because she was now swimming towards the group of six. "Hi" she called out as she stopped swimming and waved to the others. "Hello" everyone called back to her. When they reached where Karen was treading water, they stopped swimming. "Hi, Karen. My name is Jenny. Grab onto my air mattresses if you want, so you don't get too tired from treading water." Karen gratefully took hold of the mattress from the opposite side of Jenny and leaned over it. "Thanks Jenny, I was starting to get tired."

All seven of the youth continued floating out in the water, hanging onto the air mattresses and resting up. "How was lunch?" Karen asked her brother and Tomas. "Great" Greg replied, "we had hot dogs, beans, and orange soda. What did you have at home?" "Spaghetti"

Karen answered, “Mom and I were invited over to the neighbors, and they were having spaghetti and meatballs, garlic bread, and apple pie for dessert.” “Oh! I love her spaghetti” Greg exclaimed, “And I missed it?” “Not exactly” Karen replied with a smile, “They sent some home for you, since you always say how much you love it.” “Spaghetti?” Amanda said, “You should try my aunt’s spaghetti, she always makes it for us when she and our uncle come for a visit. It’s the best spaghetti I’ve ever had.” “Our neighbor makes the best we’ve ever tasted” responded Karen with a grin. “Maybe we’ll get to try her spaghetti someday” Jeremy pipped in. Karen suddenly looked nervous and looked back and forth between Tomas and her brother. “No! We didn’t tell them anything” Greg suddenly exclaimed, “We wouldn’t do that.” “What’s the matter? What didn’t you do?” Jeremy asked, “Did I say something wrong?” “No, you didn’t say anything wrong” Greg replied, “My sister was just thinking that Tomas and I might have told you where we live, that’s all.” “Oh no!” Jeremy said, “Karen, they haven’t told us where you all come from. I just meant that when we get to know each other better, maybe we’ll get to try some of each other’s spaghetti. Maybe next time we are camping here, we can bring some of my aunt’s, and you can bring some of your neighbors, and we can see which is best.” Karen seemed to relax a little after hearing Jeremy’s explanation.

"So, how about we go around behind the waterfall, and do some diving" Charlie suggested. "Alright!" Tomas exclaimed, "Can you and Jeremy give Greg and me some more lessons, to help us get better at diving?" "Are you girls coming back" Jeremy asked. "No, we'll stay out here with the air mattresses, and just relax, so you can skinny-dip some more while you're diving" Amanda answered with a giggle. "Very funny" Charlie replied, "I don't think Jeremy and I will be doing that again." "Hey, speak for yourself" Jeremy said with a chuckle, "I just might want to leave my trunks up on the ledge, and go naked again." Jenny started laughing, and grinned at her boyfriend. "You know, maybe I will come back with you, so I can watch your bare bottom as you dive into the water" she said. "I think you should just stay out here" he replied to her, "I'm not ready for an audience just yet." Jeremy offered his air mattress to Karen, who gratefully accepted it, and Charlie let Greg and Tomas use the last mattress as all four boys headed back to the ledge. "See you later" Amanda called out to them.

The four boys swam behind the waterfall and proceeded towards the steps to the ledge. When they were all standing up on the ledge, Greg looked over at Jeremy with a smile. "Were you serious, when you said you might go naked again" he inquired with a chuckle.

"Why not" Jeremy replied as he began removing his swim trunks, "I think it feels a lot better without them, so I might as well." Charlie watched his best friend strip down to his birthday suit, and shook his head. Jeremy saw his friend shaking his head back and forth. "It's no big deal" he said to him, "It's just us boys back here." "What if the girls should swim around back here?" Charlie asked. "To tell you the truth, I don't think I would really care" Jeremy replied, "I like how it feels to be free of my trunks, so I'm going nude, even if you don't want to." With that said, Jeremy finished taking off his swim trunks, tossed them to the back of the ledge, and dove into the water. Greg and Tomas looked at Charlie, and then dove off the ledge also. Charlie watched them swimming under water for a moment, then dove in after the other three.

Karen climbed up onto her air mattress and laid down on her stomach to let the sunshine wash over her exposed back side. Amanda and Jenny remained on their mattresses also, laying with their backs up also. Unlike the other two girls, Karen's bare butt was exposed to the sun as well, and she didn't seem to care that she was the only one of the three that was nude. Jenny looked over at the younger girl, and started thinking about her time at the beach four years ago, and how good it had felt. She had left the beach that day with no tan lines, and she wished she could get a tan like that again. "Why not" she said, not realizing that she was speaking out loud. "Why not what?" inquired Amanda. "Oh, sorry, I was just thinking out loud" replied Jenny. "Were you thinking about sneaking around the waterfall to see if my brother will actually be skinny-dipping?" Amanda said with a chuckle. "No, I wasn't thinking that" Jenny responded, "But he probably is you know." "No way!" exclaimed Amanda, "He wouldn't." "Yes, he would. He did it yesterday and said that he liked it. He's probably skinny-dipping again right now" Jenny said with a big grin. "You're right" Amanda confessed, "He would do it again. But what were you talking about when you said 'Why not' a moment ago." "I was thinking about the all over tan I got at that beach four years ago" Jenny said, "And how I would like to have that kind of a tan again right now."

Amanda saw Karen looking over at the two of them, and then stared at her friend. "You're thinking about going naked, right out here on the lake, aren't you?" she asked. "Why not" Jenny replied with a grin. "What if the boys were to finish diving and come out here to see you laying naked on that mattress" Amanda asked. "Well, we could all float back around the bend and further out in the lake" Jenny suggested, "We could see them if they come out from behind the waterfall, and they won't be able to see us sunbathing naked." "We? What do you mean we?" asked Amanda. "Well, I mean

Karen and me, if you don't want to get an all over tan too" answered Jenny. Karen had become very interested in the conversation by now and was watching the two older girls closely. "I already have an all over tan" Karen interjected, "But I'll be glad to join you further out, if you want me to." "Okay" Jenny responded, "Are you coming with us, Amanda?" "Oh, alright" Amanda said, "But what will you do with your swimsuit while you're sunbathing naked? You don't want to lose it you know." "I'll tie it to one of the loops on the end of the air mattress" Jenny replied, as she started removing her bikini. The three started paddling south around the bend, and further out into the lake, as soon as Jenny had her suit secured to the loop at the head of the air mattress.

When the girls were far enough out in the lake that they couldn't be clearly seen as naked, but could still see if anyone was swimming toward them, they stopped paddling, and just floated on the air mattresses. "Ah, this feels so good" Jenny exclaimed, "The warm sun all over my body." "I always think it feels good this way" Karen said, "I wouldn't ever want to sunbathe and end up with tan lines." Amanda's head popped up. "Oh, alright" she exclaimed, "I'll take my suit off to." Amanda's bikini was soon tied to the loop at the head of her mattress as well, and the three girls relaxed and enjoyed the warm sunshine on their completely exposed bodies.

The boys were having a great time behind the waterfall, diving off of the ledge and swimming around, but Jeremy kept looking at Charlie with a big grin on his face, and exclaiming how great it felt to be free, and not have a wet swimsuit on. Finally, Charlie had to give in. "Okay, you're making me feel like the odd guy here" he exclaimed, "I'm the only one with a swimsuit on, and starting to feel weird about it, so, I give up! I'll take off my trunks and join you. I'll be as naked as the day I was born, just like you." "Great" Jeremy said triumphantly, "Just toss your soggy trunks over by mine, and let's dive in again." Charlie proceeded to untie the cord of his swim trunks, and then he slipped the trunks down around his feet and stepped out of them. After tossing the wet garment at the back of the ledge, near Jeremy's now dry ones, he walked up to the edge of the ledge beside the other boys and prepared to dive into the water again. "Okay, I'm ready" he announced with a grin. The four boys dove off of the ledge together and swam around underwater for a little bit before surfacing and heading over to the steps again. Jeremy and Charlie continued giving Greg and Tomas pointers to improve their diving abilities, and they were pleased with how well the younger boys had improved over the hour and a half that they had been there in back of the waterfall. "You two are really getting the hang of this now" Jeremy finally declared. "Yeah" Charlie added with a chuckle, "Jeremy and I had better keep practicing our dive routines, or you two might suddenly get better than us." "I wonder how the girls are doing?" Jeremy said with a chuckle, while looking at his friend. "Stop it Jeremy!" exclaimed Charlie, "You're the one that wanted me to try this skinny-dipping again. Now, you say something like that to try and make me nervous. Well, I feel okay about swimming naked now, and I don't care if the girls come back here and see me naked." "It's not that" Jeremy replied, "I was really wondering about them. It's been over an hour and a half now. Do you think Amanda and Jenny are getting along okay with Greg's sister?"

"Why don't we just swim down to the edge of the waterfall and check on them" Greg suggested while treading water beside the older boys. "I guess we could do that" Jeremy said, "We'll swim around and see how all the girls are doing." "Let's split up and go to both sides of the waterfall" Tomas said, "That way we won't all four be coming around in a group." "Sounds good to me" Charlie agreed, "I'll go with you to the west end, while Jeremy and Greg go down to the east end." It was agreed, and the boys split up into two pairs to swim to opposite ends of the waterfall. Charlie and Tomas reached their end of the falls first, since they had started out closer to their end. They swam out a little past the falls and looked out across the lake. "I don't see the girls anywhere" Charlie said. "Me either" Tomas agreed. They swam out further into the lake and looked around again, and spotted Jeremy and Greg coming around on the east side of the falls. Jeremy looked around out on the lake as he and Greg came around the end of the falls. "Do you see the girls anywhere?" he asked Greg. "No" Greg replied, "Where did they go?"

The four boys started swimming closer together and further out into the lake, looking for the missing girls. They met up together and looked all around. "Where are they?" Jeremy asked of no one in particular, "They should be out here on their air mattresses." "Maybe they went back to camp for something" Charlie suggested. "I think we better go to the camp site and check on them" Jeremy said in a worried tone. The four boys started swimming for the shore together. Greg and Tomas exchanged smiles between them as they reached shallow water and wadded up onto the sandy beach. The two younger boys followed along behind the two teen boys, who started jogging quickly down the shore in the direction of their camp site. Jeremy and Charlie raced up the path to the camp, while the two younger boys stopped at the beach end of the path. Greg pointed out towards the lake, "Tomas, isn't that the girls coming this way?" he asked his friend. "Yes, it is" Tomas replied with a big grin, "and they're coming over here."

The girls came running up to the two boys standing at the end of the path to the camp site. "What's wrong, where are Charlie and Jeremy?" asked Amanda. "We saw all of you running along the beach towards camp and figured something must be wrong" Jenny added. Greg and Tomas just looked at the two teenage girls with grins on their faces and started laughing. Just then, Jeremy and Charlie came running back down the path from camp and stopped when they spotted the girls there. "Amanda, Jenny, where were you?" Jeremy inquired, "We came out from behind the waterfall and you guys were nowhere in sight. We thought you might have come back to camp, so we hurried back here." "We were worried" Charlie added. Amanda and Jenny started giggling. "What's so funny" Charlie inquired. "Well, you two must have been really worried about us" Amanda replied, "You seem to have forgotten to do something before you headed back here." Jeremy looked down at himself, and then over at Charlie, realizing what the girls were so amused about. "You guys were skinny dipping behind the falls, weren't you?" Jenny declared. Suddenly, Charlie realized what the giggling was all about. He looked over at his friend, "Jeremy, we left our swim trunks on the ledge behind the falls" he exclaimed, as his hands came down in front of his crotch.

Jeremy smiled back at his friend as he stood there in

front of his sister and his girlfriend with his male parts dangling out in plain sight, and started chuckling. “You think this is funny” Charlie exclaimed, “You and I are standing here, buck naked. Jeremy just grinned back at him. “So, what” he said, holding his hands out to the side, “The girls aren’t exactly overdressed themselves right now, in case you haven’t noticed.” His statement made Amanda suddenly look down at herself and over at Jenny. She realized that what her brother had just said was true. “Eek!” she screamed, as she tried to cover her breasts and crotch with her arms and hands, “Jenny, we forgot to put our swimsuits back on!” “Oh, well” Jenny responded without making any effort to cover herself, “It’s a little late to worry about that now, we’ve already been seen by everyone.” Jeremy looked over at Charlie and shook his head, “Don’t you think it’s a little bit too late to be hiding your stuff?” he inquired with a chuckle. “You don’t care if they see you naked?” Charlie asked. “No, I don’t” Jeremy replied, “I said back behind the waterfall that I wouldn’t care if they came back there and saw me skinny-dipping. And I think you said the same thing.” “Did I say that, too?” Charlie exclaimed with a shocked look. “Yes, you did” Jeremy replied, “And now here you are, trying to hide behind your hands, after the girls have already had a good look at you. Do you think they’ll forget what they’ve already seen?” Charlie continued to stare at his best friend as he thought about what he had just heard him say.

Slowly, the look on Charlie's face change to one of defeat, and his arms and hands slipped down to his sides.

"Oh, my, Charlie!" Amanda gasped as she stared at her boyfriend. Jenny looked over and smiled at Amanda. "Did you hear what your brother just said" she asked her friend, "The boys have already seen you and I naked. Are you going to continue standing there, trying to hide what they've already seen?" Amanda looked back at Jenny, then at her brother, and finally at Charlie. They were all accepting that they couldn't undo what had just happened. Slowly, she lowered her arms and hands, and stood there with the other six nude people. Jeremy smiled at his sister. "We haven't seen each other naked since we were little kids and had to take our baths together" he said to her, "You're even more beautiful now." "I still feel weird, standing here like this in front of my brother, my boyfriend, and two other boys" Amanda responded, "It doesn't feel right to me, to be naked like this with boys around." "I feel weird too" Charlie declared. "We're all feeling a little vulnerable right now" Jenny explained, "I felt the same way, my first time at that nude beach." "I think we'll get used to it, just like you did, Jenny" Jeremy said. "What? You're going to stay naked?" Amanda exclaimed. "Why not?" he replied, "There doesn't seem to be any reason why we shouldn't all just stay this way for the rest of the camping trip, does there?" "Well, I don't think I can do that" his sister declared, "I don't think I can just get used to being naked around other people." "Why not?" Jenny inquired, "You seemed to have gotten used to being nude around me and Karen when we were sun bathing out on the air mattresses." "Well, that was different" Amanda stammered, "We're all girls." "But you were nervous about it at first" Jenny countered, "And once you got used to it, you forgot that you were naked." "Forgot about it to the point that you rushed back here without thinking about putting on your swimsuit again" Jeremy added, "You got used to being naked around girls, I think you'll get used to going naked around boys too."

Charlie suddenly cleared his throat. "Well, I don't know about the rest of you, but I want to get back to swimming and diving again" he announced, "Jeremy, I think we should get back to the ledge again." "Sounds good to me" Jeremy responded, "Greg, Tomas, you guys coming with us?" "Yes" the two boys answered together, as they started after the two older boys that were already walking back along the beach towards the waterfall.

NATURIST EXPERIENCE

The girls watched the four boys, as they walked along the beach away from them. Amanda suddenly started giggling. “What’s funny now?” Jenny asked. Her friend glanced over at her, then turned back to watch the boys again. “I was just thinking, they all have cute butts” Amanda whispered. “Really?” Jenny responded, “You think your brother has a nice butt?” Amanda quickly looked her friend in the eyes. “I didn’t mean it that way” she muttered, “I, I just, well...” “It’s okay” Jenny giggled, “He’s a cute boy, and he does have a nice butt, and so do Charlie and the other two.” Amanda smiled again, “Yes, they all have nice butts.” “You two ARE talking about my brother’s butt too, you know” Karen pipped up. The two older girls turned red faced towards their young friend. “Oh, sorry Karen, we didn’t mean anything by what we said” Jenny apologized. Karen suddenly grinned back at them. “It’s okay” she said, “I think they all have nice butts too, even my brother.” The three girls started laughing together.

The four boys could hear the girls laughing, way back behind them, as they continued on towards the waterfall. “What do you think they’re laughing about?” Charlie asked as he glanced back behind them. “Oh, I don’t know” Jeremy replied, “Maybe they’re all laughing, because they’re watching four naked boys walking along the beach, and they're admiring how cute our butts look." Charlie gasped. "I think we should walk faster" he said, "Maybe even run. I want to get back to the ledge and get in some more diving." Charlie took off at a run along the beach, and the other three boys quickly followed after him. When they got around the bend in the shoreline, and out of sight of the girls, Charlie slowed down a little, to a fast walk. The others caught up to him in less than a minute, and Jeremy grinned at his friend. "Glad you slowed down" he said, breathing hard, "We need to be rested a little before swimming out behind the waterfall." A short way further along, and they all entered the water and started swimming in the direction of the waterfall.

The boys had been back behind the waterfall for about fifteen minutes, diving off the ledge and swimming around without swimsuits, including Charlie. Jeremy was just giving Tomas some more pointers about diving, when Greg suddenly pointed to the east side of the waterfall. "Here come the girls" he announced. All four boys looked up and saw the three girls coming around the edge of the falling water, swimming towards them. Charlie stood and waved at them. "Hey, Amanda. You coming back here to join us in some diving?" he called out. Jeremy looked at his friend and smiled. "Gee, Charlie, you seem to be a lot more comfortable like that, now" he commented. "Huh? Like what?"

Charlie replied. Jeremy, Greg, and Tomas all chuckled and pointed at where Charlie's trunks would normally be. Charlie looked down at himself and gasped. "Oh, I forgot. I still don't have my swim trunks on" he exclaimed. "Don't worry about it" Greg said, "The girls aren't wearing anything either." "How can you tell that?" Charlie inquired. "Well, if you look carefully, you can see that their swimsuits are missing." "Oh, you're right, they're still naked, too" Jeremy said, "Charlie, what are you doing?" Charlie had gone over to back of the ledge and was picking up his swim trunks. "I'm putting on my swim trunks, of course" Charlie answered. "Why?" Jeremy asked, "The girls are coming here with no swimsuits on. If you put yours on, you might make them feel bad." Charlie looked at his friend, then out at the approaching girls. "Oh, alright" he declared, "I guess they've already seen me naked anyway." "Yeah, especially when you were standing over here by me" Tomas said with a grin, "Jumping up and down and waving at them the way you were doing."

The girls swam past the boys on two air mattresses, their bare bottoms bobbing up and being exposed in the water. When the girls reached the west side of the ledge, they slid off of the air mattress and climbed up the steps to the ledge. Jenny carried the mattress up the steps with her and placed it at the back of the ledge on top of the boys' swim trunks. "We thought we'd join you boys back here" Jenny announced, "Is that okay with you?" "It's okay with me" Jeremy responded. Greg and Tomas were nodding their heads up and down in agreement with Jeremy. "Is it okay with you, Charlie" Amanda asked. "Yeah, I guess so" he answered her, staring down at the ledge. "What's wrong" Amanda asked him. "Nothing" he replied, "It's just that I'm still a little nervous about being naked around you girls." "Well, put your swim trunks on then" Amanda exclaimed, "But the rest of us are probably going to stay this way." Charlie looked up at his girlfriend and saw that she was serious. Jeremy looked at her too, a confused look on his face. "You seem to be a lot more comfortable with being naked around the rest of us" Jeremy said, "What happened to make you feel better about it?" "Jenny and I have been talking with Karen" Amanda explained, "It's like you said earlier, everyone has seen me nude already, so what's the use of trying to cover up. Besides, I think I like the feeling of going without a wet swimsuit. It feels so much nicer."

Jeremy looked over at his best friend. "Well, Charlie" he said. "Well, what" Charlie asked. "Are you going to put your swim trunks back on now, or not?" Jeremy asked. Charlie glanced around at the six other naked people that were looking at him, then looked over at his swim trunks again. He sighed and then smiled. "I guess I'll stay the way I am" he announced, "I haven't got anything to hide from the girls anymore." "Great" Jenny exclaimed, "You boys can help us girls learn to dive better, like you." "That sounds okay to me" Jeremy said, "So, who do you want helping you, Jenny?" "You, of course" she replied, as she walked up to him and gave him a little kiss on the cheek. "I want Charlie to help me" Amanda said with a grin. "What about me?" Karen asked. "Tomas and I will help you" Greg offered. "Yeah. And, Charlie and Jeremy will be here to help us help you" Tomas added, "They're on the swim team at their high school. Jeremy is the team captain."

The seven kids paired up, and the boys began instructing the girls on how to dive properly. At the end of an hour, the girls were getting quite good as beginning divers, and with some more practice and instruction would get even better over time. "Maybe Jenny and I can join the swim team this coming school year" Amanda commented. "Yeah" Jenny added, "Have there ever been any girls on the swim team before, Jeremy?" "I don't know" he answered her, "Probably not though." Charlie looked at his three close friends and frowned. Amanda saw the look on his face and stared at him. "What's the matter now, Charlie? You don't think girls should be on the swim team?" "It's not that" he said as a smile grew on his face, "I was just wondering how the other guys on the team would feel, having you two showering with us after practice and swim meets." Everyone started laughing at his comment. When the laughter died down, Jeremy looked over at his friend with a serious face. "Forget about the other guys" he said, "How will you feel, having all the other guys staring at our beautiful girlfriends?" Charlie's grin disappeared, and he looked over at the girls. "Don't worry, boys" Jenny said, "Your other team mates would probably be too nervous about girls seeing their you know what's, to stare at us. But just in case, we'll shower in the girl's locker room instead."

After another half an hour of diving and swimming, the three younger kids announced that they needed to be going home, since it was going on five o'clock already. "How far do you have to go, to get home?" asked Jenny. The three kids glanced back and forth among themselves, shaking their heads in agreement. "We can't tell you that" Karen finally answered, "We aren't allowed to tell anyone anything that would give away where we are from." "I guess that means we should head back to our camp site then" Jeremy suggested, "So we don't see which way you go, when you leave." "That would make it easier for us" Greg replied. "Okay then" Jeremy declared, "We'll start back for camp right away then. It's been nice having you all with us this afternoon though." "Yeah" Amanda said as she gave Karen a friendly hug, "It was nice, and you helped me a lot, Karen, to understand more about how being nude isn't a terrible thing." "You're welcome" Karen replied, hugging Amanda back. Jenny hugged Karen also. "Today has been a very special day with our new friends" she said, "I hope we can do this again, soon." "It's been a wonderful day, meeting you all and spending time together" Charlie stated, "I had a lot of fun." Charlie waved at the younger kids as he went to the edge of the ledge and dove into the water. When he surfaced again, he looked up at his three friends. "You guys coming" he asked. The girls stood at the edge of the ledge and smiled down at him, while Jeremy walked to the back of the ledge and grabbed the air mattress and two pairs of swim trunks.

Jeremy stepped up to the edge of the ledge and held up one of the swim trunks. "You forgetting something again, Charlie?" he said with a chuckle. Charlie looked up and groaned, "Yeah, okay. Guess you were right" he said, "I did get used to swimming naked. And, I do like it." Jeremy tossed his friends garment down to him, then waved good-bye to their new friends before jumping into the water along with the girls and the air mattress. Greg, Karen, and Tomas watched the four teenagers swim east behind the waterfall until they were out of site. "I like them" Karen declared, "They really are nice, like you two said. We'll have to come back to join them again." Greg and Tomas smiled, and nodded their heads in agreement. Five minutes later the three young kids dove into the water and headed for home.

When the four teens finally got back to the path to their camp site, they were still nude. “You boys should rinse out your swimsuits before coming up to camp” Amanda instructed them, “Jenny and I rinsed ours out already, and hung them up to dry. Jeremy handed the air mattress to his sister, and he and Charlie wadded out a little way into the water and started rinsing out their swim trunks. “What should we have for supper?” Amanda asked the boys. “Hamburgers sound good to me” replied Charlie, “And some chips.” “Okay” Jenny said, “We put more wood on the fire earlier, so we’ll put more wood on the fire and start getting the meat ready. You two come on up when you are done with your wash, and get the rest of the food supplies from the grocery bag.” “Will do” Jeremy replied, “We’ll be there in just a few minutes.” “Yeah” added Charlie, “I’m starving, so we’ll be there really quick.”

The food was prepared and eaten quite quickly, as all four of the teens were hungry after a busy day out on the lake. They spoke very little as they ate, but after they finished eating and disposed of the paper plates and utensils, they began to discuss how they felt about what they had experienced that day. “I really like skinny-dipping” Jeremy told the others, “Swimming and diving without any swimwear on was terrific, once I got past being naked around everyone else again." "I'm glad I got a chance to experience it again" Jenny said, "I know that I enjoyed my first experience, when I was twelve, but going nude again today made me remember how great it feels." "I wasn't so keen at first, when you boys saw me without my swimsuit on, but I got used to it" Amanda explained, "And after talking with Karen about naturism, I started to feel more comfortable with going nude. I stopped being scared about other people, especially boys, seeing me nude." "I'm still not real comfortable being naked with girls around" Charlie put in, "But I do have to admit that swimming without my swim trunks on is a lot more comfortable." "You just need more experience as a naturist" Amanda said with a smile, "You do realize that none of us put on clothes when we got back to camp, and we're all still nude, right?" Charlie suddenly realized that she was right, they were all naked yet. "So how about tomorrow?" Jenny asked with a grin, "Do we put clothes on, or should we go nude all day again?" "I don't know" Charlie answered. "Well, I think we should just spend the rest of the camping trip in the nude" Amanda suggested, "We've all seen each other nude, so why put on anything at all now?"

Jeremy looked around at all the others. "I think we could go naked most of the time" he said, "But we may have to wear clothes some of the time." "Like when?" his sister questioned him. "Like tomorrow" he replied, "If we are going back to explore the cave and tunnels, we may want to have clothes on, in case we come across someone else." "I don't think I want to be wearing a wet swimsuit in that cave again" Jenny declared, "It felt cold and uncomfortable. I had goose bumps the whole time we were in there this morning." "Me too" Amanda agreed, "But being nude wouldn't help with that, we need some clothes to wear in there." "That's right" Jeremy responded, "So, we need to take along some dry clothes tomorrow." "How do we do that?" Amanda inquired, "The clothes won't be dry anymore, after swimming under water through the tunnel to the cave." "Yes, they will" Charlie put in, "We just need to put them in sealed plastic bags, and then put them on when we get into the cave." "We'll need towels also" Jeremy added, "Our clothes won't be dry anymore if we put them on right after getting out of the water." "So, we need to take dry clothes and towels with us?" Amanda asked, "Do we have any bags that will keep out the water?" "Yes" Jeremy answered, "We have some large, sealable bags available." "The bags Jeremy sealed our meat in, in the cooler" Charlie continued, "We've been saving them in the recycle bag. We'll need to get them out and wash them, then let them dry so we can seal our clothes and towels in them."

Jeremy stood up and went over to the recycle bag and started pulling out the plastic bags that they would need. When he had six bags selected, he brought them over and handed one to each person, and a second one to his sister. "Six bags" he declared, "One each for our clothes, and the other two are for towels." "I don't think we can get two towels in one bag" Amanda said to her brother, "Won't we need a couple more?" "No" he answered her, "We'll share the towels, one for you girls, and one for Charlie and me." "Will these plastic bags hold all our clothes?" Jenny inquired. "Yes, if you put only a shirt and a pair of shorts in them" Jeremy answered, "We'll put all the sealed bags into my backpack, because it's water proof as well, and then put the backpack and a pair of shoes for each of us, into a large garbage bag that will be tied at the top. That should keep most everything pretty dry for us." "How do we get the garbage bag through the tunnel?" Jenny asked. Jeremy smiled. "Tomorrow, I'll go through the tunnel first, pulling the bag through, with Charlie just behind it, pushing it through" he explained, "When we've gotten through, we'll take it up to the cave and push it up on the cave floor." "Okay" the girls said in unison. "Do you girls think you can swim through the tunnel on your own this time?" Charlie asked, "Or should we come back out and follow each of you through again?" "I think we should be able to make it through on our own" Jenny replied. "Yes, I agree"

Amanda said, “I’m not afraid to swim through alone, now that I know how short a swim it will be.” “Good” her brother said, “You and Jenny can dive in and start through the tunnel, about five minutes after Charlie and I go into the tunnel. We’ll be carrying the lanterns, and you girls will have a flashlight each.”

“So, we have everything all planned then” declared Charlie. “Not quite” Amanda said with a grin, “Are we swimming through the tunnel in swimsuits, or nude?” “I think everyone can make their own decision on that” Jeremy responded. “Well, I’m going nude” declared his sister. “Me too” said Jenny. “I’m fine with going in naked” Jeremy said, “How about you Charlie?” Charlie looked around at his three friends. They were all looking at him. “Well, if you are all going to be naked, then I may as well be too.” he replied. “Let’s take the plastic bags down to the lake and clean them out, now that we’ve got everything talked out” Jeremy suggested. They all stood up and started towards the path to the beach. Jenny stopped and looked around at the others. “You know what?” she said, “We should take along our dirty clothes and rinse them out while we are down at the lake.” “Good idea” Jeremy said, “Everyone gather up their clothes that need cleaning, and take them along.” They carried the plastic bags and their clothes down the path to the lake and proceeded to clean everything until they were all finished, then they all returned to the camp site.

After returning to the camp, they all sat down around the camp fire, still nude, and continued to talk for a couple hours, while enjoying some s'mores. They were enjoying the cool night air on their skin, but after the long day they had, everyone was soon starting to feel tired, and they all decided it was time to head off to their tents, where their sleeping bags were waiting for them. Charlie looked up at the sky as they all walked over toward the tents. "The sky is starting to get kind of cloudy" he announced, "Looks like it might rain tonight, we better make sure the tents are closed up good to keep the rain out."

EXPLORING THE CAVE

The rain arrived around midnight, and all four teens were awakened by the thunder, lightning, and wind, and finally the rain started pouring down on their tents. The boys could hear the girls talking over in the other tent and decided to make sure that they were okay. Jeremy got up, unzipped the opening to their tent, and slipped out into the rain. He walked over to the girl's tent and kind of knocked on the door. "You girls doing okay in there?" he called out. The tent door quickly unzipped, and Jenny motioned for Jeremy to come in. "Come on over" he called out to Charlie, who was waiting in the opening to their tent, "Make sure to zip up the tent first though." Charlie came over a few moments later, and ducked into the girls' tent, then turned and zipped the tent opening shut.

Amanda held up the lantern and grinned at the two wet, naked boys kneeling in her tent. "You two must have dressed in a big hurry before coming over here" she said with a laugh. Jeremy stared back at his sister with a confused look on his face, then realized what she was talking about. He and Charlie had decided to try sleeping nude, and had gotten into their sleeping bags without changing into any clothes. Both boys were completely naked. "We um, decided to try sleeping naked" Jeremy explained, "Greg and Tomas said it was more comfortable to sleep without clothes on." Charlie suddenly realized what the discussion was about. "Oh gee" he exclaimed, "We forgot to put clothes on before coming over here." "That's okay" Jenny declared, "If you had worn clothes, you'd be soaking wet in them. Being nude, you'll both dry off a lot faster, and not catch a chill." "Besides" Amanda said with a smile, "Jenny and I decided to sleep nude too." They all sat around in the tent, talking and waiting for the storm to pass. The worst part of the storm was over them about an hour later, with just a light rain that continued to gently come down until around two-thirty in the morning. The boys returned to their own tent around one-thirty and crawled back into their warm sleeping bags. They were all tired by then and dozed off, with the gentle pitter patter of the rain actually helping to lull them back into a deep sleep.

Morning arrived with the chirping and singing of birds. The teenagers slowly woke and got out of their sleeping bags. When Jeremy and Charlie slipped out of their tent, they immediately headed for the boy's bathroom area. As they approached the tree line, the two girls came walking out from the girl's bathroom area, wearing nothing but a couple of big smiles. "Morning" the girls chimed together. "Good morning" Jeremy responded with a grin, "How did the two of you sleep?" "We slept pretty good after you two left" his sister replied, "and we appreciate you guys coming over to keep us company during the worst of the storm. We were pretty tired by the time you two left, so we fell asleep soon after." Charlie looked at the two girls with a serious face. "The storm? Us in your tent? Did all that really happen?" he inquired, "I thought I just dreamed it all. Especially the part about Jeremy and I forgetting to put clothes on and going over to your tent." "No, you two were completely nude. We were all sitting around in our tent, completely nude" Jenny said, "And none of us seemed the least bit uncomfortable about it." "Well" Jeremy responded, "I was a little uncomfortable at first, being soaking wet, until I dried off, then I felt completely fine about it." They all chuckled, and the girls headed back towards the tents. "We'll bring some breakfast over when we finish back here" Jeremy said.

When the boys returned from their nature call, they had the canvas grocery bag with them. Charlie retrieved some cereal from the bag and handed it out to everyone, then sat down to eat. After they had all finished eating, Amanda looked over at the boys. "Why did you bring the whole grocery bag instead of just some cereal?" she asked. "To make some sandwiches for lunch" Charlie answered, "Jeremy thought we should bring along some food for lunch when we go into the caves." "We have some sandwich meat in the cooler" Jeremy explained, "We'll each make a sandwich for ourselves and put them into the sandwich bags, then pack them along with the rest of the stuff we take into the cave." "Are we taking some drinks along too?" Jenny asked. "Yes, four bottles of water" Jeremy answered.

After preparing their sandwiches and placing them into individual sandwich bags, Jeremy packed them all together in a paper bag. "Okay, go and get the clothes you were all supposed to have packed in plastic bags last night" Jeremy instructed, "I'll get my backpack." They all returned to the firepit with their clothes, and while Jeremy put everything into the backpack, Charlie went and got a garbage bag. The backpack and ropes were placed into the garbage bag with their footwear, and then the bag was wrapped tight around the backpack and tied securely. With the camp site secured, Jeremy grabbed the garbage bag and a lantern and headed down the path to the lake. The girls followed with a flashlight each in their hands, and Charlie brought up the rear with a lantern in hand and an air mattress under his arm. The four naked teens reached the beach and turned north to head towards the waterfall. It took the four nude teens about fifteen minutes to get around the bend in the shoreline, and to where they would enter the water. Charlie placed the air mattress on the water, and Jeremy put the sealed garbage bag on the air mattress. They all entered the water and started swimming out towards the waterfall, and the ledge behind it. Jeremy had tied a twenty-foot piece of rope to the head of the air mattress, and he and Charlie pulled it along behind the group.

When they reached the steps to the ledge, behind the waterfall, the girls climbed up to the ledge, and Jeremy took the garbage bag off the mattress and up with him. Charlie came up the steps to the ledge, with the rope in hand, and they all sat down to rest for a little bit. After about five minutes, Jeremy took the rope from Charlie, and dove into the water. He swam back to the beach and stored the air mattress in the bushes, then returned to the lake and swam back out to the ledge again. He climbed up to the ledge again and sat down with the others, to rest some more. He rechecked the garbage bag, making sure that it was secured around the contents, with as little air in it as possible, to ensure that it would be easier to get the bag down to the lake bottom and through the tunnel without fighting a lot to keep it under water. After fifteen minutes, Jeremy glanced at the other three and stood up. "I'm ready to go, if you're ready" he announced. The others all got up and indicated that they were ready also.

Jeremy and Charlie walked up to the edge of the ledge. "Wait" Amanda suddenly exclaimed, "How will Jenny and I know when five minutes are up, so we can start after you two?" Jeremy smiled, took off his wrist watch, and handed it to his sister. "Put this up on your arm so it will stay" he instructed, "Jenny can watch the time and you can jump in after the five minutes have gone by." "Okay" Amanda said with a smile, as she slipped the watch up past her elbow. "Let's jump in on three" Jeremy said to his best friend. "Okay" Charlie replied. They jumped into the water on the count of three, and immediately started down to the bottom with the garbage bag in tow. When they reached the tunnel, Jeremy headed in with the end of the rope that was tied around the top of the garbage bag. Charlie went into the tunnel right behind the plastic bag, pushing it along as he went. The boys exited the other end of the tunnel about forty-five seconds after entering it and started up to the surface of the pool.

When they reached the surface, they got the garbage bag holding their clothes and lunch over to the opposite side, and up out of the water. They climbed out of the water and move the bag a few feet further into the cave, so there was room at the pool edge for people to climb out without the garbage bag getting in the way. Charlie looked at the watch he was wearing and smiled. "Two minutes gone" he said. "Good" Jeremy replied, "I'm going back out to the ledge, and I'll follow the girls through the tunnel. You go down on this end after the five minutes and hold your lantern up at the end of the tunnel so the girls can see it." "Okay" Charlie said, as Jeremy dove down into the pool of water.

Jeremy surfaced out in the lake, behind the waterfall, and swam over to the steps. He climbed up onto the ledge and looked at the girls. "How long before you two go in?" he inquired. Jenny looked at the watch on Amanda's arm. "Two minutes" she replied. "Good" he said with a smile. "Charlie will be down at the end of the tunnel with a lantern, so you have something to guide you through. I'll follow the two of you through." Amanda looked at her brother with a grin. "You worried that we might not make it in there?" she asked. "No, just want to make sure we do everything safely" he replied with a grin. "Uh huh" Amanda said, "My big brother worries about me. He cares about me." Jenny gave her friend a little push. "Of course, he cares about you" she muttered, "You're his sister. He loves you." Jeremy blushed as he looked at the two girls. "Okay, how much time left?" he asked. "Twenty-seconds" Jenny replied. "Get ready then" he instructed. When the five minutes were up, the girls jumped into the water and began swimming down to the bottom. Jeremy dove in about five seconds later, and watched his sister, and then Jenny enter the tunnel. He swam in after them, holding up his lantern to give light from behind. The girls saw the lantern light ahead of them and swam towards it. Charlie pointed upward when

Amanda exited the tunnel and followed her up as soon as Jenny came out also. Jenny was followed closely by Jeremy, and the two of them swam for the surface together.

The four teens swam over to the opposite side of the pool from where the tunnel was and grabbed the edge of the pool. The boys both hoisted themselves out of the water and stood up to help the girls out as well. They all walked around the edge of the pool to some rocks that were along the back side of the cave. Charlie carefully untied the rope, and the end of the garbage bag, then pulled the backpack out and handed it to Jeremy. Jeremy opened the backpack and started handing out the bags of clothes to everyone, while Charlie got their sandals and the rope out of the garbage bag. The girls dried off with one of the towels and then started putting on their clothes and shoes. The boys did likewise, and the empty plastic clothes bags and towels were placed back into the garbage bag. When everyone had dried off and dressed, the garbage bag was placed behind the rocks for safe keeping. Jeremy put the ropes into the backpack and then slipped the backpack on his back. "Everyone ready to explore?' he asked. "Yes" came a chorus from the other three. "Then let's get started" Jeremy said as he started walking in the direction of where he remembered the cave stairs to be located.

The four teenagers walked across the dark cave with lanterns and flashlights shining to guide them safely. They reached the west side cave wall and looked back and forward along it. "I think it's a little further down towards the end of the cave" Charlie said, "I think I can see the outline of the steps." They proceeded towards the back of the cave, and soon spotted the steps that led up to the passage that they had been in the morning before. After climbing up the steps and entering the passage, they headed back the same way they had explored the previous time. "You girls can probably turn off your flashlights for now" Jeremy suggested, "Save the batteries." The four followed the passage with just Charlie holding a lantern up in front, and Jeremy holding his up in the back. They walked upward through the passage the same way as the day before, until they reached the end again, and the entrance to the second cave that they had come to explore. As Charlie reached the second cave entrance, he glanced around into the cave like last time. "It's looks all clear" he announced as he stepped forward into the cave, "It's too dark for anyone to be inside of here."

The other three followed their friend inside of the upper cave and stopped to look around. All they could see, in the light of the two lanterns, was a light fixture suspended from the top of the cave, and some crates and boxes piled up on the floor. The cave appeared to go back a way, but they couldn't see how far beyond where their lanterns illuminated the area. "There must be a switch that turns on that light" Jeremy said, "Let's see if we can find it." The light switch wasn't too difficult to find, as it was just on the left side of the opening they had come through. Charlie flipped the switch up and the entire cavern was illuminated by two suspended lights instead of just the one. A closer look at the crates revealed that most were filled with produce, corn, apples, and sacks of potatoes. Some of the containers had covers, so the teens could not see what they contained, since they did not want to open those containers up.

There was another opening at the back of the cavern where they had entered, with a wooden door that was slightly open. They looked into the area beyond this door, but it was dark and only the outline of some furniture was distinguishable. Jenny shone her flashlight around, and they saw that this room appeared to be an office, with a couple of desks and several filing cabinets. Nothing seemed to be down at the other end of the main cavern, but the wall on the right side stopped about two-thirds of the way back. They went down and looked to the right and saw that the cavern continued on around a corner and back where there was a huge door that looked to be a garage door with more crates piled up along the wall on the left side. They all walked down to the end of this section of the cavern and checked out the large garage door. “It’s looks like a two-sided, double wide garage door” declared Charlie. He noticed a couple of rings in the center of the doors, one on each side. The rings turned out to be latches, but when he tried turning them, they were locked. “Let’s look around some more” Jeremy suggested. As they were walking back towards the other section of the cavern, Jeremy looked over at the wall and saw another opening in it. “Look, another tunnel” he exclaimed. Charlie walked over to the opening and went inside with his lantern, while the others waited for him. He returned about five minutes later, grinning from ear to ear. “It’s just a short tunnel” said Charlie, “But it has a regular size door at the end, which opens to the outside”. “Really?” said Jeremy, “That’s great, maybe it’s what we’ve been looking for, the way that Greg, Tomas, and Karen have been using to get to the lake.” “Maybe” replied Charlie, “But I think we better get moving out of here right now, because I think I hear voices coming from around the corner, on the other side of the cave.” The four of them quickly slipped into the tunnel that led to the door Charlie had found. The passage only went back about four feet, and then turned sharply to the left. They quietly made their way another four feet until they came to a steel door.

Charlie quietly eased the door open, and they all slipped out, into a clearing by the hillside, with woods all around, and a dirt road leading away from the area. Jeremy closed the door behind them, noticing that it was camouflaged to look like part of the hillside it was set into. They all headed off towards the trees and bushes on the opposite side of the small clearing. Crouching down, they waited behind the bushes, and watched the door that they had all just come out of. That's definitely a secret cave" Jeremy whispered to the others, "Look at the door we just came out of, I wouldn't know it was a door if we hadn't just come through it." "Yes, and the garage door must be hidden too" Jenny added, "Because I can't make out where that door is for sure, either." "Quiet. Someone's coming out" Charlie cautioned them. Everyone ducked down further and looked through the bushes towards where the smaller door was located and saw a man's head sticking out of the partially open door. The door closed again after the man's head disappeared back inside, and a few moments later, a wider crack suddenly appeared in the hillside a little further down the hillside. A large section of what appeared to be the hillside started to swing outward. "That's got to be the larger door" Jenny whispered. They watched as the large door swung open, and saw another man pushing it from the inside, until it was fully open. The first man they had seen looking out the smaller door a few minutes earlier, appeared in the open entry beside the one that had pushed the door open. "They must be naturists" whispered Jenny, "Neither of them is wearing any clothes." Everyone stared at the two nude men, standing in the open doorway. Then suddenly, a third man joined the first two men, and the third man was also naked.

The four teenagers remained hidden behind the bushes outside the cave and watched the three men who were wearing only shoes, as they went back inside of the cave, and out of sight. The teens could hear the men talking, their voices echoing from within the cave. After about ten minutes, Jeremy became curious, and decided to find out what the men were doing inside of the cave, and he quietly started crawling along behind the trees and bushes, towards the hillside, until he was near the cave opening. He stood up, and carefully moved along the face of the rocky hillside until he was just outside of the cave opening and peeked around the corner to see inside. His sister and friends nervously watched him from their hiding place in the bushes, and after several minutes, Jeremy suddenly darted back along the hillside to the cover of the trees and bushes. Just as he disappeared into the cover of the woods, one of the men came riding out of the cave on an ATV, but he was fully dressed now, and had several of the wooden boxes from the cave loaded onto the back of the vehicle. The other two men came out on foot, still nude, and proceeded to close up the garage door. The teens watched the door as it merged back into the hillside again, becoming unnoticeable to anyone that didn't know it was there. Jeremy had quietly made his way back to his friends by then, to join them behind the bushes. The man on the ATV waited and was finally joined by one of the other two men, who came out of the smaller door, now dressed, and got into the vehicle beside the first man. The two of them then drove down the dirt road, into the woods, and out of sight of the four teens.

"Where are they taking those boxes" asked Amanda, looking at her brother. "They filled the boxes with some produce" her brother answered, "Potatoes, corn, tomatoes, strawberries, and apples. I heard one of them say something about needing to get the boxes to a vegetable stand somewhere, by twelve o'clock." "So, that means we have about two hours before they return" Charlie announced. "Two hours for what?" Amanda asked." "To get back inside the cave" Charlie replied, looking at all of his friends. "Back inside the cave? What for" asked Jenny. "I want to explore that cave, and the tunnel going the other way" Charlie answered. "I do too" Jeremy said. "But the naturist kids are probably coming through this cave" Amanda said, "So, why should we explore down the other way yet?"

"We don't know that this is the way they come for sure" Charlie said. "And I want to find out where the passage goes to, the other way. And even if we don't do any more exploring today, we still have to go through the cave and the tunnels to get back to camp, unless we want to hike over these mountains to get there." "Oh, that's right" Jenny exclaimed. Jeremy held out his hand palm up and glanced up at the sky. "Looks like it's starting to rain again" he announced, "I definitely don't want to go hiking over the mountains in the rain." "I guess the boys are right, Amanda." Jenny said, "We might as well explore some more while it's raining. There isn't going to be much to do back at camp when it's raining. And, I want to see what's down the other way, too." "Well, I guess we may as well keep exploring, I don't want to go back to camp all by myself" Amanda said. "You wouldn't have to go back by yourself" Charlie said with a smile, "I'd go back with you. I think Jeremy and Jenny would probably go back too, if you really wanted to quit for today." "Yes, sis" Jeremy said with a smile, "I'd go back with you, but I still want to finish exploring these caves and passages, and since it's raining out now, I think it would be the best time to do it. Tomorrow will hopefully be sunny, and then we can go swimming in the lake and just relax all day." Amanda smiled at her brother, "I love you too big brother" She said as she turned to Charlie and Jenny with a grin, "Guess we better get going, we don't know how far that next tunnel goes before we'll find something, and I want to get back to camp before dark."

The group of teens made their way back over to the single door and Charlie tried to open it. "It's locked" he exclaimed. "How are we going to get back inside then" Amanda said with a gasp. "Let's try the garage door" Jeremy suggested, "Maybe it won't be locked, since those two guys will be coming back in less than two hours." They crept along the hillside until Charlie spotted a ring that was recessed into the grey, brown, and green camouflaged door. He grabbed the latch ring and turned it. "It's not locked" he whispered back to the others as he slowly pulled the door open a crack. When the door was open far enough so that he could stick his head through, Charlie poked his head in and looked around. "The lights are off again" he said with a smile, "I think the other guy must have gone away." He opened the garage door far enough to allow them all to slip inside one by one, then pulled the door closed again until the latch clicked. "Okay, stay quiet" Jeremy said as he turned on his lantern and started down towards the main part of the cavern. When they reached the turn to the main cavern, Jeremy stopped and looked carefully around the corner. He turned back to the others with a look of concern on his face. "There's a light coming from the door to the office area" he whispered, "I think the third man must be in there." "What do we do now"

Amanda asked. “We head for the passage entrance we came in here through” Charlie answered, “But we go very quietly.” Jeremy exchanged his lantern for the flashlight that Jenny had, turning off the lantern and turning on the flashlight. Charlie did likewise with Amanda, so both boys now had flashlights.

“Follow me” Jeremy whispered, as he started out around the corner. The four quietly went single file towards the light that shone through the partially open door on the opposite end of the cavern. Jeremy used the flashlight until they were about twenty feet from the door, then turned it off. Charlie turned off his flashlight also, since there was enough light from the cracked open door to let them see their way to the tunnel opening. They made their way into the passageway, and felt their way along in the diming light from behind, until they were about twenty or thirty-feet in. Jeremy finally turned on his flashlight, as did Charlie, and they headed down the passageway towards the first cave. When they were about a hundred feet along, the boys gave the flashlights back to the girls and took the lanterns again. The lanterns illuminated the passage better, and they were able to increase their pace as they went along. When they neared the opening to the original cave, Jeremy turned off his lantern, walked up to the opening, and glanced around to see into the cave. “It’s dark in there yet” he told the others, “I don’t think anyone is in there." "Let's keep going then" Charlie suggested from behind.

Jeremy turned his lantern back on and proceeded down the passage again. A short walk past the cave opening, and the passage seemed to have leveled off, and it started curving to the right. They continued on around the curve until they figured they were now going parallel to the beginning of the passage. They walked for about ten minutes more, and then the passage seemed to be getting lighter. "We may be coming to the end, it's getting lighter" Jeremy whispered back to his friends. "Either that, or we're coming to another cave where the lights are on" replied Amanda sarcastically. "It seems to be more like natural sunlight" Jeremy told her, "That would mean an exit to the outside." The passage started curving to the left, and as they walked around the curve, an opening appeared before them. "It is an exit" declared Amanda with a smile. "Yeah, but it's raining out yet" Charlie pointed out from behind her. They all walked up to the exit to stand just inside and out of the rain that was coming down. "Now what?" Jenny inquired, "Do we go out there?" "Not right now" Jeremy said, "We'll wait. Maybe the rain will stop in a little bit." "But what about those men?" Amanda asked, "What if they come down here and find us?" "The two that drove off won't be back for about another half hour or more" Charlie answered her, "And the one in the office is probably going to stay there until the other two come back. The garage door is still unlocked, and I think he's guarding the cave." "He's not guarding it very well, if we got in and past him" Amanda giggled. "He's guarding the cave, and what's in it" Jeremy told her with a smile, "He wasn't expecting four sneaky teenagers to sneak inside right away, like we did."

They decided to sit down at the mouth of the passage and wait out the rain if they could. As they sat there, Charlie suddenly looked around at the others. "Hey" he said, "Why don't we have our lunch while we're waiting?" Jeremy chuckled. "You getting hungry, just sitting here?" he asked. "As a matter of fact, yes I am" Charlie replied in a huff, "It's almost lunch time after all." The others all laughed, and Jeremy started handing out the sandwiches that they had brought along, along with the bottles of water. Charlie took a bite of his sandwich and smiled. "Oh, this is good" he declared, "Did we bring any chips along?" Jeremy grinned and reached inside of the backpack once more to take out a large sized bag of cheese puffs. "Of course, we did" he replied as he handed the bag to his friend, "With you along, I knew we would need more than just sandwiches." "Oh! Just for me then" Charlie chuckled. "Don't you even joke about it" Amanda chided him, "The rest of us will want some too. I love cheese snacks, you know." "I know it now" he said with a grin, as he put some puffs in the bag that his sandwich had come out of. He handed the larger bag over to the two girls, who set it down between them with a smile on their faces. "I may want some more of those" he mumbled with his mouth full of sandwich.

They finished eating their lunch in about fifteen minutes, but the rain was still coming down. "How long before those men might come down here?" Jenny asked. "Maybe another half an hour. Maybe more, maybe less" Jeremy answered, "We'll just have to keep an ear out for sounds of them coming this way. If it stops raining soon, we'll head out to see what's outside of this passage." "What if we hear the men coming, and it's still raining?" Amanda inquired. "Then we go out in the rain" Charlie answered from next to her. "But our clothes will get all wet if we go out in the rain" she told him. Jeremy looked over at his sister. "You're right" he said, "Maybe we should put our clothes back in the backpack and hide it somewhere in here behind some rocks. That way, if we have to run out of here and into the rain, our clothes will still be dry when we come back." Amanda frowned at her brother's comment. "I was being serious" she exclaimed. "So was he" Jenny said to her friend, "It makes perfect sense, Amanda. If we run out in the rain with our clothes on when those men come along, they'll get soaked, and we'll end up going back to camp in wet clothes. If we hide them like

Jeremy suggested, we'll have dry clothes to put back on when we head back." "But if we go out there nude, we might be seen by someone out there" Amanda exclaimed. "Amanda, we're looking for where Greg, Tomas, and Karen are going when they leave the lake. They're all naturists, and those three men were naked, so they're more than likely naturist too." Jeremy explained, "If they're all coming from out there, then I don't think we need to worry about anyone except other naturists seeing us naked."

Amanda just looked at her friend for a moment, then looked back and forth between the two boys, they all wore serious faces. "Okay" Amanda finally conceded, "I guess I don't want to walk back through cool passages and caves in wet clothes, so when we hear the men coming, we get our clothes off, right?" "Wrong" Jeremy replied, "We need to hide our clothes now, before we hear those men coming. We won't have time, once we hear them." Both boys showed no sign of amusement on their faces as they both started pulling off their shirts. Jenny, beside her, began removing her shirt also. When the boys began untying the waist cord of their shorts, Amanda decided she needed to follow their lead. Jeremy put all of their clothes into the backpack, but they kept their shoes on. Charlie went further back into the passageway to look back around the curve for anyone coming, while his friend started looking for a place to hide the backpack. Just as Jeremy located a good spot, and had put the backpack in place, Charlie came trotting back. "They're coming" he whispered to the others, "Let's go."

The four nude teenagers walked out of the passageway and into the still drizzling rain. They started walking quickly along a path that led away from the opening, and soon came to an area which had plenty of trees and brush to hide in. They slipped through an opening, and in back of some trees, crouching down to stay out of sight of anyone on the path. Moments later, the three nude men came walking along the path together, acting as if they hadn't even noticed that it was raining. "How are sales at the stand going?" the teens heard one of the men ask. "It's kind of slow today" another man replied, "The rain is keeping people from coming out right now." "It's supposed to clear up this afternoon" one of them announced, "Sales will pick up then. People love our fresh produce." The three men kept walking along the path, around a bend, and out of sight. The sound of their voices soon died off, and the teens all relaxed a little. "Can we go back to camp now?" Amanda asked, "I'm soaking wet already from being out here in the rain." "Back to camp? Just because you're getting wet in the rain?" Jenny said in answer to her, "This rain feels good to me. It's even a little warm from the hot day we're having. And, we haven't finished exploring yet." "That's right, Amanda" Jeremy added, "We need to follow those men, and see where they go. It's probably the same place that Greg, Karen, and Tomas go to."

A few minutes after the three nude men had disappeared, the teens came back out to the path, and started walking in the rain after them. When they reached the bend in the path, Charlie went ahead and looked carefully around the trees and bushes. He came back with a smile on his face. "There's a little town further down this path" he said, "The path goes around the bend, past some farm fields, and into the town." The rest all followed Charlie back around the bend, staying low. Down the path, they could still see the three men walking along, toward a group of about twelve buildings on the right side of the path. Most of the land surrounding the town was farm land, with corn and other crops growing. There was an orchard with lots of apple trees close to the town also. "Do you suppose that everyone in that town is a naturist?" Amanda asked. "I think that's probably it" Jenny replied, "Those men are walking right down into the town, still nude. I don't think they would do that if the town wasn't a naturist place." "This has to be where Greg, Tomas, and Karen all live" Charlie exclaimed, "Looks like we've solved the mystery of where they keep disappearing to." "We need to confirm that yet" Jeremy responded, “We need to be sure of it.” “How do we do that?” Amanda asked, knowing that her brother had already decided on a plan. “We’ll have to get closer to the town first” Charlie answered for his friend, “That’s what you’re thinking, right Jeremy?” “Right” Jeremy said, “We get as close to the town as we can, then watch to see if Greg, Tomas, or Karen are there. If they are, then we’ll know for sure that they live here.”

THE BIG SURPRISE

Jeremy led them down along the path towards the little town ahead, staying low and to the right side of the path, keeping an eye on the men in the distance ahead. They reached a corn field just off the path and headed over to it. Entering the field, they used the corn to hide their presence as they continued on closer to the town. By the time they reached the end of the corn field, the rain had stopped, and another field of some other crop lay ahead of them. The new field would not work to hide them, since it was filled with short green plants, probably beats or something similar. "This will have to be close enough" Jenny whispered to Jeremy, "Someone will see us if we try to go through the next field." "We can go back a little bit, and then head sideways through the rows of corn" Charlie suggested, "There's some trees and brush that way, and we might be able to get even closer." "That's where we'll head then" Jeremy agreed, "And that will take us more towards the town too." They made their way through the rows of corn to the far side of the field, and into a grove of trees, then headed towards the town again.

The grove of trees turned out to be apple trees, and it ran along behind all the houses, about four hundred feet back from the buildings in the town. Amanda looked up at the steeple on the top of the first building.

"That's a church" she gasped, "They have a church in this town." "What's wrong with that?" Jenny whispered. "Do they go to church without clothes too?" Amanda questioned in reply. "Sure, why not" Jenny said with a laugh, "Naturists can believe in God too." "Quiet" Jeremy suddenly whispered, "Someone's coming this way." The four crouched down real low as three young kids came running around the far corner of the church building, apparently playing a game of tag. Two of them continued on around to the front side of the building, while the third one veered off and away from the other two, going back the way he came from. "He got away" Charlie said with a chuckle. "How do you know it was a 'he' that got away?" Amanda asked. "Really?" Charlie said, "You can't tell the difference between boys and girls?" "Of course, I can" she replied, "I just wasn't watching them that close." "Charlie, I think the one that got away, is the one that is 'IT'." Jenny stated. "All clear now, let's go" Jeremy said, and they all started through the tree grove some more.

They had been making their way around the outskirts of the town for over an hour and had reached the other end of the little town. They had seen a lot of people going about their business in the town and working in the fields, men, women, boys, and girls, all completely naked, but had not spotted Greg, Tomas, or Karen as yet. Looking out, away from the back side of the town, they saw more high hills in the distance. "I think this town is completely surrounded by hills" Charlie concluded, "No wonder they have to go through a passageway to get out." "It's definitely not just a town in a valley" Jeremy responded, "They built this town in the middle of a big depression in the mountains. It's a perfectly secluded location." "Perfect for a naturist town" Jenny stated, "They don't have to worry about people from outside of their town coming to spy on them. They can live without clothes, and not have to worry about other people." "Until us that is" Jeremy added, "That's why Greg, Tomas, and Karen aren't allowed to tell anyone where they live." "If people from outside of here find out about this town, there will be lots of people coming here just to spy on them" Charlie said. "Well, I'm not going to tell anyone about this place" Jeremy announced, "It's a secret that I think we should keep for the people here. These people have a right to live the way they want, and if we tell anyone, it will be our fault if they lose their privacy." "Right" Jenny said, "I'm not going to tell anyone about this town either." "Me too" Amanda declared, "I'm not going to be the one to ruin it for them." "I agree" Charlie said, "I don't want anyone else to know about this place either. As a matter of fact, I think I might like to live here myself someday." Everyone stared at Charlie. "What?" he asked, "I've come to like going nude, and being free of clothes."

The teens continued out, around the rest of the town, making their way the rest of the way around the town. They'd still seen no sign of Greg, Tomas, or Karen as they made it to the end of an entire loop around the town. "Now what?" asked Amanda, "I'm getting tired, and I'm hot." "Bet you wish it would rain again, huh?" Jenny giggled as they reached the path into and out of the town again. "Yeah" Amanda replied with a grin, "That would feel really good right now. I must be filthy after walking all around the town, and through the wet fields and everything." She looked down at herself and gasped. "Oh, my" she exclaimed, "I forgot that I was nude!" "We've all been nude since we came out of that passage" Jenny chuckled, "And I don't think any of us really seemed to notice it." "I knew that I was naked" Jeremy declared, "But, I just didn't care. It feels wonderful to not have hot, sweaty clothes on right now. Can you imagine how much hotter we would feel if we were wearing clothes." "I can imagine it" Charlie said, "And when we get back to our clothes, you can leave mine in the backpack. I'm going back to camp just like I am right now, naked!" "My clothes can stay in the backpack too" Jenny added, "I'm more comfortable going nude." "Me too" Amanda declared. "Well, that makes it unanimous then" Jeremy chuckled, "I guess we've all been converted into naturists."

They all laughed as they headed back up the path

towards the passage that would take them back to the cave, and the pool back to the lake. They came to the bend in the path, chatting amongst themselves, and as they came around the corner, they met three naked kids coming from the other direction. "Oh!" exclaimed Amanda when she almost bumped into Tomas. The three young kids backed up a little bit and looked at the four naked teens. "What are you guys doing here?" exclaimed Greg, "Did you follow us?" "Follow you?" said Jeremy, "From where?" "Greg, they couldn't have followed us here" Karen said, "They weren't even out at the lake when we were there." "Oh, that's right" Greg mumbled, "But how did you find our village?" he asked the teens. "We were exploring" Jenny quickly explained, "The boys found a tunnel underwater by the ledge, and we all swam through it to a cave. We were exploring some tunnels, and found this path to the town." "You went to the village?" Karen gasped. "Not really" Charlie responded, "We saw some naked guys going into the town and thought this might be where you guys lived. We walked all the way around, staying hidden, looking to see if we could spot you." "We were up at the lake, looking for you" Tomas said. "That town back there is where you live then, right?" Jeremy asked. "Yes" Karen replied. "Well, we made sure that nobody saw us" Amanda declared, "So no one should know we were here and blame you."

Karen pointed up the path and over to the grove of trees where the four teens had hidden a couple of hours earlier. “Let’s go over there in the shade and talk” she said. “You want to talk someplace where we can’t be seen by anyone else, right?” Jeremy replied to her. Karen smiled at him, “Yes” she answered, “Plus, it will be cooler in the shade.” “I’m all for cooler” Charlie declared, “It’s hot out here in the sun, even without clothes on.” The seven kids all walked over to the shady grove and found a comfortable place in the green grass to sit. “Okay” Karen started, “First of all, thank you for not letting anyone see you. Everyone in the village knows that we have been spotted by four textile teenagers up at the lake, and they have told us to be careful not to let you find out where the village is. The reason they are all worried, is…” “We know why” Jenny interrupted, “At least we think we know why. You don’t want people outside of your town to know about it, because then you would have outsiders sneaking in to spy on you, right?” “Right” Karen replied, “We don’t want any textiles spying on us.” “You don’t have to worry about that” Jeremy stated, “We’ve all discussed it, and agreed that we don’t want to be the reason for something like that happening.” “We aren’t going to tell anyone about you or your town” Amanda declared. “Besides” Charlie interjected, “Look at us. All four of us are naked, and we like it. None of us want our friends to start thinking of us as weird, just because we became naturists ourselves, and wish we lived in your town."

Karen and the young boys looked at Charlie with big grins on their faces. Charlie started feeling uneasy as he watched them staring at him. "What" he finally exclaimed, "Do I have dirt on my face or something." "Yes, as a matter of fact, you do" Greg chuckled, "And your feet are all muddy, too." "But that isn't what surprises us" Karen said, "Of the four of you, Charlie, you seemed the least likely to want to go around nude, let alone announce that you are a naturist." Everyone now looked at him and started laughing. "Okay, okay" Charlie said, "I wasn't the only one who was nervous about it at first. Amanda didn't like being naked around anyone either." "That's true" Jeremy responded, "But she changed her mind about it yesterday, when you were still hesitant about being naked." "Okay" Charlie admitted, "I'm the last one of us four to accept being naked, I admit it. But the thing is, I did learn to like it, so stop teasing me about it, okay?" "Okay, we'll leave you alone, for now" Amanda told him with a grin. "By the way" Jeremy said, "What's the name of your town?" Karen grinned back at him. "It's called 'Village Du-Nu', which means village of the nude" she answered. "Village Du-Nu" Charlie repeated, "I like it, it fits perfectly." Everyone laughed. "That's pretty good" Karen said to him, "You pronounced it perfectly."

Karen now looked over at Jeremy again. “Jeremy, you said that you found a tunnel underwater. That you went through it to a cave and found our village when you were exploring the tunnels and caves” she said, “What underwater cave did you find?” “The one you guys are using to come and go from the lake” he answered her. “We don’t use an underwater tunnel” she replied, “Where is the tunnel you found?” “We found it behind the waterfall when we were diving” Charlie replied, “It’s to the left of the steps going up to the ledge, down at the bottom of the lake.” “We’ve never used an underwater tunnel” Greg interjected, “We use…”. Karen held up her hand to him and gave him a look that stopped him from continuing. “We aren’t supposed to tell anyone how we get to the lake” she exclaimed. “Why can’t we tell them?” Tomas asked her, “They already know another way to get here anyway.” “We still aren’t allowed to tell anyone” she replied, “We’ll have to ask for permission to tell them.” “We saw the storage room further up that passage there, too” Jenny said, pointing to the opening further up the path. “And we almost got caught in there” Amanda added, “But we slipped outside through a door when three men came along.” “What? You could have been locked out by going through that door” Greg exclaimed, “I did once.” “We got back in through the garage door” Jeremy explained, “Two of the men left on an ATV with some produce, and when we tried the garage door, it was still unlocked." "So, we got back in and followed the passage down to here" Amanda finished, "And then went around the town, keeping out of sight while looking for you guys, until we ran into you here."

"Well, we're going to have to tell our parents how you found your way here" Karen explained, "And see what they say about all this." "We were heading back to our camp site just now" Jenny said, "Can you come up to the lake tomorrow, and let us know what happens when you tell your parents?" "We'll try" Karen answered. "I just hope we didn't get you in trouble, and that we can all still be friends" Jeremy added, "Tell your parents that all four of us will keep your town a secret. We aren't even going to tell our parents." "Find out if we can come and visit your town, too" Charlie said with a grin, "I'd like see it from inside, instead of from behind trees and bushes outside of it." "Yeah, that would be great" Amanda giggled. "We would all love to visit your town if we're allowed to" Jeremy agreed. "Okay, we'll ask" Greg declared with a grin, "we'd love to show you around our town, too. Maybe you could even help us with our chores, taking care of the crops is a lot of work." "We'd love to help you with them" Jeremy answered with a smile, "As long as we don't have to wear any clothes." "Well, we have to get home now" Karen declared. "Okay" the four teens responded together. "Hope to see you tomorrow" Jenny added as the four teens headed back to the passage opening.

The three younger kids walked around the bend and started running towards the town, down the path. The four teens reached the passage in the hillside, where Jeremy retrieved his backpack. He was starting to unzip the backpack when his sister stopped him. "I don't want my clothes" she told him, "I'm fine just like this." "Me too" Jenny added, "I don't need any clothes right now." Jeremy smiled and looked at his best friend. "Don't look at me" Charlie said with a grin, "I'm just fine this way. If you want to put clothes on, go ahead, the rest of us prefer to stay naked." "We're not actually naked" Amanda corrected him, "You should say that we prefer to stay 'nude' instead. It sounds better, and Karen told me that's how naturists refer to going clothes free." "Okay" Charlie conceded as he turned to Jeremy, "The rest of us want to stay 'nude'." Jeremy grinned. "Fine with me" he replied, "I wasn't going to get dressed either. I was just going to get out some water for anyone who might want some." He handed out some water and zipped up the backpack as the four of them started up the passage towards the cave with the pool.

VISITING DU-NU

The teens returned to the cave with the pool, took off their sandals and rinsed them off in the pool water. Jeremy and Charlie made sure everything was sealed in the garbage bag again, including all the foot wear, and they were ready to take it back to camp with them. Jeremy and Charlie went into the pool with the sealed garbage bag again and took it through the tunnel. They put the garbage bag up on the ledge, then Jeremy returned to the cave pool again with just a lantern. The girls went into the pool and headed down to the tunnel again, just like when they had come into the cave for their exploring adventure. Charlie was waiting out in the lake at the end of the tunnel with a lantern for them to go towards. Jeremy followed the girls out again, and they all swam up to the surface and climbed up onto the ledge for a rest.

It was about four o'clock when they got back to camp, and they were all tired and hungry. The boys got the fire started, and the girls got out some hamburger to cook up. They never bothered to put clothes on, since it was hot out, and they were too tired. No one felt like they really needed to wear anything. After finishing super, they relaxed around the fire pit for a while, then went to the lake to rinse out their clothes and do some skinny-dipping. They returned to the camp a little after six and hung up the clothes they had rinsed out. The clothes they had left on the line that morning, were hanging there yet, still a little wet, since they had been hanging there in the rain that afternoon. The teens sat down around the fire pit again and chatted about the events of the day for a while. Around seven o'clock, they all decided to get some sleep, and headed off to their tents and sleeping bags.

Morning arrived, and the birds started singing. Jenny and Amanda came out of their tent around seven o'clock and found the boys already up, wearing their birthday suits, and getting a fire going. Jeremy looked over at the two girls and smiled. "Good morning girls, how did you sleep?" he asked. "Fine" Jenny said while stretching, "How long have you boys been up?" "We've been up since six-thirty" Charlie answered with a grin, "We thought a nice hot breakfast would be nice, after having nothing but dry cereal lately." "What are you planning?" Amanda inquired. Jeremy smiled at his sister. "Mademoiselle, for breakfast, we have planned sausage, scrambled eggs, and pancakes, with orange juice." "Oh! How long before it's ready?" she squealed. "About fifteen minutes" Charlie answered, "You have time to take care of business and get washed up." "Take care of business?" she repeated back. "Yeah, back there behind the bushes" he said. "Oh, yeah" said Amanda with a blush. "Come on" Jenny urged her friend, "I want to get back here in time for breakfast. I'm hungry." The two girls headed back into the bushes to the girl's bathroom area.

The boys got the fire going and placed the grate over the flames. They set two pans on the grate, and Charlie started putting some sausage links in one of the pans. The girls returned about ten minutes later to the smell of cooked meat, eggs, and pancakes. The sausage was wrapped in aluminum foil at the edge of the grate, to keep the meat warm while the eggs were being cooked. Jeremy had a stack of about six pancakes ready in another foil container on his side of the cooking grate. "Grab a plate and utensils" Charlie instructed the girls, "Help yourself to some good home cooked food. "Thanks" Amanda replied with a smile, as she grabbed a plate and came over to the fire pit. She looked at the sausage in the foil and then looked up at Charlie. "You boys already ate, I see" she said to Charlie, "But you left just enough food for Jenny and me." "Whoa" exclaimed Charlie, "We haven't eaten yet. All this food has to be enough for all four of us." Amanda started laughing. "Stop teasing him" Jenny scolded her friend, "The boys were nice enough to get up early and prepare a wonderful hot breakfast, and you start picking on them." "Sorry" Amanda said to Charlie with a pouty face, "Do you forgive me for being mean?" Charlie grinned back at her. "Maybe later" he replied, "After you give me an apology hug and kiss."

After they finished breakfast, and disposed of the plates, utensils, and juice containers, they started gathering up the cooking equipment to take down to the lake for cleaning. "Anyone here?" came a call from outside of the camp. "Karen? Is that you?" Jenny called back, "Yes, we're all here in camp." "Okay, we're coming up there then" Karen called out, "Hope you are all decently dressed." "Dressed? Decent?" Charlie whispered to the others, "We're all nak... I mean nude. Do we need to get dressed really quick?" "No, I think she means..." began Jenny in reply. "Oh, good, you're all dressed properly" Karen exclaimed, as she, Greg, and Tomas walked around the corner and into the camp, along with another girl. "Who's your friend?" Jeremy asked. "She's not my friend" Tomas replied, looking over at the red-haired girl, "She's my older sister, Caitlyn." Caitlyn gave her brother a little push and stepped forward. "I'm Karen and Greg's friend" she snarled at her brother. All four teens chuckled and greeted the new girl, who seemed to be around Karen's age. Karen looked at the teens with a serious face. "We talked with our parents last night and told them about you finding our village" she stated. "You didn't get in trouble, did you?" Jenny asked. "Yeah, because it wasn't your fault" Amanda added, "Charlie and my brother found the underwater tunnel, and thought we should explore it. They thought it might be how you kept disappearing all the time." "We didn't get in trouble" Greg said. "No, but our parents are a lot more curious about you now" Karen explained, "and they want to meet all of you." "So, you want us to come to your town to meet your parents?" Jeremy asked. "No" Greg answered, "They want to know if it is okay for them to come here to your camp." "Well, sure" Jeremy responded, "They can come here anytime they want to, we'd love to meet your parents."

Karen looked over the bushes in the direction of the lake. "It's okay" she called out, "They say you can come in to meet them." "What! Wait? They're already here!" Amanda exclaimed, "But we aren't dressed, we're naked!" "So are we" said a woman, as she came walking into the camp with a man following her. The two adults stood there completely nude, except for the sandals on their feet, and smiled around at the four nude teenagers. Karen chuckled, "It's alright, Amanda, we're all naturists, and nude is just normal to us." "Mom" Karen said to the woman, as she pointed to Amanda, "This is Amanda, and that is her brother Jeremy, and his friend Charlie, and Jenny, Jeremy's girlfriend." The dark-skinned woman looked at each of the teens and then introduced herself. "Glad to meet you all, my name is Kathryn, and Karen and Greg are my children" she said, "They speak very highly of all of you. And this gentleman here is Shawn, Tomas and Caitlyn's father." The red-haired man took a step forward. "Very pleased to meet you" he said, "Tomas has talked very well of you all as well." Jeremy was the first to move, as he stepped up to Kathryn and shook her hand. "We're glad to meet you also" he said, and then moved over to shake Shawn's hand as well. The other three teens came behind their impromptu leader, greeting and shaking hands with both of the adults. "We didn't come at a bad time, did we?" Kathryn asked, as she noticed the dirty cookware that the teens had put down when she had arrived. "Oh, no" Jenny answered, "We were just going down to the lake to wash some cookware is all." "I've never been camping" Kathryn said, "How do you wash the dirty cookware and dishes when you don't have a sink around?" "Oh, we'll show you" Jeremy offered, "If you want to come down to the lake with us."

The two adults agreed, and they followed the four teens to the lake, along with the four younger kids following behind them. When they reached the lake, Jeremy demonstrated, as well as explained how to wash the dirty pans and utensils with wet sand. Then they returned to the camp, rinsed everything with some bottled water, dried the items with paper towel, and then used the same paper towels to put a thin layer of oil on the pans, to keep them from rusting. "Interesting" Shawn exclaimed, "How did you learn how to do that, in a book?" "Kind of Charlie responded, "Jeremy and I are in the Boy Scouts. We go camping a lot and learned it from the scout leaders and other scouts." "So, you are both boy scouts" Kathryn declared, "I hear that boy scouts are supposed to be trustworthy and honest." "Yes, they are" Amanda responded proudly, "My brother and Charlie have been in the Boy Scouts for a long time, and they are both Eagle Scouts now." "Eagle Scouts!" Shawn repeated, "I'm impressed. That's the highest rank you can reach in the Boy Scouts, from what I've heard, and you have to be hard workers to get there." "Yes sir" Jeremy confirmed. "Well, I'm satisfied, Shawn, they seem like they can be trusted, don't you think?" Kathryn declared. "I agree" Shawn said, "I'm sure they will keep our village a secret."

"We're so glad you trust us" Jeremy stated, "We were worried that you would blame Greg, Tomas, and Karen for us finding your town, and that they would be in trouble." "They explained everything to us last night" Shawn replied, "When they mentioned the underwater tunnel, we knew it wasn't them that gave us away." "You see, none of the kids even knew about that tunnel" Kathryn added, "It hasn't been used in probably twenty-five years. Only the adults in town would remember about the tunnel, from when we used it to get to the lake." "Why don't you use it anymore?" Amanda inquired. "We created a different way to get from our town to the lake" Kathryn answered, "A way that's safer for the kids." "Karen mentioned that they didn't use the tunnel" Jenny said, "That they came and went another way. But they said it was a secret and couldn't tell anyone about it." "That's right" Shawn responded, "Everyone knows that they are not supposed to tell any textiles how to get to our village." "Textiles?" repeated Charlie, "I think Karen used that word yesterday. What's a Textile?" "A Textile" explained Kathryn, "is a person that wears textile clothing, and believes that going nude is indecent." "Oh, like my sister, Charlie, and me" exclaimed Jeremy, "up until this camping trip anyway." "What about your friend Jenny here?" Kathryn inquired. "She never believed that going nude was wrong" Jeremy answered, "She went to a nude beach with her family about four years ago, and liked it."

"So, can they come?" Greg asked his mother. Kathryn looked at Shawn. "What do you think?" she asked him. "I think it would be okay" he answered, "Unless you have a reason against it." Kathryn looked down at her son and grinned. "Yes, Greg, they can come." Greg, Tomas, and Karen suddenly started dancing up and down excitedly. "They seem pretty happy about something" Charlie observed. "Yes, they are" Kathryn responded, "They were hoping that we would agree to let you come and visit our village, and Shawn and I just told them it was alright." "Really?" Amanda exclaimed, bouncing up and down on her feet, "We can really come to your town?" "Yes" Kathryn answered with a grin, "I can see that you are just as excited about visiting, as the younger kids are." Everyone started laughing, and Amanda calmed herself down. "When is it okay to come" Jeremy asked, "And do we need to come through the tunnel again. "You can come anytime you want to, and the kids can show you another way·to get there" Shawn replied to Jeremy. "We have to get back to the village now, if you want to come along with us" Kathryn offered. "Oh, yeah. Come now" Greg pleaded, "I got chores to do yet, and you can help me with them." "Greg!" Kathryn exclaimed, "You can't ask them to come, just to help you with your chores." "No, it's okay" Charlie spoke up, "We told him yesterday that we would help with his chores, as long as we don't have to wear clothes." Kathryn chuckled at Charlie's explanation. "I think it would be fine if you wanted to work in the nude" she told him, "Come on, we'll show you how to get there using our new way."

The four teens quickly closed up their tents and followed after the two adults and four young kids, down the path from the camp to the lake. The group headed south, around the lake, until they reached the rocky wall of the mountain. They then headed west for about fifty feet and stopped to face the rock wall. The teens watched, as Shawn went up to the wall, reach into a crevice in the rock, and pulled. They heard a click and then a section of the wall separated from the rest of the wall and swung away. Behind that section of rock was an opening, and the back of the door was made of metal. Shawn motioned for everyone to go through the opening. The teens all inspected the latch as they entered the opening, to see how it worked, and when Shawn pulled the door closed behind them, a light came on to reveal a passage going into the mountain. "The lights are activated by movement" Shawn explained from behind, "But they will only come on if the door is closed. That's to prevent anyone outside from seeing the light in here at night." They continued on through the passage for about fifteen minutes, until the passage came to an end at another metal door. Shawn opened the door so they could all exit out into the open air and daylight again.

When they walked out of the mountain side, they all found themselves in a small wooded area. The adults lead the way along a path, and they soon found themselves a short walk from the path that lead down to the village. They were on the south side of the path, and the grove of trees they had sat in yesterday while talking with Karen, Greg, and Tomas, was on the north side of the path. "Wow!" Charlie exclaimed, "We were so close to that passage, yesterday." "Yes, but it's pretty well hidden" Kathryn declared. "If we had chosen to hide from those three men on this side of the path, we might have discovered it though" Jeremy responded with a grin. "I don't think so" Shawn declared, "You didn't look at the door that I closed behind all of us after we exited the mountain passage, did you?" "I looked back and couldn't see it anywhere" Amanda said, "How will we find it when we go back?" "The kids will bring you back, and through the mountain side when you leave" Kathryn answered, "After that, you should all know how to get to and from the village whenever you want to visit." "But making sure we keep it a secret from any 'Textiles' that might be around" Jeremy said with a smile. "Right" Kathryn and Shawn agreed together. "Shall we head down to the village?" Kathryn asked, "Without hiding this time." "Yes" all four teenagers replied.

Again, Kathryn led the way down the path with the rest following behind. She described things as they walked along. How the path they were on was used to transport the produce that was grown by the town, up to the storage cavern, and from there to a small retail produce stand that the town operated. "Where is the produce stand located?" Amanda asked. "It's out on the south side of highway 14, which goes to the town of Bon Amis, that I believe you four are from" answered Shawn. "Do you sell a lot of produce there?" Jeremy inquired. "Not as much as we would like" Shawn replied, “We have to try to sell a lot of it to the big grocery stores in the area, but they are all buying their produce from elsewhere, so we have to sell it pretty cheap, so as not to have it spoil.” “The produce stand sells about half of our crops” Kathryn added, “But nobody really likes working at the stand because we can’t go nude when we’re there.” “If we could find a market for all of our crops, that would be ideal” Shawn said, “But it’s hard to get a buyer, when we can’t tell the businesses where the produce is grown.” “I can see your problem” Jeremy replied, “I wonder if our mother might be willing to buy your produce, she owns a small grocery store in our town.” “She’s probably not going to be any more willing to buy from us than any of the other big grocery stores” Kathryn said, “Not without knowing where we get our produce from. And we don’t want our secret village to become know.” “Maybe if Jeremy and I talk to her” Amanda suggested, “We could tell her we know someone that has good produce to sell, and that we recommend buying from them.” “Maybe we could try that” Jeremy said, “If it’s okay with your town. We won’t tell where the town is though, that’s a secret we can’t tell her.” “As long as you keep the location of our village a secret, I don’t think it would hurt to try” Shawn responded. “We’ll see what the village leaders think about the idea” Kathryn said with a smile, “But either way, thank you for offering to help.”

The rest of the way into the village, Shawn explained what crops were growing in all the fields, and how they wanted to build greenhouses over some of the fields, so they could continue growing things all year round. "We have to have a good market for our products first though" he explained, "Before we spend any money to build green houses." As they started past the church building, Amanda stopped. "Do you go to church nude?" she asked, "Or do you dress up in you Sunday best?" Kathryn stopped and looked at her. "We all attend church in our everyday best" she replied, "We wear the finest that God gave us on our birthday, instead of man-made textile clothing." "Huh?" Amanda muttered. Jenny chuckled. "Amanda, their skin is their finest clothing. God made it for them, and they received it on the day they were born" Jenny tried to explain. "So, they go to church nude?" Amanda said. "Yes, Amanda" Kathryn replied, "I'm sorry. I was being a little vague before. As your friend said, we wear what we consider to be the finest, with nothing to hide or cover it." "That sounds good to me" Charlie said, "It's probably a lot more comfortable too. I've suffered in church many times during the summer, with the suit my mom insists I wear." "What are you going to do when we get back home" Jeremy asked his friend, "When you'll have to wear that suit again, to hide your nude body?" "I'll probably just suffer through it" Charlie answered, "But at least I'll have a week before we go to church back home." "When do you have to head back to your homes?" Kathryn inquired. "We leave on Sunday" Jeremy replied, "My mom is picking us up out on highway 22 at around three o'clock in the afternoon." "You're welcome to attend church here, if you want" Shawn suggested, "And see what it's like to go to church and not have to be all dressed up in uncomfortable clothes."

Kathryn turned right at the sidewalk leading up to the third house on the path. They followed her up to the house, where she opened the door to let them all in. Before anyone could go through the door, Greg stopped them. "Mom, I still need to do my chores, and Charlie said he would help me" Greg exclaimed, "Can't you talk to them more after we finish the chores? It's going to get hotter if we wait too long." "That's a good idea" Kathryn answered, "You and Charlie go ahead then, we'll see you when you get back." "Um, I think I would like to help Greg, too" Jeremy spoke up. "And if Karen has chores yet, Jenny and I would love to help her also" Amanda offered. "Well, the help would be appreciated" Kathryn said. "What about Caitlyn and me" Tomas inquired, "We could use some help too." Shawn looked at his son, "Tomas, you work in the same field as Greg and Karen, so they'll already be helping you" he said. "There are four of us, and four of them. We can probably work in teams, one of us each, to help each of them. That way they all can get caught up on their chores, before it gets really hot out." Shawn smiled at the teenage girl's suggestion. "You are all very generous" he said, "I'm sure our kids will really appreciate your help." "Tell you what" Kathryn declared, "When the chores are done, you all come back here for lunch, okay?"

Greg looked up at his mother. "Mom, Karen told them how good Miss Joyce's spaghetti is, and they don't think it can be better than their aunt's spaghetti. Do you suppose Miss Joyce would make spaghetti for us, and bring it over for lunch? That way, Amanda and Jeremy can see that her spaghetti is better than their aunt's." Kathryn smiled down at her son. "I'll check with her and see if she wants to make some of her spaghetti for you all" she replied, "Now you better go and get started on those chores, before it gets any warmer." "Okay mom" Greg exclaimed, "Come on Charlie, follow me." The four teens followed the four younger kids towards the fields back up the path and to the west side. When they reached a field of carrots, Greg started explaining what they needed to do. "We have to pull the weeds from around the carrots, without pulling the carrots" he explained, "If we all take one row, we'll have a lot done in no time." "You better show us what the carrots look like first" Jeremy suggested. Karen walked up to the first row in the field, and pointed to several of the green carrot tops, and pulled the weeds all around them. "That's how you do it" she said after finishing her demonstration, "Any questions?" "I got it" Amanda said as she stepped into the field to the second row, "I'll take the second row." Greg took the third row and had Charlie take the fourth row next to him. Caitlyn took the fifth row, Jenny the sixth row, Jeremy the seventh row, and Tomas got the eighth row.

They finished the first eight rows in the field in about an hour and went on to doing another eight rows in the opposite direction. Two hours after starting, they had sixteen rows of carrots all weeded. The teens started moving over to begin some more rows, but Karen stopped them. "There's only four more rows to do" she said, the rest of the field is onions. We don't have to weed them until tomorrow." Jeremy looked at the remainder of the field and saw that the she was right. "Let's split up and work from opposite ends of the field then" he suggested, "We'll work toward each other, meeting in the middle of the row." "Okay" Greg shouted out, "We can have a competition. Boys against girls." "That's a great idea" Caitlyn said, "The boys can start from the south end of the field, and we girls will start from this end." "I have a better idea" Jeremy declared, "Two girls can do this first row, two boys the second, two more girls the third row, and the last two boys do the forth row. Two boys and two girls will go down to the south end and work this way, while the rest of us can get started right away at this end. First team to finish, either boys or girls, will be the winners." Everyone thought that sounded like a good arrangement and agreed to it. "What's the prize?" Tomas asked. "The winners have to gather up the pulled weeds from the first eight rows and put them in a pile out by the road" Caitlyn suggested, "The losers have to pick up the weeds from the last twelve rows, and then take ALL the weeds over to the incinerators." "Okay, agreed" Greg exclaimed.

Charlie, Greg, Karen, and Amanda headed down to the south end of the field while the others began weeding from the north end right away. Charlie and Karen reached the north end ahead of the other two and started weeding right away. Half an hour later, the two ends were nearing each other, with the girls leading the race in both of their rows. When the girls intersected at the middle, they were finished weeding, so they stood up and shouted in triumph. They immediately went to the edge of the field, and taking one row each, the began collecting up the drying weeds and running them out to the road. The boys finally finished their rows a few minutes later and started gathering up the weeds from the last four rows of carrots in the field. The girls finished collecting weeds from their last four rows and stood by the growing pile of pulled weeds. "See you boys back at the house" the girls called out, giggling as they walked across the road. It took the boys another ten minutes to finish gathering up the last of the weeds and take them to the road. "How do we get all these weeds over to the incinerators?" Charlie gasped. Greg smiled at him. "You two wait her" he said, "Tomas and I will go and get a cart." Charlie and Jeremy sat down in some grass beside the road to wait for the younger boys to return. Greg and Tomas came back up the road with a cart about five minutes later and stopped the cart right next to the pile of weeds. It took all four boys another fifteen minutes to load all the weeds into the cart and pull it over to the incinerators a short distance away. They dumped the weeds off of the cart and spread them out to let them dry out better.

Greg smiled at the two older boys. "Thanks for helping us" he exclaimed, "It would have taken us a couple more hours to do it without you two, and Amanda and Jenny helping." "Let's go get some lunch" Tomas suggested, "It must be after twelve by now." "Yeah, lunch!" Charlie shrieked, "I'm starving." "You're always starving" Jeremy said with a laugh, "But lunch sounds like a great idea. I'm hungry too." The boys headed over to a building that served as a shower building, where they all quickly took a cool shower to clean up and cool off. They then headed back towards Greg's house, where they hoped that lunch would be ready. When they entered the house, Kathryn greeted them and told them that lunch would be there in about ten minutes. The girls were already in the dining room, sitting on chairs with towels over them, so the boys went in and joined them at the table, sitting on towel covered chairs also. "Would you boys like some nice cold lemonade?" Kathryn asked. "Yes, please" they all replied. They were all talking and enjoying the lemonade when a knock was heard at the back door. Kathryn went to the kitchen, and they could all hear her talking to another woman. Jeremy looked over at his sister with a puzzled look. "Does that voice sound familiar?" he asked her. "A little" Amanda replied, "But I don't think it could be anyone we know, not in this town."

Kathryn came back into the dining room. "Well, lunch has arrived" she announced, "I want our new friends to meet the good neighbor who prepared lunch for us, Miss Joyce." A woman came through the doorway from the kitchen with a big grin on her face. "I've been told that my spaghetti has been challenged. Well, be prepared to taste the best..." she began to say, "Oh! Oh my! What are you two doing here?" Kathryn managed to grab the large bowl of spaghetti before the woman dropped it. Jeremy sat up wide eyed at the sight of the nude woman, and Amanda gasped, then started looking around the room like a trapped animal. "Aunt Joyce!"

Jeremy managed to gasp. Everyone started looking back and forth between the shocked Miss Joyce, Amanda, and Jeremy. "Aunt Joyce!" Kathryn suddenly exclaimed, "Oh my goodness, Joyce, are these the nephew and niece that you are always bragging about?" Joyce looked at Kathryn. "Uh huh" she muttered, "My nephew Jeremy, and my niece Amanda. How in the world did they get here?" "They're the four teenagers that Greg, Karen, and Tomas met up at the lake" Kathryn explained, "They found the old under water tunnel below the ledge and started exploring until they found the village yesterday." "Aunt Joyce" Amanda finally managed to say, "You live here?" "Yes" Joyce answered, "I grew up in this village."

FAMILY HISTORY

They all heard the back door open and close at that moment, and a pair of voices called out. “Mom, are you here? We brought the garlic bread and meatballs, like you said.” Suddenly, two naked young boys walked into the room carrying a plate of bread and a bowl of meatballs. They stopped when they spotted the four older teenagers at the table, especially Jeremy and Amanda. “Mom, that’s Jeremy and Amanda” exclaimed one of the boys. “Joyce looked over at her two ten-year old twin boys. “Yes James, they are” she muttered. “When did they get here?” asked the other boy with a big grin. Jeremy grinned at the sight of his two young cousins, standing there with nothing on except sandals, beside their nude mother. “Hey, James. Hey, John” he called to them, “We’ve been camping up at the lake you told Amanda and me about. We didn’t know you lived here in Village Du-Nu.” “Hey, are we going to eat, before the food all gets cold?” Greg exclaimed, “I’m hungry.” Everyone laughed, and Kathryn had Joyce and the twins put the food on the table. “Let’s sit down and have lunch” she suggested, “We can talk while we eat.”

Everyone found a seat at the large dining room table. James and John insisted on sitting between Jeremy and Amanda. Everyone filled their plates with spaghetti, meatballs, and garlic bread, then began to eat. There were lots of moans from the kids as they enjoyed the spaghetti, until suddenly, Jeremy started laughing. "Jeremy, what's the matter?" Aunt Joyce asked, "Why are you laughing?" "The spaghetti challenge" he replied as he looked over at Karen. Karen looked confused for a moment, then started laughing also. "I don't get it, Jeremy. What's so funny about the spaghetti?" Kathryn asked. "Not the spaghetti, it's the challenge" Jeremy explained, "We told Karen that we thought our aunt made the best spaghetti, she insisted that her neighbor made the best spaghetti, and we made up this challenge." "I guess we know who makes the best spaghetti now" Karen chuckled. "Yeah" Jeremy replied with a grin, "Especially since out aunt and your neighbor are the same person." Suddenly, everyone at the table understood, and they all started chuckling.

After everyone had finished eating, they sat back and started talking. "Okay, Jeremy and Amanda, how did you two come to be here?" Aunt Joyce inquired. "We're on an eleven-day camping trip" Amanda began, "Jeremy planned the trip and chose the lake in the woods west of our town." "We saw some kids swimming in the lake, and discovered that they were skinny-dipping" Amanda added, "They were Greg, Tomas, and Karen." "But they kept vanishing, so we started searching around for how they got up there and left" Jeremy continued, "We found the ledge behind the waterfall, and when I spotted the underwater tunnel while Charlie and I were diving from the ledge, we decided to explore it, to see if it went somewhere that would explain the disappearance of those kids." "So, you found a cave and decided to explore further" Aunt Joyce said, "And then you found your way to this village." "That's about it" Jeremy said. "And how did you even know that there was a lake in those woods?" she asked, glancing over at the twins. "Well, yes" Amanda stammered, "We kind of heard about it from James and John, when you were visiting at Easter time." "They were just telling us that they knew of a great lake for swimming" Jeremy quickly interjected, "I managed to get them to tell us that it was west of our town, in the middle of some woods." "And you being the Eagle Scout that you are, were able to discover exactly where the lake was?" Aunt Joyce asked. "Yes" Jeremy answered, "And then I started planning our camping trip at the lake, because nobody else knew about it, and we wanted to have the whole lake to ourselves." Joyce looked over at Kathryn, "They're good kids" she said, "We can trust them to not tell anyone else about the village." "I know, Joyce. Shawn and I already talked to them up at the lake, after our children told us about finding the four of them just up the hill from the village" Kathryn responded, "We decided that they were trustworthy, and we've shown them the safe way to get to the village."

After Kathryn had the younger kids go outside to play for a while, the family discussion began. "Okay, Jeremy, when did you, your sister, and your friends become naturists?" Aunt Joyce asked, "Your mother never said anything about you becoming naturists." "To be honest Aunt Joyce" Amanda said, "Mom doesn't know yet. We kind of decided yesterday that we all wanted to be naturists." "Really" Joyce responded, "And how did you come to that decision, if you've never experienced naturism before?" "When we spotted Greg and Tomas swimming nude in the lake" Jeremy said, "We told them we would like to be friends, and that we already knew they were nude, and it didn't bother us. They explained about naturists, and how much better it felt to swim nude." "I kind of suggested that they should try wearing clothes" Charlie added, "They said they already had, and then they suggested that we try going nude, so we did." "The girls tried it too, when they spent some time with Karen" Jeremy explained further, "And then, we all accidently ran into each other later on, not realizing that we were all still nude." "We decided that we might as well stay the way we were" Jenny said, "After all, we had all seen each other nude then, so there was no need to hide what everyone had already seen?" "Plus, it felt a lot more comfortable without clothes on" Jeremy added. "So, your mother doesn't know that you are all camping together in the nude?" Joyce asked. "No" Amanda answered, "And we can't tell her, because then she would find out about this place, and we promised not to tell anyone about it." Joyce smiled at Kathryn, "What do you think? Should they tell their mother, now that we know who she is?" "Considering who their mother is, I think it would be okay for them to tell her" Kathryn replied with a grin.

Jeremy looked worried. "But we can't be sure that she won't tell someone else about Village Du-Nu" Jeremy exclaimed. "She hasn't told anyone else yet, so I don't think she's going to now" Aunt Joyce declared. "But," Jeremy started. "Jeremy, there's something you obviously haven't figured out about this situation" Aunt Joyce continued, "Something which may make it easier for you to tell her that you have become naturists." "Like what?" Amanda asked. "I grew up in this village" Aunt Joyce announced, "I've lived here all my life. I was born and raised by my parents here, along with my older sister." "What does that have to do with telling mom about us being naturists?" Amanda responded. "Think about it" Aunt Joyce replied with a grin, "Remember, your mother is my sister." Amanda hadn't caught on yet, but Jeremy had. "So, that means that our mom grew up here too, right?" he declared, "And since she grew up here, she already knows about this place." Amanda gasped, "Our mother grew up here? Was she a naturist, too?" "She still is a naturist" Aunt Joyce answered, "She just quit living as one, because your father didn't approve of her going nude all the time." "What do you mean, he didn't approve of it" Jeremy asked. "Well, your mother and father met in college and fell in love" Aunt Joyce began, "Your father was a very kind and friendly person, but he was never a naturist. Like a lot of people in this world, he felt that nudity was wrong, and he feared anything to do with it. When he asked your mother to marry him, she felt that she had to tell him about how she grew up, and about being a naturist. He didn't want her to continue to live a nude lifestyle, so she gave it up because she loved him. When you two were born, she had to raise you both to wear clothes also."

Jeremy and Amanda were learning a lot about their mother and father. "So, why didn't mom start raising us as naturists after dad died?" Jeremy inquired. "When your father died, your mother was totally devastated. She had to take over managing the grocery store all alone" their aunt explained, "And, since you two had always been raised wearing clothes, she figured it would be easier to just keep things the way they were, until you became adults." "So, mom gave up naturism just to please our father, and then chose not to change the way Amanda and I were used to" Jeremy concluded. "Yes" Aunt Joyce replied, "She is hoping to tell you about naturism when you are old enough to understand it better. She wants you to choose for yourself how you want to live. She plans to start living as a naturist again herself, after you two are out on your own." "I kind of wish she would have started raising us as naturists after daddy died" Amanda said, "Being nude is so much better than wearing clothes. I'm sure I would have had no problem with it." "I agree" Jeremy concurred, "I've really taken to this naturist thing." "Well, you can talk to her about naturism when you get back home" Aunt Joyce suggested. "Maybe" Jeremy said, "Amanda and I are still getting used to this, and I think we should understand more about it before we let mom know that we were going around nude with Jenny and Charlie on this camping trip." "Yeah" Amanda agreed, "We better wait and see how it feels to us when we're back home again."

Greg and Tomas suddenly came back into the room with Karen and Caitlyn close behind. "Mom, are you guys done talking yet?" Greg exclaimed, "We worked hard this morning to get our chores caught up, and we want to go up to the lake." "Go ahead" Kathryn told him, "But be careful, okay." Sure" Greg replied, "But we were hoping that Jeremy, Charlie, Amanda, and Jenny would go with us." "Oh" Kathryn said as she looked over at the four teens and Joyce, "I don't know it they are finished talking with their aunt yet." "Do you have anything else you want to ask me?" Aunt Joyce said to Jeremy and Amanda. "I can't think of anything else right now" Jeremy answered. Amanda indicated that she had nothing else right then either. "Then you four probably want to go swimming too, right?" she concluded. Jeremy and Amanda looked at their friends, "What would you like to do?' Jeremy asked. "Go swimming" Jenny answered. "We all worked hard, weeding this morning" Charlie announced, "I personally would like to go swimming with my young friends there." Joyce and Kathryn looked at each other and grinned. "Go then" Kathryn commanded, "Get out of here, and enjoy the afternoon." "Jeremy, Amanda" Aunt Joyce said, "Would you take James and John along with you, and keep an eye on them?" "Sure" Amanda answered. "I was going to ask you if they could go with us" Jeremy added, "They're great to have around." "Thank you, just have them back by six o'clock" she said, "And you two, and your two friends can join us for supper tonight." "Okay, great" Jeremy said, "We'll be there. We can't miss out on your great cooking."

Jeremy noticed a questioning look on his friends face as they were heading towards the back door to get James and John. Knowing what Charlie was wondering, he turned back to his aunt. "By-the-way, Aunt Joyce, what are you having for supper?" he asked. Aunt Joyce smiled. "Oh, I was thinking of maybe a pot roast, mashed potatoes with gravy, peas, and rolls" she replied, "And maybe some fresh apple pie with ice cream for dessert. Will that be okay with you and your friends?" "Okay? Is she kidding!" Charlie exclaimed from the kitchen. Jeremy grinned at his aunt and nodded his head in the direction of his friend, "It sounds like it would be more than okay" he answered with a laugh, "None of us has had a good home cooked meal all week, so it would be great. But be warned, my friend Charlie loves food, in case you hadn't noticed him having three helpings of your spaghetti for lunch." After they had exited the house, they could hear Aunt Joyce and Kathryn laughing together as they motioned over to the two young boys next door to come with them.

James and John both came running after the older kids. "Where're we going?" James inquired with a grin. "Swimming" Greg exclaimed, "Up at the lake." James and John both stopped walking. Jeremy spotted the disappointment on his cousins faces. "Hey, it's okay" he called back to the ten-year old twins, "Your mom asked us to take you along with us." Grins quickly replaced the frowns, and the boys ran to catch up with the eight older kids again. When they all reached the mountainside, Karen pointed out to the teenagers how to locate the secret passage door. Jeremy opened the hidden doorway, and they all proceeded through, with Charlie in the rear, closing the door behind them. Karen flipped a switch near the entrance and the passage lights came on. They continued on through the lighted passage, to the door at the other end, where Karen instructed Jeremy to open the door only a crack at first, so the lights would go out, and he could check for signs of anyone in the area that might see them all coming out of the mountainside. Karen flipped another switch near this entrance before she walked out with the others, followed by Charlie, who closed the door again. Jeremy began walking south around the lake. Karen started laughing. "Jeremy, wait" she said, "Why don't we just go swimming on this side of the lake?" Jeremy looked over at the lake and slapped his hand up against his forehead. "Of course," he said with a smile, "I guess we could do that too." Everyone laughed, and they all headed down towards the water.

Jeremy and Amanda discovered that their cousins, James and John, were pretty good swimmers for ten-year old's, but they couldn't swim as fast as the rest of them. Since they truly were very fond of the young boys, and felt responsible for them, they stayed close to them to ensure that they were safe. All ten of the youth remained on the west side of the lake, swimming around and having splash wars every now and then. After about an hour in the water, they were all starting to tire, and decided to lay out on the sandy beach for a while to rest. When Jeremy felt rested enough, he suggested that they swim out behind the waterfall and try some diving from the ledge. "We can't go out there"

James informed his cousin. "Yeah, mom says we're still too young yet to be out there, unless adults are with us." John added. "Well, would she consider Amanda, Jenny, Charlie, and me old enough to be adults?" Jeremy asked. "Yes, she would" Karen declared, "She told Caitlyn and me that when we're sixteen, we can take them out to the waterfall, if we watch them real close." "What do you think James, John. Do you want to come out with us?" Jeremy asked. The two twins grinned back at him, "Let's go!" they exclaimed together, as they both got up and ran into the water. "Whoa" exclaimed Jeremy, "First we have to set some rules. Do you both promise to listen to all four of us older teenagers, and to stay away from the waterfall itself?" "We promise" the boys answered. "Okay, now we can head out there" Jeremy said, "But stay close to the rest of us."

It took the group of kids about fifteen minutes to reach the west side of the ledge behind the water fall. They all climbed up the steps onto the ledge and sat down to rest again. "Amanda" Jeremy said to get her attention, "We need to make sure that one of us is always up here on the ledge, watching James and John, okay?" "That sounds good" Amanda replied. "What about Jenny and me?" Charlie asked his friend, "If one of us is up here, we can keep an eye on your cousins too." "I figured you two would be too busy with Greg, Tomas, Karen, and Caitlyn. They probably want to get some pointers on diving" Jeremy responded. "Wouldn't it be better if I helped Amanda keep an eye on your cousins then?" Jenny suggested, "That way you can assist Charlie with helping the others improve their diving." "I agree" Charlie chimed in, "It will be easier if both you and I take care of the diving instructions, since we're the two most experienced." "Okay" Jeremy said, "Amanda and Jenny can keep an eye on the twins, you and I will teach diving technics." They decided that Charlie would take Greg and Tomas as his students, and Jeremy would take Karen and Caitlyn."

Greg and Tomas were getting quite good at diving by now, since they had been learning from Charlie and Jeremy over the last couple of days, so Charlie started showing them how to do more complicated dives. Jeremy worked more with Caitlyn on diving, since she was pretty new to it. Karen had been diving with them for a day or two already, so she mainly kept practicing while Caitlyn got used to the basics. Pretty soon, both girls were diving about the same, so Jeremy gave them some pointers, then left them to practice for a while on their own. He went over to James and John to talk with them. "You two are pretty good swimmers already" he said to them, "Would you like to learn how to dive also?" "We sure would" they exclaimed together. "Okay then" Jeremy said, "Have either of you ever tried diving into the water before?" "No" James answered, "Mom keeps us near the shore, and you can't dive from there." "Okay" Jeremy said, "Then let's get started." Jeremy sat down on the edge of the ledge. "First thing I want you to learn is a sitting dive. You sit on the edge like I'm doing now. Then put your hands together up over your head, like this. Then you lean forward until you roll off the ledge and into the water. Keep your hands up, so they go into the water first, then your head, and finally your body. You straighten out your body as you go into the water, then curve upward towards the surface of the water again." Jeremy followed his own instructions, demonstrating the procedure for his cousins, and they applauded. He stayed out in the water as the two youngsters sat down on the ledge to try it for themselves. "Take turns, one at a time, so I can watch you" Jeremy told them.

Once each of the twins had done the sitting dive a few times, he turned them back over to his sister and girlfriend, while he went back to help Karen and Caitlyn some more. After giving more pointers to the two young girls, and observing them incorporate the changes into their dives, he left them to practice while he went back to his cousins again. James and John were doing very well and were ready for the next step in their training. "Okay" Jeremy told them, "You look like you're ready for the next step, the standing dive." "Cool" John exclaimed with a smile. Jeremy walked up to the edge of the ledge again and stood with his toes just over the edge. "It's basically the same, but you're standing up this time" he explained to them, "You stand with your toes just over the edge, hands up over your head again, and you roll your body forward and down until your hands are pointed at the water, then push gently with your feet as you roll your body towards the water. Watch me." Jeremy performed the dive with the two boys watching. When he resurfaced above water, he looked up at the waiting boys. "Okay, who's first?" he asked. "Me" John declared. "Okay, do it like you saw me do it" Jeremy said, "And don't forget to take a breath before you roll towards the water." John performed the routine, but did not roll his body properly, and ended up doing more of a belly flop instead. Jeremy quickly swam over and grabbed him, turning the boy over so his face was up and out of the water. "Ow!" that hurt" John said. "You forgot to roll your body" Jeremy responded, "You let yourself just fall off of the ledge. Let's get you back up on the ledge, and I'll demonstrate it for you again."

Jeremy demonstrated the dive two more times for the twins before letting James give it a try. James did better than his brother had, and John's second try was much better this time, with neither boy landing on their bellies. Both boys performed the standing dive several more times before Jeremy returned to his female students again. Jeremy and Charlie continued giving diving instructions for nearly an hour and a half, before they decided that everyone should rest up before they all headed back to shore. When they got back to the west side beach, it was already about four-thirty, and they all sat down on the sandy shore. Fifteen minutes later, they were all out in the water again, swimming and playing games, splashing each other, and just having a really good time. "Okay, time to head back to the village" Jeremy announced at about five-thirty. The younger kids weren't quite ready to quit swimming yet, but the older teens insisted that it was time to leave, and they all headed back towards the hidden door in the mountainside. Jeremy and Karen both made sure that there was nobody else in sight before approaching the door to the passage. Jeremy reached into a crevice in the rock, felt the latch, and opened the door. Karen entered the opening and flipped the switch on the passage wall again, then the younger kids entered, followed by the older ones. Jeremy pulled the door closed behind them and the lights came on in the passageway, so they could all find their way through the mountain, to the door on the other end.

Karen opened the door on the inner side of the mountain so that they could all exit the passageway, then she flipped the light switch to turn off the lights. "When you go back, you'll have to flip the switch on again" she instructed the four older teens, "Use the switch on the outer side to turn off the lights again, before closing the door. That way the lights aren't on all the time with both doors closed." They all proceeded to the path and followed it down towards the village. "Wow! This feels great" exclaimed Charlie, as they all walked along the path. "What does?" Amanda inquired. "Being nude." He replied, "I'm already dry, and I'm not wearing a soggy, wet swimsuit. I didn't even have to use a towel to dry off." "You're right" Amanda agreed, "I really think I'm going to like being a naturist." "You'll love it" Caitlyn told her, "And you'll really like not having tan lines, too." "Cool" Jenny exclaimed with a smile, "I've always wanted a suntan with no tan lines, but there was no place I could go where I could work on one." "Me too" Amanda said, "We live far enough out of town to be able to try it, but I was always afraid to try, because my brother was always around. Now that he and I are both naturists, I don't think I need to worry about that anymore." "Come on" Charlie exclaimed as he moved ahead of the others, "I'm hungry, and we need to shower before going to Aunt Joyce's house." Jeremy started laughing. "James, John. When we sit down to eat, better make sure you don't get between the food and Charlie. That's kind of dangerous when he's real hungry" Jeremy declared. James and John both looked at Charlie with fear and smiles on their faces. Everyone stated laughing.

They all stopped at the shower building on the way and took warm showers before continuing on. Greg and Karen had to turn off when they reached their house, saying good-bye to the others as they went inside. When the remaining group reached Aunt Joyce's, Tomas and Caitlyn continued on down the road towards where they lived and called back good-bye as well. It was ten minutes before six o'clock when the four teens and the twins entered the house. They were greeted by the fragrant smell of delicious foods coming from the kitchen. "Mom!" yelled the twins, "We're home!" Aunt Joyce came out to the front room, smiling. She looked over the group of six youth and smiled. "I see that you all showered already" she said, "I hope you're all hungry, because I've prepared a lot of food for all of us." All the kids started laughing, including Charlie. "What's so funny?" Aunt Joyce asked. "We're all starved" Jeremy replied, "We've been swimming, diving, and playing in the lake for about four hours." "And, Charlie really likes food, so don't get in his way" giggled James and John. Charlie's face started turning red. "I have a high metabolism" Charlie declared, "I eat a lot, but I'm not fat, am I?" "No, you're very slim, Charlie" Aunt Joyce said with a grin, "And I'm glad there's someone here who will enjoy my cooking, and who will eat plenty of it. I prefer not to have too many leftovers. Come on, everything is ready, I just have to put it on the table." "May I help?" asked Amanda. "Me too" Jenny added.

"Certainly girls, come on into the kitchen." Aunt Joyce answered, "The boys can grab some towels from that small table there, to put on the chairs before sitting down at the table, while we women folk get the food on the table."

When the food was all set out on the table, pot roast, mashed potatoes and gravy, peas, rolls, and milk to drink, the three women came and sat down also. After a short before-meal prayer, everyone dug in. Everyone had already gotten plenty to eat and Charlie was about to put some more meat on his plate, but Aunt Joyce suddenly cleared her throat. "Um, Charlie" she said, "Are you sure you want more pot roast? I still have apple pie and ice cream for dessert, you know. I wouldn't want you to be too full, and have to skip dessert." Charlie smiled back at his hostess. "I've got plenty of room for more of this delicious roast" he replied, "And still have some of your pie for dessert." "Don't worry, Aunt Joyce" Amanda chuckled, "My boyfriend here won't miss out on the apple pie and ice cream, trust me." "Matter of fact" Jeremy added with a grin, "I think I'll have a little more pot roast too, before dessert. Swimming makes me real hungry, especially when the food is this good." Aunt Joyce grinned at the compliment. "Okay, you boys help yourselves, I'll go and get the pie" she said, "Amanda, could you come and bring the ice cream back in for me?" "Sure, Aunt Joyce"

Amanda replied as she got up and followed her aunt. When they returned with the pie and ice cream, they discovered that James and John were eating more roast as well. "James, John, are you two still hungry too?" Aunt Joyce asked. "Swimming makes us real hungry" the two answered together with big grins.

When the boys had all finished eating their fill, the dinner plates were gathered up and taken into the kitchen. Aunt Joyce began cutting into one of the two pies that she had made, placing slices onto clean plates, while Jeremy scooped the ice cream and put it on top of the pie. Charlie had two full slices of pie, proving that he did in fact have plenty of room for dessert. After everyone was done eating, Jeremy and Charlie insisted on helping with the dishes. "We just need you to supervise" Jeremy told his aunt, "So we get everything put away in the right place." "Oh, James and John can help you with that" Aunt Joyce declared with a grin, "They know where everything goes, I think." "Mom" the twins groaned, "We always help you with the dishes, drying them and putting them away. You know that we know where everything goes." "Come on then" Jeremy said, "Charlie can bring the dishes in and put the leftovers away. I'll wash the dishes, and you two can dry and put them away." The twins hopped down from their chairs and followed Jeremy into the kitchen. The boys had all the dishes done in half an hour and returned to the women in the front room. Aunt Joyce indicated that the boys should grab their towels from the dining room chairs. "Put them down on the furniture before you sit down, like a true naturist does." The boys all sat down on their towels and relaxed after a truly wonderful meal.

"So, you said that you are camping up by the lake until Sunday" Aunt Joyce said. "Yes" Jeremy answered, "Mom is supposed to pick us up out by the road at about three o'clock in the afternoon." "But we'll be coming here to visit some more, before that" Amanda exclaimed. "Maybe we can help out in the fields some more while we're here, too" Charlie suggested, "I really liked working out in the field this morning, without any clothes on." "We would appreciate having the extra help" Aunt Joyce responded, "We don't get visitors around here very often, you know." "We could come and help out every day" suggested Jenny, "It would probably help Amanda and me with our no tan tan-line tans." "The kids in town usually do their chores in the fields early in the morning" Aunt Joyce explained, "That way they can get done before it gets really hot. And it gives them time to enjoy other activities after lunch that way. Are you sure you want to get up extra early, to get here and work in the fields?" "Maybe we could move our camp to someplace closer to the village" Jeremy said. "But then we'd have to pack everything up, then set up the camp again, and then pack up again on

Sunday" Charlie said, "Do we really want to do all that?" "I have another suggestion instead of that" Aunt Joyce said, "How about you pack everything up, bring it here and store it, then just stay here with us in the house. We have a couple of extra rooms, and you would get a chance to see what living in a naturist community is like." "Oh, that sounds good" Jenny said, "Living in a town and not having to wear any clothes, even with other people around." "Sounds great to me, too" declared Amanda. "If it's okay with Charlie, I think it's a great idea" Jeremy agreed. "It's more than okay with me" Charlie declared, "I'm a naturist now too, and if it means we get to enjoy your aunt's good cooking some more, I'm all for it." Everyone started laughing, with James and John rolling around on the floor.

EXPERIENCING DU-NU

The teens stayed and talked at Aunt Joyce's house until seven-thirty, then had to head back for their camp site, before it got too dark. When they exited the secret passage to the lake side of the mountain, Jeremy made sure the light switch was in the off position before closing the hidden door. They still had about half an hour before the sun would be going down and decided to swim across the lake instead of walking around it. The boys stayed close to the girls as they swam, in case the girls started to get tired. About three quarters of the way across, they stopped and rested until the girls were ready to swim the remaining way to the east shore. They finally reached shore, exhausted, and walked up to the camp site where the girls sat down around the cold fire pit. The fire had died out several hours before, since no one had been around since early morning to put more wood on the fire. The boys got a new fire going in the pit, and they all sat around the warm camp fire, relaxing and chatting about their day, and planning for the next day. They all agreed that they would get up as early as possible, have a quick breakfast of cereal, and then start taking down and packing up everything into the cart and backpacks. They wanted to head out around the lake to the hidden door as soon as possible, so they could get to Village Du-Nu as soon as possible. After completing their plans, they all slipped into their tents and sleeping bags, to get some sleep.

The next morning, Jeremy awoke around five-thirty to find Charlie already up and putting things in his backpack. “You’re up already?” Jeremy exclaimed, “You must be anxious to get going.” “I am” Charlie replied, “I got up around five, when I heard the girls moving around next door. You seem to be the sleepy-head today, the girls have been up for a while, too.” Jeremy quickly crawled out of his sleeping bag and stretched. Charlie already had his sleeping bag rolled up and ready to go and was just about finished putting all his personal stuff in the backpack. “You go ahead and get your stuff together” Charlie said with a grin, “I’ll go and help the girls take down their tent.” Jeremy immediately went to work, rolling up his own sleeping bag, deflating the air mattress, and putting all of his stuff into his backpack. When he finally stepped out of the tent, carrying his sleeping bag and backpack, he saw the others, still nude like himself, already rolling up the girl’s tent. “Did you sweep out all the dirt and sand before dropping the tent” Jeremy inquired. His three friends looked over at him. “We cleaned it out until it was spotless” Jenny replied with a grin. “I checked it, and they had it cleaned really good” Charlie added, “Why don’t you and the girls finish getting that tent cleaned out, while I finish packing this tent up.” The girls came over to the boy’s tent and slipped inside with a small whisk broom, while Jeremy began removing the rain cover from the tent, wiping it off and folding it up. The girls came back out of the tent and tossed the debris they had swept up, out into the brush. "You want to inspect it?" Amanda asked her brother.

Jeremy poked his head into the tent and looked all around. "Looks pretty good" he said, "Cleaner than when Charlie and I clean it after camping trips." "So, should we drop the tent?" Jenny asked with a grin. "Yes" he replied. "Wait" Amanda exclaimed, "We have to zip up the door first." After zipping up the screen and outer doors of the tent, the three of them got the tent down, and arranged so that it was ready to fold and roll up. Charlie had finished packing up the first tent, had hauled some water from the lake up and poured it on the fire pit, and he was now getting the cart cleaned out and ready to pack. They finally started packing everything into the cart. Tents and coolers went in first, then the sleeping bags, tarps, ropes, lanterns and flashlights, tools, and other miscellaneous items. The boys went over to the tree on the other side of the camp and took down the canvas grocery store. Bringing the groceries over to the cart, they removed some cereal for their breakfast and packed the rest into the cart. After eating breakfast around the cold camp fire, they threw the packaging into the recycle garbage bag, tied up the bag, and put it on top of the cart. Charlie and Jeremy then proceeded to cover the cart with the last tarp and tie it all down with a rope. They all looked around their camp site, making sure that they had packed everything, then slipped on their backpacks and marched down to the lake. Reaching the lake shore, they started walking south, to go around the lake to the secret passage on the other side that would take them to Village Du-Nu.

As they walked down the road towards the village, they saw Karen, Greg, Caitlyn, and Tomas out in a field, removing weeds from rows of what looked like lettuce. They waved and continued down to Aunt Joyce's, where they pulled the cart around to the back of the house. Jeremy knocked on the back door, and his aunt soon opened the door with a smile. "You four must have gotten up really early" she declared, "I suppose Jeremy made sure of that." "Actually, Aunt Joyce" Amanda replied with a grin, "Jeremy was the last one to wake up. Jenny and I got up a little before five and started packing our things. Charlie came over a few minutes later and showed us how to roll up the sleeping bags, then went back to his tent to start packing." "Jeremy didn't wake up until about five-thirty" Charlie added with a smile. Aunt Joyce looked at her nephew. "You all must have been very tired from all the work and play you did yesterday" she said. "I sure was" Jeremy responded, "I've never woken up after Charlie before, not on any of our camping trips." "Well, you can store your cart over in that shed" Aunt Joyce said to them, indicating a small structure in the back yard. "We have our food stuff that should probably go in the house" Jeremy replied, "Charlie and I will get them out first." With the food stuff removed from the cart, Charlie and Jeremy started pulling the cart over to the shed, while the girls started hauling the coolers and other dry goods into the house.

With the cart secured in the shed, the boys went back to the house and entered through the back door. Aunt Joyce and the girls had just finished putting the refrigerated stuff into the frig, and the dry goods into the cupboards. "Well, let me show you all to the rooms you'll be staying in for the next three days" Aunt Joyce said. She led them upstairs, and assigned one bedroom to the girls, and another to the boys. Aunt Joyce gathered up all of their clothes, so she could wash them, then directed the four teens to the field where James and John were working with two other young kids that morning. "They got up early today. They want to finish their chores, so they can spend more time with you" she told them. The four teens left the house and headed in the direction that they had been told to go. They found the twins in a field with another boy and a girl, weeding tomato plants. "Hey" Amanda called out to her two nude cousins. James and John looked up and saw the four teens walking towards them. Grins appeared on their faces as they both stood up. "What's left to do?"

Jeremy asked the four younger kids. "Yeah" Charlie declared with a smile, "Hope you have something for us to do." "We're about half done" John answered, "We have four rows of tomatoes to weed today." "What about the rest of the field?" Jeremy inquired. "We're supposed to do them tomorrow and Saturday" James answered. "Why not do it all today?" Charlie asked. James and John starred at the teen boy. "Why would we want to do that?" John asked. "Do you like doing chores?" James added. "Not really" Charlie answered the boys, "But if we finish it all today, that leaves us free to do other things for the next two days, right?"

Jeremy smiled at his cousins. "Charlie likes to get work out of the way, so he can enjoy other things" he said. "Plus, I don't mind doing chores as much, when I don't have to wear clothes. The work isn't quite so bad when I don't end up doing it in hot, sweaty clothes" Charlie explain. James and John looked confused yet. "We're all from a town where everyone has to wear clothes all the time" Jenny interjected, "Being here and not having to wear clothes is so wonderful, that it makes us feel like anything we do in the nude is fun." "Don't worry, boys" Amanda chuckled, "It's just new to us. When we get used to being nude, we'll probably start hating chores again." "Oh, okay" James said, "You had us worried for a little bit, but if we can get the next two days off from chores, then let's try to finish the whole field." "You're from another village?" asked the young girl that was working with James and John. "Yes" Amanda answered, "My name is Amanda and this is my brother, Jeremy. These other two are our friends Jenny and Charlie. "Amanda and Jeremy are our cousins" John pointed out to his friends. "These are our friends, Beth and her brother Ben" James said, "They always work in the same field with us." "We're all glad to meet you" Jeremy said, offering his hand to the two new acquaintances. Beth and Ben shook the hands of the four teenagers, and then they all went back to work weeding the tomatoes. Each teen went to the end of the rows that the four younger kids were working on, and helped finish those rows, then each of the eight proceeded to a new row each.

The four teenagers had become good at weeding from their experience the previous day and were able to keep up with the four younger kids. The entire tomato field was completed by ten-thirty, and after they hauled all the extracted weeds to the disposal area, the eight proceeded to the shower building and cleaned up. The four teens, and James and John said good-bye to Beth and Ben and walked back to Aunt Joyce's. When they all came walking in through the back door, Aunt Joyce was in the kitchen, finishing up with folding clothes. "Oh, you're finally back" she exclaimed, "I was going to come and check on you all when I finished folding these clothes. You've been gone a lot longer than I figured you would." "We did extra weeding in the tomato field" James declared with a grin. "Yeah" John said, "Jeremy, Amanda, and their friends helped us to finished the whole field." "What? You weeded the entire field?" Aunt Joyce gasped. "Yes, my boyfriend here suggested we do the whole field" Amanda replied, as she put her arm around Charlie "He thought we might have the next couple of days off that way." "Well, good work" Aunt Joyce said, "But I don't know if James and John will be able to take the next two days off. The boys, Beth, and Ben have fallen behind in their weeding chores, they still need to catch up on their work yet." "Aw, mom" John and James whined. "I'm sorry, boys, but you knew that you still had work to catch up on" Aunt Joyce declared, "You should have told the others before letting them think you were getting ahead on your chores, instead of just catching up a little bit."

Jeremy looked at his Aunt. "How far behind are they?" he asked. "Well, they were three days behind, before today. Now I guess they are only one day behind" she answered. Jeremy looked at the other teens. "What do you think?" he asked them, "If we help them again tomorrow, like we did today, they should be caught up, maybe even a day ahead." "I'm in" Charlie replied with a grin. "Count us in too" the girls chimed together. "That should give them Saturday off then, right Aunt

Joyce?" Jeremy asked. Aunt Joyce looked at the hopeful faces of her two sons and smiled. "Yes, that would get them caught up, and a day ahead" she replied, "And it's very generous of you four to offer to help." "Hey, we have to earn our keep" Charlie exclaimed with a grin, "A little hard work in exchange for your delicious, home cooked meals." Aunt Joyce smiled, "You're such a charmer, Charlie" she said, "Amanda, you better hang onto this one." Amanda grinned at her aunt, "I'll do my best, Aunt Joyce." "Okay, I need to finish getting something ready for lunch" Aunt Joyce declared, "You kids can take your clothes up to your rooms and pack them for Sunday." The four teens grabbed their clean clothes and headed upstairs to put them into their backpacks. James and John went along, and after the teens finished storing their clothes, invited the teens to come and see their room. When the six returned downstairs, there were a couple of picnic baskets sitting on the dining room table, along with a cooler. Aunt Joyce came out of the kitchen as they entered the room. "Are you all ready to go?" she asked.

The four teens all glanced around at each other with confusion showing on their faces. "Where are we going?" Jeremy asked his aunt. "Oh, I thought James and John might have told you already" she replied, "We're going to the village park for a pot luck lunch." "A pot luck lunch?" Amanda asked. "Yes" Aunt Joyce replied, "Today is June fourth, the date that our little village was founded. The whole village celebrates with a pot luck in the park every year. You'll get to meet a lot of the people there today, but the celebration party is strictly formal." "Formal!" exclaimed Amanda, "All we have with us is every day clothes." "Don't worry, dear" her aunt chuckled, "Everyone just wears their very best birthday suits." All the others watched as the look on Amanda's face slowly changed from confusion to comprehension, and then to a grin. "Oh, I get it" Amanda finally exclaimed, "To a naturist, formal still means nude." "Yes, Amanda" Aunt Joyce chuckled, "But clean also, freshly showered, with only shoes on. Now, we better get going, or we'll be late for the pot luck and Charlie there might have to go hungry. Almost everyone has been out working in the fields all morning, so they're bound to all be hungry also."

The park was already filled with people when they arrived, and everyone was nude, except for shoes and smiles. Greg, Karen, Tomas, Caitlyn, Beth, and Ben all rushed over to welcome the four teens. Shawn and Kathryn came over also, to say hello again. Aunt Joyce and Kathryn started taking the four teens around to introduced them to some friends. All the people they met were very friendly and welcoming. Jeremy notice Charlie starting to look worried. "What's the matter?" he asked his friend. "Huh? What?" Charlie stammered,

"Oh! I was just noticing that everyone seems to be lining up at the food tables. Maybe we should get in line too." "Charlie" Aunt Joyce chuckled, "I was just joking about running out of food, there's plenty of food. Every time we have a pot luck around here, we end up with a lot of food leftover. We'll probably be taking some home with us." "Oh good" Charlie responded, "But I'm still really hungry, and I'd like to get in line. We only had dry cereal for breakfast you know." "Dry cereal? Is that all?" Aunt Joyce gasped, "Why didn't you have more than that?" "We wanted to get here to the village as quickly as possible" Amanda responded, "And we didn't want to start a fire that we'd end up having to put out before leaving the camp, so we agreed to have cereal for breakfast." "Well, let's get over in the food line then" Aunt Joyce declared, "Before Charlie faints from hunger."

They all quickly walked over and got in line to get some food, Charlie leading the way. As they stood in line, several people introduced themselves to the four teenagers, asking them if they were the young people visiting in the village. When they finally got to the first of three food tables, they were amazed by the large assortment of food there. There was a variety of casseroles, ham, some fried chicken, turkey, sandwiches, vegetables, chips, fruits, and breads. The last table was covered with desserts of all kinds, and their mouths watered at the sight. Charlie and the others filled their plates with all kinds of food, then Aunt Joyce led them over to a couple of empty tables. They all sat down on the towels that they had brought along, and then dug into the food on their plates. They were all finishing off their first plates of food when three teenage boys walked up to the group and introduced themselves as Tim, Joe, and Dan. They invited the teens to join in on the volleyball games that would be starting in a little while. Jeremy and Charlie accepted the invitation, saying they would be there as soon as they were finished eating. The girls declined, since it appeared that all the participants were going to be boys, deciding instead to join some girls that were chatting a short distance away. Charlie and Jeremy got up from the table and headed back over to the food table for seconds, since the line was almost gone now. After finishing off their second plates of food, Jeremy, Charlie, James, and John all headed over to where the volleyball game was starting up already.

James and John joined the other spectators sitting off to the sides of the sand volleyball court, while Jeremy and Charlie were asked to join the team that Tim and the other two boys were on. Neither of the boys had ever played volleyball in a sand court before, and it took them a while to get used to it. Their team lost the first game, and two teams of adult men took to the volleyball court to play a new game. Jeremy and Charlie sat down on the side of the court with James and John, and the three boys that had invited them to play came over to join them. "Sorry about how badly we played" Jeremy expressed to the three boys, "Charlie and I have never played volleyball on sand before." "You did pretty good for your first time on sand" Tim replied. "Yeah" Joe added, "But you might want to play without shoes in the next game. Sometimes it's easier to get used to the sand, if you can feel what you're standing on." "Thanks" Jeremy said, "We'll try it without shoes next time, if we get to play again." "If?" Tim said, "We'll be playing again right after this game." "Cool" Charlie exclaimed, "Do we have time to run and get a drink?" "Sure" Tim answered, "This game will be going on for about half an hour to an hour yet."

Charlie got up, followed by Jeremy, James, and John, and they headed back to the picnic table where Aunt Joyce and Kathryn were sitting and talking with some other ladies. As the boys approached the group of ladies, Aunt Joyce saw them coming and reached into the cooler next to her. She smiled and held up bottles of water for the boys. "You must be thirsty" she said, "Did you win your volleyball game?" "No" Charlie replied, "But we'll be playing again, in the next game." "Well, maybe I'll come over and watch you play" Aunt Joyce said. "I'll come too" Kathryn added, "And maybe

I'll see if Karen and Greg want to come and watch, if I can find them." "They're probably over at the water slide" John suggested. "You want us to go and get them?" James asked. "No, that's alright" Kathryn replied with a smile, "I'll go over there myself, and ask them if they want to come watch the game." "Well, we better get back over to the volleyball court" Jeremy declared, "So we can rest up for our next game." The two teen boys headed back over to the volleyball court again. James and John stayed back at the picnic table, to come with Aunt Joyce in a little bit.

Jeremy and Charlie returned to the volleyball court and sat down with the three other boys from their team. "You got any other pointers for us?" Jeremy asked, as he sipped some cool water from his bottle. "Well, you have to remember that the sand gives way when you jump" Tim explained, "You don't have to push as much when playing on solid ground, but playing in sand takes a little more leg muscle." "We got the leg muscle" Charlie told him, "Jeremy and I are on the swim team back at school, and we do a lot of diving." "Cool" Dan exclaimed, "Then you got the strength, you just need to get used to pushing up a little harder from the sand." "You two seemed to be getting used to the sand towards the end of the first game anyway" Tim added, "This next game you'll do a lot better. We may even win this time." The current game in progress lasted another half hour, and then it was time for Jeremy, Charlie, and their team to play again. The team that won against them the last time came onto the court. "We play the same team again" Tim commented, "But on the opposite side of the net this time." "They're good" Charlie commented. "Yeah" Joe responded, "All the players on that team practice and play together all the time. They actually go all over, to play in nude volleyball tournaments." "And you think we have a chance to win against them?" Jeremy exclaimed. "Yeah" Tim answered with a smile, "Our team goes to those tournaments too, but we lost a few of our best players when they moved to another state. With Jake over there, and you two, we have a full team again."

The teams got into position on the sand court. Jeremy saw his aunt and cousins sitting down over on the sideline, along with Jenny, Amanda, Kathryn, Karen, and Greg. "Hey, there's Tomas and Caitlyn with their dad" Charlie exclaimed, pointing to the three of them on the opposite side of the court from Aunt Joyce and the others. "Yeah" Jeremy responded, "And I see Beth and Ben arriving over there. That's probably their mom and dad with them." "Get ready!" called Tim, "Games about to start." Their team was serving first, since the opposing team had won against them in their last game. Tim served the ball over the net, into the middle of the other team court. The ball was tapped almost straight up by the back row middle player, who had stepped forward. He bent down to allow another player from the back row to come up and hit the ball up to a player in the front row. The player on the front row jumped up high and attempted to spike the ball down on their side, but Joe intercepted the ball and knocked it up and to his right. The ball was coming to Jeremy and he was ready. He bumped the ball up to Dan in the front row middle, who returned the ball to the other team by spiking it down in front of the back row middle player. The player tried to intercept the ball again, but missed it, and the ball landed in the sand. One point for their team. Lots of people on the sidelines cheered for them. Joe, who was on Jeremy's left side, patted him on the shoulder. "Good job" he said to Jeremy, "We were just warming up in the first game. Now we'll show them how the game is really played." Jeremy grinned at the compliment.

Tim served the ball again, and got it just over the net, so that when the opposing team player hit it, the ball went back to their side under the net. "That's two points for us" exclaimed Charlie, from the front row, "We got them on the run now." "Don't get over confident" Dan told Charlie, "We got a long way to go, to win this game." Charlie nodded back at Dan. "Sorry he responded, "It's just that we're starting out so good this time." Tim served the next two balls, one gaining them yet a third point, but the fourth one was finally returned after several times back and forth and missed by their team. No point for the other team, since their team had served, but now the opposing team was going to be serving. The ball was served to them, returned back over the net and returned to them again. The ball went back and forth between the two sides for what seemed like a long time but was actually only a few minutes. Finally, the ball was bumped up for Charlie to hit it, and he spiked the ball almost straight down in front of the opposing team player right on the other side of the net. The other team player looked back at Charlie with a confused look, then grinned. "Nicely played" he told Charlie, "I thought you would hit it further over, so I wasn't ready. Next time, I'll be ready for you. You're a better player than I thought you were. You must have been slacking off in that first game." "Nah" Charlie replied with a grin, "That was just my friend's and my first time playing on a sand court."

Charlie and Jeremy were playing a lot better this second game, and their team was leading after forty minutes with a score of nineteen to seventeen. Charlie was back in the front row again, across from the same player. When the ball was hit up to him, he tried spiking the ball the same way he had done at the beginning of the game. The opposing player was ready this time and knocked the ball back to one of his other players, who knocked it back up to him so that he could in turn spike the ball down on Charlie's side of the net, right in front of Charlie. The smile that had been present on Charlie's face for a while now, suddenly disappeared. He starred over at the player on the other side of the net. "I told you I'd be ready the next time" the boy told Charlie. Charlie just stood there with a confused look on his face, then a grin spread across his face. "Yeah, you warned me" he replied to the boy, "I guess I got a little over confident, and figured I could get you again with the same play." The other boy grinned back. "I told you I thought you were a good player" he explained, "I'll be ready for whatever you got from now on. I'm going to be on my guard." "Me too" Charlie replied with a chuckle. The other team served three more times, leaving the score now at nineteen to twenty. Their team rotated and Charlie was in the serving position.

"Serving, nineteen, twenty" Charlie called out as he hit the ball over the net. The other team returned the ball, with it going to Jeremy. He hit the ball up to Dan in the right front row, who bumped it up over the net so that Jake could jump up and hit the ball to the middle left side of the other court for a point. "Serving, twenty, twenty" Charlie called, as he served the ball again. This time the ball was kept in play for nearly three minutes before Dan was able to spike the ball down just inside of the boundary line of the opposing teams court. Charlie was smiling again, as he served the ball once more. "Serving, twenty-one, twenty" he called out. The ball was quickly returned by the other team, with it landing in the sand near Charlie, who had been unprepared for it to come back to him so quickly. The other team served the ball three times, scoring two points, and leaving the score at twenty-one to twenty-two. Dan served the ball two times, bringing the score to a tie at twenty-two to twenty-two. The spectators were really enjoying this game, cheering on the teams that they favored to win. The opposing team was up to serve again. If they scored two points, the game would be over, since the winning team was required to win by two points. The ball came over the net to Charlie, but he was ready this time, and bumped the ball up to Jake, who in turn bumped it over to Jeremy. Jeremy jumped, hit the ball hard, and sent it into the sand on the other team's side.

Jake served the ball over the net. The other team hit the ball three times, setting it up just right. The ball came to Charlie in the back-left corner. He hit the ball up high to Joe, who bumped it up and over to Jeremy. Jeremy jumped high, spiked the ball down, and watched as the player on the other side of the net dropped and hit the ball back up again. Another player jumped up to spike the ball back on their side of the net, but Tim jumped up and blocked the hit, sending the ball back to the other side and in the sand. "Serving, twenty-three, twenty-two, game point" called out Jake as he served the ball over the net again. The ball came back over to them again and they returned it back over the net to the other team. The ball kept going back and forth over the net for almost five minutes. Both teams were getting tired, you could see it in how they were slowing down. Jeremy was trying to stay out of the action as much as possible, only hitting the ball easily over to another player when he had to. Finally, he nodded to Joe, and then to the back-row players. The ball came over the net, back to Charlie. Charlie quickly sent the ball up to the front row where Joe bumped it up and over to Jeremy. Jeremy launched himself up, took aim at the ball in the air, and slammed it down on the other side of the net. The opposing player, exhausted from the five-minute volleying of the ball, just missed the speeding ball, and it hit the sand and bounced back away from the net. "Game" one of the judges shouted. The crowd around the volleyball court cheered and applauded. "A most spectacular game" the judge declared.

The players on both teams walked up to the net to shake hands. "Good game" everyone declared back and forth. Both teams found a shady place together under some trees and sat down to rest and cool off. They could see the adult men's teams starting to play another game back on the court, but they weren't really watching them. "Hey" one of the other team players called over to Charlie, “My name is Dave. I told you I’d be keeping my eyes on you. You played really good, once your over confidence was gone.” “Yeah” Charlie replied with a grin, “Thanks for helping me come down to earth again, and start playing better. My name’s Charlie.” All the other team players looked over at Dave with serious faces. “Hey, don’t look at me like that” he exclaimed to his fellow team mates, “We didn’t lose the game because I crushed his over confidence. We lost because they’re a really good team. We’re going to have to work hard to win the next game against them.” “Next Game!” exclaimed Jeremy and Charlie. “We have to play another game?” Charlie asked. “Of course,” Tim chuckled, “we’re tied, one game each. We have to play a tie-breaker game after the men finish playing again, so you better rest up, cool off, and get ready.” “I’m going to need some fuel to keep me going through another game” Charlie declared. Just at that moment, Aunt Joyce, Kathryn, and the others showed up with several platters full of sandwiches and desserts.

Both teams thanked the women and kids for all the food they had brought over, along with some water. The twelve volleyball players all grabbed a sandwich to eat. After the sandwiches were eaten, they all had a couple of desserts, to get their sugar levels back up, and be ready for the next game. “You all played a terrific game out there” Kathryn announced, “Best game we’ve seen here in several years." "Yes" Aunt Joyce said, "It's been a long time since we've seen a volleyball game go into over-time like that. There'll be a pretty big crowd of spectators gathered around for your tie-breaker game." They all turned their attention over to the men's volleyball game that was going on. "Hey, isn't that Tomas' father playing out there?" Charlie asked, pointing to one of the team players. "Yes, that's my dad" Tomas proudly declared, "He plays pretty well, doesn't he?" "Yes, he does" Jeremy replied. "He's considered to be the best volleyball player out there" Dave said, "He's the team captain, and he coaches all the youth teams in the village as well." The men's game went on for about another fifteen minutes, with Shawn's team winning. "Do they have to play another game after us?" Charlie asked. "No, they don't" Tim answered, "The same team won both games, so a tie-breaker isn't required." "Fifteen minutes until the teen boy's tie-breaker game" announced one of the volleyball judges, repeating his announcement two more times to be sure everyone had heard him.

Tim looked at his fellow team mates. "We better get ready for the game" he said, "Start with some stretches to loosen up. Anyone that needs to go to the bathroom had better go now, because there's no potty breaks during the game." Everyone on both teams started stretching and after a few minutes, most of them got up and headed for the restrooms a short distance away. They still had a few minutes before the game was to start. "Are you going to wear shoes for this game?" Tim asked Jeremy and Charlie, "Now that you're used to playing in the sand." "Not me" Charlie answered, "I think I like it better without shoes." Me too" Jeremy replied, "Bare footed and completely nude, that's how I want to play." "Well, put on some more sunscreen before we start" Joe suggested, "You probably sweated off most of what you had on before that last game." Charlie and Jeremy agreed, and started applying sunscreen to themselves. When they had all but their backs done, they did each other's backs to complete the protection from the sun. Aunt Joyce came over with a towel. "Here, you two, wipe your hands on this" she said, "You don't want your hands to be greasy when playing volleyball." They wiped the sunscreen off of the palms of their hands and handed the towel back to Jeremy's aunt. "Players! Take your positions" came the announcement, "The game begins in one minute."

Jeremy and Charlie's team had won the coin toss and would be serving first. Tim looked at his team members. "Remember, first team to reach fifteen or higher with a two-point lead will win" he declared, "Play your best." The entire team prepared for the start. Tim served the first ball of the game to the center of the other team's court. The ball was returned and went back and forth over the net several times before scoring the first point of the game for their team. The ball was served again and came back quickly into the sand of their court. The opposing team took to serving and ended up scoring two points before having to give up the serve to Charlie. Charlie got to serve two times, gaining one point before the other team served three times, and brought the score up to two to four. Their team served once with no additional point, and four serves later, from the other team, and the score was now two to seven. “Come on team” Tim hollered, “They're half way there already, we need to concentrate.” Dan started serving, and the rest of the team showed their determination, as seven serves later, the score was up to eight to seven. Three serves from the other team and the score was at eight to nine. Jake served next for their team, and when the other team got the serve back again, the score was up to ten to nine. The other team scored only one point this time around, but Jeremy and Charlie's team failed to add to their score during their serve. The other team started serving again, and managed to gain another four points this time, bringing the score up to ten to fourteen.

The determination to win became evident in the team at this point, since the other team only needed one more point to win now. It was Jeremy's turn to serve, and he felt the pressure. Concentrating, he put the ball into play. His team performed exceptionally well, and scored the point. The next two serves scored points as well, and the score was now at thirteen to fourteen. They scored two more points during the next three serves, so the score was up to fifteen to fourteen. The other team was up to serve now, and the ball came over to Joe. He bumped the ball up to Charlie, who set it up for Dan. Dan jumped above the net to spike the ball, but when he hit the ball, the player on the opposite side blocked the hit and knocked it back into the sand on their side again. The score was tied now at fifteen, and the other team was still serving. Everyone was tired at this point, as the game had been going on for over half an hour already. The next serve came to Jeremy, who hit the ball high up to Dan in the opposite corner of their court. Dan bumped the ball up high, over Charlie's head and to Tim. Tim hit the ball hard over the net, but a player on the other team managed to get it and send it up to the front row, where his team mate immediately spiked the ball down in the middle of their team. The score now stood at fifteen to sixteen. One more point to the other team, and the game would be over. The serve came over to Joe, who hit it up to the front row, where Charlie smacked it over the net. The ball was hit up to the opposing players at the net, where one player set the ball up and another spiked it down to the sand for a point, and a win.

Jeremy and Charlie stood there with the other team players, disappointed in their loss. "Game and match to team one" the judge announced, "An excellent exhibition by both teams. Thank you." The players walked up to the net again to shake hands with the opposing team. When Charlie and Dave shook hands, Dave held onto Charlie's hand. "You do play an excellent game of volleyball" he told Charlie, and Jeremy who was right behind Charlie, "I don't know where Tim found two such skilled players, but you gave my team a pretty good workout, and had me worried. I hope we can get to know each other better, once you get settled in." "Get settle in?" Charlie questioned. "Yeah, you two are new in the village, right?" Dave said. "We don't live here in Village Du-Nu" Charlie responded. "What?" Dave exclaimed, "You don't live here? Where are you from then?" "We're from the town of Bon Amis east of here" Jeremy explained, as members of both teams gathered all around Charlie and himself. "We were camping up at the lake" Charlie continued, "We went exploring, and found our way here." "Does anyone else from the village know about you?" Tim asked. "Oh, sure" Charlie answered, "Jeremy's Aunt Joyce lives here. We're staying at her house until we leave on Sunday." "Kathryn and Shawn know about us too" Jeremy added, "And of course their kids." "Oh" Dave said, "I suppose if they all know, then you're okay. We're not supposed to tell anyone from outside of the village about where we live." "We know" Charlie responded, "And none of us plans to tell anyone else about this place. Not me or Jeremy, or Jeremy's sister Amanda or his girlfriend Jenny." "Well, we might tell my mom" Jeremy interjected. "No, you can't tell her" Tim exclaimed, "If she finds out about us here, she might tell others, and then everyone will want to come here to stare at us."

"Jeremy and Amanda's mom won't tell anyone about Village Du-Nu" Charlie chuckled. "How do you know that for sure?" Joe asked. Jeremy smiled around at everyone. "Because she already knows about this place" he explained, "We found out that our mom actually grew up here in Village Du-Nu, just like my Aunt Joyce, and my cousins James and John." "Your mom grew up here, of course" Tim said, "Joyce is always talking about her sister, and her nephew and niece, and how someday they might all be living here again." "Well, maybe we might want to live here" Jeremy responded, "Amanda and I really like this place, and we've come to like not wearing clothes. But when we get home, we'll have to see if anything changes. If we decide that we don't want to live here, we'll still keep this place a secret. And Aunt Joyce told us that my mom plans on moving back here after my sister and I have moved away from home, after school." "I sure hope you all decide to come here to live" Tim said with a grin, "We need good volleyball players like you and Charlie, to give some good competition to Dave and his team." Everyone started laughing and headed up to the picnic tables for some refreshment, especially since there was ice cream being served after the volleyball games concluded.

Everyone was tired when they finally got home from the village park, and the celebration. Jeremy and Charlie carried the sleeping James and John upstairs and put them into their beds while Amanda and Jenny watched from the doorway. Then the four teens went to their rooms and crawled into bed. Everyone slept very well that night, after a long and exhausting day of work and play. It felt wonderful, living in a naturist village.

WORK AND PLAY IN DU-NU

The next morning, Aunt Joyce came upstairs and woke everyone up just after seven o'clock. They reluctantly got out of bed and headed down to the kitchen. "Isn't it nice to just get out of bed and go" Amanda giggled, "No clothes to pick out and put on." "And everything you're wearing is so coordinated" Jenny chuckled. Aunt Joyce had breakfast already on the table for them. Scrambled eggs, sausage, and toast, with orange juice and milk to drink. They had all brought their towels with them, and they placed them on the chairs before sitting down to eat. Aunt Joyce chuckled at the sight. "What's funny, Aunt Joyce?" asked Amanda. "Just that you are all getting trained really well as naturists" she replied, "I didn't even have to remind you to sit on towels." "Why do naturists always sit on towels anyway?" Charlie mumbled with his mouth full of eggs. "It's for sanitary reasons, Charlie" Aunt Joyce responded, "You wouldn't want to sit down where someone else's bare butt has been, without your towel between your butt and the seat, would you?" He thought about that for a few seconds before answering. "I guess not" he said with a frown and then went back to eating. "What field do we have to weed today?" James asked his mother. "You have the potato field to do today" Aunt Joyce replied, "Do you think that the six of you, plus Beth and Ben, will be able to complete the entire field?" "We'll sure try our best" Jeremy declared.

After everyone was finished eating, they all started putting on sunscreen. James and John did each other's back, Jenny and Amanda did each other, and Charlie and Jeremy did each other. Ten minutes before eight, they all left the house with James and John leading the way to the potato field. Beth and Ben were just arriving as the six got to the field. Splitting into two groups of four, each group went to opposite ends of the field, and started working on the first four rows, towards the middle where they would all meet. It took them forty-five minutes to complete the first four rows and haul the weeds over to the incinerators. They returned to the field and each one of them took one of the eight remaining rows for themselves. When they finished those eight rows, they would be done for the day, and have Saturday off from chores. It took them an hour and forty-five minutes to finish off the field and haul all the weeds over to the incinerators. Beth and Ben headed for the showers before they headed back home. "James, John" Jeremy said, "You two can go and take showers, and then go home too. The four of us are going to go and help Karen, Greg, Tomas, and Caitlyn in their field." "Can't we come and help too?" John asked. "Yeah, can't we help too?" James said. "You don't have to do that" Amanda said with a smile. "But we want to" the twins chorused together. "You like doing chores now?" Charlie teased, "We must be rubbing off on you two." "If you really want to help, we won't stop you from coming along" Jeremy responded, "But if you start getting tired, you should go shower, then go home and rest, while waiting for the rest of us to finish."

The six walked over to the cucumber field and found the four other youth weeding away. "How's it going?" Charlie called out as they all approached. "We've already started on tomorrows work" Karen answered, "We're a fourth of the way through, we only have these four rows left." How about we help you" Jeremy offered, "Maybe you'll get done before lunch that way." "Sure" the four responded. The four teens went to the end of the rows that the four youth were working on and began weeding towards them. James and John were given the task of collecting up all the pulled weeds and piling them up at the edge of the road. It only took about half an hour to complete the weeding, then the ten of them gathered up the weeds and hauled them over to the incinerators. "I need a shower" Jenny declared. "Me too" said Amanda. "I think we all need to take showers" Jeremy exclaimed. "Yeah, we're all hot and stinky" Charlie said with a laugh. They all headed for the shower building, where they took warm showers to clean up and then cool showers to cool off a little. It was fifteen minutes to twelve, almost lunch time, so they all headed off to their homes for lunch.

James, John, and the four teenagers all walked into the house and called out to Aunt Joyce that they were back. Aunt Joyce came out of the kitchen. "Finally, your back" she exclaimed, "I was wondering what was taking you so long again today. I figured that you would all be back around eleven." "We went and helped Greg and Karen's team with their field" James and John said with grins on their faces. "What?" Aunt Joyce gasped, "Who are you two? My boys hate doing chores in the field. What did you do with my two wonderful little boys?" "Mom!" the two twins moaned, "We just wanted to go along and help when Jeremy, Amanda, Charlie, and Jenny said they were going to help them." "Well, you four teenagers sure are having a positive influence on my boys" she declared, "I would love to have you around to influence them some more." Maybe we can come here to visit you, now that we've become naturists" Amanda said with a smile. "That would be nice" her aunt responded. "What's for lunch?" Charlie suddenly asked, "I'm..." "HUNGRY!" everyone said along with him. Charlie's face turned red. "Well, yeah. I am" he said. "I've got some soup on the stove, and some sandwiches" Aunt Joyce announced, "Everyone take a seat around the dining room table.

Amanda and Jenny helped get lunch by setting the table and helping Aunt Joyce bring in all the food. They all sat down and started eating. “So, what do you have planned for this afternoon?” Aunt Joyce asked. “Swimming!” the twins chorused together, “We want to go to the lake and swim.” “James, John” Aunt Joyce exclaimed, “I was asking our guests what THEIR plans were, not what you wanted.” The teens all looked from Aunt Joyce to the twins. “We were actually hoping that James and John might show us around the village a little” Amanda said. “If they would be willing to take us on a tour, then we’ll go swimming with them afterwards, up at the lake” Charlie added. The twins looked at each other, then over at their mother. “Would that be okay?” John asked his mother. She looked back at her sons with a smile. “Yes, that would be fine” she replied, “But you should also invite Karen and Greg along. They might like to show off our little village too.” “That would be great” Jeremy said, “We could see if Tomas, Caitlyn, Beth, and Ben would like to come also.”

Aunt Joyce made a quick call and returned to the dining room table. They finished up their lunch, and the boys had started doing the dishes out in the kitchen, when there was a knock at the back door. Karen and Greg came in and saw the boys washing dishes. “You’re just in time” Jeremy exclaimed, “Girls go in the dining room while boys do the dishes.” Karen grinned at her brother. "Looks like you've got work to do" she told him as she walked out of the kitchen giggling. Greg looked at the other boys with a worried look. "Don't worry, Greg, the four of us have a routine, and you don't have to help" Jeremy said, "Just sit down in here and wait for us to finish, or you can go into the dining room with the girls to wait." Greg put the towel that he was carrying on a kitchen chair and sat down. "Tomas is coming with us" Greg declared, "I don't know about Caitlyn. We can stop and pick Tomas up when we go by his house." "What about Beth and Ben?" Charlie inquired. "They aren't in the village this afternoon" Greg answered, "Their mom took them into town for a dentist appointment." "Oh, yuck" Charlie responded, "I'll bet they didn't really want to go, did then." "You got that right" Karen said from the doorway to the dining room, "They don't mind having their teeth cleaned, but they hate having to put on clothes to go to town." "We used to have a dentist living here in our village" James declared, "But he moved to another state. He's Bill and Grant's father, the two boys that used to be on Tim's volleyball team."

With the dishes done, the boys went into the dining room to get the girls. "Dishes are done and put away" declared Charlie with a smile, "You girls ready to go?" "Yes" answered Amanda as she stood up, "Let's go have a good look at this village where I'm going to move to after school." "You've already decided that?" Aunt Joyce asked. "I'm pretty sure" she replied, "After I finish college, I want to try and move here to live." "I don't know about me, yet" Jeremy stated, "I need to get to college first, then graduate, and then see how I feel. I'll want to find a job, and I don't know if there'll be an engineering job close enough to here, so I can commute from here." "That's good thinking, Jeremy" Aunt Joyce said, "Plan for your future, but don't try to set anything in concrete just yet. Your mother never planned to move away from the village she grew up in, but she fell in love with your father, and that affected her plans." "Well, let's go already" exclaimed James and John together. "We want to show you the village, and then go swimming" John added. "So, lead on" Amanda said with a chuckle, "You're the tour guides after all." "Hey, I didn't get a tour map" Charlie complained with a laugh. "Funny, Charlie. Very funny" Jeremy said as he followed the twins out the door, "Come on, let's go."

The young kids took the four teens north to the edge of the village, stopping on the way to have Tomas join them, and Caitlyn had decided to come along with them also. "This grove of fruit trees goes all around the village" Karen said, "But you already know that, right?" "Yes" Jenny answered, "We went through the trees the other day, when we walked around the village." "And you saw all the crop fields on the inside of the grove?'

Karen asked. "Yes" Amanda said, "We saw corn, potatoes, cucumbers, carrots, lettuce, peas, tomatoes, cabbage, broccoli, and cauliflower." "Well, we have fruits growing in fields on the other side of this part of the fruit trees" Karen explained, "Just past the hedge on the back side of the grove." "Fruits?" Charlie said, "What kind?" "We got strawberries" Greg exclaimed. "And raspberries" added James. "And blueberries" said John. "And cantaloupe and watermelon" finished Tomas with a grin. "Wow" exclaimed Jeremy, "You got everything except farm animals." "We have them too" Caitlyn informed them, "But they're all further north, away from the town, so the smell doesn't bother everyone in the village." "There are two farm houses about a mile north of here" Karen added, "That's were some villagers live, so they can take care of the cows, pigs, and chickens. There are some wheat and hay fields around the farms too, so the animals have food to eat." "You do have everything here then" Amanda declared.

They followed the path to the back of the grove where it intersected another road that went to the left and the right, going all around the backside of the grove. "This other road lets us get the apples we pick loaded into carts to haul out to sell" Karen explained, "Following the road we're on will take us further north to the farms." They walked north on the road for about half an hour before they spotted the farm houses, one on each side of the road. As they got closer, they spotted cows out in fenced off fields. “I can tell that we’re close to the farms now” Jeremy declared, “It smells like we’re out in farm land now.” Ten minutes later they were on the road in front of the two farm houses, and they saw a woman out in the front yard of one house, weeding a flower bed. “Hello Jeanne” Caitlyn called out to her. The woman stood up and came over to the inside of the gate that the ten kids were standing outside of. “Hello Caitlyn, Karen, Tomas, and Greg” the woman said, “Is that James and John, the twins with you?” “Yes” Caitlyn replied, “And we have their cousins, Jeremy and Amanda, and their friends, Jenny and Charlie with us.” “Oh, yes” Jeanne said, “I recognize the two older boys, they were playing volleyball at the park yesterday. They were on the team playing against my Dave’s team.”

“You’re Dave’s mother?” Charlie said, “I’m Charlie. I got to talk to Dave between games yesterday. He’s a really good player.” “He talked about you last night too” Jeanne said, “He said you were a good player too, and he wouldn’t mind having you play on his team. Are you all here to see Dave?” “No, we’re being given a tour of the village and area around it” Jeremy explained as he motioned to himself and the other three teens, “We’re not from the village, we’re from Bon Amis, the town east of here, we’re just visiting until Sunday.” “Visiting?”

Jeanne said with a concerned look. “Yes” Amanda chimed in, “James and John’s mother is our Aunt Joyce, and our mother grew up here in Village Du-Nu.” “Oh, then your mother must be Grace” Jeanne exclaimed, “I grew up with your mother and your aunt. We were very good friends. I was so sad to hear that your mother wasn’t going to be coming back here after college.” “We just found out that our mother grew up here, yesterday” Jeremy said, “Amanda and I wish we could have grown up here, but I guess our father didn’t want that.” “Well, welcome to our village, I’m glad you got to visit us” Jeanne said, “And say hello to your mother for me.” “She doesn’t know we are here” Amanda explained, “We were camping up by the lake and found our way here while exploring an underwater tunnel behind the waterfall.” “We promised not to tell anyone else about the village” Jeremy added. “Not even your mother?” Jeanne asked. “We’ll see about that when we get back home on Sunday” Jeremy said, “Right now I don’t think we will say anything, for a while at least.”

“We have to be going back to the village now, Jeanne” Karen said, “When we finish showing them most everything, we’re going to go swimming up at the lake.” “Okay, have fun” Jeanne replied, “I’ll let Dave know that you stopped by, Charlie.” “Thanks” Charlie responded, “Nice meeting you.” They all waved good-bye as they turned and headed back along the road on their way back to town. When they reached the village again, it was around two-thirty, and the younger kids were anxious to go to the lake. Jeremy had the kids go and inform their parents that they were going up to the lake, before they started up to the mountain side. They all started applying sunscreen to themselves on the way up the path, helping each other to get the lotion on each other's backs. Karen opened the hidden door on the village side and they all started through the lighted passage. Jeremy reached the lake side of the passage first and carefully opened the door on that side and looked all around outside, to be sure no one else would see the ten of them coming out of the side of the mountain. They all immediately ran to the lake and into the cool water. They swam around in the water for about fifteen minutes, then everyone decided that they would like to go out to the ledge and practice their diving. A fifteen-minute swim, and they were all sitting on the ledge, resting up.

Greg was the first one to finally get up, go to the edge of the ledge, and dive in. The rest all followed him and started diving into the water also, except for the twins and Jeremy. When Jenny came back up on the ledge, Jeremy asked her if she would stay on the ledge while he went into the water and observed James and John diving in. "Sure" Jenny agreed, "I'll help you with teaching them some more diving." Jeremy dove into the water and resurfaced quickly, then had the twins dive in one at a time so he could see how well they were doing at diving. John dove in first, just like Jeremy had taught the boys. Toes over the edge of the ledge, arms and hands up over his head, bending forward and rolling forward into the water. James waited until his brother was out of the way and then dove in himself. Jeremy followed the boys up onto the ledge and indicated that Jenny could go ahead and dive in if she wanted to. "You both did very well" he praised the twins, "Now I want to see how well you can just jump into the water, but in a certain way." "A certain way?" James inquired. "Yes" Jeremy replied, "I want you to stand on the edge of the ledge like you do when diving, but instead of rolling forward and going hands first into the water, I want you to jump up and out into the water. I want to see how far out you can jump, and go in feet first, but don't jump out into the waterfall."

Both boys stared back at him. "We can't jump that far" John exclaimed, "The waterfall is way too far out." "Well, I just wanted to make sure" Jeremy responded with a grin, "Just in case you have super strength or something." "You don't really think we have super strength" John said, "You're just joshing us." "I don't know" Jeremy replied with a straight face, "You're both a couple of super cool cousins, and super-fast learners, so you might have other super powers too." "Well, you're a super cool cousin, too" James declared. "Guess it must run in your family" said Charlie as he came up to the boys, "Your cousin Amanda is super pretty, super smart, and super cool also." Jeremy and the twins stared at Charlie. "Really?" Jeremy replied, "She's super pretty, sure. Maybe even super cool, but what makes you say she's super smart?" "Well" answered Charlie with a grin, "She must be, since she chose me as her boyfriend." All four of them started laughing at that comment. "What's so funny" Amanda asked from behind them, startling everyone. "Huh? How long have you been there?" Charlie stammered. "Long enough to hear that I'm from a super family" she declared, "And just so you know, Charlie, I had to choose you as my boyfriend." Charlie eyed her carefully. "You had to?" he said. "Yes" she replied, "Who else would a smart, super pretty, super cool girl chose, except a super boyfriend like you." "Okay, James and John, you better show me your jumps now" Jeremy announced, "It's getting a little too thick up here right now, and the water might help rinse some of the sticky stuff off of us."

James walked up to the edge and prepared to jump. "Bend your legs a little at the knees" Jeremy instructed, "It will help you jump further. "Okay" James replied with a giggle, as he bent at the knees, "But it might be harder to not jump into the waterfall this way." He landed in the water feet first, about four feet from the ledge.

"That's excellent" Jeremy praised him. John positioned himself at the edge next and bent at the knees. He looked back at Jeremy and smiled. "I remember" he said with a chuckle, "Stay out of the waterfall." He jumped, and landed right where his brother had a moment before. "Great jump" Jeremy declared when his cousin resurfaced, "Now, both of you can come back up here and I'll instruct you on your next dive."

The two young boys got back up on the ledge, ready to learn more about diving from their older cousin. "Okay" Jeremy said to them, "This time, you'll be diving off almost the same way as you did before, but this time I want you to push your bodies up and forward. Bend your bodies over like when you did the last standing dives. You'll want to get bent over enough so that when you start going down again, you have your hands up over your heads and pointing down towards the water. I'm going to demonstrate for you, so watch carefully. If you don't do it right, you'll end up doing a belly flop." Charlie stepped forward to the edge of the ledge. "I'll demonstrate it for you" he said to the twins. James and John watched closely as Charlie launched off of the ledge, arched in the air, and came down in the water hands first and gliding into the water. When Charlie resurfaced, the twins were applauding him, along with everyone else up on the ledge. "That was really good" Tomas called out to Charlie, "I think that was the best dive I've seen you do here." "Nah, it was just another dive" Charlie replied with a red face. "No, it wasn't" Jeremy said, "That really was an exceptional dive. Perfect launch, perfect form, and perfect entry into the water." "Do you really think so" Charlie asked. "Yes" Jeremy replied with a grin, "I guess you were listening when I described how to do it to my cousins. You demonstrated exactly how it should look when performed right." Charlie frowned at his friend, not knowing if he was being teased or not, and swam over to the steps.

Charlie climbed up onto the ledge and came over to Jeremy. "Now, I'll demonstrate for you" Jeremy told the twins, "Watch carefully again, okay." "Okay" the two boys answered. Jeremy went through the dive steps and launched off of the ledge and into the water. When he surfaced in the water, he looked up at James and John. "Do you think you're ready to try it now? He asked them. "I am" John exclaimed. "Me too" James said, "But I think Charlie's dive was a little better than yours, Jeremy." Jeremy stared at his cousin. "He's right, big brother" Amanda declared, "Charlie's dive was a little more graceful than yours." "Really?" Jeremy said with a frown. "Sorry, Jeremy" Jenny chimed in, "They're right, Charlie dove a little better than you, not that there was anything wrong with your dive." He stared up at everyone on the ledge and observed that they were all shaking their heads in confirmation of the dive appraisals. “Well, I guess I’ve been neglecting my diving practice” he exclaimed with a smile, “I’ll have to start practicing a lot more after we get James and John there diving properly.” Jeremy remained in the water while the twins performed the dive one at a time. Both boys did fairly well on their first tries, although they were both a little between a dive and a belly flop. A little more instruction from Charlie, a little rest to recuperate, and both boys were ready to try again. They performed a few more dives under close supervision, before being left to practice on their own.

Everyone continued to dive and jump off of the ledge for about another hour, Jeremy especially, until the teens decided that they should rest for a while, and then head back to shore. None of the younger kids complained about going to the beach, since they were all starting to get a little tired. They all rested for about fifteen minutes, then swam back to shore and rested again on the sand, talking about how well everyone was diving after Charlie and Jeremy’s help to learn some techniques. “You all still think that Charlie’s one dive was better than mine” Jeremy finally asked. “Yes” everyone exclaimed, practically in unison. “But don’t worry about it” Charlie said with a chuckle, “You’ll get better with more practice. And someday you may be as good as me.” “Boo!” everyone exclaimed. Amanda looked over at her boyfriend. “Charlie, that wasn’t funny” she told him with a smile, “Your sense of humor needs some work. Maybe it means you’re getting hungry. You need some nice hot food to refuel you.” Charlie grinned. “Yeah” he replied, “Food. Charlie need food.” Everyone started laughing, and Charlie apologized to Jeremy for his bad joke a few minutes earlier. “That’s okay” Jeremy replied, “I do need to practice some more. I really do love teaching the kids to dive, but I’ve been letting my own practice lapse a little.” “Well, I think you should be able to practice more now” Charlie told him, “All the kids just need to practice on their own now, and perfect what they’ve learned from us. We need to start practicing ourselves, or they may get to be better than their teachers.” “You’re right” Jeremy agreed, “Tomorrow, we just let them practice on their own.”

The ten kids swam and played games in the lake, resting on the sandy beach occasionally, for almost another hour, then they headed back for the village. They all stopped at the shower building on the way home, and took some nice warm showers, then dried off in the open air as they continued walking along the road. Greg and Karen left the group as they all passed their house, waving good-bye. Caitlyn and Tomas continued on down the road, saying good-bye as the teens and the twins turned to go up to Aunt Joyce’s house. When they came in the front door, Aunt Joyce came out of the dining room. "Oh, good" Aunt Joyce said, "You're all back in time for supper." "Was there any doubt that we wouldn't be here for supper?" Charlie inquired with a grin. Aunt Joyce looked at him and started laughing. "No, I guess not, Charlie" she said, "Why don't you all grab some dry towels and have a seat at the dining room table. Supper will be ready in about ten minutes." The six youth had just sat down when there was a knock at the back door. "James, can you answer the door?" Aunt Joyce called out. James got up and went to the back door. When he opened it, there stood Greg and Karen with their parents. "Hi" Greg said. "Are we in time for supper?" asked Kathryn with a smile. James looked over at his mother. "It's Greg, Karen, and their mom and dad" he declared. "Oh, good" Joyce said, "They're joining us for supper, let them in." Aunt Joyce went over to the door while wiping her hands on a towel. "You're just in time" she said to Kathryn, "I've got everything here ready to put on the table." "I brought a couple of pies for dessert" Kathryn said, "Apple and cherry."

Kathryn helped Joyce put everything on the dining room table, while her husband, Jamal set up a folding table that he had brought along, in the entryway between the living room and dining room. "James, John, Karen, and Greg, you'll be sitting at the small table here" Joyce announced as she put a table cloth over the folding table, "The rest of us will be at the big table." She grabbed the plates, utensils, and glasses from the corner of the dining room table and placed them on the small table for the four younger kids. Kathryn walked over to her husband and put her arm around his neck. "Amanda, Jeremy, Jenny, and Charlie, this is my husband, Jamal" she said, pointing to each of the teens as she introduced them. "Glad to meet you all" Jamal responded, "I've been hearing a lot about you from my son and daughter." The four teens expressed their pleasure in meeting Greg and Karen's father, and they all sat down at the table. Aunt Joyce and Kathryn finished putting all the food on the table and sat down also. Jamal gave the blessing before they started digging into the food. They had meatloaf, mashed potatoes and gravy, peas, and rolls.

Jamal's eyes started getting really big as he watched the four teens eating. He was especially fascinated by Charlie, who seemed to be the biggest eater. "You all seem to be pretty hungry" he said, "we worked you pretty hard today, I hear." "They started out weeding an entire field of potatoes with James, John, Beth, and Ben this morning" Joyce said. "Then they came over and helped Greg, Tomas, Caitlyn, and me with the cucumber field" Karen announced. "We took them on a tour of the village after lunch, way out to the farms" added Greg.

"And then, they all spent the rest of the afternoon up at the lake, swimming" finished up Aunt Joyce. "You've had a busy day then" Jamal exclaimed, "And you're all probably famished." "Especially, Charlie" Amanda replied with a chuckle. "Yeah, I'm a bottomless pit when it comes to food" Charlie declared between mouthfuls. Everyone laughed. "Food doesn't go to waste very much with my Charlie around" Amanda said as she hugged her boyfriend. "I hear that both Charlie and Jeremy are pretty good divers" Jamal said, "And that they have been teaching some of the younger kids in the village how to dive." "We're on the school swim team" Jeremy responded, "And we've enjoyed helping all our friends to be better at diving." "Jeremy is our swim team captain" Charlie declared, "He's the best swimmer and diver on the team." Jeremy blushed a little. "I used to be the best diver on the team" he said, "Charlie passed me by this afternoon with a perfect dive. I have six witnesses who will attest to that."

After supper, the four younger kids went outside to play, while the teens and adults went into the living room to chat for a while. The teens hadn't met Jamal before that evening, because he had been away on village business, trying to find markets for all their produce. The teens kept talking about what they liked about the village, expressing how much they enjoyed not having to wear any clothing. They asked questions and received answers from the three adults, until a little after nine o'clock, when the four kids came back in through the back door. "Is it nine o'clock yet" James asked his mother. "Yes, it's a little after nine" she answered, "Time for you and your brother to head off to bed." "Ah mom!" John exclaimed, "Do we have to?" "Yes" Aunt Joyce said, "You've been working and playing hard all day. You need to get a good night's sleep." Reluctantly, the two boys said good night and headed up the stairs to their bedroom. "I think we should probably head home and get our two off to bed also" Kathryn said to her husband. "Yes" he replied, "And I would like to get a good night's sleep too." Kathryn and Jamal got up and thanked Joyce for inviting them over for supper. "Is everything arranged for tomorrow?" Joyce asked Kathryn. "Yes" she replied, "It's all set. We can head out at nine-thirty in the morning." "See you tomorrow then" Joyce replied. Kathryn, Jamal, Karen, and Greg all left through the back door saying good-bye, and Aunt Joyce turned to the four teens. "I would guess that you four are rather tired by now also" she said, "I know that I am." The teens agreed, and they headed upstairs to their bedrooms, to get some sleep.

PICNIC AT THE LAKE

The four teens slept quite well during the night, after all the work and play from the day before, and having been up until about nine-thirty. They didn't wake up until seven-thirty, when James and John came into the boy's bedroom, and Aunt Joyce went into the girl's bedroom, to wake them all up. Still being half asleep after the young boys had left, Jeremy and Charlie sat up on opposite sides of the bed and started looking around for their clothes. "Hey, where are my..." Charlie began, then stopped and started chuckling. He saw Jeremy looking around, confused. "You looking for your clothes? he asked his friend. "Yeah" Jeremy replied, then his eyes popped open and he looked first at himself and then at his nude friend. "Oh, yeah" he exclaimed, "We don't need clothes, we're in Village Du-Nu!" The boys got up and left the room. As they walked down the hall toward the stairs, and were breathing in the delicious smell of breakfast cooking, the girls walked out of their room, giggling. "What's funny" Charlie inquired. "We woke up and started looking for our clothes" Amanda answered, "Then we realized that we don't need any." "You've been going nude for four whole days, and now you start looking for clothes to wear, that's weird" Jeremy stated. "Why is it weird?" asked his sister. "Because" Charlie chuckled, "We got up and started looking for our clothes too." They all came down the stairs laughing together, and walked into the dining room.

Aunt Joyce was just placing a platter of scrambled eggs, and a plate of sausage links on the table, beside a bowl of hash browns and plate of toast. “Well, it sounds like you four are in good spirits” she said, “What’s so amusing?” “Something happened to all of us when we got up” Amanda responded, “Something that that you and the twins have probably never experienced.” “Oh?” Aunt Joyce declared with a grin, “Let me guess. You all got up and started looking around for clothes to wear, then remembered that you’ve been going without clothes for several days already.” “How did you know that?” Charlie asked, “Are you psychic?” “No, it’s just something most new naturists experience occasionally, until they get used to being naturists” Aunt Joyce replied, “Nothing really unusual. But when you get used to being nude, you’ll have to be careful, so you don’t go out in the textile world without clothes on.” “We’re going on a picnic today” declared John, with his mouth full of eggs. “John, don’t talk with your mouth full” scolded his mother. “We’re going on a picnic?” Charlie asked of John, “Where?” John finished the eggs in his mouth and grinned at the four teens. “At the lake” he said, “A big picnic. With all of us, and Greg, Karen, and their mom and dad, and Tomas and Caitlyn with their dad, and Ben, Beth, and their mom.” A man walked out of the kitchen at that moment and into the dining room. "All of us, includes me" he said with a grin. "Uncle Frank!" exclaimed Jeremy and Amanda together.

"When did you get here" asked Jeremy, "Aunt Joyce said you were away on business for the village. "I was" Uncle Frank answered, "I finished up early and got back late last night, after you were already in bed. Your aunt told me about having visitors in the village, and that she and Kathryn were planning a picnic for today, with most of the friends that you've mad, so I kind of invited myself along. I refuse to miss out on your aunt's fried chicken and potato salad, you know." "Yummy, fried chicken and potato salad" Charlie repeated. "Now, let me see" Uncle Frank declared, "You must be Charlie, right?" Charlie turned red faced. "Y-yes" he replied, "I'm Jeremy's friend." "I've heard a little bit about you" Uncle Frank said with a smile, "I'm glad to hear that there's someone else here besides me, who knows how to enjoy good food. I'll have some competition." Charlie looked confused. Aunt Joyce started chuckling, along with the twins, Amanda, and Jeremy. "Charlie" she began, "My husband here loves food too, and he may be an even bigger eater than you, so if you want to keep your title of the biggest eater, you'll have to work hard for it today." "Now let me see" Uncle Frank said, "Since I obviously know my niece and nephew already, and Charlie and I have now been introduced, that leaves this other lovely young lady, who must be Jenny." "Yes sir" Jenny replied. "She's my girlfriend already, Uncle Frank" Jeremy stated with a smile, "And you've already got Aunt Joyce, so don't try luring her away from me, okay?" "Okay" he replied, putting his arm around their aunt, "I'm kind of stuck on this beautiful gal here anyway."

After finishing breakfast, it was time to head for the village park, where all the families were going to meet before heading up to the lake. They left the house, and Shawn, Caitlyn, and Tomas were coming up the road. They waited for them, and walked to the park together. Arriving at the park, they saw Beth and Ben waiting with their mother. They chatted for about five minutes before Kathryn, Jamal, Karen, and Greg arrived, and then all eighteen started up the road to the mountain side secret door and passage. The entire group arrived at the lake around ten o'clock and setup the picnic in the large open area that the teens had found seven days earlier. The open area bordered the lake on the east side and had a large firepit near some large boulders. "We'll need some wood for a fire" Shawn announced, "Who wants to help with gathering some?" "There's a couple piles of dry wood on the path that goes south of here" Charlie exclaimed, "And another pile to the north." "How do you know that?" Uncle Frank inquired. "We made the piles of wood" Jeremy exclaimed, "When we were exploring all around the lake, we gathered up good fire wood and left piles of it all around the lake." "Well, that should make it easier and quicker to get a fire going" Shawn said with a smile. The three men headed south to gather that wood up and Jeremy and Charlie headed north to get the wood in that direction.

The two teen boys arrived back in the clearing ahead of the three men and piled their wood up a short distance from the fire pit. Kathryn gave them some newspaper and matches, so by the time the men returned, the boys had the fire started already. The men piled their wood with the wood the boys had gathered, checked the fire that was going, and then went to sit down on the blankets. "Can we go swimming now?" Tomas asked, "I want to go out to the ledge and practice my diving." The parents all decided that it would be okay for the kids to go swimming, but not out to the ledge until after they had eaten lunch. Tomas and the other young kids were disappointed that they had to wait to do diving until later, but accepted the explanation that since it was already ten-thirty and it would take twenty minutes to swim out to the ledge and twenty minutes to get back to shore, they would only have less than an hour out there, before having to return for lunch.

All the kids and teens ran out into the lake, splashing

as they entered into the water. Uncle Frank and Aunt Joyce, Kathryn and Jamal, and Shawn and Sarah remained on the blankets back on shore, talking. The adults watched how the younger kids and teens played together out in the water, splashing each other for a while and then starting a game of tag. "I never thought Jeremy and Amanda would ever accept naturism" Jack said to Joyce, "Not with their father insisting on them being raised as textiles." "Imagine how shocked I was" Joyce said, "To walk into Kathryn's dining room with lunch for some kids that had been discovered camping up here at the lake, and seeing my nephew and niece sitting at the table with nothing on except the horrified looks on their faces. I almost dropped that big bowl of spaghetti that I was carrying." "I was caught off guard too" Kathryn interjected, "Here I have four nude teens visiting me, you walk into the house, and they shriek 'Aunt Joyce' at you. I was horrified at the thought of having given away your secret about being a naturist." "Well, at least James and John had no problem with the surprise" Joyce responded, "They simply welcomed their cousins to the village, like true naturists. Didn't even blink at seeing Jeremy and Amanda here, and nude." "Did you think it would catch them off guard" Jack asked, "They have always wondered why Grace and the teens are never nude when we visit, and why they aren't allowed to go nude either."

"Well, they sure have taken to the naturist lifestyle" Kathryn chuckled, "When Shawn and I came up to visit them in their camp across the lake, all four of those teens were as naked as the day that they were born." "Yeah" Shawn added, "Although, they were a bit nervous about being nude in front of a couple of adults, at first." "But they got used to it real fast as we talked with them" Kathryn said, "And when we invited them to the village for lunch, none of them gave it a second thought that they were nude. They just followed us to the village as if they had been naturists all their lives." "They probably got that from Grace" Joyce stated, "Grace would never talk against nudity, and she wouldn't let their father either. She wanted them to decide how they felt, on their own." "She's going to be mighty surprised, when the kids get back home" Jack declared, "And find out that they have become naturists." "I don't know if they will tell her or not" Joyce replied, "Not right away anyhow. They seem nervous about letting Grace know that they were camping in the nude with their best friends, who are now their girl and boyfriends." "Well, I hope they tell your sister" Jack exclaimed, "It would be nice to be able to go nude when we go to visit them at their house." "It would be even nicer if they could come here for a visit" Joyce responded.

Around eleven-thirty, the three men began getting

the fire pit ready for cooking. They hauled a large cooking grate out from behind the boulders by the fire pit, rubbed it down with sand, and then rinsed it off in the lake before placing it over the fire. Hamburger patties and hotdogs were placed on the grate to start cooking, and the rest of the food was placed out on the blankets. The smell of the cooking meat soon reached the kids out in the water, and they started swimming for the shore. Everyone filled their plates with whatever they wanted to eat. Charlie had two pieces of still warm fried chicken, potato salad, beans, chips, and a roll on his first plate of food, and a hamburger, more beans, and chips on his second plateful. Uncle Jack matched the teen boy, except he had a hotdog as well as a hamburger on his second plate. Everyone watched the pair eating. They were obviously competing to see who could eat the most. Charlie had some watermelon and one piece of Aunt Joyce's apple pie for dessert, while Jack managed to consume only two pieces of pie, one apple and the other a piece of Sarah's cherry pie.

All the leftovers were put away for later, and everyone sat or laid back on the blankets to rest and digest what they had eaten. An hour later, the kids started hinting that they were ready to get back into the lake. They were told that they could swim off the shore of the camp site, but not go out to the ledge yet for another hour. Tomas and Greg started to protest, but Charlie headed off their complaints. "We need to give our stomachs another hour to digest the food yet" he announced, "We don't want to be diving off the cliff, hit the water a little wrong, and end up losing our lunch out there in the water. At least I don't want to be diving into water that has regurgitated food floating around in it." "Oh, yuck" exclaimed the girls, all together. "What's regurgitated food?" John asked. "It's food that you throw back up" explained Greg, "Like when you have the flu." "Oh" John said, "I guess maybe we should wait for a while longer then." All the kids were in total agreement now, and calmly returned to playing in the water just off shore for a while. "Charlie sure knew how to get the others to agree to wait a while" Shawn commented. "I think, maybe, he wasn't really feeling like going diving just yet, himself" Kathryn said, "After what he ate for lunch, he's probably still a little too full to want to go out to the ledge." "What do you think?" Joyce asked her husband. "Definitely" Jack replied, "I know I don't feel like swimming all the way out there, the way I feel right now." "And I see that Charlie is just kind of relaxing in the water" Sarah commented.

After the second hour was up, the young boys came back up on shore again. "Can we swim out to the ledge now" Tomas inquired. "If Charlie and Jeremy think it's okay" Shawn answered him, "They seem to be more knowledgeable about when to begin diving after eating." "Our swim team coach says not to eat for at least two hours before swim meets and practice" Jeremy exclaimed, "I think it would be okay for us now, unless someone still feels a little over full yet." The adults all agreed that the young kids could indeed go out to the ledge behind the waterfall, and do some diving, and the young boys were happy again. The three adult men and all the boys began swimming out to the waterfall, around the west end, and over to the steps. They all climbed up onto the ledge and sat down to rest from the swim out. The girls had all decided to remain back on shore with the women and go out to the ledge later, when it wasn't so crowded. "That's probably a good idea" Aunt Joyce had declared, "Ten boys and men out there will be plenty."

After a short rest on the ledge, the younger boys were ready to begin diving into the water. "Watch me dive in" Tomas exclaimed to his father. Shawn watched his son walk up to the edge of the ledge, ready himself, and then jump up and off of the ledge. He was very impressed with how well his son did and when Tomas resurfaced and faced his father from the water, he was complemented on his dive. "You want to see me dive?" Greg asked his father. "Sure" Jamal answered, "Let me see how well you do." Greg went up to the edge of the ledge and launched himself off and into the water. When he surfaced, his father likewise expressed how impressed he was as well. "It's our turn, now" James exclaimed, "Watch me dad!" His father watched him dive into the water, and then John after him. When they surfaced, he smiled down at them in the water. "That was very good" he told them, "I didn't even know that you could dive at all yet." "Jeremy and Charlie have been teaching us" John explained, "They've been helping all of us learn to dive." Uncle Jack turned to Ben and looked expectantly at the young boy. "Would you like for us to watch you dive now too?" he asked. Ben shook his head and looked down at the stone ledge. "I don't know how to dive" he answered. "This is Ben's first time here with us" Greg interjected, "He hasn't been able to learn how to dive like the rest of us." James looked over at Ben. "I'll bet my cousin would show you how" he told his friend, "He showed John and me."

Ben looked up and over at Jeremy. Jeremy looked back at him and smiled. "Would you like to learn how to dive?" he asked the young boy. Ben seemed a little shy and did not answer. "I'm not very good at diving either" Jamal declared, "Would you be willing to give me some instructions too, Jeremy?" "I know your uncle there was on a swim team in college" Shawn said, "But I could use some help to get better myself, if you're going to be teaching Ben and Jamal." "Well, if Charlie helps, I suppose we could hold a little beginner's class for the three of you" Jeremy replied. "Sure thing, I'll help out" Charlie said. "What do you say, Ben" Shawn asked the boy, "You want to join the class with us?" Ben looked over at the rest of the boys and men and nodded his head yes. "I'm not sure if I heard you, Ben" Jeremy chuckled, "You obviously do not have any loose rocks in your head, as my school swim coach says, so I can't hear any rattling in there, and you'll have to speak up." Ben smiled back at Jeremy. "Yes, I want to learn to dive, too" he declared, "Sir!" Jeremy looked shocked at the "Sir" part for a moment, until Uncle Jack started chuckling. "You should know that Ben's father used to be in the marines" he told Jeremy, "Ben has been brought up to be very respectful to his elders and teachers, and to address them as sir or mam." Jeremy smiled back at the young boy again. "Okay then, those not in the class may stay down here by the steps, the rest of us will go down to the east end and get started.

Jeremy instructed Ben, and the two men on how to sit on the edge of the ledge, hold their hands up over their heads, and roll into the water. He then jumped into the water and waited for the young boy to follow his directions until he entered the water. Jeremy was right there when Ben resurfaced with a grin on his face. "That was very good" he told the boy, "You did even better than your class mates." "Really?" Ben asked. "Yes" Jeremy whispered, "But let's not say anything to them." "You don't have to say anything to me" Jamal suddenly whispered from behind them, "I know I didn't do very good that time, but I'm way out of practice, and I've put on a few pounds since I was Ben's age." Ben giggled. "You'll all improve, as you get used to the dive" Jeremy chuckled, and then maybe we can go on to the standing dive." The four of them swam over to the steps, making sure that the other four boys and one man held off on diving while they all passed by the area. When they got up on the ledge again, and down to their class area, they all sat down to rest for five minutes. The next attempt at the rolling dive, Charlie demonstrated before the students attempted the dive again. Charlie waited in the water, and was there when Ben surfaced out in the water again. "Good, very good" Charlie exclaimed, "All of you did very good." They all swam back to the steps and went up to the class area again, to try the dive again.

Charlie and Jeremy took turns, one of them in the water and one up on the ledge, for the next four dives that their students did. Each successive dive got better until Jeremy decided to move on to the standing dive. Once again, he explained the procedure of the dive, then demonstrated it. One at a time, starting with Shawn, then Jamal, and finally Ben, they all did the standing dive. "Ouch" Ben exclaimed when he surfaced after his turn diving, "That kind of hurt a little." "You were off in your form a little" Jeremy told him, "John did the same thing on his first standing dive, too." "Will you show me again, how to do it right" Ben inquired. "Of, course I will" Jeremy answered him, "Charlie and I will work with you until you have it just right. You'll be diving as well as the other boys in no time at all, if you keep working at it." Several more dives later, and all the students were performing the standing dive well enough to move on to the next step. "Okay" Jeremy finally announced, "It's time to go on to the next step." He explained that they would be jumping up a little bit before rolling forward and down into the water. He demonstrated the dive, followed by Charlie demonstrating it right after him. "Now remember" Jeremy stated, "Take a breath before jumping off the ledge, and roll forward and down so you don't do a belly flop." The three students all did the dive really well on their first attempt, with no belly flops at all. They continued to practice their diving for about another half an hour, resting up every few dives, so they wouldn't get too tired.

The girls all showed up behind the waterfall around three-thirty, and announced that it was their turn to use the ledge. The younger boys were all a little disappointed, but knew that they had to give the girls a chance to use the ledge also, to be fair. Greg looked out at his mom and grinned. "Hey mom, watch me dive" he exclaimed. Kathryn watched her son, and was impressed. Next, Tomas dove in, followed by James and

John for their Aunt Joyce. Shawn, Jamal, and Uncle Jack then dove in and started swimming back to the shore with Greg, Tomas, James, and John, leaving the girls to use the ledge. Jeremy, Charlie, and Ben all remained back at the ledge so that Ben could improve his newly developed skill of diving. Ben demonstrated how well he could dive now, and all the women were impressed. "You dive pretty good" Beth exclaimed, "I didn't even know that you knew how." Ben grinned back at his sister. "I just learned" he said, "Jeremy and Charlie are good teachers." "I'm impressed too" Sarah said to her son, "For just having learned how, you dive very well." "We want him to keep practicing for a little while longer" Charlie said, "So we can be sure he has it really good." "Beth" Sarah said, looking at her daughter, "I know you said you knew how to dive, but could I see you do one?"

Beth stood up at the edge of the ledge and prepared to dive off and into the water. She felt a little nervous with everyone watching her, and Jeremy noticed her nervousness. "Beth" he said to her, "You seem to be a little nervous with all of us watching you. Would you like some advice on how to relax a little?" "Sure" she answered. "Okay" Jeremy said with a grin, "Our swim couch always tells us, that to relax before a dive, just try to imagine all the people watching you, as being in only their underwear." Everyone except Jeremy started slowly chuckling until they were all shaking with laughter. Jeremy looked around at everyone with a bewildered look on his face. Beth stood and looked back at Jeremy with a grin on her face. "Thanks Jeremy, but I'm not sure what underwear actually look like." Suddenly, Jeremy realized why everyone thought his suggestion was so funny. He slapped his hand to his forehead and groaned. "Oh!" he exclaimed, "How stupid of me. Everyone here is naked!" Beth turned and jumped off of the ledge, gracefully diving into the water with no problems at all. She surfaced, wiped the water from her face and eyes, then floated out in the water with her eyes fully open. "Oh my" she exclaimed, "My imagination has gone wild. I seem to be seeing everyone up there as naked."

Beth returned up to the ledge and went over to Jeremy and Charlie. "Well, how did I do" she asked, "Do you have any suggestions on how I can improve?" Jeremy pointed his thumb over at Charlie. "I'll let my friend here answer that" he replied, "He did a dive yesterday that everyone thought was better than mine. Plus, I'm still trying to get my foot out of my mouth, after that last suggestion I gave you." Charlie chuckled. "Okay, buddy. You work with Ben some more and I'll give Beth a couple pointers, not that she needs much help. That dive was really good." Jeremy worked with Ben for about fifteen minutes more, then told him to just keep practicing whenever he could, and he would improve more. Charlie gave Beth a couple of pointers which she tried and was pleased with. The other girls were all jumping and diving into the water also, until Jeremy thought that the last three boys should join the other guys back in shallower water or on shore. Ben wanted to stay out at the ledge and practice some more, and the girls agreed to keep an eye on him until they all returned to the beach for supper. Jeremy followed Charlie into the water, both of them preforming near perfect dives, and then began swimming off around the waterfall.

The two teen boys got back to the beach and found the rest of the guys all relaxing on the beach, sitting and laying out on the blankets, and some towels, in the sun. Jeremy grabbed the towel that he had brought along and laid it out in a nice sunny spot, then laid down in the sun to rest. Charlie went over to the picnic basket that Aunt Joyce had brought along and started looking inside of it. "Looking for something?" Uncle Jack suddenly asked him. Charlie jumped. "I um, I was just looking" Charlie nervously answered. "Yeah, I did the same thing when I got back here" Uncle Jack said with a chuckle, "The piece of chicken that leaped into my hand when I was looking inside of that basket was really tasty." Charlie stared back at the man for a moment, then smiled as he brought his hand out of the basket clutching a drumstick. “Oh my, looks like some chicken jumped into your hand too” Uncle Jack said with a laugh, “Best way to handle that my boy, is to just eat it.” All the guys on the beach started laughing except Charlie, who had taken the man’s advice and bit into the piece of chicken, his mouth being full of the meat.

The women and girls all returned to the beach around four-forty-five and walked up onto the beach and sat down on towels to rest. “Did you all have a good time in back of the waterfall?” Jamal asked. “Yes, we did” Kathryn answered him, “All the girls are really good at diving. And Ben is getting really good at it too, for his first day at it.” “I want to thank you” Sarah addressed the two teen boys, “For helping Ben and Beth with learning to dive so well, especially Ben. He never seemed interested in diving until today. He just doesn’t want to quit now.” “I think he was just a little nervous about trying it” Jeremy replied, “But I think he felt better about learning to dive, when he found out that Jamal and Shawn needed some instructions too.” “What?” Kathryn exclaimed, looking over at her husband, “You needed instructions in diving? I thought you were a team captain on your swim team in high school.” Jamal just grinned back at his wife. “I think he was just trying to put Ben at ease, just like I was” Shawn said with a chuckle, “We saw how nervous Ben was, being the only one out there that didn’t know how to dive.” Ben looked between the two smiling men. “You two already knew how to dive?” he asked, “You just acted like you needed help, so I would join you in the class?” “They didn’t mean to fool you to embarrass you” Sarah explained to her son. “We just didn’t want you to feel like you were alone” Shawn said, “Plus, I know I wasn’t very good on that first dive we did. I heard Jeremy tell you that you did better than Jamal and me, and he was right.” Ben was grinning from ear to ear. “Can we go back out to the ledge and do some more diving after supper” he asked.

Jeremy looked at the young boy shaking his head. “I don’t think we’ll be doing any more diving today” he said to Ben, “We’ll be eating supper pretty soon.” “Yes, and by the time you finish eating supper and wait two hours again, it will be close to eight o’clock” Sarah explained to her son, “It will be getting too dark by then. You’ll have about an hour after eating, to play in the water here by the beach though, before we have to head back home.” Ben looked disappointed. “So, I won’t get to do any more diving again” he grumbled, “Jeremy and Charlie are going back home tomorrow, and we aren’t allowed by the waterfall without an adult with us.” “Hey, maybe Shawn, Jack, and I can take some time to go with you all to the lake sometimes” Jamal suggested, “I kind of liked diving off the ledge back there, and I really liked seeing how good you all have gotten at diving." "I'm willing to come up here at least once a week" Shawn volunteered. "I will too" Jack offered, "Providing I'm not off on business for the village, that is." "There" Jamal said, "We'll all try to get up here with you kids as often as we can. And I think there might be some other parents around who wouldn't mind taking some time off from the fields, to cool off at the lake here." All the kids were very enthusiastic about the idea of having adults to accompany them out to the waterfall so they could continue practicing their diving.

With the talk about the kids getting the opportunity to get in some more diving practice after the four teens had left completed, the three women decided it was time for them all to eat. The men stoked up the fire in the pit, and placed the cleaned cooking grate over it to start cooking some meats for supper. Aunt Joyce got the chicken out and placed it on the buffet blanket for supper. "I could have sworn there was more chicken left than that after lunch" she commented, "Some wild animals must have come around here since lunch, and gotten into the leftover chicken. She was looking at her husband and Charlie as she said that. They were both looking around everywhere except in her direction. "I ate some of the chicken, Miss Joyce" Greg spoke up, "And so did John and James. We were really hungry after diving, and it was really good." Aunt Joyce smiled and started laughing, along with the rest of the group. Supper was served up about ten minutes later, after the hotdogs and hamburgers were ready. Charlie and Uncle Jack of course were competing to see who would eat the most again.

After they had finished eating supper, everyone rested for about half an hour, with Charlie and Uncle Jack coming back to get more food a couple of times. Finally, the women decided it was time to pack up the rest of the food, and send the children and men out into the lake to swim for a little while. At around seven fifteen, Kathryn called out to the swimmers that it was time to come in and head back to the village for the night. All the younger kids seemed a little depressed on the walk back to the village, due to the fact that they all knew that the four teenagers would be leaving for their own homes the next day. They all stopped at the shower building to wash up, so that they would be clean for church the following morning, then everyone said good-bye as they separated outside the building to go to their own individual homes. It was after eight o'clock when Jeremy, Amanda, Jenny, and Charlie walked into Uncle Jack and Aunt Joyce's house with James and John. They were all tired from a long day at the lake, and said good-night to each other as they each headed off to bed for the night. "I wish we could stay longer" Amanda whispered to the others after James and John had gone into their bedroom. “I do too” Jeremy replied, “But we have to get back and help mom out in the store on Monday.” “Are you going to tell your mom about finding the village she grew up in?” asked Jenny. “I don’t think we’ll know that until we get home and see how things go” Jeremy answered. “Yeah” Amanda added, “We’ll have to wait and see.”

THE FINAL CAMPING DAY

The next morning, Jeremy got up at seven o'clock, and quietly left the bedroom to head downstairs. He figured that Aunt Joyce would be up and getting breakfast ready for everyone, and he was right. He walked into the kitchen to find her cooking up sausage and scrambled eggs. "Anything I can help you with" he asked from behind her. "Oh, Jeremy" she gasped, "You startled me. I didn't think anyone else would be up yet." "I couldn't sleep any longer Aunt Joyce" he replied, "I keep thinking about how nice it is here in Du-Nu, and how much I'd love to stay longer." "I understand" she responded, giving him a hug, "It's been so wonderful to have you, Amanda, and your friends here for a visit." "What time is church?" Jeremy inquired. "Service starts at nine o'clock" she replied. "Is there anything I can help you with, for breakfast?" he repeated. Aunt Joyce smiled at him. "You could make the toast and butter it" she told him. He took the loaf of bread and put a couple of slices in the toaster.

At seven-thirty, breakfast was almost ready and his aunt instructed Jeremy to go upstairs and wake up James, John, and his friends. Jeremy walked up the stairs and went into the twin's room first. Once the twins were awake, they went with him to wake up Charlie. "Watch how quickly he wakes up when you say something about food" Jeremy whispered to his cousins. He walked over to the bed. "Hey, Charlie, it's time to get up" Jeremy said to his sleeping friend, "Breakfast is ready." Charlie opened his eyes and sat up in bed. He looked around and saw Jeremy and the twins looking at him, blinking his eyes. "Did you say breakfast was ready?" he asked, as he climbed out of bed. "Yes" Jeremy answered, "But you need to get dressed first, you're not wearing anything." "So, what" Charlie responded with a laugh, "Nobody around here is wearing anything, who cares. Let's go eat, I'm hungry." Charlie and the twins headed down the stairs to the dining room, while Jeremy went to the girl's room to wake them up. When he got downstairs, Uncle Jack, Charlie, and the twins were already seated at the table with a plate of eggs, sausage, and toast. The twins were seated on opposite sides of their father. Aunt Joyce came in from the kitchen and set a pitcher of orange juice on the table. "Are the girls up yet?" she asked Jeremy, "Church is in just over an hour." "Yes, we're up" announced Amanda as she and Jenny walked into the dining room. "Well, sit down and help yourself to some breakfast, we'll have to leave in about thirty minutes" Aunt Joyce said. The teens all got seated at the table and started helping themselves to the food on the table. "I hope I cooked enough" Aunt Joyce giggled, "With two big eaters at the table, I may have to cook up some more food if this isn't enough." Jack and Charlie both looked at her and smiled.

When they all finished eating, Jeremy, Charlie, James, and John all started in on the dishes. Jack watched the four boys as they worked the same routine as on the previous nights, with Charlie taking the dirty dishes out to the kitchen where Jeremy washed and rinsed them, then James and John dried and put them away. When all the dishes had been cleared from the table, Charlie helped the twins with putting the clean dishes up in the higher cupboards. "They work well together" Joyce commented to her husband, when she saw him watching the boys work, "I'll miss having those two boys doing the dishes for me, you know?" It was twenty-five minutes past eight when all the dishes were done and put away, and Joyce told the kids it was time to leave for church. They all grabbed their towels and headed out the front door, all of them wearing their best birthday suits and big smiles. When they reached the church, there weren't a lot of people there yet. "Mom, how come we came so early?" James asked. "I wanted to take our guests back to meet the pastor before church service begins" she replied. She motioned for the teens to follow her and took them up to the front of the little church, then left and over through a side door. As they entered the church office through the door, the four teens spotted a man who was just slipping on a clergy stole. "Pastor Alvin" Aunt Joyce said, "I'd like you to meet my nephew and niece, and their two friends." The pastor turned around and extended his hand. "Well, glad to meet..." he began, then stopped and just stared at the four teens. "Pastor Alvin!" Amanda exclaimed as she strategically covered specific parts of her body with her hands and arm, "What are you doing here?"

Pastor Alvin quickly regained his own composure and looked back and forth between the four nude teens. "Amanda, Jeremy, Jenny, and Charlie?" he declared, "I'm the visiting pastor here this week. What are you four doing here? I don't remember seeing any of you here before." "We were on a camping trip up at the lake" Jeremy casually replied, "We found our way here while exploring, and have been staying at Aunt Joyce's for the past few days." "Really?" Pastor Adam said, "Well, will miracles never cease. I can tell by your sister's reaction to seeing me here, that she hasn't been around naturists very long." "I thought it a good idea to bring them back here to meet you before church" Aunt Joyce explained, "So the service wouldn't be disturbed by the five of you seeing each other in the sanctuary for the first time." "A very good idea, Joyce" the pastor responded, "I'm glad you did, it seems that Amanda will need to get used to me being here, the most." Everyone looked at Amanda, still trying to cover herself. "Amanda" Pastor Alvin said to her, "I've been preaching here in the village of Du-Nu for several years now, twice a month. I'm quite used to seeing nude men, women, and children. You don't have to hide from me, like Eve did from God in the Garden of Eden." Amanda eyed the pastor. "It just doesn't seem right to me though" she told him, "You're my pastor back home, and I'm used to wearing clothes in front of you."

Pastor Alvin smiled at her. "You'd like to run back to your Aunt Joyce's and put some clothes on I gather" he said to her. Amanda nodded her head in the affirmative. "Well the church service is about to start" he declared, "But I have an idea that might help you out. "We need an acolyte to light the candles on the alter, and put them out again at the end of the service. The acolyte has the option of wearing a robe, would you like to act as the acolyte today?" Amanda nodded her head in the affirmative again. The pastor took a white robe from out of a cabinet and handed it to Amanda. "You may slip this on in the bathroom over there" he said, "Then come out and we'll get you started. You can go out and sit in the pew with your aunt and uncle, after lighting the candles. At the end service, you put the candles out and return the robe back here to the office while I greet everyone at the front of the church." Amanda went into the bathroom to change into the robe. "She needs to get used to the idea of being nude around a pastor" Aunt Joyce whispered. "Yes" Pastor Alvin agreed, "I think that seeing me in my vestments is the hardest part for her." "Maybe you would like to come over for lunch after the service" Aunt Joyce suggested, "You can talk with her and the others then, before they have to leave this afternoon." "I think that would be a wonderful idea" he responded, "I'll be there around eleven."

Aunt Joyce guided the other three teenagers back out into the church and they all sat down in one of the front pews together. Amanda came out dressed in the white robe a few minutes later and proceeded to light the candles on the alter. When all the candles were lighted, she extinguished the lighter and walked out to sit in the pew alongside of her aunt. She felt embarrassed about being embarrassed over her nudity in front of the pastor, but she couldn't help how she felt. She kept looking over at her brother and friends, they seemed to have adjusted to being nude in church with their regular pastor preaching. Jeremy and Charlie were boys, she understood that they wouldn't have as much trouble with it, but Jenny also seemed perfectly fine with sitting here in church, nude. Aunt Joyce saw how upset her niece was and put her arm around her shoulders. She leaned her head over so her mouth was next to Amanda's ear. "Don't feel bad" she whispered, "Seeing Pastor Alvin here was a pretty big shock to you. Your mother has told me how much respect you have for him, so it's only reasonable that you will need more time to get used to him being here." Amanda smiled back at her aunt, then leaned over and gave her a big hug.

The church service was similar to the ones she had attended back home, and Amanda soon began to relax and participate as if she were back home. During the service, she kept thinking about how she had reacted to seeing Pastor Alvin, and him seeing her nude. She was the one who had reacted with embarrassment, he hadn't reacted at all to it. If he hadn't cared that she was nude, why had she. The more she thought about it, the more she realized that Aunt Joyce was probably right. She thought very highly of Pastor Alvin, and had felt bad about being seen nude by him. She had been going nude in front of everyone for several days now, even total strangers, and had not felt like she was doing anything wrong. Why should she feel any different around her pastor, especially when he obviously didn't think she was doing anything sinful? She started to feel restless wearing the robe, when everyone else in the congregation was nude. Aunt Joyce noticed her restlessness and looked over at her. "Are you alright?" she whispered. "Yes" Amanda whispered back, "I just wish I wasn't wearing this robe." Aunt Joyce reached over and unzipped the full-length zipper of the robe. "Just slip it off" she whispered. Amanda slowly slipped the robe off of her shoulders and let it slide down behind her, that felt a lot better she thought to herself. She looked back at her aunt. "Thank you" she whispered.

When the service came to an end, and the closing song was being sung, Amanda got up with the candle snuffer ready, and walked up to the alter. As she was putting the candles out, she glanced over at Pastor Alvin. He smiled back at her and nodded his head. She grinned back at him and finished putting the rest of the candles out, then returned to the pew, gathered up the acolyte robe, and walked back to the church office where she put the robe and candle lighter back in the cabinet. She came out of the office, and Aunt Joyce, Uncle Jack, and the rest were waiting for her. “You feeling better, sis?” Jeremy asked with concern. “Yes” Amanda declared, “I feel wonderful now. It was silly of me to be embarrassed in front of the pastor, there’s nothing wrong with going nude.” They all left the pew and got in back of the rest of the congregation that was walking down the aisle to the exit. They all walked back to the exit and shook hands with the pastor. “I’m glad to see that you have overcome your embarrassment” Pastor Alvin whispered to Amanda. “Me too” she responded, “I’m sorry for the way I reacted.” “That’s alright child” the pastor replied with a smile, “I understand. It was just the shock of seeing your favorite pastor.” Amanda grinned. “Yeah” she giggled. “We’ll see you at eleven” Aunt Joyce said to the pastor, as she shook his hand and they all headed home.

At just before eleven o'clock, a knock sounded at the front door of Uncle Jack and Aunt Joyce's house. Aunt Joyce went to the door, opened it and welcomed Pastor Alvin inside. "Pastor, please come in. If you would like to have a seat, lunch will be ready in about half an hour" she said. Pastor Alvin came inside. "Hello everyone" he said as he placed a towel on one of the chairs and sat down. The four teens mumbled "Hello" back to the pastor, otherwise they all just sat and starred at him. "Something smells good" the pastor added, "But then, Joyce always seems to have something tasty cooking whenever I come for a visit." "That's true" Uncle Jack" agreed, "And she's the best cook I've ever come across." "So, does that mean you married me for my cooking skills?" Joyce inquired of her husband. "That's just one of the many things I married you for" he answered, "The most significant thing of course is that I am in love with you." Aunt Joyce grinned and excused herself to check on the source of all the good smells coming from the kitchen. "Know what pastor" James suddenly exclaimed, "John and I learned how to dive this week." "Really?" Pastor Alvin replied. "Yes, Jeremy and Charlie taught us" John added. "And they taught Greg, Karen, Tomas, Caitlyn, Beth, and Ben, too" James said.

"Well, it sounds to me like your cousins had a busy week, with all of you youngsters learning to dive from them" Pastor Alvin declared as he turned to look at the four teens that were still staring at him, "What else have you four done this week, Jeremy?" "Wh..what?" Jeremy stammered. "You four seem to be staring at the pastor" Uncle Jack declared. "It's alright, Jack. I probably have something spilled on my suit somewhere" the pastor chuckled. "Suit?" Charlie said, "What suit?" "Why, my birthday suit of course" he replied. "Pastor, you aren't wearing a suit" Amanda exclaimed, "You're nude." "Yes, exactly" Pastor Alvin responded, "I'm wearing my best birthday suit. It was made for me by the same tailor that made Adam's first suit." "Adam who?" inquired Charlie. "Adam, like in Adam and Eve" Jenny giggled, "Right Pastor?" "Right" the pastor replied, "It's the original one that God gave me when I was born. Anyway, I was asking Jeremy what you all have been doing this week, besides teaching the kids around here to dive." "We helped out in the fields a little" Charlie said. "Charlie and I played on a volleyball team at the village celebration, too" Jeremy added, "Our team only won one game out of three though." "But it was our first time playing on a sand volleyball court" Charlie declared, "Everyone said we did pretty good for our first time."

"Are any of you uncomfortable with me being nude?" Pastor Alvin asked the four teens, "If so, I have some clothes here in my briefcase." "No. No, Pastor" Jenny said, "I don't think any of us are uncomfortable." "No,

Pastor, Jenny is right" Amanda added, "We're just not used to seeing our pastor this way. We just need a little time to get used to it is all. Like I had to get used to being nude in church with you there this morning." "I was glad to see you overcome your embarrassment" Pastor Alvin responded. "Me too" Amanda replied with a smile, "I realized that being nude around you, was no different than being nude around my brother and friends, my aunt and uncle, my cousins, and the whole village of Du-Nu." "Good" Pastor Alvin declared, "I'm glad you are getting comfortable with your own skin. Just be sure you don't get too comfortable when you are back home. We don't want you to come to church services back in Bon Amis, like this. There are some people in the congregation back there who would be shocked and appalled by your being nude."

Charlie looked at the pastor. "How come you aren't shocked by nudity?" he asked. "Well" the pastor responded, "Why should I be shocked by it?" "Doesn't the bible say that it's wrong?" Charlie asked. "I don't know" Pastor Alvin replied, "Do you know of any place in the bible that specifically says nudity is wrong?" "No, I don't" Charlie answered, "Do you know of any?" "I can't say that I do" Pastor Alvin said, "The bible says God created Adam and Eve and put them in the garden naked. God only gave them aprons to wear for protection, when they were thrown out of the Garden of Eden, but clothes have become more than protection now, many people actually seem to worship clothing, and think that the fancier the clothes they wear, the better person they are. They frown upon nudity, and believe that everyone should live by the eleventh commandment. God sees right through those fancy clothes, he sees everyone as we truly are, sinful, but forgiven." "What's the eleventh commandment?" Charlie asked, "I always thought there were only ten commandments." The pastor chuckled. "God gave Moses the original ten commandments, Charlie" he answered, "But man has made up extra commandments to suit his own ideas." "Thou shalt not go nude!" exclaimed Uncle Jack, "The man-made commandment of self-righteous men." Aunt Joyce came back into the living room at that point and announced that lunch was ready. Everyone got up and proceeded to the dining room with their towels.

Aunt Joyce had prepared a delicious meal of turkey, mashed potatoes and gravy, corn, a fruit salad, and rolls. Pastor Alvin said a prayer after everyone was seated and then they all proceeded to fill their plates with food. Pastor Alvin turned out to be another person who loved to eat good food and provided Uncle Jack and Charlie a good challenge for biggest eater. For dessert, there was blueberry pie with ice cream, and then it was time to clean up. Aunt Joyce took care of putting all the leftovers away, while Charlie cleared the table, Jeremy washed and rinsed the dishes, and James and John dried and put the dishes away. Uncle Jack saw the pastor watching the four teens doing the dishes. "Joyce says they've been doing the dishes like that since they got here" he explained, "They seem to have developed an efficient routine for cleaning up the dishes." "Yes, they have" Pastor Alvin agreed, "I'll have to remember how well they work together, the next time they come to a church dinner. They would be a great help in the kitchen after eating."

When the dishes were done, the pastor visited some more with everyone, answering the four teens questions as well as he could. At one o'clock, Aunt Joyce told the teens that it was time to get their stuff together, so they could leave for their appointment, to be picked up and taken back home. Pastor Alvin also had to be going, and offered to walk up to the storage cave with them. Jeremy and Charlie went out to the shed in the back yard, got the cart out and brought it over to the back door of the house. The empty coolers were loaded into the cart and then the boys tied the tarp down over the top again. Each teen had their backpack, with their personal items and clothes, plus a couple bottles of water. Uncle Jack and the twins were staying back at the house, so they hugged the four teens and said their good-byes. The four teens followed Aunt Joyce and the pastor up the road to the mountain passage that the teens had come through on the day that they had first found Village Du-Nu. They reached the storage cave at fifteen minutes to two o'clock and Pastor Alvin said good-bye, got into his car, and drove off down the dirt road.

"We have to get the cart into the back of the pickup" Aunt Joyce declared, "There is a ramp over there in the corner of the cave that should work." Jeremy and Charlie located the ramp and brought it to the large cave opening, while Aunt Joyce walked out to a cove off of the dirt road and came back to the cave in a pickup. With the ramp secured in place at the end of the pickup, the boys pulled and pushed the cart up into the back. They slid the ramp into the back of the pickup also and secured everything. Jeremy and Charlie got into the bed of the pickup with the cart, and Jenny and Amanda got into the front seat of the pickup next to Aunt Joyce. The drive around the mountain to the east side of the woods took about half an hour. Joyce parked the car at the side of the road and stopped the teens from getting out of the pickup. "There's something you should all do before you unload the cart" she announced with a smile. "What?" Amanda asked. "Get dressed" Aunt Joyce said with a chuckle, "You're all still nude. You might want to get dressed, in case someone happens to drive by along the highway." "Oh, you're right" Amanda chuckled,

"Although I'd rather stay the way I am right now, if I could."

The teens all got out of the pickup on the woods side, took shirts and pants out of their backpacks, and slipped into the clothing. Once they were all dressed, the boys proceeded to unload the cart from the pickup. After storing the ramp in the back of the pickup again, and closing the tail gate, they all gave Aunt Joyce a hug, and thanked her for having them stay with her. Jeremy and Amanda gave her a kiss good-bye as well, and tearfully waved fair-well as she turned the truck around and headed back for Village Du-Nu. Jeremy started pulling the cart towards the woods. "Where are you going" Charlie asked with a chuckle, "We're not starting our camping trip today, we're supposed to be going home." "I know" Jeremy replied with a smile, "I just thought it might be a little cooler in the woods, then out in the sun." The other three thought that was a good idea, and followed him to the edge of the woods and some shade.

They all sat down on some grass, took out a bottle of water and started sipping the cool liquid. About twenty-five minutes later, Amanda jumped up and pointed down the road. "I think that's mom coming" she said. Everyone else got up and looked down the road. "Yup, that's mom's pickup" Jeremy confirmed as he grabbed the pull handle of the cart. They all began walking back to the road, and arrived about ten minutes after the pickup came to a stop. Grace had the tail gate open already and the ramp pulled out. Jeremy and Charlie secured the ramp in place and then pushed and pulled the cart up into the back of the pickup. With everything loaded and tied down, the boys climbed into the bed beside the cart again, and the girls got into the cab of the pickup beside Amanda's mother. Grace turned the pickup around and started driving back towards town. "Did you all have a good time camping?" she asked. Amanda started giggling, along with Jenny. "What's so funny?" Grace inquired. "We had a great time" Amanda replied, "Jenny is now Jeremy's girlfriend, and Charlie is now my boyfriend." "Well, I'm glad to hear that my children finally have someone special included in their lives" Grace said, "But I hope you're both ready to go back to work tomorrow."

They dropped Charlie off at his house. "See you later" he said to them all. "Okay, see you" Amanda replied, blowing him a kiss as her mother started driving away. Jenny's house was past where Jeremy lived with his mother and sister, so they decided to go home, so Jeremy could get all the camping stuff put away. He got the cart unloaded from the pickup when they got home. "I'll see you" he told Jenny. "Okay" she replied red faced. Jeremy's mother drove back down the driveway with Jenny and Amanda in the seat beside her. When the truck turned onto the road and went out of sight, Jeremy pulled the cart into the garage, then took the ramp back to the storage shed and stored it. Going back to the garage, he began unloading the cart, storing all the tents, sleeping bags, tarps, and other stuff. He returned the cart to the storage shed also, and then went into the house.

Amanda and his mother drove up the driveway again about ten minutes later and came into the house. “Everything put away already?” Mrs. Andersen asked. “Yup, I got everything all taken care of” he answered. “You forgot your backpack in the pickup” Amanda said as she handed it to him. “Thanks” he replied as he took it from her, “I’ll take it up to my room right away.” Mrs. Andersen and her two teenagers went into town to have supper at a restaurant that evening, then returned home to watch some television until nine o’clock. Jeremy and Amanda had been up early that morning, in order to attend church, and they were both feeling a little tired. “I’m going to bed” Jeremy announced, “I’m pretty tired, and I have to get up early to go to work tomorrow morning.” “Me too” Amanda said, “See you in the morning, mom.” “Good-night you two” their mother replied, “Breakfast will be ready at seven, make sure you set your alarm clocks.” “Okay, mom” they both answered, “Good-night.”

Jeremy went to the bathroom, then to his bedroom. He slipped off his shoes and socks, then took off his shirt and pants. "It feels good to get out of those clothes" he thought to himself as he climbed into bed and turned off the table lamp. Amanda went to her room and slipped out of all her clothes also. "I hate wearing clothes" she thought, "I'm going to have to get used to wearing them again though, I suppose." Both teens drifted off to sleep, enjoying the feel of the clean sheets against their bare skin.

NO TAN LINES

The next morning, Amanda woke up to her alarm clock going off at six-thirty. She climbed out of bed, visited the bathroom, and then got dressed for work. She came out of her bedroom just as her brother walked out of his. They looked at each and walked down the hall to the stairs. "I feel so uncomfortable in these clothes" Amanda whispered to her brother. "Yeah, I know" Jeremy whispered back, "That's why I decided to go commando today." Amanda stopped and looked at Jeremy. "What's that mean?" she asked. He smiled at her and chuckled, "It means that I'm not wearing any underwear" he replied. Amanda smiled back at him. "Then I guess I'm a commando right now, too" she giggled. "Jeremy, Amanda!" their mother yelled from downstairs, "Breakfast is almost ready! Are you two up yet?" "Yes mother" Amanda said as she walked into the kitchen, "We're both up." "Like army commandos" chuckled Jeremy. Grace looked at her children, confused. "We're just having breakfast today, then going to work at the store" she said, "We're not going to war."

After breakfast, Jeremy gathered up the dirty dishes, took them over to the sink, and started washing them. Amanda came over and began drying the dishes as Jeremy put them into the dish rack. Grace starred at her son and daughter. “Okay, what’s up?” she asked, “Why are you two doing the dishes?” “We just realized how much you do for us” Amanda replied, “And we want to start helping out a little more around here.” Grace smiled, “That’s very sweet of you” she said, “I appreciate it.” After the dishes were washed and put away, it was time to head for the grocery store. When they arrived, Grace went to the office with Amanda to get the cash drawers for the registers, while Jeremy grabbed a clipboard and started going up and down the aisles, to see what items needed to be stocked. When he got to the produce area, he was shocked to discover that there were a lot of items that were low or completely gone, and needed restocking immediately.

Jeremy went back to the stock room, grabbed a stocking cart, and went to get the items that were needed out in the produce section. He found that the items he needed the most, were not available, they were out of most items. He went and found his mother at the front of the store, putting the cash drawers into the registers. “Mom, we have a problem in the produce section” he exclaimed. “Oh, I forgot to tell you about that” Grace responded, “The regular produce supplier didn’t get here last Friday, their driver quit.” “When will they get here with our order then?” Jeremy inquired. “They have to keep on schedule with deliveries to their other customers.” His mother answered, “They asked the other drivers if one of them would put in overtime to make deliveries to us, but no one volunteered. They're trying to find a new driver, and hope to get us a delivery by this Friday." "But, we're out of some items now" Jeremy gasped, "We need to get some produce in right away." "I know" Grace said, "And I'm going to work on it after we get the store open." "Mom, I heard that there's a place out on highway 14 that sells produce" Amanda suddenly exclaimed.

Grace's eyes opened wide. "Well, yes, I know of the place" she said, "I suppose I could check and see if they have enough to cover us until Friday. I'll give them a call." "Will they have a phone out there?" Jeremy said while trying to conceal a smile, "Otherwise you'll have to drive all the way out there, and if they don't have anything, it would be a waste of time." "I know who the owner of the stand is" Grace replied, "I can call them to see about some produce." "You'd better hurry, mom" Jeremy responded, "People will want to know if we have produce coming in or not, or they'll go to the big supermarket on the east side of town." Grace finished getting the cash drawers into the tills, then headed back to the office again. She came out about ten minutes later with a grin on her face. "They'll be delivering it later this morning" she said. "What's the name of the company" Jeremy asked. "I don't think they have a name" Grace replied, "But a man named Shawn will be delivering the produce here."

The store opened at nine o'clock while Jeremy was stocking the produce section the best that he could. He then started restocking other shelf items until he got a page over the intercom system saying that 'Shawn' was waiting at the stock room delivery door. He almost ran to the back of the store. Entering the stockroom, he saw Shawn standing just inside the loading bay. Looking around, he saw no one else within ear shot of them. "Shawn, great to see you" Jeremy whispered. "Nice to see you" Shawn responded with a smile and a hand shake, "Your mother calling for some produce was kind of a surprise." "Our regular supplier lost a driver and couldn't make their regular delivery last Friday" Jeremy explained with a grin, "We really needed to get some product into the store." "Well, at least we got a good order from your mother for today" Shawn said in a disappointed voice. "Not if Amanda and I can help it" Jeremy chuckled, "This is just the opening we need, to talk mom into changing to you as our produce supplier. The other company comes from about sixty miles away, and the product isn't nearly as fresh as what you can get to us." "You think you can convince her to switch" Shawn asked with a smile. "I'm sure going to try" Jeremy replied, "As long as you can supply all that we need, I think she'll give you a try."

He and Shawn unloaded everything from the truck, then Jeremy started loading up a stock cart to take some of the produce out to the front of the store. “I need to get some of this out front, fast” Jeremy explained. Shawn grabbed another cart and began filling it up too. “I’ll help you get started, before I leave” he said. “Thanks” Jeremy replied, “The sooner we get fresh produce out to the customers, the sooner I can get their opinions of the quality, and pass that on to my mom.” They finished stocking of the produce section and Jeremy thanked Shawn again. “Good luck with your mother” Shawn said as he prepared to leave. “Thanks” Jeremy said, “With this quality of produce, I’m sure that our customers will be overjoyed, and that’ll make it easier to convince mom to change suppliers. By the way, do you have a company name?” Shawn smiled, and handed Jeremy a slip of paper. “Name of the company is at the top of the invoice” he said with a grin. Jeremy unfolded the paper and looked at the heading. “Du-Nu Fresh Produce” it said in bold lettering at the top. “Good name” Jeremy said with a grin.

Jeremy took the invoice to his mother in the office. “They already delivered the order?” she asked. “Yes” Jeremy answered, “And the produce section is already stocked.” “Well, you’re being pretty efficient today” she complimented him. “Well, the man that delivered everything helped me get the product out front” Jeremy replied, “And, the company name is on the top of the invoice.” Grace looked at the invoice and read the name out loud. “Du-Nu Fresh Produce” she said. “Kind of a cool name, huh?” Jeremy asked with a smile, “Du-Nu means nude, in French. It probably means they grow everything organically, without using chemicals.” “Yes, that’s probably what it means” his mother replied, her face turning a little red. “Their product looks a lot fresher than what we normally get” Jeremy offered, “I’m going to see what the customers think.” “That’s a good idea” Grace responded, “If the customers are pleased with the product, and we can get delivery like today, I may see if we can switch to them as our main supplier. I’ll come out and see what kind of quality you’re talking about.”

Grace followed her son to the produce section where customers were already looking over the product. “Hello, ladies” Jeremy greeted them, “Is there anything I can do to assist you?” The three ladies all turned to face Jeremy and his mom. “The produce looks a lot fresher than usual” one of the ladies stated, “Do you have a new supplier?” “These vegetables are even fresher than what the supermarket on the east side of town carries” another woman commented, “Are you going to be carrying this produce all the time now?” “We’re trying out a new supplier” Grace replied, “We may be switching to them permanently, if they continue to supply the same quality product." "You're Mrs. Marsh from school" Jeremy said to the third woman. "Yes, I am" she replied, "And you're Jeremy Andersen, captain of the school swim team." "Yes" Jeremy replied, "That's me." "Do you work here?" Mrs. Marsh asked. "Kind of" Jeremy answered with a grin, "My mom here owns the store, and my sister Amanda and I work here with her during the summer." "Well, I just sold my house last week, and I'm waiting to move into my new home, so I'm staying with my friend here and came along with her to check out the local grocery store" Mrs. Marsh said. "Well, welcome to our store" Grace responded, "If there's anything you need help with, just ask Jeremy or myself. We want our customers to be happy with the service here."

Grace smiled at her son. "I'll be in the office if you need me, Jeremy" she told him, "I want to place another order for produce with this new company, and cancel our order from the old one." "Okay, mom" Jeremy replied with a grin, "I better get back to my work of stocking the shelves again." The night shift came in just before four o'clock, including the store's assistant manager, so Grace was able to concentrate on counting the receipts for the day. At four-thirty, Grace had all the registers closed out except for one. She placed a fresh drawer in that register and had the night cashier take over for Amanda, checking customers out. She took the last drawer to the office to count it, and after finishing, locked it in the safe with the others. She prepared the deposit for the bank and was ready to leave. "Okay" she declared, "Let's get going. We'll drop the deposit off at the bank on our way home."

They arrived home at five-thirty and Grace went to see about starting supper for them. Amanda and Jeremy headed upstairs to get cleaned up and change clothes. Amanda insisted that Jeremy should take his shower first, since he had been sweating all day while stocking the shelves, coolers, and freezers, and carrying out groceries for the customers. "You saying that I stink" he asked her. "No, no!" she replied with a smile, "Well, maybe a little." "Yeah, thanks" he responded with a smile, "I agree though, I haven't had a shower since Saturday." Jeremy grabbed a towel from the linen closet in the hall and went into the bathroom. Amanda went to her room across the hall and stripped off all her clothes, grabbed a book, and laid down on the bed to wait for Jeremy to finish in the bathroom. "Oh!" she mumbled to herself, "It feels so good to be out of those clothes." Jeremy stripped out of his clothes in the bathroom and dropped them down the laundry chute, then started the water in the shower and got in. He began washing up with soap and a wash cloth, then proceeded to shampoo his hair. When he finished showering, he grabbed the towel from the towel rack and began to dry off.

Grace, down in the kitchen, was trying to decide what to make for supper, hotdogs or spaghetti. She finally decided to let the kids decide and headed upstairs. She heard water running in the bathroom, so knew that one of the kids was already in the shower. She glanced in through Jeremy's open bedroom door, and saw that he wasn't there. "Good" she thought to herself, "He's the one that needed a shower the most." She continued on to Amanda's bedroom and gently knocked on the door. "Who is it?" Amanda called from inside. "Your mother" Grace called out as she opened the door and stepped inside. She froze in place when she saw her daughter starting to get up off of the bed. "Hi, Mom, what did you want" Amanda asked, as she stood up. Grace starred at her daughter, open mouthed. "Amanda! You're naked!" she exclaimed, "You should put on a robe or something." Amanda looked at herself. "Oh, sorry mom" she said as she turned and reached for the robe that was laying on a chair next to the bed, "I was waiting for Jeremy to finish in the bathroom. I guess I forgot to put on my robe." "I came up to ask you and Jeremy what you wanted for supper" Grace muttered as she watched her daughter slipping on the robe. Amanda saw the confused look on her mother's face. "Is there something wrong, mom?" Amanda asked. Just at that moment, the bathroom door opened out in the hallway.

Jeremy had finished drying off, so he tossed the damp towel down the laundry chute as he opened the bathroom door and stepped out into the hallway. "Hey, Amanda!" he called, "I'm all finished in the b-bath…" He froze in place when he spotted his mother looking at him through Amanda's open bedroom door. "M-Mom" he gasped, when he realized that he was still completely nude yet, out in the hallway. He quickly covered his crotch with both hands and started looking around for something to cover himself with. Grace starred at her naked son in the hallway. "Jeremy" she gasped, "Why are you out in the hallway with nothing on?" "Mom" he mumbled, "I just took a shower. I took off my sweaty clothes in the bathroom and tossed them down the laundry chute. All I had left with me was a towel, and I tossed that down the chute too, when I finished drying off." Grace frowned at her son. "Well, you better go put on some clothes, don't you think" his mother chuckled. "Y-yes" Jeremy replied as he quickly walked into his own bedroom and closed the door behind him. Grace watched her son's bare butt as he walked into his room. Amanda saw the frown on her mother's face as she continued to stare at Jeremy's closed door. "I think spaghetti would be good for supper" she mumbled to her mother. "Huh. What?" Grace muttered back. "Jeremy" Amanda called out to her brother, "Mom wants to know what we would like for supper, spaghetti or hotdogs?" "Spaghetti sounds really good" Jeremy replied from behind the door. Grace looked at her daughter, then headed down the hallway with the confused look still showing on her face. “Supper should be ready in about twenty minutes” she called back.

Amanda took a quick shower and dried off, all the time thinking about how her mother had seen her laying nude on the bed, and then Jeremy coming out of the bathroom with nothing on. She slipped her robe back on, dropped the damp towel in the laundry chute, then exited the bathroom to cross the hall and knock on Jeremy’s bedroom door. Jeremy opened the door a few seconds later, wearing a t-shirt and jean shorts. Amanda walked into her brother’s bedroom and closed the door behind her. “Do you think I’m in trouble with mom?” Jeremy asked. “If you are, then so am I” Amanda replied, “Mom found me laying on the bed with nothing on.” “Yeah, but I came walking out of the bathroom, naked” he responded, “Did you see the look on her face as she stared at me, standing nude in the hall?” “I don’t know if she is upset with us, or not” Amanda responded, “But she seemed confused about something.” “Yeah” Jeremy said, “Guess we’ll find out if we’re in trouble when we go down for supper.” “Yeah” Amanda agreed, “I better get dressed before we go downstairs.” Amanda went to her room and dressed, going so far as to put on underwear also. When she came out of the bedroom, Jeremy was waiting. “What do we tell her?” Amanda asked him. “The only thing we can” her brother replied, “We’ll have to tell her the truth.” They walked downstairs and into the kitchen, where their mother was sitting at the table. Supper was ready, the spaghetti and garlic bread waiting on the table.

“Sit down” Grace said, “Supper’s ready.” As Grace started putting the spaghetti on their plates, Jeremy decided he had to say something. “Mom, I’m sorry about what happened upstairs a little bit ago. I should have taken a robe to the bathroom with me, or just kept the towel around me until I was in my room.” “It’s okay, Jeremy, I understand” his mother replied, “You were tired and in a hurry. You absent-mindedly forgot your robe, and when you dropped your towel down the chute like you normally do, you had no choice except to walk out as you were.” “Maybe I could have called out to have Amanda bring me another towel” he suggested. “Jeremy” Grace said, “you didn’t even seem to care that you were naked, until you saw me looking at you, and Amanda acted the same way. She didn’t realize she was naked either, when I came into her room.” Grace finished filling their plates with the spaghetti. “Garlic bread?” she asked them. “Yes, please” Amanda answered. “Me too, please” Jeremy said. “So, mom” Amanda hesitantly began, “You aren’t upset with us about what happened upstairs? Because you had a really strange look on your face.” “No, I’m not upset with either of you, I've seen both of you without clothes on before, although you were a lot younger at the time and not so well developed" Grace replied while smiling at her son. Jeremy saw her smiling at him as she said the last part, and his face turned red. "But I am curious about something I noticed" she added. "Curious about what?" Jeremy mumbled with his mouth full of spaghetti.

Their mother looked back and forth between the two teens. "Well, I noticed that you both seem to have gotten some good tans while camping" Grace replied, "I'm just wondering how come neither of you seems to have any tan lines." Jeremy choked a little on the food in his mouth and started coughing. Amanda's hand froze in place with the fork half way to her mouth. "Um, tan lines" Amanda muttered. "Yes" her mother replied, "You see, your skin tends to get darker when you spend time out in the sunshine. All but the parts of your body that are covered by your swimsuit or your clothing. When I saw both of you upstairs, I noticed that neither of you seem to have the areas of lighter skin that I would expect to see, and I'm curious as to why that is." The two teens sat starring at their mother, not knowing how to go about explaining the absence of tan lines on their bodies. Grace smiled at her two children. "For now, you should eat your food, before it gets cold" she told them, "You can tell me 'ALL' about your camping trip after we finish eating."

When they had finished supper, and the dishes had been done, Grace motioned for the two teens to follow her to the family room. She sat down in a recliner and indicated that they should sit on the sofa across from her. "I think it's time for me to hear about your camping trip" she said. Jeremy and Amanda sat down on the edge of the sofa and looked down towards the floor. They remained like that for several minutes before Jeremy decided to speak. "Mom, we didn't do anything that we are ashamed of or wrong" he began, "Amanda, Jenny, Charlie, and I decided to become naturists after we met some kids that were skinny-dipping in the lake." "They were around twelve or so, and we became friends with them" Amanda added. Their mother looked at the two of them. "So, you just decided to become naturists because you met some other naturists on your camping trip" she stated, "And what else did you do besides skinny-dip?" Jeremy looked up at his mother. "Nothing bad, mom. And, we didn't decide to be naturists for just this camping trip" he exclaimed, "We all decided it after several days, and we want to be naturists from now on." "Those kids we saw were younger than the four of us" Amanda explained, "And they kept disappearing when they saw us, so we started exploring around the lake to see where they were vanishing to." "And that's how we found our way to Village Du-Nu" Jeremy exclaimed.

Grace gasped, realizing that they had found the place where she had grown up.

"You found Village Du-Nu? How could you find the secret passage through the mountain?" Grace asked, "That door is too well hidden. You must have seen those kids going through it." "No, we didn't find that door" Jeremy replied, "We found another way to the village." Grace looked confused. "Jeremy and Charlie found an underwater tunnel behind the waterfall" Amanda explained, "We all went through it and found our way to Village Du-Nu." Grace gasped again. "You swam through that old tunnel?" she exclaimed, "No one has used it in years." "We did" Amanda replied with a grin, "We went through it, and started to explore one morning, then went back to the lake and spent the afternoon with the young kids." "The two boys, Greg and Tomas, convinced me to try skinny-dipping in back of the waterfall" Jeremy said, "And I talked Charlie into trying it too." "And the third kid, Karen, talked Jenny and me into sunbathing nude on air mattresses, out on the lake" Amanda added. The two teens took turns continuing to give a brief description of everything that happened on the entire camping trip. They described how the boys had come to accidentally run into the girls while they were all nude, and how they decided to stay nude and try the naturist way for the rest of the week. They described how they had first met Aunt Joyce and the twins in the village, had helped the twins and the other kids out in the fields, and stayed with Aunt Joyce for several days, all while going nude.

Grace sat back in the recliner, shocked. "And I was worried about how to explain to you about me being a naturist" she exclaimed, "And here you two manage to discover naturism all by yourselves, and take to it like a fish to water." Jeremy and Amanda watched their mother, to see if she was going to react badly to anything they had told her. "Mom?" Amanda suddenly said, "We weren't trying to keep this a secret from you, we just wanted to wait until we could figure out how to tell you." "Well, I kind of forced the issue, didn't I" Grace declared, "You and your friends were pretty good detectives to find your way to my home town, but I'm a good detective, too. I knew that you had been going nude on your camping trip as soon as I saw you without tan lines upstairs." "Mom" Amanda cautiously spoke, "Aunt Joyce told us you wanted to tell us about being a naturist, and that you wanted to move back to Du-Nu. Now that we already know about naturism, what are you going to do?" Grace looked at her daughter. "I don't know" she replied, "I hadn't planned to move back there for a long time yet, and I don't know if I'm ready to move back yet." "Why not?" Jeremy inquired, "It'll be like falling off your bike, you just have to get back on and start riding again." "Maybe you can start out by being a naturist, just at home" Amanda suggested, "Jeremy and I would be fine with it, especially since we'd love to not have to wear these clothes all the time, ourselves."

Grace looked at her kids. "I don't know how I feel about being nude around my own children, it would feel so weird" she said. Jeremy looked at his mother for a little bit. "Well, could Amanda and I go nude around the house?" he asked, "And when you get used to seeing us nude all the time, maybe you'll feel like you can live as a naturist again." Grace smiled. "If the two of you want to go clothes free around here, I think that would be okay" she responded, "But it might be a long time before I feel ready to join you." "Alright" exclaimed Amanda as she stood up and started pulling her shirt up over her head. Grace watched her daughter strip out of her clothes, then stand there stretching out her arms. "I'm free!" Amanda declared, "Free of those uncomfortable clothes." Grace looked over at Jeremy. "It's hard to believe that she and Charlie were the last hold outs to try going nude?" he chuckled. "How about you?" Grace asked, "Are you as anxious to get out of your clothes and be free, too?" "Yes" he answered as he stood up. Moments later, Jeremy stood totally exposed before his mother and sister. "It feels wonderful to not be confined to scratchy textile clothes" he exclaimed with a grin.

Grace settled back in the recliner and turned on the

television. Amanda suddenly had an idea, and she went into the hall to make a quick telephone call before returning to the family room to watch the television with her mother and her brother. An hour later, a knock came at the back door. Amanda quickly got up and ran for the door. "Amanda!" yelled Grace, "Wait, you can't go to the door like that!" Grace watched, horrified, as her daughter opened the door while completely nude. "Jenny!" exclaimed Amanda, feigning surprise, "How good to see you. And Charlie. Come on in, Jeremy and my mom are in the family room." Grace's eyes opened wide, as the two visitors came walking in through the back door with only shoes on. "Good evening Mrs. Andersen" the two kids said together as they looked at her, grinning. "Hello" Grace responded, "Nice to um, see you two again." "Mom" said Amanda, "Jeremy and I did mention that Jenny and Charlie were naturists now too, right? So, I figured it would be okay for them to be nude over here also. Is that alright with you?" "Well, I guess this has become a naturist home now" Grace declared, "They can dress however they want when visiting." "Thank you" Charlie exclaimed, "I haven't told my parents about becoming a naturist yet, and I was suffocating at home, having to wear clothes all the time." Jeremy started laughing. "And Charlie was the one that took the most convincing" he stated. Everyone started laughing.

Over the next week, Jenny and Charlie came over

almost every night, sometimes joining the Andersen's for supper. They would strip off their clothes as soon as they got around to the back of the house, and enter through the back door. Grace watched the four teens play games in the family room, but they spent most of their time out in the backyard, around and in the swimming pool. She joined them at the pool a lot, but always wore a swimsuit. That weekend, Jenny and Charlie came on Friday evening and were going to stay for the entire weekend. Grace only had to work in the grocery store on Saturday morning, since the store closed at noon, and the kids did not work that weekend at all. It turned out to be a very busy morning, and she had to help with restocking some of the produce once, and work at a cash register the rest of the time. The last customer was let out of the store around twenty after twelve, and she still had to count all the cash drawers, do some paperwork, and take the daily deposit to the bank.

By the time Grace got home from work, it was after two in the afternoon. She was tired and felt in need of a nice long shower. She went to her bedroom on the first floor and had just stripped out of her clothes when Amanda came into the room. "You're home kind of late, mom" Amanda stated, "We were beginning to worry about you." "Sorry, it was very busy at the store this morning" Grace explained, "The last customer left at a quarter after twelve, and I still had the cash drawers to count and paperwork to finish. I'm going to take a shower, and then relax." "Okay, mom" Amanda said, "Jeremy made some chicken for lunch, and we left some for you in the oven, if you're hungry." "Thanks" her mother replied, "Where is everyone else?" "Jeremy is getting his car out, we're all going to go to a movie in town" Amanda replied, "Do you want to come with?" "No, you kids go ahead" Grace answered, "I'll just rest up while you are all gone."

Grace got into the shower and let the warm water cascade down over her tired body. After twenty minutes in the shower, she felt her stomach starting to growl. "I better get something to eat" she thought to herself. She got out of the shower and dried off. She was about to get out some clean clothes to put on, but stopped. "The kids are all gone" she thought, "I don't really need to get dressed right now. I think I'll have lunch first." She walked out to the kitchen completely nude, and it felt wonderful. The chicken in the oven smelled delicious. She got a plate, took the pot out of the oven, and put some chicken on her plate, along with some of the peas and some rice that were staying warm in pots on top of the stove. She sat down on a chair at the table, after putting a clean hand town down first, and began eating. "Um, this is really good" she thought, "Jeremy is a really good cook. I may have to let him start making supper for us occasionally."

After finishing off seconds on the chicken, Grace put the dirty dishes in the sink, and the leftovers in the refrigerator. "Let's see" she thought to herself, "If the movie started at three, and it's three-thirty now, I have about ninety minutes or more before the kids get back, maybe I can relax by the pool and work on my tan." She started back to her bedroom to get her swimsuit. "What am I doing?" she said to herself, "I don't need a swimsuit when I'm here all alone. Maybe I'll try being a naturist while the kids are gone." She decided to stay nude for about an hour or so, grabbed a towel from the linen closet, and headed for the backyard with nothing except sandals on. She stepped out the patio door into the sunlight and felt the warm sunshine on her skin. "Oh, it's been a long time since I felt my entire body warmed by the sun like this" she whispered to herself. Walking up to the pool, she looked at the glistening water and then jumped in. After a few laps back and forth across the length of the pool, she got out of the water and stood in the warm air, applying sunscreen, before lying down on a lounge chair. After about twenty minutes of lying face up, Grace turned over on her stomach to work on tanning her back, and then turned back over on her back again about twenty minutes later. She felt extremely relaxed as she laid back with her eyes closed, enjoying the warm sunshine.

"Cannon ball!" Grace heard someone yell. She opened her eyes and sat up, just in time to see Charlie jumping off of the diving board across the pool, and make a tremendous splash. She actually felt a few drops of cool water land on her feet. "Nice one" she heard Jeremy call out, "Now it's my turn." She watched her son climb up on the board, run to the end of it, bounce once and launch himself up over the water. His splash was even bigger, and she felt drops of water land on her legs. She spotted her daughter and Jenny in the water on this end of the pool. "How was the movie?" she called out to the two girls. "It was okay" Amanda answered, "But I would have enjoyed it more if we weren't required to wear clothes in the theatre." "Everything would be better, if you could do it without clothes" Grace stated. "How was the chicken?" her son asked as his head popped up beside Jenny, "I used your recipe, with a few modifications." "You changed my recipe?" Grace gasped, "I thought I had a really good recipe, just the way it was. Now, you're going to have to tell me what you changed, so I can change the recipe when I make it." "He's a pretty good cook, isn't he?" Amanda exclaimed with a grin, "Who would have guessed that he could even make something edible."

"What time is it anyway?" Grace asked. "It's a little after five-thirty, Mrs. Andersen" Charlie stated as he walked up and sat down on another lounge chair. "Oh" Grace gasped, "I should get supper started then." "No need to do that" Amanda giggled, "We figured you were pretty tired when we saw you sleeping out here, so Jeremy and Jenny already started making supper." "She means that we put a couple of frozen pizzas in the oven about ten minutes ago" Jeremy said with a chuckle, "They should be ready in about another ten minutes, so we should go and put some plates on the table." Grace watched her son and his girlfriend walk over and enter the house. "Oh!" she gasped, looking down at herself after remembering, "I'm not dressed. I was going to get dressed before you all got back from the movie." Grace got up from the lounge chair and started walking toward the house. "Mom" Amanda said, "You've been nude out here with us for about half an hour. You aren't going to put on clothes now?" Grace smiled at her daughter. "Of course, not" she replied, "But Jeremy is waving for us to come in for supper." Amanda and Charlie followed Grace inside and over to the dining room table. Grace put her towel down on a chair and sat down. "I guess I may as well stay nude from now on" she declared, "I seem to have overcome my difficulty with being nude around you kids, so, I'm officially back to being a naturist again." "Great" exclaimed Jeremy, "That means we have a fully naturist home now."

A NEW FUTURE

After supper, Grace excused herself and went back to her bedroom. "Is she putting on her clothes now?" Jeremy whispered to the others. "I don't think so" Jenny said, "You heard her say that she was back to being a naturist again." After getting all the dishes cleaned up, the four teens went back out to the pool area and relaxed on the lounge chairs. About an hour later, Grace came out of the house, still wearing only sandals, plus a big grin. "Sorry, but I decided that I needed to make a phone call" Grace declared, "I called your Aunt Joyce to let her know that you told me about your trip, and that we'd like to come for a visit. How do you feel about spending the Fourth of July weekend in Village Du-Nu?" "Really?" Jeremy exclaimed. "That would be great" Amanda added, "But what about the store?" "I'll have the night shift work on Friday morning and close at noon" their mother replied, "The store will be closed on Saturday, the forth, and the store is normally closed on Sundays. We'll leave on Friday morning, and return directly to work the following Monday morning." "But what about Jenny and Charlie" Jeremy asked, "I was hoping to spend the weekend with Jenny around." "And Charlie and I kind of wanted to spend time together also" Amanda said. "Well, if they can get permission, they can come with us" Grace answered, "But we'll need to take along one tent and sleeping bags then."

"I'm sure I can get permission" Jenny stated, "My family hasn't made any plans for the holiday yet, and they know that I want to spend the holiday with my boyfriend. "I'll have to ask my dad" Charlie said, "But I don't think he will care if I'm gone. He's been telling me that I need to spend more time with this beautiful girl, and to treat her good so I don't lose her. I think he likes my choice in girlfriends." "Great" Grace declared, "Then we'll make plans for all five of us to go together. You two can confirm, once you have parental permission." "This will be great" Amanda exclaimed, "A whole weekend without clothes. And, we can go nude anywhere in the town, not just at home." "Speaking of home" Grace said, "I should probably tell you that we may be moving to another town this fall." "What?" Jeremy gasped, "Move to another town! But Jenny just became my girlfriend, how far away is the town, and what about the store?" "The town is Village Du-Nu" Grace replied with a smile, "Your Aunt Joyce says that the house we grew up in is still vacant, and she and I inherited it after our parents died. I'll buy her half of the house." "We're moving to Du-Nu?" gasped Amanda. "Yes, but we'll have to fix up the house before we can move into it" Grace explained, "But between your Uncle Jack, Jeremy, and some of the other men in the village, we should be able to move in before school starts."

"How big is the house" Jeremy inquired. "It's three

bedrooms and a bathroom upstairs, plus one bedroom and a bathroom downstairs, with a front room, dining room, and kitchen" Grace answered, "It's about the same size as your Uncle Jack and Aunt Joyce's house. We'll be taking a look at it when we visit on the Fourth of July, to see how much work will actually need to be done, and order the material for the repairs." "Where will we be going to school?" asked Amanda, "They don't have a high school in Du-Nu." Grace replied, "You'll still be going to Bon Amis High School. You'll just be driving to and from the village each day, instead of from this house, and you'll have to get up a little earlier. So, what do you think?" "I think life has suddenly become really good" Amanda declared. "And I think I'm going to have a really great senior year" Jeremy exclaimed with a grin.

The End

About The Author

G James Quandt, born in the Midwest part of the United States, grew up in a small town with four siblings. At an early age, he day-dreamed and created stories in his mind, but his parents encouraged him to concentrate on school studies. His limited knowledge of nudists while growing up, was obtained from distorted images presented in the media of television, but as an adult he found chat rooms on the internet, and learned the true ideals of naturism from actual naturists.

Searching the internet, James noted that naturism does not involve participation in lewd activities, as many uninformed people believe, but is simply a belief that nudity is the natural state of humans, and not wrong. Finding that there were naturist organizations all over the world (local, national, and international), he decided to join a local club. He wished to learn first-hand about naturism, and he nervously attended a volleyball activity of the club. He observed how at ease everyone seemed to be while playing volleyball without clothing, and after several volleyball activities, decided to join the national organizations as well.

After moving to Texas, James visited “Hippy Hollow”, a legal, clothing-optional beach. He began day-dreaming about a naturist themed story, and started typing the story into a computer. He wanted to create a story showing the innocence of naturism, while providing readers with some entertainment in the form of a mystery. Once completed, his story was published in ebook and paperback formats at Amazon. "Mystery of The Vanishing Skinny-Dippers" was released in December of 2018.

If you liked the story, please feel free to leave a review with your book retailer, encouraging others to read the book.

Printed in Great Britain
by Amazon